# BOOKS BY JAMES WHITE

*The Secret Visitor* (1957)
*Second Ending* (1962)
*Deadly Litter* (1964)
*Escape Orbit* (1965)
*The Watch Below* (1966)
*All Judgement Fled* (1968)
*The Aliens among Us* (1969)
*Tomorrow Is Too Far* (1971)
*Dark Inferno* (1972)
*The Dream Millennium* (1974)
*Monsters and Medics* (1977)
*Underkill* (1979)
*Future Past* (1982)
*Federation World* (1988)
*The Silent Stars Go By* (1991)
*The White Papers* (1996)

## THE SECTOR GENERAL SERIES

*Hospital Station* (1962)
*Star Surgeon* (1963)
*Major Operation* (1971)
*Ambulance Ship* (1979)
*Sector General* (1983)
*Star Healer* (1985)
*Code Blue—Emergency* (1987)
*The Genocidal Healer* (1992)
*The Galactic Gourmet* (Tor, 1996)
*Final Diagnosis* (Tor, 1997)
*Mind Changer* (Tor, 1998)

# MIND CHANGER

## A SECTOR GENERAL NOVEL

## JAMES WHITE

**TOR**®

A TOM DOHERTY ASSOCIATES BOOK
NEW YORK

MIND CHANGER

Edited by Teresa Nielsen Hayden

A Tor Book
Published by Tom Doherty Associates, LLC
175 Fifth Avenue
New York, NY 10010

www.tor.com

Tor® is a registered trademark of Tom Doherty Associates, LLC.

ISBN: 0-812-54196-0
Library of Congress Catalog Card Number: 98-23620

First edition: November 1998
First mass market edition: September 1999

Printed in the United States of America

0  9  8  7  6  5  4  3  2  1

# MIND
## CHANGER

# CHAPTER 1

**F**ar out on the galactic rim, where star systems were sparse and the darkness close to absolute, Sector Twelve General Hospital hung in space. Too vast by far to be considered a space station, too small to be called a metal moon, in its three hundred and eighty-four levels were reproduced the environments of all the intelligent species known to the Galactic Federation, a biological spectrum ranging from the ultra-frigid methane life-forms through the more normal oxygen- and chlorine-breathing types up to the exotic beings who lived by the direct conversion of hard radiation. Its thousands of viewports were constantly ablaze with lighting in the dazzling variety and intensity necessary for the visual sensors of its extraterrestrial patients and staff, so that to approaching ships the great hospital resembled a gigantic Christmas tree.

The most brilliant feature of all was the flashing pattern of warning beacons outlining the perimeter of the fusion reactors. But for the next few hours the real source of power within the vast establishment would lie behind a group of three yellow, lighted panels of moderate intensity on Level Thirty-Nine—although,

O'Mara thought cynically, the people wielding that power would have been the first to make token denials of that fact.

But today he was receiving some very confusing signals from the beings who were standing, sitting, hanging, or otherwise reclining at ease around the big table. Something unusual had happened or was about to happen, or Skempton would not have been able to ensure this full attendance. By the nature of things within this medical madhouse that meant a surprise, almost certainly an unpleasant surprise, for someone here. As he stared slowly at the others in turn, he knew that the DBDGs present, as well as the few ETs who had learned how to read Earth-human facial expressions, were aware of his irritation.

With the exception of the hospital's administrator, Colonel Skempton, and himself, they were the hospital's medical elite, diagnosticians all and the heads of their respective departments. This was the first monthly Meeting of Diagnosticians that he could recall where all staff members had turned up and were staring at the colonel in silence instead of complaining loudly to each other about having better things to do elsewhere.

Definitely, O'Mara thought, the surprise was going to be an unpleasant one.

Around the big table the silence deepened until the quiet bubbling sound from the environmental protection vehicle of the water-breathing Diagnostician Vosan began to sound loud. Inside its protective chlorine envelope, Lachlichi twitched disgustingly but silently, and the highly refrigerated sphere containing Diagnostician Semlic radiated a supercooled silence, while the tentacles of Diagnostician Camuth, the Creppelian octopoid, made impatient, slapping noises against the floor. The others were warm-blooded oxygen-breathers who did not need to wear environmental protection, or even clothing apart from their badges of medical rank, with the exception of the three Earth-humans present. Diagnostician Conway had on his surgical white coveralls, while Colonel

Skempton and himself wore their dark green Monitor Corps uniforms. It was the colonel who finally broke the silence by clearing his throat.

As he knew it would, the Kelgian diagnostician, Yursedth, reacted at once. Its mobile, silvery fur rippled into angry eddies as it said loudly, "That noise illustrates the basic design flaw in your Earth-human physiology, Colonel, that of having the functions of respiration and speech served by the same air passage. Surely you can exercise some voluntary control over the process when you prepare to speak, and refrain from making that disgusting sound."

The concepts of politeness, diplomacy, or otherwise hiding the truth were totally alien to Kelgians because, to another member of their species, the movements of their highly mobile fur expressed exactly what they were thinking and feeling from second to second, so that trying to vocalize a different message would have been a stupid waste of their time. Skempton ignored the outburst, as did everyone else in the room, and spoke.

"Before we get down to the routine business," he said, and added with a small, dry laugh, "if anything about this medical menagerie can be described as routine, I have two important announcements to make. They are the results of discussions and decisions taken at the highest level, that of the Federation's Medical Council and the subcommittee tasked with the supply, maintenance, and administration of Sector General. These decisions are irreversible, not subject to debate or amendment and, naturally, they will not please everyone."

He had the precise, colorless voice of a bookkeeper, O'Mara thought dryly, although over the years the excellence of his bookkeeping had earned him the highest nonmedical position in the hospital. As Skempton paused for a moment to look slowly around the table, his expression remained emotionless and his gaze lingered on O'Mara for perhaps an additional millisecond. But

O'Mara was too good a psychologist to be blind and deaf to the other's body language.

The decisions, whatever they were, had certainly pleased Colonel Skempton.

"My first announcement," the colonel resumed, "is that I shall be relinquishing my position as the hospital's administrator and will shortly be leaving Sector General. This was not my decision, but as a serving Monitor Corps officer I have to go when and where I'm told. I am being appointed to a similar, but I think a much easier job, in the multi-species Monitor Corps base at Retlin on Nidia, with the substantive rank of fleet commander. I am not unhappy about this move because, large and well-appointed as our recreation level is, it is too small to include a proper golf course. So I look forward to relearning the game after twenty years' lack of practice . . ." He looked at O'Mara for a moment before ending, ". . . and playing it on real grass under a real sky."

O'Mara was the only other person in the hospital who knew about, and had helped the other to fight, his continuing war against claustrophobia and its related neuroses—a common enough problem among the hospital staff, especially with newly arrived trainees. In Skempton's case the war had gone well, although it had never been truly won.

Without changing his expression, he gave the colonel a nod of sympathy, understanding, and congratulation that was too brief for the others to see.

"Isn't that the game where Earth-humans knock a small ball into a slightly larger hole with a stick?" said Yursedth with a disapproving ruffle of its fur. "Our children play a game like that; the adults have more important things to do. But your promotion and anticipated juvenile pleasures, Colonel, are both well deserved."

Coming from a Kelgian, it was a highly complimentary speech. Everyone else around the table made the untranslatable sounds that were the extraterrestrial equivalents of murmurs of agreement.

The colonel dipped his head briefly in acknowledgment, then went on, "Before naming my successor, who has already been chosen, I must first inform you about two important changes in the job specification. Henceforth the position of hospital administrator will no longer be filled by a serving officer of the Monitor Corps but by a senior member of the medical staff. The reason the Federation's Medical Council gives for this is . . ."

Chairs, benches, and support frames creaked as their occupants changed position suddenly to stare at Thornnastor, the diagnostician-in-charge of Pathology and the acknowledged senior member of the medical hierarchy. Thornnastor, who did not use furniture because its species did everything including sleeping on their six elephantine feet, used its four extensible eyes to stare back at all of them simultaneously.

It stamped two of its feet for emphasis, and when the loose equipment about the room had stopped rattling, it said, "Don't look at me. With respect, Colonel, I'm a pathologist, not a glorified supplies clerk. If I have been considered for the position, I respectfully decline it."

Skempton ignored the interruption and continued, ". . . is that someone with medical experience and a detailed understanding of the medical needs of the hospital—rather than a Service-indoctrinated, glorified supplies clerk, even one with my lengthy experience in the job—will eventually occupy the position. The new appointee will have to satisfy the Federation's Medical Council, but more importantly our own medical staff, regarding his, her, or its fitness for the post . . ."

Inside its ultra-refrigerated protective sphere, the tiny, crystalline entity that was Diagnostician Semlic spoke in a voice like the amplified but ineffably sweet chiming of colliding snowflakes. From their translator packs came the words "Who the hell is it?"

"The first of the new-style hospital administrators," Skempton replied, looking directly at O'Mara with an expression that was sympathetic rather than congratulatory, "will be our chief psychologist."

For a moment surprise left O'Mara incapable of speech, a condition so rare that he could not remember the last time it had happened, but he did not allow his feelings to show in either his expression or his voice.

"I'm not qualified," he said firmly.

Before the colonel could reply, Ergandhir, the Melfan diagnostician, raised one of its thin, exoskeletal limbs and began clicking the pincers loudly together for attention.

"I agree," it said. "Major O'Mara is not qualified. Shortly after joining the hospital I was surprised to discover that it had no formal medical training or qualifications, but that it was virtually running the place, and that in real terms its authority, with respect, Colonel, exceeded your own. But you have just stated that the appointee must be medically qualified, so you appear to be contradicting yourself. Are you waiving that requirement in O'Mara's case? If for some reason you are already changing the rules . . ."

It had been an even longer time, O'Mara thought with angry embarrassment, since anyone had so much as dared mention his lack of medical training to his face, much less publicly and in such distinguished company. He thought about using a few pungent and appropriate words that would lift the skin off Ergandhir's back, even though as a Melfan that area was covered only by a bony carapace. But the other was still talking.

". . . Its time served in Sector General exceeds that of everyone in this room," Erghandir was saying, "because it joined Sector General before the final assembly of the structure was complete. Since then, as head of the Department of Other-Species Psychology, it has held the place together by showing the inhabitants of this medical madhouse how to live and work together as a unit. Its experience in this respect is unequaled. But I have an orderly mind, Colonel. I would like to know why you make rules one moment and break them the next—although, needless to say, I have no problem with your choice of administrator."

Around the table there were more untranslatable noises signifying approval. Yursedth said, "It has never been a requirement that the administrator be popular."

Their reaction gave O'Mara a warm feeling of surprise and pleasure, which he did not allow to show in his face because that would have been a totally uncharacteristic reaction from the most disliked person in the hospital, but he decided that the nonexistent skin on Ergandhir's back was safe. He nodded toward the Kelgian, then looked steadily at Skempton.

"Yursedth is correct," he said. "But I repeat, Colonel, I am still not qualified. My experience in procuring medical and maintenance supplies is nil. In this area the job is far beyond my level of competence." In a very disrespectful voice he added, "I, too, will respectfully decline."

"You will *not* decline," said the other firmly, "because the alternative would mean you leaving Sector General at once. Besides, my department is efficient and my staff are very good, good enough to make me feel redundant most of the time, and they will take care of all the routine matters involving procurement and transportation of supplies, with or without supervision. You must be left free to do the more important and urgent work—which, we believe, you are uniquely qualified to do."

"Which is?" said O'Mara.

Skempton stared back at him but appeared to be ducking the question. Obviously there was something he was finding it difficult to say, something which O'Mara might not like to hear.

The colonel went on. "I've no intention of breaking all the new rules on the first day. As I have already said, this is to be a civil appointment. You will therefore have to resign your rank of major in the Monitor Corps. This should be no hardship since it was originally given to you for purely administrative reasons and Corps discipline never has meant anything to you, especially . . ." He smiled faintly. ". . . in the matter of obeying the orders of senior officers. You will, of course, retain your position as head of Multi-Species Psychology because henceforth the positions of administrator and chief psychologist are to be merged into one. But as a civilian administrator you will not have to accept orders from any other person within the hospital, which is simply regularizing the unofficial situation as it is now, and obey only the one general directive of the Federation's Medical Council . . ."

"Which is?" O'Mara broke in again, this time making no attempt to conceal his impatience. If there was anything he disliked, it was having to repeat a simple question.

The other hesitated, forced a smile, then said, "The good news is that your appointment will be temporary. It will last only for as long as it takes for you to select, evaluate, and fully train your successor."

For a moment there were so many excited, other-species voices speaking at once that his translator was making the derisive beeping sound that signaled input overload. O'Mara did not speak until everyone was quiet again.

"And the bad news?" he said.

Skempton looked very uncomfortable, but his voice was steady as he replied, "You have given exemplary service to this hospital for a very long time, Major, or I should say, ex-Major O'Mara. I fully agree with the majority of the Medical Council who say that, in the early years especially, it could not have functioned without you. But choosing and grooming your successor to a level of excellence that is as close as possible to your own may well be the most important and professionally challenging project you will ever undertake. And when you have completed it to your own satisfaction . . ."

The colonel paused. When he went on, his expression, O'Mara thought, showed an odd mixture of reluctance, sympathy, and deep anxiety, as if he was experiencing both sorrow and the expectation of an imminent emotional eruption.

"Well, Administrator O'Mara," he ended awkwardly, "I have already said that you have served this hospital for a very long time. As soon as you have completed this assignment, you will be required to leave and take your long-overdue retirement."

# CHAPTER 2

O'Mara remained silent for the rest of the meeting and left for his quarters before any of those who had waited behind could congratulate or commiserate with him on his promotion and forced retirement, but he knew that his bad manners would be considered entirely in character. Although he had shown no outward reaction to his sudden elevation and limited future in Sector General, the news had shaken him badly. A certainty that had supported his entire professional life was to be taken away from him and, as soon as possible, he needed to settle down for a lengthy period of reappraisal. As the hospital's administrator his authority was such that he could absent himself for as long as he thought necessary for him to come to terms with a major problem that was both professional and emotional, but as the chief psychologist he could not spare the time right now.

He remained in his rooms only long enough to remove the insignia of rank from his uniform. As he did so he realized for the first time that, apart from a few sleepsuits, he did not have anything to wear that was not Monitor Corps issue.

On the way to his office he scarcely noticed the pre-lunch crowd of multi-species medical and maintenance staff thronging the corridors leading to the dining hall. The heavyweight Tralthans and Hudlars and the species driving environmental protection vehicles, and the Melfans, whose wide-spreading, bony limbs could cause painful bruising of the shins, he avoided as a matter of long habit, and the smaller life-forms he ignored because they avoided him. Even the species who said that they couldn't tell one Earth-human from another knew the green-clad being with the grey head fur as the chief psychologist. He did not speak to any of them, and they knew better than to speak to him unless an emotional emergency of some kind was involved.

Padre Lioren and Cha Thrat were still at lunch, so Braithwaite was alone in the outer office.

"I heard about your appointment a few minutes ago," said the lieutenant. He stood up quickly behind his console and smiled, but he knew better than to try to shake hands. "Congratulations, sir."

O'Mara wasn't surprised. The hospital grapevine was an extremely rapid, if not always accurate, channel of communication. He scowled.

"Don't worry, Lieutenant," he said. "I won't allow my new eminence to change me in any way. And you don't have to call me 'sir' anymore. As a civilian it is a courtesy I no longer expect."

Braithwaite's eyes flickered toward the undecorated collar and empty shoulder tabs on O'Mara's tunic; then they returned to his face.

Still smiling, he said, "Force of habit. Besides, I have been known to extend that same courtesy to members of the civilian staff, if they deserve it. But, well, how do you feel about it, sir?"

Braithwaite's tone sounded concerned as well as curious, O'Mara noted, so perhaps his customary dour lack of expression had slipped a little. He ignored the question but contrived to answer it anyway.

"If my aging and no doubt untrustworthy memory serves me

correctly," he said sourly, "Cresk-Sar has a half-hour appointment with me in twenty-five minutes. Use the time to refuel in the dining hall. As soon as the senior physician leaves, I want to see all three of you together to discuss in detail my feelings about this situation and how it will affect the department. Meanwhile, Lieutenant, sit down and finish those psych file updates."

As usual, Gurronsevas had ensured that his lunch would be the most enjoyable period of the day. The chief dietician and former renowned multi-species *chef de cuisine* had caused an awful lot of trouble during its first few weeks at Sector General, and had come very close to being pitched out on its large, Tralthan ear, so it was continually trying to return the favor it thought it owed him for saving it from that fate. It was a good time to think unpleasant thoughts and allow the pleasure of the meal to dilute them.

Occasionally he had thought about his age and the dreadful inevitability of his having to retire someday from Sector General, the world he had helped build and the only life he had known since his early twenties. He had been an immensely strong young man then, and over the years his fitness checks had been optimum, until recently. Now old Thornnastor, who must be nearly as advanced in years as he was if one allowed for the lengthier Tralthan life span, and young Conway were forever hinting that he should take it easier, slow down and reduce his workload. By accident Gurronsevas had let slip the fact that it had been necessary to modify several of its sauces to disguise the taste of the supportive medication that was now being included daily in O'Mara's food intake. He was returning the dishes, all empty if not quite licked clean, to the insulated serving tray when the attention signal on his console beeped at him.

"Yes?" he said.

"Senior Physician Cresk-Sar is here, sir," said Cha Thrat in its deep, Sommaradvan voice. "Are you ready for it?"

"Yes," he said again.

Cresk-Sar opened the door and waddled quickly into the

room like a hyperactive teddy bear. It was barely a meter tall, with tiny eyes that were almost hidden by tightly curled facial fur that was tinged around its mouth and ears with grey, as was the longer body hair that poked out in untidy tufts between the straps of its equipment harness. *Aging is happening to all of us,* O'Mara thought sadly. The Nidian senior tutor was the most frequent visitor to his office but, thankfully, it brought with it only the problems of its students.

O'Mara keyed his board for the latest trainee psych reports and pointed at the edge of a recliner that had been designed for a Melfan but that should be comfortable enough for a short meeting. If it wasn't, then Cresk-Sar could always take the option of making it shorter.

"Your latest batch of trainees seems to be a pretty average bunch," he said, turning aside from his screen. "There is the usual incidence of anxiety neuroses regarding underperformance during the coming examinations, professional inadequacy when faced with treating their first other-species patients, and, of course, their conviction that never ever will they learn to fully understand the thought processes of their medical-colleagues-to-be. They are right, of course, but that doesn't stop you or any of the other seniors from doing your jobs. And yes, there is one of them, a Tralthan, for God's sake, who is reporting dreams indicative of the fear—well-controlled, I admit—associated with possible sexual molestation and penetration by one or more of its other-species colleagues. What could a six-legged, tentacled elephant possibly fear from a bunch of Kelgians, Melfans, Nidians, and one Earth-human female, all of whom are less than one-quarter of its body mass?"

Cresk-Sar made a barking sound that did not translate, its Nidian equivalent of laughter. "As we know, sir, large muscles do not preclude emotional sensitivity."

O'Mara knew that very well, but it was a sensitivity he had tried to hide over the years. Irritated at having an old wound opened, he said sharply, "I don't anticipate any serious emotional problems developing among this lot, Senior Physician. Or are you about to tell me I'm wrong?"

"Yes," said Cresk-Sar, fidgeting on the edge of the Melfan recliner. "I mean, not exactly. It's . . . The problem is mine."

For a long moment O'Mara stared at the other in silence. The thick, overall covering of fur made reading its expression impossible, except for the tiny, dark eyes and the body language, which were signaling tension and distress. He softened his tone to an extent that those who thought they knew him would not have believed possible.

"Take your time, Cresk-Sar."

But the other did not want to take its time, because its staccato, Nidian speech poured out like the barking of an agitated dog. "It's Crang-Suvi," it said, "and me. She is the only other Nidian in the class. She's very young, with dark-red fur and a voice and personality that, that . . . Dammit, she's a Nidian male's wish-fulfillment dream. But she seems to be basically insecure for reasons which you know about and probably understand far better than I do. . . ."

While the other was talking, O'Mara had called up Crang-Suvi's psych file, and he did understand. Even though Cresk-Sar was repeating much of what was showing on the screen, he listened patiently without interrupting.

". . . She is a Graduate of Excellence from Sanator Five," the senior tutor went on, "which is Nidia's foremost teaching hospital. Any hospital on a dozen planets, or the Corps' medical service, would be glad to have her but, like everyone else in her class, she has always had her mind set on making it as a Sector General graduate and applying for a staff position here. She is intelligent, able, caring, unusually beautiful, shows no marked signs of xenophobia, and is used to getting what she wants. Personally, I've no doubt at all that Crang-Suvi will make it, but I can't tell her so because that would be unfair to the other trainees. But she isn't so sure and, within a week of her arrival, she indicated that she would like to increase her chances by providing sexual favors to her senior tutor. She says that the age differential is unimportant, and she refuses to take no for an answer. . . ."

O'Mara held up his hand. "Has sexual contact taken place between you?"

"No," said Cresk-Sar.

"Why not?" said O'Mara.

The other hesitated for a moment, during which O'Mara thought that at least the matter involved two beings of the same species; otherwise, if word of the affair had got out, it would have become really messy and a matter for someone's resignation. In the circumstances they both knew that the hospital's long-serving and most highly experienced tutor would not normally have been the one to resign—unless, of course, the situation had reached the stage of emotional involvement where they both felt it necessary to leave together. That would be bad, he thought, for Cresk-Sar, Crang-Suvi, and Sector General, but otherwise gifted and intelligent people did stupid things at times.

"Take your time," he said again.

Cresk-Sar made a loud, self-irritated sound that did not translate; then it answered his original question.

"There are four reasons why not," it said miserably. "She is less than one-third of my age. She gives no promise of a permanent or even a lengthy relationship. I would be taking an unfair and selfish advantage of what would be a very pleasant situation, which would not influence the result of her finals one bit, although the psychological effect on her classmates, who would have difficulty believing that she was not being given an unfair advantage, would not be good. And, well, there is Surgeon-Lieutenant Warnagh-Lut, who would not like it. Do you know about Warnagh-Lut?"

"Not officially," said O'Mara dryly. His department took official cognizance of an event or activity only when it was highlighted in orange or red on the relevant psych file.

The other went on, "She—Warnagh-Lut, that is—is closer to

me in age and temperamentally much more suitable. But as a serving medical officer, even though her department is responsible for looking after the Corps maintenance personnel at the hospital, she could be sent anywhere in the galaxy at short notice. Had this not been so, we would have proclaimed our life-mate status long since. But now Crang-Suvi has, well, disturbed things. You understand?"

O'Mara nodded. He said, "You, and your continued mental well-being, are more valuable to this establishment than any trainee, no matter how gifted. It can be returned to its home world immediately, with or without an explanation. Right?"

"No!" said Cresk-Sar vehemently. "That isn't necessary. Besides, it would be a terrible waste of future medical talent. I just want Crang-Suvi off my back, or whatever. I've tried to do it, but she just ignores me and, well, it's very difficult to ignore her. Could you just make her understand the situation and, well, talk to her like a stern father? In my trainee days, I seem to remember you doing that to me more than once."

Feeling relieved, O'Mara nodded again. He approved of people with problems who provided their own solutions.

"I can do that for you, of course," he replied. "But initially I think Cha Thrat should approach your little disturbance before the chief psychologist has to take official notice of this particular misdemeanor, which would mean an official reprimand going on its training record. Cha Thrat is also female, and thankfully the only Sommaradvan in the hospital, so it will be more sympathetic. The department will handle it."

Deliberately he had followed the hospital practice of referring to Crang-Suvi and Cha Thrat as "it" because, to a member of any other species, the difference was considered unimportant unless there were clinical reasons for specifying another being's sex. In many cases the visual differences were hard to detect, and much trouble and emotional distress had been caused in the early days by other-species members of the staff being mistakenly identified in company. So he called everyone who was not an Earth-human man or woman "it" regardless of sex, while the other-species staff did likewise where Earth-human males and females were involved. Besides, he thought dryly, it was much handier when the other species concerned had more than one sex.

But now that the other's problem was being solved it was time, O'Mara thought, that he stepped back into character. There was no sense in giving the impression that he was going soft.

In a brisk, dismissive voice he said, "Is there anything or anyone else bothering you, Doctor?"

"No, sir," the other replied, slipping from the high edge of the Melfan recliner onto the floor and turning to leave. "But I would like to congratulate you on your new appointment. It is well-deserved."

O'Mara inclined his head; then on impulse he said, "In my new capacity as administrator I can see to it that the Monitor Corps allows your Warnagh-Lut to remain in Sector General indefinitely, if that is what you both wish." He smiled sourly and added, "After all, there is no point in me having ultimate power if I don't occasionally abuse it."

Cresk-Sar gave an untranslatable bark of thanks and waddled hurriedly out of the office as if it had good and urgent news to tell someone. O'Mara sighed in self-irritation. *Watch it,* he told himself, *you are definitely going soft.* Then he keyed the attention signal to the outer office and held it down until Braithwaite replied.

"In here, all of you. Now."

# CHAPTER 3

They trooped in single file into the big inner office in reverse order of seniority. The Tarlan ex-surgeon-captain and present Padre Lioren was first, followed by the Sommaradvan former warrior-surgeon Cha Thrat, with O'Mara's principal assistant, Braithwaite, bringing up the rear. O'Mara waved a hand loosely toward the furniture.

"This will take time," he said. "Find a place to sit."

Braithwaite was lucky in that there was one Earth-human chair; the others had to settle for the best they could find, because the Sommaradvan and Tarlan cultures had yet to be discovered when the room had been furnished. No doubt Maintenance, who argued that anything that was not an emergency had to be considered low priority, would get around to remedying the discrepancy one of these years.

While O'Mara pretended to stare down at his large, blunt-fingered hands on the desk before him, he watched them through lowered brows as they settled themselves comfortably or uncomfortably and stopped fidgeting. He was thinking that one didn't have to have a history of insanity to work in Other-Species Psychology, but that precondition conferred certain advantages, even where their chief was concerned. Every member of his staff was flawed in some respect, but today he was regarding them all clinically and dispassionately from a completely new viewpoint.

Braithwaite looked relaxed, self-assured, and incredibly neat. Even when he was leaning back onto his shoulder blades in an armchair, his uniform gave the impression that he was about to undergo a fleet commander's inspection. Cha Thrat was a physiological classification DCNF whose large, cone-shaped body possessed four stubby legs, four medial arms, and another four arms at shoulder level that were thinner with hands terminating in finer, more sensitive digits. Physically, Lioren resembled Cha Thrat except that its body, legs, and arms were longer and less muscular, but the resemblance was no closer than that between a giraffe and a horse.

O'Mara raised his head. "I want to discuss briefly my promotion to administrator," he said, "and its effect on the future work of this department, the change of emphasis in certain of your duties that will become necessary, and what I expect from all of you as a result. Feel free to interrupt if you are quite sure you have something of value to say. But I shall begin by talking, in order of length of service and experience, about you."

He waited until a second bout of fidgeting had abated, then went on, "I know that you have all broken the rules by sneaking a look at one another's confidential psych files, so what I say should not cause embarrassment. If it does, tough. Braithwaite first."

Without changing his position in the deep armchair, the lieutenant somehow gave the impression that he had come to attention.

"You," he went on briskly, "deal well with the office staff and routine and you are good with people regardless of species. When sympathy is needed you are sympathetic, firm when the being concerned isn't doing enough to help solve his, her, or its problem, and you never, ever lose your temper. To your present superior you are respectful without being subservient, and you gently but firmly re-

sist any attempt at bullying. As my principal assistant you're close
to ideal. Intelligent, efficient, adaptable, dedicated, uncomplaining,
and completely lacking in ambition. In spite of completing your
medical training here, you refused to take the Corps exams for
surgeon-lieutenant. You have found your niche in Other-Species
Psychology and you don't want to go anywhere or do anything else.
When you were offered a major promotion off-hospital you turned
it down.

"But enough of the compliments, Lieutenant," he went on.
"On and under the surface your personality is so well adjusted that
it is almost frightening. Your only defect is that in one respect you
are a total and abject coward. You want to be and you are a trusted
and resourceful second-in-command who enjoys the power and
advantages that the position confers, but you are intensely afraid of
taking the ultimate responsibility that would go with the top job."

Without the smallest change of expression, Braithwaite nodded. He was a man who was comfortable with the truth about himself. O'Mara turned to Cha Thrat.

"Unlike the lieutenant," he said, "you are not afraid of anything. On Sommaradva you were a leading warrior-surgeon who,
in spite of your patient being the first other-species entity you had
ever seen, was able to intervene surgically and save the life of a leading member of the contact team. Because of the team's gratitude,
plus the fact that they wanted to do the Sommaradvan authorities
a favor because the contact was not going well, you were sent here
as a trainee, in spite of hospital objections, for political rather than
medical reasons.

"In the event your surgical ability and technique were acceptable," he continued sourly, "but your strict adherence to Sommaradvan medical ethics was not. You were free to attend lectures,
but soon nobody would accept you for practical work on the wards.
We found you a job as a trainee in Maintenance, where you did well
and became popular with a large number of the junior-grade medical and maintenance staff trainees until you messed up there, too.

I'm not quite sure how you ended up here. Some people think I took pity on you.

"Some people," he added dryly as he turned toward Lioren, "don't know me very well."

He paused for a long moment, thinking about what he should say to this entity who had suffered and was still suffering. O'Mara's words and manner toward a patient and a colleague were different. With an emotionally distressed person he could be as gentle and sympathetic as the situation required, but to a mentally healthy nonpatient he preferred to relax and be his normal, bad-tempered, sarcastic self. In spite of the Tarlan's continued good progress over the past two years, Lioren fell somewhere into the grey area between therapist and patient. But whatever he said, the Padre would accept it without complaint because it would consider that it deserved every physical and mental cruelty it would ever receive.

When Lioren had joined Sector General he had been a Wearer of the Blue Cloak, Tarla's equivalent of Earth's Nobel Prize for Medicine, and it had shown itself to be an unusually able and dedicated other-species physician and surgeon before transferring to the Monitor Corps' medical service, where its promotion to surgeon-captain had been deservedly rapid.

Then had come the terrible Cromsaggar Incident.

While it was in charge of a disaster-relief operation on Cromsag involving urgent treatment for a planetwide epidemic, a mistake had occurred that had virtually decimated the surviving population. As a result it was court-martialed for professional negligence and exonerated. But it had disagreed with the findings of the court, felt that it deserved the ultimate penalty, that it would never be able to forgive itself, and it had made a solemn promise that it would never again practice its beloved medical arts for the rest of its life, which it did not expect to last for more than a few days. With the aid of O'Mara's highly unorthodox therapy, it had been able to forgive itself in part and extend its life expectancy, but Tarlans did not take their solemn promises lightly so it had never nor would it ever practice medicine on any being again.

Instead it had learned to sublimate its need to alleviate the suffering of others by bringing to them not the healing knife but the gentle, understanding, and sympathetic words, words that really meant something because the recipients knew beyond any possible doubt that they came from a person whose suffering had been so much greater than their own.

In every hospital, O'Mara knew, there were always patients whose condition was more serious than one's own, so that the less serious cases found hope and consolation, and even felt themselves fortunate, in the knowledge that they were not as bad as that poor bugger down the ward.

It was a psychological truism that had enabled Lioren to put his mental anguish to constructive use. Its preferences were the truly hopeless cases, patients or staff members who were mentally distressed and did not respond to normal psychotherapy, or who were in desperate need of spiritual consolation, or who were terminally ill and afraid. It had turned its brilliant mind to gaining a basic knowledge of all the religious beliefs and practices known within the Galactic Federation, which on average numbered twelve to every inhabited planet. Its results, considering the difficult emotional area it had made its own, were exceptionally good.

Moral cowardice in an embarrassing situation, O'Mara decided finally, was the first refuge of the intelligent. He went on, "Padre, everyone knows everything about you and you are beyond embarrassment, so talking about you would be a waste of my time and breath. The point I'm making is that to begin with, all of you were flawed in some respect, but that has not affected the quality of your work in the department. To the contrary, it has given you a greater sensitivity and insight where your patients are concerned. But as a result of my recent promotion, from now on I expect you to do better, and much more.

"In case the grapevine omitted the details," he continued,

looking at them in turn, "my current position is this: I have been appointed administrator while retaining my position and duties of chief psychologist for the interim period necessary for me to find, evaluate, train, and choose my successor, who will also be expected to perform both jobs. It has been decided that in future the entity who holds this position must be a civilian, so that he, she, or it will not be influenced by the Monitor Corps, as well as having formal medical training and experience in other-species psychology to enable it to understand and satisfy the peculiar medical and non-medical needs of this establishment. Because of its importance and the unusual nature of the qualification required, the position has been advertised on all the professional nets. Much of my time will be taken up familiarizing myself with my new duties while you help me winnow out the wishful thinkers, preferably at long range, so that we can short-list and concentrate on the one or two who might possibly measure up for the job."

He nodded curtly to indicate that the meeting was over, then said, "Don't bother asking questions until you've had a chance to think about them. From now on I'll be watching you closely and hitting you with a few surprises from time to time. Cha Thrat, Lioren, if you're tired, go rest in the outer office. Braithwaite, I have a job for you."

As the others were leaving, he went on, "Lieutenant, Diagnostician Yursedth is due in half an hour. It is having troublesome dreams and waking episodes of psychosomatic peripheral neuropathy associated with one of its Educator tapes. Talk to it, identify and erase the culprit tape, then reimpress a same-species tape with what you consider to be a more amenable personality with a similar medical background. I shall be picking the retiring administrator's brains for the rest of the afternoon and, no doubt, trying to duck invitations to his farewell party."

He held Braithwaite's eyes for a moment, but he did not allow the sympathy he was feeling to reach his voice as he went on, "The Yursedth case could be tricky, and this will be the first time that you've erased and reimpressed a tape without supervision. If you have a problem with it, Lieutenant, don't call me. This one will be entirely your responsibility."

Braithwaite nodded and turned to follow the others. His carriage was erect, his uniform was impeccable, his features were without expression, but his face looked very pale. O'Mara sighed, closed his eyes, and tried to remember the mechanics of interviewing a candidate for a difficult and responsible job.

As they had applied to himself.

# CHAPTER 4

It had been the same office, but those days the walls had been covered only by sickly green anticorrosive paint rather than a selection of restful landscapes from a dozen worlds, and instead of the extraterrestrial furniture that made the present office look like a medieval torture chamber, there had been only two hard, upright chairs on opposite sides of a bench whose plastic worktop was buried under an untidy heap of printouts. Major Craythorne had occupied one chair and O'Mara the other.

That job interview, with the breaks necessary for eating, sleeping, and long periods of work experience, lasted for three years.

Suddenly he was back to the there and then, feeling the anxiety or perhaps it was the last hurried, undigested meal heavy in his stomach. Again he was smelling the supposedly odorless paint and hearing the high-pitched, intermittent sound of a nearby power drill that was forcing the major to swear mildly and pause from time to time.

"You have to remember, O'Mara," said Craythorne, not for the first time, "that your face and manner do not invite trust, and your features show no depth or subtlety of mind even though we both know those qualities are there, and that on several occasions you have tinkered curatively with troubled other-species personalities. On the surface your consultation technique is crude but effective, so crude that your poor patient has no idea how deeply and sensitively he, she, or it has been probed and manipulated while you are appearing to bully them. Have you ever considered trying to be, well, insincerely polite?"

O'Mara sighed in angry impatience, but silently with his mouth open so that the other couldn't detect it, then said, "You're familiar with the Earth saying, sir, about trying to make a silk purse out of a sow's ear? You know I don't work well in an atmosphere of insincere friendliness."

Craythorne nodded calmly, but whether it was in answer to the question or the statement was unclear, so probably it was to both. He said, "Forget it for now, O'Mara. Your next assignment is to settle in a group of Kelgians. With them insincerity or politeness would be a waste of time because both concepts are completely alien to them. You'll feel right at home. Have you any prior experience with that species?"

O'Mara shook his head.

The major smiled. "If I had time to tell you about them, which unfortunately I don't right now, you wouldn't believe me. They arrive in two hours. Before meeting them you should brief yourself on the library computer . . ."

In the corridor outside their doorless office, someone dropped something heavy and metallic that made the whole room ring like a discordant bell. Craythorne winced and ended calmly, ". . . which, fortunately, is one of the few facilities in this place that is up and running."

The major was a man O'Mara would have dearly liked to hate, but couldn't because he was so damned likable. No matter how or why one of his subordinates messed up, he never lost his temper. Instead he just looked so disappointed that the culprits felt so sorry they never made the same mistake again. His manner was polished, invariably correct, and the greying hair and thin, sensitive features could have belonged to a career diplomat. Even in the issue coveralls he looked impeccable. It was as if the ever-present mixture of oily grime and metallic dust that stained everyone else's clothing did not so much as dare approach his. He gave the impression of being, and truly was, a good man. He had opened up a job for O'Mara when all O'Mara's options had closed.

"Major," said O'Mara enviously, "how the hell did you get this way?"

The other smiled again and shook his head. "You keep trying to probe my hidden inner depths, and I yours. But trying to practice psychoanalysis on each other's deeply buried psychoses is a waste of time, because as psychologists we don't have any. We're supposed to be sane, well-integrated personalities. It's in our contracts."

"Your contract, maybe . . ." O'Mara began.

Before he could go on, Craythorne said in a tone of gentle dismissal, "If you aren't familiar with the new library computer consoles, there are plenty of mad geniuses working down there who will be glad to help you out."

Only a few of the freight elevators were working and they were usually so full of men and equipment that it wasn't worth spending time waiting for a chance to squeeze into one. Besides, he was used to threading his way through many miles of corridors still under construction that were identified only by their hospital level and corridor numbers daubed with paint at the intersections. He slowed his pace to go around a couple of large, sweating and swearing men in Monitor Corps green coveralls, one of them a sergeant, who had been installing a heavy length of ceiling ducting, one end of which had fallen onto the floor. The NCO called out to him as he was passing.

"You," he said sharply, "help us lift this damn thing into position again and hold it. I'll show you where it fits . . ."

It was obvious where it fitted. Without speaking, O'Mara pulled a nearby bench into a more convenient position, lifted the loose end of the ducting onto the top surface, and jumped up himself. Then he lifted it without effort to the ceiling and held it accurately in position while the other two secured it.

"Thanks, friend," said the sergeant. "Obviously you know what you're doing and I need you here for a couple of hours. Whatever else you you were about to do, forget it."

O'Mara shook his head and jumped to the floor.

"It's okay," said the sergeant in a manner suggesting that he was unused to receiving negative responses. "I'll fix it with your squad leader. On this job the Corps instructions take precedence over those given by civilian contractor supervisors."

"Sorry," said O'Mara, turning to go. "I really have to be somewhere else."

"Hold it right there," said the other angrily. "Have you some kind of difficulty in comprehension . . . ? What is it, Bates?"

The sergeant broke off as O'Mara turned back to look at him. It would not have been the first time that he had had to win an argument with his fists. But that had been in the bad old days and Craythorne would not like it if he started doing it again. Besides, the second Corpsman, Bates, was staring at his face and tugging urgently at the sergeant's sleeve.

"I know this one, Sarge," he said in a respectful undertone. "Forget it."

O'Mara turned away again to resume his interrupted journey to the library. He had gone about twenty yards along the corridor when he heard the sergeant saying loudly, "He's Major Craythorne's assistant, you say? But what the hell is a bloody psychologist doing with muscles like *that*?"

It was a question that had been asked many times by many people during O'Mara's life, and the answer, based on visual evidence alone, was usually provided by the questioner, who took one look and saw no reason to listen to anything he had to say.

Since his early teens, O'Mara's life had been a series of such frustrations. He had lost both parents when he was three and his aunt, probably because of ill health plus the fact that he had been a really obnoxious child, had not given him the support needed against adults and superiors who kept telling him what he should be and do with his life.

Teachers took one look, relegated him to the sports field, and considered his efforts to study an interesting and unnecessary anomaly. Later a succession of company personnel officers could not believe that a young man with such square, ugly features and shoulders so huge that they made his head look moronically small by comparison could be really interested in brainy stuff like electronics, medicine, or psychology. He had gone into space in the hope of finding a different situation and more flexible minds there, but in vain. Despite constant efforts during interviews to impress people with his quite considerable intelligence, they were too impressed by his muscle power to listen and his applications were invariably stamped APPROVED SUITABLE FOR HEAVY SUSTAINED LABOR. So he had gone from one space construction job to another, always working with people whose minds as well as their bodies were muscle-bound, and ending with this one on the final assembly of Sector Twelve General Hospital. Here he had decided to relieve the physical monotony by using his intelligence to secretly tinker with other people's minds.

It was not something one did to one's friends, he thought, but then he had never had any.

One piece of covert therapy performed on an Earth-human workmate, plus some very rule-of-thumb treatment he had given to a space-orphaned and emotionally disturbed Hudlar infant weighing half a ton, had brought him to Craythorne's attention. Not only had the investigating officer exonerated him of all blame in causing the accident that had killed the baby's parents, but the ensuing trial had uncovered the finer details of his curative tinkering with the emotional problems of a seriously neurotic workmate and had impressed the other to the extent that the major had offered him, for a trial period that would last only until he showed himself incapable of doing it, a job where brains rather than his overlarge muscles were needed. It had turned out to be the hardest and most satisfying job he had ever had.

It was a job he didn't want to lose.

But satisfying the major this time, he realized as soon as the library data on the Kelgian species and culture began to unroll, would not be easy. Of course, neither had any of his recent assignments. That first other-species job had nearly killed him at the time, but there were days when he found himself wishing that he had nothing more complicated to do than feed, bathe, and baby-sit half a ton of squalling Hudlar infant.

Two hours later he was waiting inside Personnel Lock F on Level Thirty-Seven and watching the first Kelgians he had ever seen, other than in the library pictures, come crawling toward him along the boarding tube. *At least they are warm-blooded oxygen-breathers like me,* he thought dryly, but that was the only point of similarity.

They were like fat, silver-furred caterpillars averaging more than two meters from conical head to upturned tail, undulating forward on twelve pairs of stubby feet, although the four sets closest to the head were slightly longer, thinner, and terminated in delicate, pink hands. Their tiny, tightly grouped facial features were too alien to be readable, but, he had learned, the involuntary motion of the highly mobile fur that tufted, spiked, or rippled in waves along their entire body surface told everyone, or at least every other Kelgian, exactly what they were feeling from moment to moment. The result was that telling a lie or even trying to shade the truth was a complete waste of time where their species was concerned.

The Kelgians were soft and visually appealing creatures. Had they been scaled down by a factor of ten, as a boy he would not have minded keeping one as a pet, if he had been allowed to keep pets.

He backed away a little as they moved out of the boarding

tube and began spreading around him in a semicircle. They had raised their bodies upright and were balancing on their rearmost four legs, and their heads were curved forward so that their tiny faces were at eye level. It felt as though he were being surrounded by a bunch of furry question marks.

So far as he was concerned, O'Mara realized with a stirring of butterflies in his stomach, he was close to being in a first-contact situation. If he should do or say something wrong, it was unlikely that he would cause an interstellar war to start. The Kelgians were reputed to be a highly intelligent, technologically advanced, and civilized species who probably knew more about Earth-humans than he did about them and they would, he hoped, make allowances.

Faced with this situation, what would the cool and impeccably mannered Major Craythorne say and do?

O'Mara held out his hand toward the nearest Kelgian, then abruptly brought it back to his side. The library computer had not mentioned this form of physical greeting. With two-handed people of Earth it was a sign of friendship and trust, a legacy of a time when it made good sense for people meeting for the first time to grab and thereby immobilize each other's weapon hand. But the Kelgians' hands were ridiculously tiny and there were too many of them. O'Mara had the feeling that he had just avoided making his first mistake.

Instead he said slowly and clearly, "My name is O'Mara. Did you have a comfortable trip, and would you prefer to see—"

"My name is Crenneth," the one facing him broke in, its fur stirring restively. "The ship accommodation was cramped and uncomfortable and the food terrible. The speech of the Earth-human crew was rapid and precise. Why are you speaking so slowly? We do not have a problem with verbal comprehension. Do you?"

O'Mara choked, cleared his throat, and said, "No."

"Are you a Healer?" Crenneth asked. "If so, what is your level of seniority?"

"No," said O'Mara again. "A, a psychologist." Silently he added, *Without qualifications.*

"Then you are a Healer of the Mind," the other persisted. "What's the difference?"

"We can discuss the difference when there is more time," he replied, deciding that he was not going to reveal his lack of formal training, or anything else of a personal nature, to this inquisitive, outsized caterpillar on first acquaintance. He went on, "Earlier I was about to ask if you would prefer to see your living quarters, or visit the dining hall first? Your personal effects are being moved to your quarters as we speak."

"I'm hungry," said one of the others, its fur rising in spikes. "After that indigestible ship food, your dining hall is bound to be an improvement."

"There are no guarantees," said O'Mara dryly.

Crenneth rippled its fur. In a manner which suggested that it was the Kelgian spokesperson and the one with the rank, it said, "Our quarters first. You lead the way, O'Mara. Are Earth-humans able to talk while they walk? I expect balancing a long, upright body on only two feet requires some concentration. Does jerking your head up and down like that indicate a negative or an affirmative reply?"

"Affirmative," he replied as they moved off. He had the feeling that Crenneth was about to speak again but had stopped itself. They were approaching the end of a long, unpainted corridor and from both branches of the intersection came the increasing sounds of hammering and drilling interspersed with shouted Earth-human voices.

When they reached the intersection he saw that the corridor in both directions was scattered with wall and ceiling scaffolding units containing men with paint applicators or thin sheets of sharp-edged metal which they were swinging around with little regard for the safety of passersby. More panels lay flat on the scaffolding, their sharp edges projecting beyond the work surfaces into the corridor. O'Mara was about to tell the Kelgians to halt, but they were already hanging back, their fur tufting and rippling in a way that suggested great agitation.

He faced into the slightly less cluttered corridor and looked for someone in authority. But he could see no Monitor Corps coveralls or insignia of rank to read, so obviously the men were employed by one of the civilian contractors. He filled his lungs.

"Men!" he shouted above the background noise. "I want to speak to your squad leader. Now."

A large, red-faced man jumped down from a section of scaffolding about twenty yards away and dodged quickly between the intervening equipment to stand facing him. The red facial coloration, O'Mara decided, was due to irritation as well as hard work. He tried the Craythorne approach.

"Sorry for the inconvenience," he said, nodding along the corridor, "when you're obviously busy. I'm taking a group of newly arrived Kelgian nurses to their quarters on Forty-Three, and I would like you to clear a path for them through the—"

"The hell you would," the other broke in, looking past O'Mara's shoulder for a moment. "I've got just two hours to finish this stretch of corridor. Take them to the dining hall and feed them lettuce, or whatever else overgrown caterpillars eat, until then. Otherwise go up to Fifty-One, the freight elevator is supposed to be working to that level now, and the ramps down to Forty-Nine are clear. Then if you take a left past the—"

While the squad leader had been talking, O'Mara had decided that he could not go around for the reasons that neither of them could be completely sure that the way would be clear and he did not want his party diverting all over the hospital while trying to find a way to their quarters. He shook his head.

"Going around is not an option," said O'Mara.

"Who d'you think you're ordering around?" the squad leader said angrily. "Get your trainees out of here and stop wasting my time."

The men working nearby had stopped to listen, followed by the ones who were farther down the line. It was as if a strange wave of silence were rolling slowly down the corridor.

"Your scaffolding, especially the sections with wall plating projecting over the edges, is on wheels," said O'Mara in what he hoped was a quiet, reasonable voice. "It can be easily moved against one wall to let my people pass in safety. The same applies to the paint and other loose stuff lying around, which you will have to stow and take away soon, anyway. I'll lend a hand to move it."

Deliberately the squad leader did not lower his voice. He said, "No you won't, because you don't give me orders and you're not coming this way. Move off. Just who the hell d'you think you are, anyway?"

O'Mara tried hard to keep his temper in check and his voice low. Two more of the men nearest to them had jumped to the floor and were moving to join their boss. He waited until they were close; then he looked them up and down and nodded to each before speaking.

"I don't have an identity problem," he said, "so I know that my name is O'Mara. In case I'm tempted to report this matter later, it would be better not to know your names. My trainees will move along this corridor, without trouble, I trust, because we do not want to give other-species medical staff a bad impression. Please clear a path for them. I'm afraid I must insist."

*Craythorne would approve of my gentlemanly manner and phraseology,* he thought. Not so the squad leader. He gave O'Mara specific instructions where a brainless, overmuscled gorilla trying to use fancy language should go and the various physiologically impossible acts he should perform on himself when he got there, regrettably in language that was clear enough to be processed by the Kelgians' translators. O'Mara had had more than enough of people who held it to be a law of nature that brains and brawn were mutually exclusive, and he felt a terrible urge to finish the argument their way, with his fists, head, and feet. He held up one hand.

"Enough," he said in a cold, quiet voice that cut the other off in midword. "If this argument is about to become physical, which I would rather it didn't, we have twelve nurses available whose training covers the treatment of the three, or maybe more, Earth-human casualties that will result. It is your move."

*Craythorne,* he thought, *would certainly not approve of me now.*

# CHAPTER 5

For a few seconds there was total silence in the corridor. The squad leader's face was darkening toward purple. The man on his right was smiling and the one on his left was looking thoughtful but not afraid; his hand moved toward his boss's arm as if to restrain him, then he let it fall again. This one, O'Mara thought, was able to think even if, for the sake of a peaceful life, he was in the habit of letting the squad leader do the thinking for him.

As space construction workers they were highly paid but, so far as the majority of them were concerned, not highly intelligent or well educated. They didn't have to be. But their ignorance was a temporary condition that could be relieved. O'Mara nodded to the man on the left to show that his words were for him as well as for his boss before returning his attention to the squad leader. Regretfully, he thought, *I'll try to do it Craythorne's way one more time.*

"While we're all thinking about what to do next," he said, allowing a smile to touch the corners of his mouth, "there is something you should know about Kelgians—if, that is, some of you are meeting them for the first time. Physically they are not very strong. Apart from the delicate bone structure of the spine and brain casing, they are made up of soft muscle tissue in broad, circular bands along their body length. These muscles need a lot of blood and the veins are close to the skin, which means that even a small surface wound is serious for them because their mobile fur makes it difficult to control the bleeding. The effect on the fur is even more serious . . ."

It sounded as if he knew what he was talking about, but he was simply paraphrasing the introductory material, intended for primary-school children, on Kelgian physiology from the library. But the man on the right was frowning in concentration, the thoughtful one on the left was staring at the Kelgians, and the squad leader's face was shading through red to pink.

". . . because the fur is their most expressive and, to them, beautiful feature," he went on quickly. "To every other Kelgian the fur movements are an extension of their spoken language that shows exactly what they are thinking and feeling. For example, a male can't hide his feelings for a female or, whether or not she returns them, hers for him. They can never be coy or play hard to get. The fur is very sensitive. If it is injured or damaged in any way, it is the equivalent of a severe physical disfigurement or bad facial scarring to us. A scarred Kelgian would, well, have great difficulty finding a mate . . ."

"I wish it was that simple with our women," the one who had been concentrating broke in. The thoughtful one added, "So you're saying that if they get cut by sharp edges of plating, or get their fur smeared with paint or oil, the ladies are in bad trouble." Without waiting for O'Mara to reply, he said, "Boss, do we clear a path for them?"

The squad leader hesitated. His face had returned to its natural color, but plainly he was a man who did not like losing an argument. It was time to give him back the initiative, O'Mara thought, and appeal to the better side of his nature, if he had one.

"They have been traveling for a long time," he said, "and some of them badly need to use the, ah, facilities in their quarters." He grinned. "Your corridor is messed up enough as it is."

The other hesitated, then guffawed loudly. "Right, O'Mara, you've got it. Far be it from me to get a lady into serious trouble. Give us ten minutes."

There was only one small holdup while the party was moving in single file along the cleared section of corridor. Word had been passed down the line that a party of other-species nurses were going through and the men began whistling. Crenneth wanted to know the meaning of the strange, untranslatable noise. O'Mara decided to hide behind the literal truth.

He said, "It is a sound they make when the think another person is beautiful."

"Oh, that's all right then," said Crenneth. "Are we expected to whistle back?"

It was ten minutes later when they were entering the brightly painted and completed section containing the Kelgian living quarters that Crenneth spoke again. It said, "For your information we are not, at our ages, subject to involuntary incontinence, if that is what you were suggesting back there. I did not allow any of my people to correct you because your situation at the time seemed uncertain and an interruption might not have been helpful. But there is a question I wanted to ask earlier."

"Ask it now," said O'Mara.

"Why are you, a Healer of the Mind, showing us the way to our accommodation," it said, "rather than a person of lesser professional rank? Are you curious about a species you are meeting for the first time? Or do you have professional reasons for observing our behavior?"

For a moment he wondered how the ultra-polite Craythorne

would have responded to questions like that. But he wasn't the major and he would feel more comfortable if he started out the way he intended to proceed or, if he messed up, how he would very shortly finish. Besides, the library material had stated several times that politeness, like tact or telling lies, was a concept that Kelgians did not understand and they found its use both confusing and irritating.

"Yes to both questions," said O'Mara. "You are among the first of the other-species medical staff to arrive here. I wanted to make your acquaintance as soon as possible since in the future I may, or may not, be called on to treat you in my professional capacity, or possibly to have some of you expelled from the hospital as psychologically unsuitable for service here. You will appreciate that my first impressions of your behavior could be important."

Crenneth remained silent while its agitated fur told everyone but O'Mara what exactly it was feeling. It could not tell a lie, but there was nothing to stop its exercising the option of silence.

From somewhere among the group following them a voice said, "It thinks we're all mad." Another said, "After the higher nursing examinations and psychological fitness tests we had to take before we were even allowed to volunteer for this place, I think it's right."

They did not understand politeness, diplomacy, or the many other ways Earth-humans had of hiding the fact that they were lying, O'Mara thought, but surely it must be possible to ease the exact and perhaps frightening truth with an honest compliment.

He looked at Crenneth and raised his voice so that everyone else would hear him as he said, "From an objective viewpoint, you *are* all mad. However, an unusually high degree of dedication, unselfishness, and the placing of the health and future welfare of others before your own individual happiness are allowable neuroses. In fact, the fabric of galactic civilization is based on them.

"But."

They had reached the entrances to their quarters but it seemed that none of them wanted to go inside. Instead they stood around him, watching and listening while their fur did things that were incomprehensible to him, at least for the present.

Very seriously, he said, "You are all filled with enthusiasm and dedication and the noblest qualities of your profession, but that may not be enough. When this hospital goes into full operation there will be upward of sixty different life-forms, with sixty different sets of species' behavioral characteristics, body odors, and ways of looking at life, on the medical and maintenance staff. Living space will be at a premium, so you will be working, eating, and, on our communal recreation level, playing together. A very high degree of species adaptability on the social level will be required.

"Undoubtedly some of you will encounter serious psychological problems," he went on, "whether you think so right now or not. Given even the highest qualities of mutual respect and tolerance you hold for your colleagues on the staff, there will still be occasions when inter-species friction occurs. Potentially dangerous situations will arise, through ignorance or misunderstanding, or, more seriously, a being could develop an unsuspected xenophobia which could affect its professional capabilities, its mental stability, or both. A Melfan medic, for example, who had a subconscious fear of the furry vermin with lethal stings that are native to its planet, might not be able to bring to bear on a Kelgian patient the proper degree of clinical detachment required for its treatment. Since Melfans are a six-limbed, exoskeletal species, some of you might feel the same way about them."

O'Mara paused for a moment, but there was no response. They were watching him in absolute silence, even though their fur was rippling and whipping about as if an unfelt gale were blowing along the corridor.

He went on, "Updated training reports and psych profiles will be maintained in our other-species psychology department, whose purpose is the earliest possible dete. ion and eradication of such problems or, if therapy fails, the removal of the individual concerned from the hospital before the situation can develop into open conflict. Guarding against such wrong, unhealthy, or intolerant thinking is a duty which the department will perform with great zeal, so much so that that it will irritate or anger you to the extent that you may want to tell us, sometimes to our faces, exactly what you think of us. But justifiable invective we do not consider to be a symptom of wrong thinking."

Earth-humans might have laughed politely at his attempted pleasantry; then he remembered that Kelgians always said exactly what they thought.

"Your sleep will be troubled with nightmares, perhaps sex-based fears or fantasies so terrifying that you do not yet believe them possible. When you awaken from them you will be expected to go on duty and work with these nightmares, and make friends with them, or learn to respect and obey them if they happen to be your superiors. If you have a problem with this, as a last resort you may request psychological assistance. But if you have understood the implications of what I have been telling you, you already know that it would be better for everyone concerned if you solved these problems yourselves.

"After you have had time to settle in," he continued, "you will be contacted by the Earth-human senior tutor, Dr. Mannen, regarding your sleeping, eating, training, and lecture schedules. He has a dog, a nonsapient, nonhostile Earth quadruped which he will expect you to acknowledge, or perhaps admire even though it has no medical training. . . ."

*Like me,* he added silently.

"You will find Dr. Mannen to be an excellent teacher, friendly, helpful, and with a personality that is more pleasant than my own—"

"That's the best news we've heard today," said one of the Kelgians behind Crenneth.

O'Mara ignored it. As he turned to go he gestured toward their waiting quarters and ended, "Good luck with your studies. Professionally, I hope never to see any of you again."

"Thank you, O'Mara," said Crenneth, with a sudden ripple of its fur. "We also hope never to see you again."

# CHAPTER 6

The reason for their forthright language and behavior, he had decided there and, then, was that in Kelgians the physiology and psychology, the fur and the feelings of the mind that controlled it, were difficult to separate. Unlike other species, who had to depend on words alone to communicate, they did not have to carry the psychological baggage of lies, or of having to hide their true feelings from others, or the stress of not knowing the truth about what other people were thinking about them. The Kelgian emotional life was beautifully simple. And now, almost fifty years since he had first met that first group of them, he still had a warm and special regard for them even though he could never admit to such a thing. Apart from Prilicla, their single Cinrusskin empath, who knew more about the hidden contents of O'Mara's mind than did anyone else in the hospital, the Kelgians were his favorite species in Sector General, because they said what they thought and everyone knew exactly where they were with them.

They were his kind of people.

O'Mara sighed, opened his eyes, and completed the process of easing himself back into present space and time. It was necessary that he see Colonel Skempton, and he had to go at once if he was going to leave Braithwaite to deal alone with their latest psychological hot potato. He left via the outer office without talking to anyone.

The administrator's private office was much larger and more luxuriously appointed than O'Mara's in the Psychology Department. The floor covering was so deep and soft that one waded through rather than walked over it, and there was a greater variety of other-species' furniture that really was comfortable for beings who had occasion to use it. Behind the enormous, tidy desk, which was empty except for its inset console and communications screens, there were two chairs instead of the one that was usually there. They both looked as sinfully comfortable as the extraterrestrial relaxers. Skempton pointed at the empty one beside him.

"There was no need to tidy up your desk just for me," said O'Mara dryly as he sat down. They both knew that the colonel had a neatness fetish and that his desk always looked that way. He swiveled his chair to face O'Mara and stared directly at his chest for a few seconds without speaking.

"As you have seen," said O'Mara caustically, "I'm still wearing my uniform with the insignia removed. This is not because I yearn for my former rank or have any deep attachment to the Monitor Corps, or for any other sentimental or psychological reason. There are just too many people in this place who can't tell one Earth-human from another, but they think of me as the one with grey hair and a Monitor green uniform who doesn't bother to wish anyone the time of day. I'm wearing it as a simple aid to identification, so you don't have to commiserate or avoid hurting my bruised feelings because I don't have any, bruised or otherwise. And as a civilian I don't even have to call you 'sir' . . ."

"I don't remember you ever calling me 'sir,'" Skempton broke in, smiling. "But as the new civilian administrator everyone, including as a courtesy the military personnel, will call you 'sir' at all times, whether they feel respect for you in any given situation or not. Do you handle megalomania well, O'Mara?"

". . . so if you have instructions, advice, warnings, or other unclassifiable knowledge you wish to share with me," O'Mara continued, ignoring the interruption, "let's cut to it at once. I would appreciate your advice even though I probably won't take it. Then you can formally introduce me to your staff, having first indicated which heads I should pat or the asses, if any, I should kick. Right?

"And the megalomania will be a temporary condition," he added sourly, "because so is this new job."

Skempton nodded sympathetically. "Choosing and training a successor capable of filling your shoes could take time," he said seriously, "so your temporary job could last for as long as you need. Or even want."

"Are you trying to compliment me," said O'Mara, "or lead me into temptation?"

"Yes, twice," said the colonel. "But seriously, the hardest part of the new job is being pleasant, and firm, too, of course, with everyone. In this office you won't be dealing with emotionally troubled patients, they will all *know* that they are saner, more intelligent, and fully capable of doing this job better than you can. Maybe some of them are, but they are too high in their comfortable medical specialties to seriously consider ousting you. They will come to you with legitimate requests for equipment, medical supplies, or additional staff that have, they will insist, much more merit than the similar requests of their colleagues.

"You will listen to them," he went on, "and tell them exactly what you think of them, but always under your breath, and do whatever is humanly, or nonhumanly, possible. Considering the resources of the Federation and the Monitor Corps, that is quite a lot. The ones who know exactly what they need will tell you without wasting time. You will give them what they want or tell them gently why they can't have it until the week after next, or whenever, and find a compromise solution to their particular problem. But with the others you will listen and be diplomatic, I hope, and do nothing at all."

He gave O'Mara a worried smile and continued, "This is because all they want to do is talk to you, and complain about the nasty things they think their colleagues are saying behind their backs, or about the apparent and sometimes real attempts certain other department heads are making at empire-building by grabbing their unfair share of the top trainees. Or they will complain about the difficulties of fitting their workload into the allotted time, or stuff like that. Basically it is just high-level griping which you will listen to with an occasional sympathetic or encouraging word as appropriate or, in extreme cases, a promise to look into it as soon as your own workload allows. But usually you won't even have to say or promise anything, or do anything that your subordinate staff can't do or aren't already doing."

When Skempton paused for breath, O'Mara made a pretense of sounding shocked and said, "And is that what our respected chief administrator has been doing for the past twelve years?"

"Shameful, isn't it?" said the colonel, laughing for the first time. The process smoothed away the worry lines in his face and relaxed his mouth so that for a moment he looked younger than O'Mara had ever seen him since he had taken over the administration of the hospital. He went on, "There are moments of drama when I have to earn my salary, when saying and doing nothing isn't enough. But the point I'm making is that, regardless of their size, shape, species, or rank, listening will be the most important part of your job. Mostly you'll just have to listen and make appropriate noises while they talk out and solve their own problems and go away happy until the next time."

Suddenly O'Mara found himself laughing, too, although he could not remember how long it had been since he had done that. He said dryly, "That sounds very like what I do in Other-Species Psychology."

"Maybe that," said Skempton, "is why they gave you my job in the first place."

Irritated with himself, O'Mara allowed his features to fall back into their usual unfriendly configuration. He said, "Are you trying to compliment me again? There's no reason to waste time on pleas-antries when you're leaving the place and can't hope to benefit from them. Have you anything else to tell me about the job? Or have you any more helpful advice to give me?"

Skempton's smile faded and his tone became businesslike as he said, "No more advice, only information. The first applicant for your job arrives in three days' time. It is Dr. Cerdal, a Cemmeccan, physiological classification DBKR, and the first member of its species to come to Sector General. It was asked to donate a mind recording for the Educator tape program, so it thinks it's good. So do the Federation medical and psychiatric examiners who put it on their short list. So far it has been the only suitable candidate. What you think and the action you take will, of course, be up to you."

O'Mara nodded. The colonel turned and keyed his console before going on, "Whatever you may finally decide, you should know that the position of Administrator of Sector Twelve General Hospital is the most sought-after post in the field of multi-species medicine. The would-be candidates are important enough to exert political as well as medical influence, which is why the Federa-tion's medical examiners are winnowing out the hopeless hopefuls from the few who might stand a chance, so that you can assess and/or train the applicants without being swayed by external influences—if, that is, it's possible to influence you with anything or anybody.

"The data on Cerdal's qualifications, experience, and behavior before the examiners will be copied to you for later study. Mainte-nance has Cerdal's quarters ready for it, nothing lavish even though it is an important being on its home world, and we'll leave the rest to you. Sorry for dropping you in at the deep end . . ."

"This place," said O'Mara, "is one perpetual deep end. It always has been."

The colonel's smile returned briefly as he continued, "By the time Dr. Cerdal arrives, I shall be on my way to Nidia and a future of being an ever more high-ranking military bookkeeper on a world where the only deep ends will be sand bunkers and water traps."

Gruffly, O'Mara said, "I wish the fleet commander joy of them."

Skempton inclined his head and glanced at his watch. "Thank you," he said. "I don't see you as a golfer, O'Mara. What does our feared and respected chief psychologist do with himself when he isn't being feared and respected?"

O'Mara just shook his head.

"We all wonder about that, you know," Skempton said, "and some of the ideas put forward are unusual and colorful and, well, weird enough to arouse your professional concern. Where do you take your leaves, dammit, and what do you do there? This is probably my last chance to find out."

O'Mara shook his head again.

"Once I considered requesting a covert trace on you," the other went on, glancing again at his wrist. "But you know me better than I know myself, O'Mara, so I couldn't justify bringing in Monitor internal security just to satisfy my morbid curiosity regarding the possible misbehavior of a reticent colleague who . . ."

"You've been looking at your watch," O'Mara broke in. "If you've nothing else to tell me, I'll stop wasting your time."

"No, O'Mara," said Skempton with a sudden, broad smile, "I'm wasting *your* time. I'm supposed to keep you talking here until some people arrive. Thornnastor, Conway, Murchison, Prilicla, and any of the other diagnosticians or seniors who aren't in OR. They're bringing some special stuff that was brewed by Chief Dietician Gurronsevas, a concoction used widely on Orligia that has a blanket contraindication for all warm-blooded oxygen-breathers. You won't be able to dodge them the way you did after this morning's meeting, because they'll be here any second now. In fact, that must be Thornnastor's feet I hear in the corridor outside. This time I'm afraid you're stuck with us.

"But don't worry," he went on, plainly enjoying O'Mara's discomfort, "it shouldn't last for more than two or three hours. It's just an excuse for a party, but they also want to congratulate us properly on our new appointments, wish us well, and say nice things about my service here. They'll be trying to say nice things about you, too."

"I don't envy them their job."

# CHAPTER 7

If anything, O'Mara thought, Dr. Cerdal resembled a Kelgian, although the resemblance was not close. The Cemmeccan's caterpillar-like body was shorter and more heavily built and, rather than multiple legs, there were ten wide, semicircular bands of padded muscle spaced along its underside for ambulation and its fur was long, immobile, and jet black rather than silver. The four arms that grew from just below its large, round head and stretched backward for nearly half the length of its body were black and looked thin because they were completely hairless. The body fur continued forward without thinning to cover its face, so that the only features visible were its large, black eyes, and when it opened its mouth, it displayed an oral cavity and teeth that were also deepest black. According to the library computer there had been sound, evolutionary reasons for the body coloration, but to O'Mara it seemed that Cerdal was absorbing all the ambient light in the office like an organic black hole.

Rather than use his big, new administrator's office, O'Mara had decided to hold the initial interview in the Psychology Department. There were three reasons for this. A gratuitous display of his new, lavish workplace would have been a waste of time and a great unkindness if the candidate was unsuccessful; all the training records and psyche files that it would be using were in the old office; and anyway, it was possible that Cerdal would be equally uncomfortable in either office until Maintenance provided some Cemmeccan furniture.

O'Mara tried to imagine how his predecessor Craythorne would have handled this situation while at the same time remembering all the advice Thornnastor, Skempton, Prilicla, and even young Conway, who was going a touch grey at the temples these days, had given him on how an administrator should behave while interviewing a high-level candidate. He took a deep breath and worked the long-unused facial muscles to produce a pleasant expression even though the other might not be able to read it.

"I am Chief Psychologist and Administrator O'Mara," he said briskly, and with a nod to his left and right continued, "and these are my assistants, Padre and former Surgeon-Captain Lioren of Tarla, and the Sommaradvan former warrior-surgeon Cha Thrat. My principal assistant, Lieutenant Braithwaite, is manning the outer office. He is monitoring this interview and may put in a relevant comment or question. The proceedings will be informal and you may speak freely or interrupt at any time.

"For the present that is all you need to know about us," he ended, smiling, "but we need to know everything about you. Please speak."

Dr. Cerdal lay with the forward half of its body supported on part of a Melfan cradle so as to bring its head level with those of the interviewers. For several seconds it kept its jet-black Cemmeccan eyes only on O'Mara before the first low, gurgling words of its native speech came through their translators.

"First an observation, and questions," it said. "I am being interviewed for the most important post in this establishment, as was expected, by the present incumbent. But why am I to be questioned by and in the presence of subordinates? I had assumed the position to be one carrying complete authority and full responsibility for decision making. Is this authority and responsibility to be diluted? Is the position of administrator in fact a committee? Or is it that the present incumbent requires some form of moral support?"

Cha Thrat made a sound that did not translate, Lioren turned all four of its eyes in Cerdal's direction, and O'Mara pressed his lips tightly together to contain a verbal explosion. Perhaps, he thought angrily, the Cemmeccans were closer to the Kelgians than he had realized. This one appeared not, or maybe it was pretending not, to understand the concepts of diplomacy, tact, or even a simple show of respect for authority. It was the Padre, who was obviously having similar thoughts, who spoke first.

"My study of the Cemmeccan material in our library did not suggest that you belong to a particularly impolite species," it said. "Would you like to correct me, or comment?"

Cerdal's attention moved, reluctantly, O'Mara thought, to Lioren. It said, "I understand, and at times appreciate, polite behavior. But in essence politeness is a social lubricant that smooths, but more often conceals, the rough surfaces of interpersonal contact that could be a later cause of conflict. No doubt there will be future cases here where the softer and more gentle contact will be the indicated therapy. During the present proceedings, however, I believe that a complete and honest response to questions will be of more long-term benefit to me than a pretense of subservience and obeisance. I do not believe that I am here to waste time."

From the desk communicator came the sound of Braithwaite clearing his throat. The lieutenant said, "Has the candidate, as an additional preparation for this interview, studied the hearsay evidence available to it regarding the similar behavioral characteristics of Administrator O'Mara in the hope that modeling itself on the present incumbent will increase its chances of landing the job?"

"Of course," said Cerdal without hesitation.

His anger had faded, but O'Mara chose to remain silent because the others were asking the questions he would have asked. And Cerdal, he thought, was handling itself well.

"Dr. Cerdal," said Cha Thrat, speaking for the first time, "since you may be the only Cemmeccan at the hospital for a long time, the future cases here that you mentioned earlier will involve beings not of your species. How many other-species patients have you treated?"

"Before I answer that question," Cerdal replied, "you must understand that I was on the staff of the largest one-species Cemmeccan hospital, which also had provision for the limited treatment of emergency admissions from the principal star-traveling species sent to us from the nearby spaceport. There was no provision for chlorine- or methane-breathers or the more exotic life-forms. I treated five cases, two surgically with Educator-tape assistance and three with psychotherapy."

"It is the latter three which interest us," said Cha Thrat. Without even a glance toward O'Mara for permission, it went on, "May we have the clinical details? A brief outline will suffice."

Cha Thrat was enjoying this, O'Mara thought. As a warrior-surgeon it was probably more highly placed in its Sommaradvan medical hierarchy than the candidate had been on Cemmecca, and it was letting its feelings show. He remained silent.

"The Melfan was a space-accident casualty," Cerdal replied, answering Cha Thrat although its eyes remained on O'Mara, "whose limbs had to be broken to enable it to fit into a tiny, species-unsuitable survival pod. A colleague repaired the physical damage, but as soon as it had regained partial mobility it made repeated attempts to escape from its room, and its emotional disturbance was so marked that it would or could not tell us what was wrong. I decided that our Cemmeccan accommodation, which for physiological reasons tends to be small and low-ceilinged and cramped by Melfan standards, was a factor which had reinforced the psychological damage caused by its recent confinement in a physiologically unsuitable survival pod. I moved the patient, together with its treatment frame and medical sensors, into an open, treeless area of our hospital's park. Within a few weeks it made a full recovery, both from its physical injuries and an associated manic claustrophobia, and was discharged.

"It is fortunate that the Melfan exoskeleton is waterproof," it added, "because it rains a lot on Cemmecca."

If it was an attempt at humor, O'Mara noted with approval, it was ignored by everyone. Lioren said, "Please continue."

"The second case was an Orligian with a history of stress-related illnesses associated with its job, a very responsible but temporary one, setting up the computer interface between our planetary network and the Monitor Corps establishment on Cemmecca. Questioning revealed that it was unmated and intensely dedicated to its work, which had involved its having to travel between many worlds during its entire adult life. I decided that the cause of its problem was mental fatigue combined with severe homesickness. But my investigation revealed that it wanted to return to the time as well as the place of its youth, so that the lengthy period of rest and recuperation on its home world that I prescribed was not entirely successful, although it was able to resume its off-planet career.

"The third case was a young, recuperating Kelgian who had sustained burn damage to its fur," Cerdal went on. "The area affected was small, but the delicate network of underlying nerve and muscle responsible for fur mobility was destroyed with no possibility of regeneration so that the patient, and every other member of its species, considered it to be grossly and permanently disfigured. Bearing in mind the part that the mobility of their emotion-sensitive fur plays in the courtship, coupling, and long-term mating process, the patient knew that it could never attract a life-mate or even join in the briefest of temporary liaisons, and it developed an increasingly severe, sex-based urge toward further self-damage which, had the attempts been successful, would have left its body in an even more disfigured state.

"It was treated for nearly a year," Cerdal went on, "during which it returned to its work specialty, but always working on Cemmecca and never appearing among other Kelgians. The periodicity of its attempts at self-disfigurement has been reduced. But it is not a successful case. Therapy continues."

Although none of them would ever know why, it was a very sensitive subject where O'Mara himself was concerned. He was glad when Braithwaite's voice broke the silence.

"On the subject of sex-based urges," said the lieutenant, "you will be the hospital's only Cemmeccan. Will this be a problem for you? If it will be, please describe how you plan to handle it or, if it won't be, why not?"

Cerdal's attention remained firmly on O'Mara as it replied, "One or more of you must already have informed yourselves regarding my species' mechanism of reproduction. But in case one or more of you are ignorant of the process I shall describe it briefly. Since none of you belong to my species and your interest is, I hope, clinical, I can do so with the minimum of embarrassment."

Cha Thrat moved two of its upper hands together in the sign of Sommaradvan apology, a gesture which was probably lost on the Cemmeccan, and said, "Please go on."

"There are three sexes," said Cerdal. "Two, whose function roughly approximates that of the male and female among bisexual species, and the mother. All are, of course, sapient, but in general the male equivalent tends to be less willing to accept the long-term responsibility of raising children and has to be influenced in subtle ways to become a parent by entering the mother person with his partner. Sexual coupling and procreation takes place between both partners inside the mother, who also takes part and who, making allowances for the increased body weight of the couple and the growing fetus, continues with normal day-to-day activities. When parturition takes place and the couple with their child are expelled, the mother ceases to have any further part in the proceedings. The period that the couple and their developing offspring spend inside the mother is said to be an intensely pleasurable time. I have not yet had the experience myself.

"As a rule the mothers are psychologically very stable personalities," Cerdal went on, "but occasionally there is a physical dysfunction in the rather crowded womb equivalent which necessitates surgical intervention. When this occurs the surgeon, completely encased in an operating garment so that it will not inadvertently contribute genetic material to the fetus or receive pleasure sensations from the mother, also enters for the briefest time necessary to repair the damage. There are sometimes psychological problems with male- or female-equivalent parents who wish to remain in or reenter the mother, but such cases are rare."

It paused for a moment. When nobody spoke, it added, "My own sexual needs have, I believe, been sublimated to my lifelong dedication to the profession of healing minds. While I will be the only member of my species in Sector General, the mechanics of Cemmeccan sex are such that I do not believe that I would ever be tempted to experiment sexually with the members of other species . . ."

"Thank God for that," said Lioren softly.

". . . so that now and in the future," it went on, "my entire mind, indeed my entire physical and mental output, will be devoted solely to the work of this hospital."

O'Mara stared at Cerdal for a few seconds while the Cemmeccan stared back. He was quite happy to let Lioren make the running.

"You will realize, Dr. Cerdal," said the Padre, "that your other-species experience is grossly inadequate for the duties you will be called on to perform here, and that you will need training if you are to have any hope of performing them to the standard required. This interview is not in itself of major importance. Much more depends on the assessment of your psychological reactions, general proficiency in dealing with patients whose minds are beyond anything in your previous experience, and the control or lack of it of your xenophobia on the conscious and unconscious levels during training."

"I understand," said Cerdal. It was still looking at O'Mara.

"Your training," Lioren continued, "will be given principally by what you may consider to be the subordinate members of this department, Braithwaite, Cha Thrat, and myself. We will be advising and more often as not criticizing and telling you where you went wrong. Will you have a problem with that?"

"No," said the Cemmeccan. "At least, not until my training is complete and my appointment to the job is confirmed. Then I may have critical words of my own to say. But I must repeat my earlier question."

"Go on," said Lioren.

Obviously choosing its words with care and with its attention still focused on O'Mara, Cerdal continued, "I am being considered for the most senior and responsible position in the hospital. Why then is this interview being conducted not by the present incumbent but by underlings? To a person of my high professional standing I find this demeaning, even insulting, unless there is a very good reason or excuse for your behavior. Bearing in mind the grey coloration of your head fur, is it possible that you are no longer capable of performing your duties adequately and require more youthful assistance? This would be a completely acceptable excuse."

Beside him Cha Thrat and Lioren were still as statues, and on the communicator he could hear Braithwaite making noises which suggested that someone was strangling him. All of them were waiting for a verbal explosion of nuclear proportions, but O'Mara had a contrary streak that delighted in doing the unexpected.

He smiled and said, "A possibility you have not considered, Dr. Cerdal, is that I am conducting not one interview but four, and that my assistants, unknown to themselves until this moment, are your fellow candidates for the job."

Before anyone could speak, O'Mara raised a hand and looked at each of them in turn. He said, "Spare me your token protestations of inadequacy. False modesty makes me sick. Your experience with this department's work makes all of your prime candidates as my replacement, as do your qualifications in medicine. The fact that the lieutenant's medical knowledge is rusty from disuse, and Cha Thrat is not allowed to practice here, and Lioren, for personal reasons, has forbidden itself to practice, is unimportant. The administrator will not be expected to treat patients.

"Cha Thrat, Padre," he continued briskly, "I know exactly how much you have to do. Continue doing it. Braithwaite, free some time to show Dr. Cerdal around what it hopes will be its future empire. And remember, I will be watching and from time to time testing all of you. Your future promotion depends on your increased levels of professional competence, behavior under stress, and my own personal whim . . ."

He allowed his face to crack into one of its rare smiles.

". . . not necessarily in that order of importance," he ended. "Your preliminary interviews are over. You may go."

# CHAPTER 8

Close on half a century earlier, the idea of promotion was something that O'Mara had not felt happy about—although, to be honest with himself, the fact that it had never been offered might have played a large part in forming that feeling. Now, for the first time in his working life, he was being offered one and his first reaction was to shake his head. Vigorously.

"A facial expression reflecting pleasure," said Major Craythorne gravely, "and a simple word of thanks with a few questions tacked on regarding your exact status, job description, and increased level of pay is what I expected from you, not an outright refusal. This is the first step on a ladder you must have wanted to climb all your life, O'Mara, and with your proven capabilities the succeeding steps will be easier. What are you afraid of?"

Craythorne sighed, wrinkled his nose, and in a gentle, apologetic voice said, "I'd ask you to sit down for a while and talk about this, but you're filthy and you stink to high heaven as would the chair when the next person comes in to sit on it, so I'm afraid you'll have to take the good news on your feet. What the hell were you doing?"

"I was helping clear the blocked waste-disposal system on Level Thirty-Three when your—"

"What possible reason," the Major broke in, "did my xenopsychology assistant have for clearing blocked latrines?"

"Four reasons," O'Mara replied. "The squad leader had been called away; his men didn't know what the hell they were doing, while I had, ah, previous experience in the job; I didn't have anything urgent to do at the time; and, well, they asked me nicely for a change."

Like everything else about him, Craythorne's irritation was gentle and controlled. He said, "Listen carefully to me, O'Mara. You are never again to perform menial tasks like that just because you happen to have previous experience in them, or because you are asked nicely. From now on I want your position within this establishment to be clear to everyone. That is why I'm inducting you into the Monitor Corps and giving you an immediate promotion to . . ."

He broke off and added, "At last it looks as if you're going to say something. Very likely it will be offensive, but say it anyway before you blow a fuse."

O'Mara took a deep breath and strove vainly for internal calm. He could almost feel his face radiating deep into the infrared. After a moment he said, "Sir, I'm not happy with the idea of promotion in a civilian job mostly because, unlike you, I don't have the good manners or the knack of giving orders without also giving offense, or maybe even starting a fight. If absolutely necessary I could try to improve my manners, lengthen my temper, and learn to live with that situation. But joining a routine-indoctrinated and discipline-oriented organization like the Monitor Corps, and going through basic training and having to stand at attention and salute and . . . You know I don't take orders very well, so I wouldn't last a week. I've no wish to be personally offensive—"

"If it helps explain your obviously strong feelings in the matter," Craythorne broke in, "you have permission to be personally offensive. Within reason."

"All right," said O'Mara, staring into a pair of eyes which, he had found over the years, had the disconcerting ability to stare back without wavering. "In the civilian sector I've had painful experience with nominal superiors who made a pretense at the habit of command but who needed their nominal subordinates to keep their nose, or a less delicate body orifice, wiped clean. If I did join the Corps and some NCO or officer, present company excepted, told me to do something that I knew to be wrong, and I could be severely disciplined for not doing it, well . . . Sir, joining the Monitor Corps is not an option."

Craythorne was still holding his eyes as he said quietly, "Joining the Corps is the only option, O'Mara, if you wish to remain in Sector General. I know you well enough to feel sure that, faced with the prospect of leaving, you will exert a considerable amount of self-control in order to remain here. Right?"

O'Mara swallowed and for a moment he couldn't speak. The thought of leaving the hospital, with its nice or normally nasty construction crews and its increasingly weird intake of doctors and medical trainees, to return to the space construction gangs whose brains, if not actually dead, had never been given the opportunity to live, was too terrible to contemplate. He was beginning to develop a proprietary, almost a parental interest in the place and its people, and he knew that being forced to leave it would hurt more than anything in his short and already hurt-filled life.

But as a Corpsman O'Mara didn't know if he was capable of that much self-control.

"I thought so," said the major. He gave O'Mara a brief, sympathetic smile of encouragement and went on, "For your information, the construction of the hospital is within a few weeks of completion and the civil contractors and their people are rapidly being phased out. Henceforth the Monitor Corps will be wholly responsible for all aspects of supply, maintenance, power requirements, supply logistics, catering, and so on. The only civilians here will be the medical staff, which is why, considering your lack of formal medical training, you have no choice but to be one of us. To stay here you must be a medic or a member of the Corps. I'm not breaking any rules, because for this place they haven't been written yet; I'm just bending them a little.

"As the ranking officer on site," Craythorne went on, his smile broadening, "I have applied for and received permission to waive the usual basic-training procedures. I can't imagine you ever needing to know about space ordnance or riot-control weapons here, so you are joining us as a specialist in other-species psychology and will continue with the work you are doing now. You will not have to worry about junior NCOs telling you what to do, although it might be a good idea to listen to their advice if or when they give it . . ."

The major sat back in his chair, his face becoming politely stern.

". . . but you will, however, obey orders," he went on. "Especially mine. The first one is to clean up and call on Maintenance Technician Wenalont on Level Fifty-One, Room Eighteen. It has already altered the issue uniforms and kit to your measurements, which it has had for the past two weeks, and reports them ready for fitting." He glanced at his watch. "Then at fifteen hundred hours precisely I want you back here for an important technical briefing from a medical VIP, and looking and smelling a lot more presentable. It will be a long session so don't skip lunch."

O'Mara's mind and tongue were still paralyzed by surprise. He nodded wordlessly and turned to go. Craythorne wrapped a knuckle gently against the top of his desk.

"And if I ever hear of you cleaning latrines again," he added, "you and your service career will both be terminated on the spot. Do you understand me, Lieutenant O'Mara?"

On the way to Level Fifty-One the main corridors were clear

of major obstructions and, he noticed since the major had drawn his attention to the reason for it, the remaining equipment-installation jobs were being done by people in Monitor green coveralls while the only civilians he passed were wearing medical insignia and whites if they were wearing anything at all. He was already worrying about what exactly he should say and how he should say it to this Wenalont character, but in the event it was the other who did all the talking.

"I am Technical Sergeant Wenalont, sir," it said briskly. "As a Melfan I haven't much use for clothing, since my exoskeleton is impervious to all but the most severe climatic changes, but my hobby is tailoring and the fitting of wearing apparel to weird and unusual body configurations. No offense is intended, I meant weird and unusual to me. We will begin from the epidermis out, with the undergarment and the tubular coverings for the feet and lower legs. Please strip off, sir."

*I'm not supposed to take orders from NCOs,* thought O'Mara, feeling his face growing warm. But then, he told himself, if they were preceded by "please" and he was called "sir" it was not technically an order.

"Now we will fit the outer garments," the sergeant went on a few moments later, "that is, the coveralls which serve as the working uniform, and the uniform proper. Once I have ensured that the fit is smart and comfortable, duplicates of all these garments will be sent to your new quarters on the officers' level . . ."

He felt Wenalont's hard, bony wrists against the sides of his head as it pulled, settled, and straightened each garment onto his shoulders and neck. It never stopped talking about fastenings, insignia, and the types and proper positioning of antigravity or weapons belts and equipment harness. Then suddenly it was over. The sergeant grasped him firmly by the upper arms and rotated him to face the full-length mirror.

The man looking back at him was dressed in the full, dark-green uniform with the Monitor Corps crest glittering on the collar and the insignia of rank and space service emblem decorating the shoulder tabs, one of which retained his neatly folded beret. O'Mara had expected the sight to make him feel ridiculous. He didn't know how he felt exactly, but ridiculous was not one of the feelings.

He wondered if his sudden surge of mixed feelings was due to the fact that for the first time in his life as a quarrelsome, intellectually frustrated, and friendless loner he had become, without changing these characteristics one bit, a person who belonged to something. He dragged his mind back to the sergeant, who was talking again.

"The fit, sir," said Wenalont, moving around and staring him up and down with its large, insectile eyes, "is very good, neat without being constricting. You are unusually large and heavily muscled for an Earth-human male. If you were to appear dressed like that in the dining hall, I feel sure that the Earth-human females on the medical staff would be greatly impressed. But may I offer a word of advice, sir?"

The idea of him trying to impress female medics was so ridiculous that he almost laughed out loud. Instead he tried to be polite, as he thought Major Craythorne would have liked him to be, and said, "Please do."

"It is regarding service dress protocol and saluting," the sergeant went on. "In the space service we do not go in much for the exchange of such compliments because of the restricted living and working environment. As well, by the nature of things there are many fewer officers than there are other ranks, so that their subordinates would have to salute them perhaps three or four times a day while they would have to return these compliments hundreds of times a day, which can be time-wasting, irritating, and physically tiring for the officer concerned. As a simple verbal expression of respect, the word 'sir' or its other-species equivalent, and the wearing of issue coveralls with appropriate insignia patches, is considered acceptable. The only exception is during occasions such as inspec-

tions or visits by high-ranking Corps officers or government offi-
cials when the full uniform must be worn and all the military cour-
tesies performed.

"I hope you aren't disappointed, sir," the sergeant went on,
"but if you were to go to lunch in full uniform instead of coveralls,
every subordinate you met or passed would stop whatever they
were doing to exchange salutes with you, so that you would need to
eat one-handed. But if that is what you desire—"

"No!" O'Mara broke in, and then for the first time in many
years he laughed out loud. "I'm relieved, not disappointed. And,
well, thank you for your help and advice, Sergeant. Unless you need
me for anything else, I'll change into coveralls again at once because
I'm pushed for time."

"A moment before you change," said the other. "My congratulations on your commission, sir."

One of the sergeant's long, shiny, sticklike and multi-jointed
forelimbs swept out sideways and upward to come to a rigid halt
beside its head and, for the first time in his life, O'Mara found himself returning a salute.

He did not have to undergo the embarrassing experience
again, even though the dining hall for warm-blooded oxygen-
breathers was crowded with Corps and medical personnel. His crisp
new coveralls with their bright, painfully clean patches denoting his
rank and departmental insignia, O'Mara was relieved to find,
aroused no comment or even notice. During dessert he was joined
by a trainee nurse who had asked politely to take the empty place
at his table, but as it was a Tralthan with four times his body mass
and six elephantine feet, he doubted that it had been attracted by
his uniform.

# CHAPTER 9

**E**ven though the operating theater's occupants were all warm-blooded oxygen-breathers, it was clear that the atmosphere of stress and tension in the place could have been cut with a blunt scalpel. The bony features of the Melfan surgeon in charge of the team were incapable of registering any expression, as was the dome-like head of its massive Tralthan assistant, but the mobile fur of the Kelgian anesthetist was twitching and tufting violently. The only person in the room who looked composed was the Earth-human who was the deeply unconscious patient.

The Melfan raised a forelimb and clicked its pincers together for attention.

"I should have no need to remind you of how important the next twenty minutes are to the future of other-species surgery," it said with a glance toward the overhead vision recorder, "or that this is considered to be one of the simplest procedures that are performed routinely in many thousands of hospitals throughout the patient's home planet and on other Earth-seeded colony worlds. The diagnosis has been confirmed as a clinical condition which, due to the patient's delay in reaching hospital, has become life-threatening and requires immediate surgery. Are we all ready? Then let's have it out."

The blade of the scalpel, its handle designed to fit precisely the Melfan pincer, flashed brightly as it caught the overhead lighting; then the reflection became pink-tinged as it made a longitudinal incision in the right lower quadrant of the abdomen.

"Normally a shorter incision would suffice," said the Melfan, "but we're not trying to impress anyone with the minimal size and neatness of the work here. This is strange country to all of us and I want to give myself room to look around. Ah, there is a thick layer of adipose tissue overlying the musculature, we'll have to go deeper. Control that bleeding, please. Quickly, Doctor. Clear the operative field, I can't see what I'm doing."

There was a low, faintly derisive sound as the delicate tips of two of the Tralthan assistant's tentacles holding the suction instrument moved in from the side briefly before withdrawing again a few seconds later to reveal the upper surface of the ascending colon at the bottom of the shallow, red crevice that was the wound.

"Thank you," said the Melfan surgeon, laying aside the scalpel. "Now we will tie off and excise the . . . Where the hell is it?"

"I don't see it, either, sir," said the Tralthan. "Could it be attached to the underside of the colon or—"

"We've studied the anatomy of this life-form closely for a week," the Melfan broke in, "so we shouldn't have to do this. Oh, very well. Library, display physiological classification DBDG, abdominal area, Earth-human male. Highlight position of the appendix."

A few seconds later the large wall screen facing them lit up with the requested picture, the lower end of the ascending colon and the appendix projecting downward from it enclosed by a circle of red light.

"That's where it is," said the Melfan, pointing with its free pincer at the outlined area, "and that is where we went in. But it isn't here."

"Sir," said its assistant, "the literature suggested that on Earth-humans this could be the simplest of all surgical procedures lasting only a few minutes, or one that can be taxing, difficult, and lengthy. This is because, and I may be quoting inaccurately from memory, the normally healthy organ, which is thinner than a digit and only two to eight inches in length, when diseased, inflamed, and filled with pus can be enlarged to many times that size. If this happens, the organ is very mobile and may grow toward one of a number of other organs within the abdominal cavity, so that the patient's symptoms appear to involve a different organ. I'm still quoting from memory, but this can make an accurate diagnosis difficult. Is it possible that the case has been misdiagnosed?"

Without looking up, the Melfan said, "I am constantly referring to the same memories, Doctor. But what a stupid set of internal plumbing these Earth-human DBDGs have. One wonders how their species was able to survive and evolve intelligence. But no, for now we will assume that the diagnosis was correct. My problem, that whether the appendix is short and thin or lengthy, greatly distended, and growing into another area, or has perhaps become entangled with the small intestine, is that I can't find either it or its attachment point to the bowel. Suggestions would be welcome, Doctor."

There was a long pause before its assistant said, "I realize that it doesn't appear to be either diseased or inflamed, but is it possible that the short length of organ visible to us is, in fact, a part of the distended appendix rather than the bowel? After all, it is in the correct position."

There was another period of silence. The Kelgian anesthetist's fur rippled with impatience. It said, "The patient's condition is stable, Doctors, but it could terminate from old age while we wait."

Ignoring the remark as one did with Kelgians, the Melfan went on, "I'm going to extend the incision in both directions so as to see more of this area of bowel, which will enable me to lift it into the operative field and find the attachment point even if it is hiding on the underside. After which we will release it from any adhesions or local entanglements and deliver it into the wound where we will tie off, incise, and complete the procedure. Here we go. Be ready with suction, Doctor."

The incision was enlarged, its edges pulled apart, and the bowel lifted higher in the operative field.

"Still nothing visible," said the Melfan. "Doctor, your digits have more tactual sensitivity. Go underneath and see if you can feel anything."

"Nothing, sir," said the Tralthan.

The Melfan hesitated a moment, then said, "I'll extend the incision again. We'll save a few moments if you keep holding it. But carefully, it's very slippery . . . Don't grab for it! Let *go!*"

Its surgical assistant had laid aside the instrument that had held the section of bowel above the wound while the other hand continued to hold it gently and firmly in position. But not firmly enough. Suddenly the bowel slipped between the Tralthan's digits and it made an instinctive grab for it, but succeeded only in pulling it higher above the operative field and into the path of the surgeon's scalpel. A four-inch long incision appeared suddenly on the bowel which gaped open and began leaking its liquid contents.

"So now we're faced with doing a bowel repair and we still haven't found the appendix yet," said the Melfan surgeon angrily. "This, this is not going well. This minor operation is fast becoming a major disaster."

It used a phrase that its translator, which had probably been programmed by people with less colorful Melfan vocabularies, refused to accept. Then it looked up directly into the vision recorder.

"Enough," it said, "I'm withdrawing from this one before we end up killing the patient. Same-species standby team, take over!"

Within seconds the OR door hissed open to admit three Earth-humans, already masked and gowned, and a floater bearing a tray of ergonomically suited instruments. Quickly the Melfan, Tralthan, and Kelgian medics withdrew from the table. Their places were taken by the new arrivals, who immediately went to work.

As the original team were filing quietly out of the room, the big wall screen in Craythorne's office went dark as Councillor Davantry ended the playback and swung around to face them.

Davantry was a small, aging, soft-spoken Earth-human whose expression was grave and without the smallest trace of condescension—the kind of person who, like O'Mara's chief, had the ability to make an order sound as if he were requesting a favor. He did not look at all like a god but, as he was a senior member of the Galactic Federation's Central Medical Council, Craythorne had suggested that it would be a good idea to treat him as if he were. So far the major had not dared ask the purpose of the equipment in the opened, well-padded container in the center of the office floor.

O'Mara had the uneasy feeling that he was a god about to ask a favor that they could not refuse.

The councillor sighed and said, "You have just viewed one of several multi-species surgical experiments. It was also a horror story. Fortunately, none of the patients concerned terminated, although several came very close to it. There are many more such horror stories, if you want to view them. But they all make the same point, that practicing medicine and surgery—especially surgery—across the species divide is dangerous and, well, is a problem almost impossible of solution."

O'Mara nodded and waited for a moment to give Craythorne the chance to respond; then he said, "I note the qualifier, sir. Does it mean that you have found one?"

"It means that there are two possible solutions, Lieutenant," said Davantry, "Neither of which I particularly like. One is straightforward and probably unworkable, the other is simpler but, well, psychologically tricky. But first let us consider the reason for this hospital's existence, which is to receive and treat the sick and injured of the sixty-odd intelligent species that compose the Galactic Federation. In the light of the experiment you have just seen, and discounting the few species who don't travel in space, this would mean staffing the hospital with complete teams of physicians, surgeons, and medical and technical support staff of virtually every known life-form, on the off chance that a member of any one of those species would arrive needing treatment. It would be the same as providing sixty different one-species hospitals inside one structure. Sector General is big but not that big. It could be done but, to do it that way, the proportion of patients to staff would be ridiculously low and criminally wasteful of medical personnel, the majority of whom would have nothing to do but hang around waiting for a same-species patient to arrive. Inter-species conflicts could arise through sheer boredom."

"More likely," said Craythorne with feeling, "another interstellar war. But you have another solution, sir?"

"Or perhaps, Major," said Davantry, pointing at the opened crate, "I have more horror stories for you. They involve, or will involve, cross-species memory transfer."

Craythorne leaned forward in his chair, looking excited. "There's been a lot about it in the literature recently," he said. "Very interesting stuff, sir. It would be the ideal solution, but I thought the procedure was still experimental. Has the technique been perfected?"

"Not quite," Davantry replied with a small smile. "We were hoping that would be done at Sector General."

"Oh," said Craythorne. O'Mara said the same but under his breath. Davantry smiled again, and divided his attention between them as he spoke.

"This hospital," he said in a very serious voice, "will be equipped to treat every known form of intelligent life. But we have just proved beyond doubt that no single individual can hold in his, her, or its brain even a fraction of the vast amount of physiological data necessary for this purpose. Surgical dexterity is a matter of ability and training but, we have discovered, the complete knowledge of an other-species patient's physiology and metabolism can only be furnished by means of a complete memory transfer of the mind of a leading medical authority in the relevant field of the patient's own species into the brain of the physician-in-charge, who can belong to any other species provided it has hands and eyes and has the required surgical training. With the help of what, because the original name is polysyllabic and cumbersome, we are calling an Educator tape, any medically trained being can treat any patient regardless of species.

"The Educator-tape application system," he went on with a nod toward the opened container, "can impress a mind recording on the recipient's brain within a few minutes, and be erased just as easily when the indicated treatment for the patient has been completed. The equipment and procedure has been thoroughly tested and the user is completely safe in that there is no physical trauma. But there is another problem."

"Why am I not surprised?" said O'Mara. He thought he had been speaking under his breath, but Craythorne looked at him warningly while Councillor Davantry pretended not to hear and continued speaking.

"It is this," he went on. "The tapes do not impart only physiological knowledge; the entire memory, personal and professional experience, and personality of the entity who donated the tape are transferred as well, and we know that all too often the top specialists in the medical or any other field can be aggressive, self-opinionated, and generally obnoxious people, because that is how most of them rose to eminence. Geniuses are rarely charming people. So in effect the tape's would-be recipient must subject himself voluntarily to a drastic but temporary form of schizophrenia because another personality, an authoritive, forceful, and completely alien personality, is apparently sharing his mind. If the recipient's mind is not also strong-willed and well integrated, especially if the tape is in place for several days, it will feel as if the donor mind is fighting for and perhaps threatening to gain control over it."

Davantry looked steadily at Craythorne and O'Mara for a moment, raised his hands slightly, then let them fall again onto his lap.

"With the tape donor's complete personality," he went on, "are included all its pet peeves, bad habits, and major or minor phobias. For the long-term recipient, the different food preferences can be a difficulty and, during periods of sleep, alien dreams, nightmares, and particularly other-species sexual fantasies can be a real problem, although none of the previous subjects suffered lasting mental damage. But before your department administers a mind-transfer tape all this must be explained to the would-be recipient, especially to the first volunteer."

There was a long silence. O'Mara stared at Craythorne, who stared back at him for a moment before looking back to Davantry. The major's expression remained calm, composed, and quietly attentive, but when he spoke his face had lightened a shade.

"Since my department will be responsible for conducting these mind transfers," he said calmly, "it follows that I should have firsthand knowledge of the psychological problems involved so that, logically, I should be the first volunteer."

Davantry shook his head firmly. "If you insist, you may be the second volunteer, Major," he said, "or preferably the twenty-second. I will need to demonstrate the mind-transfer procedure to you, and to have your training and experience available in your own stable and unaltered mind in case something goes wrong with the subject. I'm just a glorified meditech, not a trained psychologist.

"A subordinate," he added, looking at O'Mara, "or even someone from outside your department is preferable. But he, she, or it must be a volunteer."

"With the earlier subjects," said O'Mara, looking right back, "what were the short- and long-term effects?"

"Short-term," Councillor Davantry replied, "there was a marked lack of physical coordination, vertigo, and pronounced mental confusion. Usually the first two diminish or disappear within a few minutes. The third can reduce or increase over the space of a few hours or days, depending on the subject's mental flexibility and strength of will. That's why I want a trained therapist standing by, in case the subject panics or suffers other emotional problems, so that the mind tape can be erased without delay."

O'Mara's mouth was already opening but Craythorne broke in sharply before he could respond.

"Think about it for a moment, Lieutenant O'Mara," he said. "You don't have to do this."

"I know that, sir," said O'Mara, "but I will anyway."

Later O'Mara was to wonder why he spoke as he did, at once and without any trace of hesitation. He had always liked trying to understand other people's minds on an amateur basis, and now he had the chance to look at an extraterrestrial's mind from the inside. Or maybe it was his new rank and position, with its responsibilities as well as privileges, that had gone to his head. More likely he was just being stupid.

It was too late for him to retract while Councillor Davantry was showing the major how to adjust the open-mesh lightweight helmet and connections to the contours of an Earth-human cranium and calibrate the associated items of equipment that were now winking, clicking, and humming on top of Craythorne's desk. He was surprised by the gentleness of Davantry's touch and astonished when this medical god placed a hand on his shoulder and gave it a reassuring squeeze.

"Good luck, Lieutenant," he said. "Major, switch on."

His view of the office and occupants was blotted out by a sudden flash of light which faded quickly to be replaced with a flickering sensation, as if the scene were an unfamiliar image on a faulty viewscreen, before it settled into stillness.

"How do you feel, Lieutenant O'Mara?" said Davantry. "Confused? Frightened? Both?"

"Yes. No," he snapped. "Not both. I, I know a lot of stuff I've no business knowing, mostly medical information, and a lot of people, extraterrestrials, I definitely don't know. You look ridiculous standing there. Flat, less three-dimensional. And you haven't any fur to tell me what you are feeling and thinking."

Davantry nodded and smiled. "I'm thinking that you are doing very well," he said. "Stand up and walk around your chair a few times, then try to walk to the office door and back."

As soon as he stood up the room tilted alarmingly. He had to grab the ridiculous piece of furniture he had been sitting on to keep his balance and later while he was walking awkwardly around it. Then he steadied himself, tried not to look down at a floor that was much too far away, and moved toward the door.

He barely made it, because he was suddenly falling forward and had to put out his hands to the door surface to steady himself, but he still couldn't stop himself from dropping painfully onto his knees. Then he climbed awkwardly to his feet, straightened up, and turned so that his back was propped securely against the door before he looked back at the suddenly distant chair and the two Earth-humans.

The one called Craythorne was watching him, the two semi-circles of facial fur above its eyes drawn down in what some alien group of memories deep within his mind identified as a frown of concern. The other one nodded, showed its teeth briefly in what the same area of memory suggested was a smile of reassurance, and spoke.

"Very good, Lieutenant," it said. "Now walk back again."

"Don't be stupid," said O'Mara angrily. "I've only got two bloody feet!"

"I know," said the other gently, "but try anyway."

O'Mara used words that he did not remember knowing, steadied himself, and walked carefully into the middle of the room. He had gone only a few paces when he felt himself swaying to one side. Instinctively he raised and extended sideways his two thick, ungainly, Earth-human arms. For some reason this enabled him to maintain his balance until he reached the chair. He dropped onto it and used more words that he hadn't known he knew.

The older Earth-human reached forward and flipped a switch on the side of O'Mara's helmet. Without it changing appearance in any way, the office and the people in it were suddenly familiar again.

"That's enough for now, Lieutenant," said Davantry briskly. "Your mind tape has been erased. But you'll want to discuss the experience with the major before you run more tests. Remember to extend the exposure time gradually until you are comfortable with your mind partner and are quite sure of which one of you is boss. . . ."

To Craythorne he went on, "A good initial session, Major, and from now on you'll be teaching yourselves. I have to return to my ship now; a councillor's work is never done. Contact me only if you run into a serious problem."

He was moving toward the door when the major said quickly, "Sir, my apologies. I hope you weren't offended by the lieutenant's disrespectful language and—"

Councillor Davantry raised a hand without turning. "Don't worry about it, Major. Lieutenant O'Mara wasn't quite himself. He was disrespectful, outspoken, and abusive because he had a Kelgian senior physician riding his mind, and Kelgians always behave that way."

When the door had closed behind him, Craythorne laughed softly.

"I suppose that was not the right time," he said, "to tell him that Lieutenant O'Mara always behaves that way, too."

# CHAPTER 10

**T**hen as well as now there had been problems with Educator tapes, O'Mara thought dourly, except that with the passage of time the problems were more familiar and much more numerous, and now it was he rather than Craythorne who had the rank and ultimate responsibility for solving them—even when, as now, he was able to dump some of them onto his chief assistant. In that respect at least, nothing had changed.

"Braithwaite," said O'Mara sourly, "how the blazes do you always manage to look so neat? The only creases in your uniform are where they're supposed to be, the vertical ones in your pants. Is it Monitor Corps conditioning, something in your DNA, or have you sold your soul to some sartorial devil?"

The lieutenant knew a rhetorical question when he heard one and replied with a polite smile.

"All right," said O'Mara. "Diagnostician Yursedth. What happened?"

Braithwaite smiled again and said, "Initially there was a frank exchange of views. It said that, considering its position within the hospital, it deserved the attention of the chief psychologist. I told it that was so, normally, but as the new administrator you had more urgent matters to attend to and were being forced to delegate. It became personally uncomplimentary, toward both of us, and some of the phrases from the Tralthan component of its mind were particularly . . . inventive. But after a few minutes letting off steam, it agreed to talk to a substandard psychiatrist, me."

"And," said O'Mara.

"Currently it carries four Educator tapes," said the lieutenant, "Tralthan, Melfan, Dwerlan, and Earth-human. I checked the donors' psych profiles and none of them seemed as if they would be particularly hard to live with, especially for a strong-willed Kelgian like Yursedth who has years of experience with mind transfers. Its own psych file shows nothing suspect in its past. As for the troublesome dreams, which are causing mental distress of nightmare proportions during sleep and continual worry for hours subsequent to waking, I can find no cause for them. The same applies to the bouts of peripheral neuropathy, which are almost certainly associated with the main problem because they so closely resemble the nightmares. If there is a culprit tape, as you called it, I couldn't identify it. This is a strange one, sir, because there is no obvious reason why the subject's problem should exist."

O'Mara nodded. "You didn't expect me to hand you an easy one, Lieutenant," he said. "What are you doing about this nonexistent problem?"

"The subject is becoming increasingly distressed," said Braithwaite, "and I don't want to waste time duplicating someone else's work, especially yours. Yursedth wouldn't tell me, at the time it was still annoyed because it wasn't being treated by you, whether you had already initiated any kind of therapy. Have you?"

O'Mara shook his head. "I barely glanced through Yursedth's file to check on its current workload," he said, "which was about normal for a diagnostician of its seniority. The original question stands, Lieutenant: what are you going to do?"

Braithwaite was silent for a moment, and then he said, "I already checked for stress due to overwork and found nothing unusual. I'm going to get it to talk about its dreams and psychosomatic episodes again, and listen even more carefully this time. If nothing else occurs to me, I'll suggest erasing the Melfan tape. If any of the Educator tapes are causing the trouble it is likely, well, slightly more likely, to be that one. As you know, sir, while the Melfans have very precise and accurate muscle control and positional sense, but the exoskeletal structures covering their limbs and digits have no sense of touch. It is probably a forlorn hope, but that might equate with Yursedth's waking loss of sensation in its limbs and other areas of its body and its persistent nightmares. One of them, the one that seems to trouble it most, is about it being in a hospital OR on Melf and unable to operate because of an unexplained, creeping paralysis. I would then erase the Melfan tape and, before impressing another, observe and question the subject closely for a few days or weeks, to see whether or not the troublesome symptoms were still present or receding. I would do the same with the other tapes in turn and, if that didn't work, I'd erase all of them and observe the effects. If any."

O'Mara sat back in his chair and kept his face expressionless. Everyone on the staff knew that Yursedth had teaching duties as well as ongoing surgical commitments using its own medical experience as well as that of its four other-species mind partners. Time, as well as considerable personal mental disruption, was required to acclimatize mentally after the erasure of long-term tapes, which was why junior medics were not allowed to retain them for more than a few hours after use. Much more time and considerable emotional hassle would be needed for Yursedth's mind, which subjectively would feel suddenly empty, to accommodate the alien knowledge and feelings of four new mind partners. But Braithwaite knew all this.

Deliberately, O'Mara decided to give a noncommittal, unhelpful answer. He said, "I can only imagine what Yursedth will say about that."

"I didn't have to imagine," said Braithwaite feelingly. "It told me what it thought in detail when I told it what I intended to do, purely as a last resort. I hoped that would concentrate, well, scare its mind to the extent of producing a reaction that would furnish a clue to the basic problem. It didn't. Apart from the verbal abuse it said that it would ask for a second opinion. Yours."

"And you said?" O'Mara prompted.

"That you had given me sole responsibility for its case and that if you did speak to it, that was the first thing you would say," the lieutenant replied, then hesitated. "I don't know what the second thing would be."

"The same as the first," said O'Mara carefully. "I expect you to talk to me about the case and report progress, if any. If you consider it necessary you may discuss it with your colleagues in the outer office, but not to the extent that you would be dividing the responsibility for treatment. I am not going to advise or second-guess you with Yursedth. So don't worry, Lieutenant, this psychological hot, medium-roasted, or cold mashed potato is all yours."

"But I am worrying, sir," said Braithwaite, "mostly about my proposed line of treatment. I was ashamed of even suggesting it. Just wiping all four mind partners is, is *crude*, like amputating a leg on the off chance of curing a sprained ankle. I want to try something a little more sophisticated, and I'm not asking for advice . . ."

"Good," said O'Mara, "because you wouldn't get it."

". . . but I would appreciate your technical supervision," Braithwaite went on, "during a tape impression of Yursedth's suspect Melfan mind partner into another subject. Instead of working from subjective verbal data secondhand, I'd like to have a close look around that Melfan donor's mind myself from the inside—"

"*No!*"

Braithwaite looked surprised. "I know we don't usually do it, sir," he said, "and that technically it's against the rules, but I believe this to be a special problem which I might not be able to solve in any other way without wasting several days or weeks of Yursedth's teaching and operating time as well as subjecting it to a lot of emotional hassle. With respect, sir, it was you who made the rules and, from what I've heard, broke them all before they could be made official."

That was then, O'Mara remembered, during the early years before Craythorne and the newly promoted and eager Lieutenant O'Mara knew what they were doing. He had insisted on doing more while knowing much less than the major and he still carried the mental scars, many of them willingly, to prove it. *We lived,* as the old Chinese curse phrased it, *in interesting times.* He shook his head.

"No," he repeated in a conversational tone, "because the staff in this department are expected to be more or less sane. Failing that, they are expected at very least to know exactly who and what they are at all times and in all circumstances. To function effectively a therapist in this place must retain his, her, or its mental objectivity. That cannot be done if you assimilate and go probing into a donor mind that may be psychologically suspect because the experience, no matter how hard you tried to be objective, is intensely and dangerously subjective. A form of insidious psychological merging takes place, and traces of the emotional involvement with the donor entity remain even after the tape has been erased. You know the rule and, if you've temporarily forgotten it, I'm reminding you now. If you go exploring in alien mental territory, Lieutenant, you might bring back mental mud on your boots. So your mind, such as it is, must remain exclusively your own."

O'Mara paused for a moment to stare hard into the other's eyes. Without raising his voice he added, "If one of my staff was to break that rule, they would need to urgently consider other work options. Is that clearly understood?"

"Yes, sir," said Braithwaite. "But what about the diagnosticians and seniors who carry anything up to six long-term tapes each?

Were they told the psychological reason for that rule, and about the risks?"

O'Mara shook his head. "No," he said, "because the risk for them is nil, or at most very slight. All they are interested in is obtaining the other-species tape donor's medical knowledge and experience for use in a current op or research project. The personality of the entity sharing their minds, be it nice, nasty, egocentric, or whatever, is something they try hard to ignore because they are physicians and surgeons who have neither the inclination nor the time to waste on delving into the reasons for their mind partner's emotional behavior. The donor's subconscious surfaces often enough when they sleep, or for some other reason lose concentration and awareness of their own identity. But when this happens they instinctively fight it and are, therefore, safe. To be sure of that we always check periodically for any sudden change in their psych profiles during long-term mind impressions.

"But you want to dive into the middle of an other-species mind," he went on seriously, "perhaps a disturbed alien mind who may already have had psychiatric assistance from a therapist of its own species to control its psychoses. That is asking for serious trouble because neuroses and psychoses are subjective experiences which, unlike other-species pathogens, can be passed from one intelligent and disturbed mind to another that is more or less sane. If that were to happen to you, the only hope of a cure would be to bring in a therapist of the mind partner's species as well as one of your own, me, to clean up the mess. Right now, and for the foreseeable future, I don't have the time."

"Sorry, sir," said Braithwaite. "Until you gave me the Yursedth case, I just accepted your general instruction about not taking Educator tapes without realizing the reasoning behind it. I'm still tempted by the thought of going into and viewing an alien mental landscape from the inside, and maybe help clear away some of the weeds, but . . . well, I'll resist the temptation."

O'Mara nodded. He said, "Your job, and everyone else's in this department, is to clear away mental weeds. But you will continue to do it by using your knowledge and experience and the tools of observation and verbal probing and your own Earth-human, or Sommaradvan or Tarlan as the case may be, processes of deduction while at all times remaining yourselves. I won't ask if you understand me, Lieutenant, because if you don't, you're fired."

"I do understand, sir," said Braithwaite, looking chastened but as cool and impeccable as ever. "But I don't understand why you reacted so strongly when I mentioned the idea. Have you yourself been inside a disturbed, alien mind, sir, and have you firsthand experience with the long-term problems?"

A few days ago Braithwaite would not have dared ask such a question. Plainly the acquisition of full responsibility was bringing out some of the lieutenant's hidden strengths. O'Mara remained silent.

"With respect," the lieutenant went on calmly, "that could be the reason for your complete lack of social contact with the staff over the years, and your general antisocial behavior, which has made you the most disliked as well as the most professionally respected person in the hospital. It is difficult to believe that you like that situation. Would you care to comment, sir?"

For a moment O'Mara stared into the other's eyes, which, he was pleased to see, stared right back. Then he sighed and deliberately looked at his watch.

"Was there anything else you want to ask me, Lieutenant," he said, "before you leave?"

Braithwaite departed, his curiosity unsatisfied, and O'Mara tried to concentrate on moving the mounting pile of administrative detail, which his two jobs had caused to double in size. But instead his mind kept sliding away from the now and into the then.

*Increasing bouts of stupid nostalgia,* he thought sourly, *is a neurosis of the senile.*

# CHAPTER 11

The Lieutenant O'Mara in his mind picture had been less self-assured in his speech and manner, the appearance of his uniform fell into the gray area between untidy and disheveled, and it was Major Craythorne who looked as if he had stepped out of a Monitor Corps recruiting program. Then the conversation had been similar but the instructions, which Craythorne had the habit of disguising as friendly advice, were much less forceful. Part of the reason for that, he remembered, was that at the time neither of them knew what they were talking about.

"I wonder," said Craythorne apologetically, "if you would be kind enough to investigate a dispute of some kind going on between trainees on Level One-Eleven. I don't know what it's about because the parties concerned haven't approached me officially, but the maintenance chief in the area says he's heard quieter riots. Inter-species friction must not be allowed to develop. Look into it, would you, and see if you can ..."

"Knock a few heads together until they see sense?" asked O'Mara.

Craythorne shook his head. ". . . talk some unofficial sense into them before it comes to our official attention and someone is expelled from the hospital. The disputants are Tralthans and Melfans, so the cranial-contact therapy you suggest would be impracticable, even for you."

"Figure of speech," O'Mara muttered.

"I know," said the major. "And both of us should be handling this one, but for the first time I'm making it your responsibility and will require you to turn in a full report and recommendations. Sorry about that. Trainees Edanelt and Vosan are taking more of my therapy time than I'd estimated."

"Transference," said O'Mara.

"Transference?"

O'Mara grinned. "I've been learning the professional vocabulary," he said, "and even know what most of the words mean. And I overheard them talking about you in the dining hall. Professionally, both of them have the greatest possible confidence in you. They think you are kindly, sensitive, and understanding and, on the personal side, they see you as a close friend rather than a therapist. I couldn't support the truth of these verbal statements because it's difficult to read the facial expression of a being who wears its skull on the outside, but Edanelt said that if you hadn't been an extraterrestrial—from its standpoint, that is—it would willingly carry your eggs . . ."

He was interrupted by a quiet laugh from the major, who said, "Well, it's nice to be appreciated."

"Not always, sir," said O'Mara. "This isn't a laughing matter. If you weren't so nice all the time to everybody, medical staff, subordinates, and especially me, people wouldn't take advantage of your good nature. Everybody likes you, naturally, because they think you are a soft touch. What I'm trying to say is that if you were more unfriendly, or even nasty sometimes, the demands on your time by people who just want a friendly chat rather than being in urgent need of therapy would be significantly reduced."

For a moment Craythorne stared down at his desk. When he looked up he was frowning.

"Lieutenant O'Mara," he said, "*please* stop trying to psycho-analyze your superior officer. Prying into and trying to tinker with my mind, while doubtless interesting, is a waste of time that you must put to better use. I realise that you learned your other-species psychology the hard way, initially by baby-sitting a Hudlar for three weeks, but knocking some sense into people, while simple and direct, is not the indicated procedure in all cases. 'Subtlety' is also in the vocabulary you've been studying. Learn its meaning and try practicing it more often.

"And another thing," he went on. "If you look unkempt that's the way people will expect you to think. It's probably too much to expect that you'll wear it with pride, but that uniform is supposed to look functional and smart. On you it looks as if you've taken a shortcut through the maintenance tunnels in it, which you probably have. Comb your hair as if you meant it and try shaving more often. At least three times a week would be nice. The problem on One-Eleven needs attention. You may go."

O'Mara's thumb was on the door button when Craythorne spoke from behind him.

"Am I being nasty enough, Lieutenant?"

"Not bad, sir," said O'Mara, "but you need more practice."

One-Eleven had been the first accommodation level to be completed and fully furnished to the requirements of five different other-species life-forms. The Maintenance Department was quietly but intensely proud of it and had promised that real soon, or at least as soon as possible, the other uncompleted and partially occupied accommodation levels would be brought up to the same standard of comfort. Since One-Eleven's completion it had been the hospital's most desirable place to live, but now, it seemed, the neighborhood was fast going to hell.

He already knew who the offenders were, but made his first

calls in the side corridors housing the innocent bystanders. Perhaps the major would have considered this a subtle approach.

In the short corridor accommodating the Kelgian DBLFs, the first few door IDs were flagged ABSENT, ON DUTY or SLEEPING, DO NOT DISTURB. The fourth said OCCUPIED, but several minutes of almost continuous thumb pressure passed before the door was opened by a Kelgian wearing large, padded headphones which it was lifting from its ears. Behind it he could see a lighted screen showing clinically nasty things being performed deep inside a species whose organs he couldn't identify.

The Kelgian ruffled its fur irritably at him and said, "I'm studying. Didn't hear you. What do you want?"

"Information," he replied, falling into the other's direct mode of speech, "regarding complaints of high levels of organic noise in this area. Have you been inconvenienced by it?"

"Yes, but not now," said the Kelgian. "My species has a low tolerance for being vivisected by Melfan pincers or trampled to death by Tralthan feet, so I was afraid to attempt to reduce the noise level at the source by remonstrating with them . . ." It tapped an earphone with one of its tiny fingers. ". . . so I took other measures. Go away."

Its door hissed shut before O'Mara could finish saying, "Thank you."

A few minutes later he was trying to talk to one of the Eurilian MSVKs, a storklike, tripedal nonflier whose atrophied wings were flapping so furiously that they all but lifted it into the air anyway, and whose angry, twittering speech didn't allow him to get a word in edgewise.

". . . and you've got to *do* something about this!" the Euril was saying, not for the first time. "Somehow you've got to stop that infernal racket. It isn't too bad when they visit each other's rooms to talk over lectures, or whatever else they do. You hear the Tralthans rumbling at each other sometimes when they get excited and raise their voices, and the Melfans sound as if they're beating their walls with sticks, but that's just a noise nuisance and bearable. But then they go back to their rooms to settle for the night. It's quiet for maybe an hour and we begin to feel safe. But when they start falling asleep the noise nearly blows me off my sleeping perch. And when they open their doors and the Tralthans and Melfans start complaining to each other about the noise they're both making keeping the other party awake, by then everybody is awake and we're lucky to get any sleep for the rest of the night. Or until next day during lectures when the tutors have harsh things to say to us for being inattentive. It's quiet now because they are settling themselves to sleep, but any minute now . . . I'm not equipped to inflict physical damage, but more and more often I feel like murdering one of them, any one of them. You've got to do something before somebody bigger and stronger than I am does."

O'Mara held up both hands placatingly. This was worse than he had been led to believe. For a moment he considered trying for a soft, conciliatory, Craythorne-type approach, then decided against it. The trouble that was developing here was much too serious for that. He would have to be tough.

"When you applied for a position here," he said firmly, "you knew that you would have to work and live with persons of many different species. Are you no longer able to do that?"

The Euril didn't reply. To O'Mara the expression on its feathered, birdlike face was unreadable, but he felt that the other was looking uneasy. Maybe hinting that it might be asked to leave Sector General was an unnecessary psychological overkill, especially as it was one of the injured parties.

Gently, he went on, "Don't worry, that would be a measure of last resort. Did you complain person to person, and explain your problem to them directly?"

"I tried once, with one of the Tralthans," the Euril replied. "It said it was sorry, but that many members of its species made noises in their sleep, that they couldn't help it and that the only way to stop making the noises was for them to stop breathing. It sounded very irritated, the way we all are when we don't get enough sleep. I didn't want to risk irritating again someone with twelve times my body mass, and decided that complaining to the Melfans, who aren't as big but are more excitable than Tralthans, would be better. It wasn't. The one I spoke to used words that the translator wasn't programmed to accept. Now I don't talk to any of them."

"But surely you talk to them during lectures," said O'Mara, "or on the wards, in the dining hall, or on the recreation level?"

"A little," the other replied. "But then it's mostly answering questions from the tutor or charge nurse, or talking to wide-awake patients. If any of them make sleeping noises they do it somewhere else in the hospital, not here in study block. The dining hall is big enough to let everyone dine among their own people, so we don't have to watch some of the others' disgusting eating habits. The same goes for the rec deck. It's better, and much more comfortable for us, if we stay away from them and them from us. Not just the snoring Tralthans and clattering Melfans, I mean everybody else."

O'Mara started to speak, then decided against it because he could think of nothing constructive to say. The situation was much worse than he had thought.

One pint-sized furry Nidian still looked much like any other to O'Mara, but with the one who opened its door to him it was immediately obvious that the reverse did not hold true.

"You're that other Earth-human psychologist, O'Mara," it said. Even through the translator it sounded as if it were barking angrily at him. "What is a psychologist going to do about that damned noise? Tell me to think beautiful, positive thoughts and ignore it? Suggest I OD on tranquilizers? Move the source to the other side of the galaxy? What?"

"I agree," said O'Mara, fighting an urge not to bark back at the irate little teddy bear, "that you have a legitimate complaint—"

"No!" snapped the Nidian. "I have a legitimate *request*. I want to be moved out of here. There's Nidian accommodation on Level One-Fourteen, I've seen Maintenance working on it."

"Level One-Fourteen isn't just for Nidians," said O'Mara quietly, but the other wasn't listening to him.

"They haven't finished the interior furnishings yet," it went on, "and it won't be nearly as comfortable as this place. But with a bunk and a chair and a console I'll be able to study in peace, and during sleep periods Maintenance are considerate enough to stop hammering and drilling, so at night it will be quiet . . ."

It was interrupted by a low, intermittent, growling sound from farther along the corridor that rose slowly in pitch and volume like a modulated foghorn before fading away. But the silence lasted only for the few moments necessary to lull a listener into thinking that it had gone away for good. The sound was muffled to an unknown extent by the sleeper's room walls, but at times it was so deep that it seemed as if the accompanying subsonics were vibrating the bones as well as the eardrums. Before O'Mara could speak there was a new sound, a slow, irregular clicking like amplified castanets. The short periods of silence during the Tralthan snoring were filled by the Melfan sleeping sounds and vice versa. The noises weren't all that loud, but together they were so nerve-shredding and insistent that O'Mara found himself clenching his teeth.

"I rest my case," barked the Nidian. "Well, what are you going to do about it?"

O'Mara remained silent, because right then he didn't know how to answer. Another set of amplified castanets were starting up, but they faltered and died. A door hissed open and a Melfan emerged and moved diagonally across the corridor to stab at a door call button with a bony pincer. A blocky Tralthan head and forebody appeared and they exchanged complaints about wanting to sleep in loud rumbling and clicking conversations interspersed with beeps because their translators had not been programmed to accept some of the words they were using. O'Mara shook his head.

"The Earth-human word that applies here," said the Nidian as it closed its door, "is 'chicken.' "

For a few minutes O'Mara watched the two quarreling ETs until he was sure that the dire threats of violence would be verbal rather than physical. He told himself that he was not being a moral coward, but he wasn't sure that he entirely believed himself. Trying to talk sense to those two when he didn't know how to solve the problem would simply increase the level of noise, especially if they made him lose his temper. Before he talked to them he needed to know what he was talking about.

He had to see a doctor.

It would have to be a friendly, approachable, closemouthed doctor, he decided, who was neither a Tralthan nor a Melfan but who knew a lot about the behavior of other-species staff under stress.

# CHAPTER 12

Senior Tutor Mannen was an Earth-human male DBDG whose age was indeterminate because his wrinkled, balding scalp was completely at odds with the fresh, youthful features visible from his eyebrows down. On the desk before him lay a neat pile of opened lecture folders and tapes, and frolicking around his feet there was a small, brown and white and very well house-trained puppy. The puppy went everywhere with him, except into OR, and there was a rumor, never officially denied by Mannen himself, that they slept together. The senior tutor looked up from his work, pointed to a chair, inclined his head in recognition, and waited.

O'Mara hesitated, then said, "Is your pup settling in okay, Doctor?"

Mannen nodded. "If you're sucking up to me through my dog," he said, grinning, "you must want a favor, right? You were lucky to catch me between lectures. What can I do for you . . ." He looked at his watch. ". . . during the next nine and a half minutes?"

"These days," said O'Mara sadly, "everybody is a psychologist. Sir, it's just that I need a little physiological or perhaps medical information on the Tralthan and Melfan life-forms. And, in confidence, your advice on how best to use it. My problem is this . . ."

Quickly he described the serious interpersonal situation that was developing on Level One-Eleven, including the close to xenophobic reactions of the innocent-bystander life-forms. Suddenly Mannen held up one hand and with the other began tapping keys on his communicator.

"This is going to take more than nine minutes," he said briskly. "Lecture Room Eighteen? I will be unavoidably delayed. Tell trainee Yursedth to take over the class until I arrive. Off." To O'Mara he went on wryly, "The trouble with this place is that it accepts only the highest grade of applicants. Yursedth thinks it knows more about Kelgian obstetrics than I do, and it could well be right. Taking over the class for a while and making the senior tutor feel redundant is something it will enjoy, although its classmates certainly won't. But enough of my troubles. Let us move to your problem."

Mannen paused and a rueful expression passed briefly over his face as he went on, "As yet nobody has fallen asleep during lectures. A few of the normally boisterous ones have been quieter than usual but mistakenly, I now realize, I thought that they were paying more attention, although I couldn't understand why the marks of these attentive ones were hitting the deck. So you see, the problem is mine as well as yours in that it can seriously affect future student training. Do you have a solution in mind for it, Lieutenant?"

O'Mara shook his head, then nodded uncertainly. He said, "Sir, only if there is a way to treat snoring, psychologically, medically, or surgically."

"Snoring, and its other-species equivalents, afflicts around five percent of the galaxy's sapient life-forms," said Mannen. "It is in no way an abnormal or a life-threatening condition, except possibly when the sound drives a sleep-deprived partner to acts of physical violence. It isn't due to a psychological disturbance; most snorers are quite sane, so that it cannot, so far as I know, be treated with psychotherapy. Every planet has its traditional cures, none of which are effective, or those which do work only by waking the person when he, she, or it begins snoring, which means the subject is deprived of sleep. That it not what we want here.

"Regarding the mechanics of snoring," Mannen went on, slipping into his lecturing mode, "in Earth-humans it is due to the palate relaxing and dropping during unconsciousness while lying on the back. With Tralthans, who do everything including sleep on their feet, there is a similar relaxation of the muscles which intermittently short-circuits the expelled air from the four breathing passages into the airway used for speech; they call it 'night-talking without words.' The physiological cause of the Melfan sleep rattle is much more complex and very interesting. . . . Sorry, Lieutenant, your only interest here is in stopping the condition, not studying how it works. Has anything I've said been helpful?"

O'Mara maintained a diplomatic silence.

"Thought so," said Mannen dryly. "Regarding surgical intervention, this is a possibility in all of the cases but not an option. We can't order our trainees to undergo unnecessary and in some species risky surgery just because they're noisy sleepers. We'd soon run short on Sector General applicants and anyway, the Federation's Medical Council wouldn't allow it. I think the solution will have to be technical rather than medical, separation by distance or greatly increased sound attenuation at source. Well?"

O'Mara thought for a moment. Then he said, "When the hospital is fully operational, the medical and maintenance staff are going to be really packed in. Putting distance between snorers and nonsnorers will not be an option either, but you must already know that, sir. When I checked with Maintenance, they told me that the level of personnel soundproofing in the Tralthan and Melfan quarters had already been increased to the maximum conducive to normal living requirements. Any more and the music or dialogue on the occupants' entertainment channels, even their own conversations, would be so off-pitch and muffled that . . . well, they'd feel like they were in padded cells and they wouldn't like that one bit."

"What about using hush fields?" said Mannen.

"I know about them, sir," O'Mara replied. "Most of the wards have one, to sonically isolate a case whose audible output is causing distress to the other patients. Psychology is a small department and there are budgetary considerations. Maintenance says they are hellishly expensive."

"They are," Mannen agreed. "But don't look as if all your relatives had just died. By comparison, Training Department has an obscenely large budget. Some of it could be spent to ensure me of a continued supply of wakeful and attentive students, so don't bother thanking me. Just tell me how many units you think you'll need and I'll talk to Major Craythorne about ordering them as soon as possible. Your problem is solved, so why are you still wearing that dissatisfied expression?"

"Sorry, sir," said O'Mara, "but you've solved only part of the trouble, or will have in a few weeks or months from now when the units are installed. But that isn't tackling the more serious underlying problem."

"Go on," said Mannen.

O'Mara tried hard to sound as if he wasn't lecturing as he went on, "We know that lack of sleep causes short-term irritability that can, unless it is countered, grow into something more permanent and much worse. I've already detected the beginning of an intense xenophobic reaction in the Kelgian, Eurilian, and Nidian trainees I spoke to, and that is really dangerous. In time there will be members of sixty-odd, some of them very odd, intelligent species working here. They should not be collected into their own little same-species enclaves, with tight circles of same-species friends, all sharing in same-species social and recreational activities. This is expected to be the galaxy's biggest and best multi-species hospital. If it is to work as it should then the staff has got to mix, and not only at lectures or on the wards . . ."

He stopped as Mannen held up one hand again and said, "Lieutenant, I'm not your grandmother, but if I was I'd tell you not to teach me to suck eggs."

"Sorry, sir," said O'Mara. "It's something I feel strongly about."

Mannen nodded and looked at his watch. "Right. What else do you want from me?"

"I would like you to start conning your students," O'Mara said quickly. "I don't mean tell them lies exactly, just shade the truth a little. And spend a few minutes of every lecture, longer if you can manage it, asking them about their personal feelings and progress rather than their clinical work. Be like a stern father no matter what size they are. You can say that you've noticed that some of them are looking tired and are falling behind in their studies but you are aware of the reason. Tell them about the hush-field units which will be installed in the quarters of those who really need them, but the process will be a gradual one over the coming months and, regrettably, some of them will have to make the best of the situation until then. Without saying so directly, suggest that their ability to adapt to this situation, and to understand the needs, behavior, and feelings of their other-species colleagues, can have a very beneficial effect on their grades, and that the last few of them to have their rooms fitted with hush fields can feel deservedly proud of themselves.

"As yet I haven't discussed this idea with my chief," he went on quickly, "but when I do, I'm sure Major Craythorne will be glad to talk to and encourage them along the same lines. He's much better than I am at that sort of thing."

"I disagree," said Mannen. "Is that all?"

O'Mara hesitated. "No, sir. I don't know how, but is it possible for you to modify the content of your lectures and study assignments so that one student, or students, have more understanding, or perhaps background knowledge regarding a particular assignment than the others, so that for the best results they will be forced to use a lot more of their free time outside of lectures and ward duties to exchange this knowledge and, well, be forced into using their free time to mix with each other to talk shop? They have to be forced, I mean encouraged, to mix. Is this possible?"

"Possible," said Mannen, "but not easy. It would mean reorganizing my whole . . . Lieutenant, you've got a nasty, devious mind."

Pleased, O'Mara nodded. "I'm a psychologist, sir."

The other gave him a long look under lowered brows, then went on, "Right, your ideas are workable and I'll do as you suggest. I'm not a psychologist, but as a clinical tutor of long experience I know when someone is trying to hide something from me. What else is in your nasty, devious mind, Lieutenant?"

O'Mara felt his face growing warm. He hesitated, then said, "I'd rather not say, sir. The major has given me full responsibility for this one and my idea is a bit unusual, and comes under the heading of a crude but effective solution. I haven't thought it through properly and it might not work, so I think it's better that you don't know the details."

Mannen nodded, looked at his watch again, and got quickly to his feet. "Just try not to wreck the hospital," he said.

"I won't, sir," said O'Mara as he rose to leave. Under his breath he added, *At least, not all of it.*

His next stop was at his quarters, where he changed into his oldest and most stained set of coveralls, the ones that the laundry was continually sending him notes about suggesting that they should be sent without delay to the incinerator. It was likely that Major Craythorne would not be pleased by what he intended to do, and he didn't want to make matters worse by ruining another uniform. Besides, he needed to find his way among the service tunnels under the dining hall, and that could not be done quickly if one wanted to stay clean.

He found Technician Lenneth working on one of the battery of cleaning, food-delivery, and systems-checking robots in its charge. It was wearing two sets of coveralls. Kelgians were inclined to be overprotective where their silver fur was concerned.

"O'Mara," said Lennenth, "what do you want?"

"I want you to do me a big favor," he replied.

"Earth-humans don't always say what they mean," said Lennenth. "Do you mean you want me to return the big favor you did for me?"

O'Mara shook his head. "You are under no obligation to do anything for me," he said. "If you simply return that favor, we're quits. But if you do this one for me, we'll each owe the other a favor and that might come in useful in the future. Do you agree?"

"O'Mara, you're making my head hurt," said Lennenth. "Your help with the Tralthan waste-pumping system failure under Ward Fifteen earned me a promotion, so either way, I'll do it. What exactly do you want done?"

"First," he said, "are you still responsible for the dining-area cleaning and maintenance? Especially for driving that big cleaning vehicle?"

"Yes," said the Kelgian, "and yes."

"Good," said O'Mara. "On your next cleanup shift, which is six hours from now, I want to drive it. I'll need your advice about maneuvering the brute between the table spaces, but this is what I plan to do. . . ."

As he went on speaking, Lennenth's fur moved so violently that its coveralls looked as if they had been stuffed with maddened weasels. Its fur was still twitching uncontrollably when he stopped talking and the other found its voice.

"They'll kick us both off the hospital for this!" it said. "O'Mara, I think you need therapy."

"I don't think they'll kick us off the hospital," said O'Mara, "and certainly not both of us. We'll work out the details later, but you will be temporarily detached from your dining-area duties and sent to do something in a public area that will keep you busy for a couple of hours, so you will not be directly involved. I'll put the order in writing, but you are not to show it to anyone unless the idea goes sour and they try to blame you.

"After all," he added, smiling, "a mere technician, even a newly promoted technician first class, cannot disobey the direct order of a lieutenant."

During the ensuing six hours before the dastardly deed was done, O'Mara tried to sleep or at least rest, in vain. Instead, he used the time to write his report and recommendations to Craythorne in advance of the event. He tried to make it as neat, clear, and concise as he could, because the major had a tidy mind and, as well, it might well be the last report he would ever write in Sector General.

But when he placed the report on the major's desk next morning, Craythorne barely glanced at the title page before pushing it aside. It was the first time he had seen the other angry as Craythorne said grimly, "Thank you, O'Mara, but I haven't time to read it now. Something more urgent and serious has come up. Someone has trashed the dining area, uprooted most of the furniture by tearing it off its floor attachments. A big cleaning and repair vehicle was used and it wasn't an accident. This looks as if it was deliberately planned vandalism by a person or persons unknown while the technician in charge was absent. The damage can be repaired easily enough, but I want you to go down there and find out what the hell happened and why."

"I know what happened, and why," said O'Mara. "It's in my report, sir."

Craythorne blinked slowly; then, without taking his eyes off O'Mara, he reached sideways and pulled the report in front of him again. He said, "Then obviously I have time to read it now. Sit down, Lieutenant."

There were five pages and the major didn't speak until he had finished reading the last one. Then he placed his elbows on the desk, cupped his forehead in both hands for a moment, then looked up and said, "O'Mara, when you mentioned knocking people's heads together to make them see sense, I thought you were joking."

"Sir, I'm not knocking heads together," O'Mara protested, "just forcing them close enough to talk, which they will have to do if they eat together. The damage in the dining area was precisely calculated so that there will not be enough physiologically suitable furniture for any given species to dine without having to make use of other-species tables, chairs, or whatever. They'll probably argue or quarrel at first, have nasty things to say about each others' eating habits, but they will talk and get to understand and make allowances for each other instead of isolating themselves into tight and potentially hostile same-species groups. Senior Tutor Mannen is restructuring his lectures so that, in their off-duty periods, they will be forced together to talk shop if they want optimum exam results.

"As well," O'Mara went on excitedly, "he is helping fund hushfield installations for some of the sleeping quarters that will need them although, if my idea works out and they really begin to understand and accept each other, eating habits, sleeping noises, warts and all, we may not need many of them. But what we do need is enough time to allow the process to work."

"Which is why," Craythorne said, tapping the report, "you want the table repairs to be delayed for as long as possible."

"Yes, sir," said O'Mara quickly. "But I need your help there. I don't have the rank to tell Maintenance to slow down, but you have. Regarding the trainees, what I thought we might do is introduce a little professional competitiveness into the process. The Educator tapes are about to be introduced, initially to senior staff members, although the trainees will be keen to try them, too. Maybe we, through Dr. Mannen, could suggest that the impression of an other-species mind tape is a landmark event, a high professional compliment, and that trainees who do not make an effort to fully understand the thought processes and behavior of their colleagues might not be considered suitable for the impression of other-species mind partners.

"In the meantime," he continued, "we could plant the idea that anyone who is averse to using physically unsuitable table furniture and talking to other-species friends and colleagues is, well, something of a sissy. Or the ET equivalent."

Craythorne nodded. "And you also want to rearrange the staff duty schedules, and particularly their mealtimes, so that there are never enough empty same-species tables to go round. We might even make that situation permanent as part of the other-species social acclimatization process. Maintenance would have a lot of complaints, but Maintenance always has a lot of complaints. It will be inconvenient at first but soon the constant shortage of tables will be accepted as a continuing fact of hospital life."

He tapped the report again. "I like this, O'Mara. Your recommendations will be put into effect at once. Well done."

O'Mara nodded. He was so pleased and relieved that no words would come.

Craythorne went on, "You handled this situation so well, but in such a direct, unorthodox fashion, that at the moment I'm reluctant to give you another problem to solve. But one thing surprises me."

"Sir?"

"Yes," said the other. "You have never struck me, Lieutenant, as the type of person to whom anyone would want to do a favor."

As he was leaving the office, Craythorne added, "Ignore the last remark, O'Mara, I'm still trying to be nasty."

# CHAPTER 13

**C**raythorne's reluctance to give him another assignment lasted for all of three days. The major was busy smoothing the administrational wrinkles out of the nonrepairable dining-area project, so they were rarely in the department at the same time. It came as no surprise that the latest job came in the form of the cover-page summary of a trainee psych file and a note in Craythorne's terrible handwriting. He read the file first.

> Subject: THORNNASTOR. Physiological classification FGLI; species Tralthan; age, 87 Earth standard years with a normal life-expectancy of 150 years; graduate with honors University of Howth Medical School on Traltha; served 12 years as medical consultant on multi-species space construction projects in the Ballildon, Corso, and Lentallet systems; no close family or nonfamily emotional ties; accepted for advanced multi-species surgical training Sector General; first trainee to undergo an other-

species Educator tape impression with no reported aftereffects, and permission has been given to retain the
tape until its current medical project is completed, following successful completion of which it will be offered
a position on the permanent staff at senior-physician
level; previous clinical studies and ward work exemplary,
but a marked deterioration has been noted over the past
three weeks; psychological investigation requested by Senior Tutor Mannen before finalizing its promotion. Present living quarters Level 111, Room 18.

The note said, "Maybe it's just homesick, or at 87 is having a
midlife crisis. Talk to it, find out what if anything is going wrong in
its mind, but leave the hobnailed boots in your quarters."

Plainly, O'Mara thought, Craythorne was still trying hard to
be nasty.

Unless it was on the recreation deck or socializing somewhere,
Thornnastor's duty schedule placed it in its quarters an hour before
it was due to retire for the night. As he left the elevator on One-
Eleven and found the right door number, he wondered if it was
one of the snorers. He heard and felt the deck vibration as it approached and opened its door.

"My name is O'Mara," he said, trying not to feel intimidated
by a highly intelligent six-legged elephant who might or might not
be emotionally disturbed, "from the Other-Species Psychology Department. If it's convenient, I'd like to talk to you."

"I know of you, O'Mara," said Thornnastor. "Come in. The inconvenience will be all yours if you have no prior experience of my
species' lack of furniture. I suggest that you sit on the edge of the
sleeping pit."

Thornnastor's accommodation was a large, empty cube rendered small by the size of the occupant. The walls were covered
by pictures of home-world scenery and images too strange for

O'Mara to even guess at what they might be, and a few trailing pieces of strong-smelling, decorative vegetation that partly concealed the door to the bathroom. A thick, semicircular shelf carrying a lighted viewscreen, a recorder, and lecture tapes was the only piece of furniture that projected from the walls. The deep, rectangular, Tralthan-sized sleeping recess in the center of the floor was entered by a sloping ramp. O'Mara moved down the ramp until the edge of the floor was level with the back of his knees, half turned, and sat down. He pressed his palms briefly into the thick, soft material that covered the floor.

"Thank you," he said, trying to find something complimentary to say. "This is very comfortable."

"My species does not require a high level of physical comfort," said Thornnastor. "The padding is there to deaden the sound of my footfalls so as not to inconvenience my neighbors with sound pollution. While I welcome a legitimate interruption in my studies . . ." It pointed a tentacle at the lighted viewscreen. ". . . I would prefer it not to be a waste of time."

The mind tape it was carrying had been donated by a Kelgian, O'Mara thought, and it was obvious that the host's behavior was being influenced by the donor, so a polite, roundabout approach would also be redundant.

"I've no intention of wasting your time or mine," he said. "Senior Tutor Mannen has asked me to talk about the recent deterioration in your work which, because it has previously been of such a high standard, is causing us concern. The continuing decline became apparent a few days after you were impressed with a Kelgian DBLF mind tape, so we suspect a psychological component to your problem. Would you care to comment?"

Thornnastor turned one of its eyes in the direction of the viewscreen, followed by a tentacle tip, which switched it off; then all four of its eyes curled down to look at O'Mara. A few moments passed without a reply.

"If you are taking time to make a considered and accurate answer," said O'Mara, "I can wait. But if you are unwilling to speak, why not?"

The Tralthan made a muted, foghorn sound that did not translate and otherwise remained silent. O'Mara sighed.

"There have been complaints of noise in this area during rest periods," he went on. "The matter is being dealt with. But sleep deprivation can seriously affect the ability to concentrate. Is that the problem?"

"No," said Thornnastor.

"Is the behavior or a lack of understanding of your colleagues or the teaching staff affecting you?" he continued. "Has anything they have done or said made you feel insecure? Are you having an emotional or perhaps a sexual involvement with someone?"

"No," the Tralthan repeated.

"Then has it something to do with the mind tape?" he persisted.

The other remained silent.

*I should have studied dentistry,* he thought. *This is like pulling teeth.*

"Plainly there is a problem with your Educator tape," said O'Mara patiently, "which it is my job to help you solve. But we can't solve it unless I know what it is. I have the feeling that you would like to talk about it. Please do so."

Thornnastor made another untranslatable sound so deep that it seemed to vibrate his bones. Then it said, "This is stupid, ridiculous. There's no reason why I should feel this way."

"Whether or not it is stupid or ridiculous," said O'Mara, "is a purely subjective judgment on your part and as such has questionable value, as is the apparent lack of reason for your present feelings. Take as much time as you need to describe those feelings."

The Tralthan raised and stamped the floor with its two middle feet. O'Mara felt the vibration even through the floor padding.

In a Tralthan, he reassured himself, it was supposed to be a sign of extreme irritation, perhaps of self-irritation in this case. It was also an indication, he hoped, that the other was going to speak.

"I am being afflicted with intense feelings of homesickness," said Thornnastor in a low, ashamed voice, "for people and a planet I have never known. I'm supposed to have a stable, well-integrated mind. It is ridiculous and stupid to feel this way."

*So it* was *the mind tape,* O'Mara thought. At least he knew where the problem lay, and that, according to the unwritten laws of Major Craythorne, meant that he had taken the first step toward solving it. But it was beginning to look as if he was trying to analyze two patients here, the one presently looming over him and the tape donor at the other end of the galaxy who might not even be alive.

He said, "Not necessarily. The trouble may lie in the tape donor's mind rather than yours. You know that mind from the inside. Tell me about it."

"No," said Thornnastor. He waited but that was all it would say. For some reason Thornnastor had gone into silent mode again.

"This isn't helping either of us," said O'Mara. "Why won't you tell me about this person's mind? The communication is privileged and nothing you can tell me will have any possible effect on a tape donor whose mind is just a recording that cannot be hurt or helped or changed in any way, and who may well be dead by now. You are intelligent enough to be aware of this. Well?"

There was another long silence. He tried again.

"Regardless of species," said O'Mara, "the beings who are invited to provide our mind tapes are the top people in their home worlds' medical profession. But individuals who climb to the top, as we both know, are not always nice people. You already know that it is not just the donor's medical or surgical skill that is impressed on a recipient's mind, it is all of the memories, feelings, pet hates, prejudices, and psychological hangups, if any, that are transferred as well. You are required to ignore, for the period that the donor tape is in your mind and as far as you are able, all this nonmedical baggage and concentrate only on the medical material you need for your current project. Nobody thinks this is easy, and I can only imagine what—"

"You can have no understanding of what an other-species mind tape feels like," Thornnastor broke in, "unless you take the same mind impression. How otherwise can you possibly know or feel what I'm feeling?"

Even though it was a legitimate question, O'Mara had to control his irritation as he replied, "I was impressed with a mind tape only once, and briefly, to become acquainted with the mental disorientation that occurs when a completely alien personality is sharing one's mind, so you're wrong in thinking that I'm completely ignorant of the effects. But I am forbidden to take your tape or any other because it is my job as an Earth-human therapist to be objective, well-balanced, and self-aware so that I can work to remove the emotional problems in your mind. With an other-species mind partner muddying the mental water that would not be easy. This is the department's policy. I don't need to know what your tape donor felt in its past but what you are feeling now. Is this clear?"

"Yes."

"Then talk to me," said O'Mara.

"No."

O'Mara took a deep breath that would enable him to say harsh things in a loud voice, then changed his mind and spoke quietly. He said, "Among Earth-humans there is a disrespectful but fairly accurate name given to people in my profession. It is 'headshrinker.' As the name suggests, my job is to shrink heads, to make the minds within them respond to the real world rather than live in a flawed reality of their own, and not swell them with flattery.

"Now," he went on, "I have no medical training and, therefore, no real appreciation of your professional qualifications except through hospital gossip and the hearsay evidence of your colleagues and superiors, all of whom speak well of you. It seems that you are highly proficient as a surgeon, have the ability to inspire subordinate staff to perform to the same level of proficiency, and are species-adaptable, imaginative, and justifiably ambitious. If your current progress continues you will shortly be appointed to the permanent staff here with the rank of senior physician, thus skipping the two intervening trainee levels. But enough of the flattery."

O'Mara paused for a moment. He knew that the other was unlikely to be able to read Earth-human facial expressions, but he hoped the serious tone in his voice would get through the translator as he went on, "This appointment will require the continuing impression and erasure of the mind tapes necessary for the treatment of your future other-species patients, but it will definitely be withheld if you aren't able to cope with your first experience of having a mind partner. Thornnastor, I am here to help you cope. Is the emotional problem you are experiencing so serious and mentally disabling that you *want* to give up a promising career in medicine because of it?"

"No," said Thornnastor.

"Again I remind you," O'Mara continued, "my interest in anything you tell me is purely clinical. Anything I learn will be a privileged communication, and I shall not be judgmental or feel shocked by anything you say. Now, is there something in your tape donor's mind that has triggered past memories or experiences of your own, something about which you now feel ashamed?"

"No," said the other loudly.

"Calm yourself," said O'Mara. "I had no intention of giving offense. But I do need information. You said that you felt intense feelings of homesickness, for friends you never met and places you have never been and, initially, you appeared to feel shame over these feelings. Is it your mind partner who feels this shame or—"

"No," said Thornnastor again.

"So it's you who feels the shame," said O'Mara. "Tell me why you feel it, in your own words and time. Tell me what is wrong with you, or what you think is wrong with you, because you are the only person who can give me a clue to what that is."

"No."

O'Mara took a deep breath then let it out slowly. He said, "Thornnastor, I am becoming very irritated by your continuing use of that word. If you won't talk to me about the problem, will you at least tell me why?"

"For three reasons," said Thornnastor. "You are not a medic and would not appreciate my special difficulty, and you cannot know the complete workings of my mind or those of my mind partner. With respect and apologies, O'Mara, you are wasting your time here. There is nothing you can do to help me."

O'Mara nodded. "Possibly not," he said. "But I can be patient and talk all around the problem, perhaps attack it from different directions. Would that help?"

"No," said Thornnastor.

At least, O'Mara thought sourly as he left the Tralthan's quarters, the other's replies had been consistently negative. But if there was one thing he hated it was being told what he could or could not do.

When he returned to the department there was a message for him saying that Craythorne would be absent from his office for the next two hours. That, he thought, should give him enough time to read more than the first page of Thornnastor's psych file and to study the available information on the entity who had donated that troublesome mind tape.

But the Tralthan's file revealed much that was new and nothing that was useful. It seemed that Thornnastor was an exemplary trainee, a self-starter from the beginning, able, serious, strong-willed, and with an unusually stable and well integrated mind of which it was justifiably proud. Although it was otherwise polite and well-behaved in its same- and other-species contacts, the pride showed in its tendency to argue with its tutors during lectures, when it had the irritating habit of usually proving them wrong.

The information on Thornnastor could have been a copy of the material that appeared in all of the senior medical staff's psych files. Barring unforeseen accidents, it was the psychological profile of a person who was heading for the top of its professional tree. The personal information on its mind partner, a Kelgian DBLF called Marrasarah, was sparse but interesting.

It began with a general explanation of the Educator-tape system and its uses followed by a warning to the effect that the donors of the mind tapes were not to be contacted for consultation regarding the material they had donated, or for any other purpose, unless their own express permission or that of a close relative was obtained. And even then the request would have to be investigated and approved by a special subcommittee of the Galactic Medical Council set up for the protection of the privacy of mind tape donors.

The principal reason for this many-layered protection was simply the passage of time. A person with the necessary eminence in its field to be invited to donate a mind tape was, in the usual course of events, at its professional and mental peak and already of advanced years. Such a being would not want to be subjected to the general hassle of questioning, no matter how polite and respectful the questioners were, regarding details of the mental legacy it had left by rising younger medics trying to second-guess it, especially if the donor mind in question had begun to age-deteriorate during the time since the tape had been made. O'Mara could understand that. It was simply a matter of showing consideration for the feelings of the old who had once been great.

But the interesting part was that Marrasarah wasn't old. Instead it had been a brilliant and gifted young medical hotshot. No details were given regarding its meteoric progress in its chosen field. The cause listed for its ridiculously early retirement was "personal and emotional reasons resulting from burn injuries." But in its case the strictures regarding noncontact were repeated and underlined.

O'Mara looked at the mind-tape container inside its file for a long time. It was obvious that Marrasarah had suffered a major emotional upheaval of some kind and had been seriously and perhaps permanently affected by it. But its professional knowledge and experience had been so valuable that it had been invited to make the tape before it retired—on the assumption, O'Mara supposed, that any future recipient would either be strong-willed enough to concentrate on the medical component and ignore the associated emotional problems or, if the psychological content was too troublesome, simply withdraw from the case, have the tape erased at the earliest opportunity, and take another that had fewer problems. But from what he knew of Thornnastor's personality, the Tralthan was too proud and pigheaded to do that.

Even though he could explain the situation to Mannen and have Thornnastor excused from the case, he knew that the Tralthan would not want to put its promotion prospects on hold until another opportunity occurred. From what he knew of the other, it would also feel afraid that it would not be able to adapt to the next mind tape, either, and that its career as an other-species surgeon in Sector General would be at an end. It had probably decided that it was better to know the worst as soon as possible. O'Mara could sympathize with that feeling, but his sympathy alone wouldn't solve the problem.

He could only do that by getting into the stubbornly uncommunicative Thornnastor's mind, and the only path open to him was through the mind of the brilliant but seriously disturbed Marrasarah. He shook his head and took a long look at his watch.

Craythorne was due back within half an hour. He could wait, make his report, discuss his idea for treatment with his superior, who would warn him of the psychological risks and almost certainly order him not to proceed. Or he could do what he wanted to do in a few minutes before the major had a chance to forbid it.

The trick with any really close decision, he told himself as he moved with slow deliberation to the Educator-tape couch, donned the helmet, and pushed the Marrasarah mind tape into its slot, was to weigh the probabilities very carefully but not for too long.

Indecision could paralyze some people.

# CHAPTER 14

For the first few minutes the sensations were exactly the same as those he had felt after Councillor Davantry had administered that first Kelgian mind tape. There was the same feeling that he was looking at a strange office from a distance too high above the floor, and the same sensation of vertigo because he was balancing on two long, Earth-human legs rather than the twelve stubby ones possessed by Kelgians. But the disorientation and dizziness passed quickly and were replaced by something much worse. It was so bad that he was forced to sit down and fight desperately to retain control of the personality that was O'Mara.

*Poor Thornnastor,* he thought, *if this is what it has to contend with.* He tried not to think *Poor me* because the reason he was feeling this way was nobody's fault but his own.

Unlike the Tralthan, he did not believe that he had a brilliant, stable, and well-integrated mind. But he had always had the reputation for being as stubborn as a mule, or one of its off-world equivalents, and he had never, ever allowed another person to do his thinking, or in this case his feeling, for him. Gradually but not completely he began to regain control over his mind.

Now he could understand why Thornnastor wouldn't talk to him. A combination of the Tralthan's professional pride and that of its even prouder mind partner precluded that, together with the emotional distress that had spilled over from Marrasarah's tortured mind. In spite of its physical and mental suffering, the Kelgian's mind had been sane when it had donated the tape. And it, too, had been a fighter and every bit as stubborn as O'Mara. But it had been suffering then, just as Thornnastor and himself were suffering now, but without the option of having its intensity of sorrow, anger, bitter personal loss, and a mess of associated emotions erased. Marrasarah had not deserved to be caught in that accidental lab fire that had destroyed much of its fur, but then history was full of nice people who got what they didn't deserve and nobody, including himself, could do anything about that except feel bad.

But Thornnastor wasn't history, at least not yet, and it was O'Mara's job to do something about that if the Tralthan was not to become a minor entry as a promising failure in the annals of Sector General.

He began walking around the office because regular, noncerebral activity had always helped his mind to work better, and now it was working overtime. He stopped only long enough to call Mannen, who fortunately could see him immediately, and to leave a message for his chief saying that he was going to talk to the senior tutor regarding the Thornnastor assignment.

Craythorne would have no worries about that, but if he had told the other what he had just done and about the idea for treatment he would be trying to sell Mannen, the major would have been worried sick.

As soon as he entered, Mannen looked up from his desk and pointed at a chair that was suitable, but not comfortable, for Earth-human occupation and waited.

"About Thornnastor . . ." O'Mara began.

"So you've discovered what's wrong with my star trainee?" Mannen broke in. "That's good."

"Yes," said O'Mara, "but it isn't good."

Mannen was trying unsuccessfully to hide his disappointment. He said, "We'd hate to lose that one, Lieutenant. But go on."

O'Mara was choosing his words with care so that he could hide the truth without actually telling a lie as he said, "Thornnastor was completely uncooperative during our interview and refused to tell me, except briefly and in the most general terms, why the Kelgian mind tape was causing it such intense emotional distress. With some patients we find an initial lack of cooperation, even outright hostility, and allowances are made for this, especially when the reason for the behavior is fully understood. But hostility in a patient doesn't preclude us attempting to treat it or—"

"Wait," Mannen broke in. "Just now you told me that Thornnastor wouldn't talk, except in general terms, about its troubles or its mind partner. How then did you come to fully understand its behavior? Did Major Craythorne allow you to take the same mind tape? And isn't that, well, unusual?"

*Obviously,* thought O'Mara, *I didn't choose my words carefully enough to hide anything, or the other was smart enough to see right through them.* He said, "I couldn't think of any other way of helping Thornnastor with its problem. The major doesn't know I've taken the tape. It isn't unusual, it's forbidden."

"I knew that," said Mannen, "but it isn't any of my business what rules you break. But did you hint back there that curative therapy is possible? If so, what will the treatment entail, and will Thornnastor be able to perform its operation by noon tomorrow?"

"The treatment is radical, untried, and, well, risky," O'Mara replied. "But if it goes as I expect it will, your star trainee, who is my patient, should be able to operate."

There was an edge of sarcasm in the other's voice as he said, "You *are* going to tell me what you intend to do?"

"Yes, sir," said O'Mara. "But the pride Thornnastor has in its professional ability, and the intense embarrassment it is feeling over what it believes is its impending failure, is the reason for its silence. A similar degree of pride, plus a truly horrendous load of despair, anger, and deep, personal sorrow, it has inherited via the Kelgian Educator tape. Thornnastor has an unusually powerful mind that is also extremely sensitive. If it had been less sensitive to the medical condition it is sharing through its mind partner, and had less of that resultant fellow-species sympathy it feels toward its forthcoming Kelgian patient, it might have been able to ignore the nonmedical material in Marrasarah's mind tape and we would have had no trouble. But, well, as things stand I shall tell it that no report of this case will ever appear outside the department's confidential files, and there will be no future verbal discussion among the parties concerned. Naturally, I'll have to make a detailed report on the case to Major Craythorne, which will probably land me in trouble, but I don't want to do that until the therapy is complete. Sir, can I ask you not to—"

"Of course," Mannen broke in. "Until then my lips are sealed. But what the hell are you intending to *do?*"

As O'Mara began telling him the other's mouth opened to interrupt him and remained open without speaking until he had finished. Then Mannen closed his mouth so hard that his teeth came together with an audible click. He shook his head. O'Mara hoped it was in silent puzzlement rather than complete negation.

"Let me be sure I understand you, O'Mara," he said finally. "Thornnastor is having problems with its first mind transfer, so you want to give it three mind tapes to contend with?"

"Three more," O'Mara corrected. "It will be four tapes altogether. And if you know the kinds of patients Thornnastor is most likely to have assigned to it in the near future, I'd like your advice on the species concerned so that the process will serve as a brief introduction to its mind partners to be. This is a matter of simple mathematics as well as psychology. With four tapes occupying its mind at once, the effect of their extraneous emotional material will be diluted to a quarter, especially during the op when it will have to concentrate on abstracting only the required medical information. Following the operation the tapes, all of them, will be erased and Thornnastor's mind will be back to normal with its pride intact and without it having suffered any professional embarrassment. I think it is a simple, direct, elegant solution to the . . ."

Mannen held up one hand. "The word that comes most readily to my mind," he said dryly, "is 'simpleminded.' Thornnastor has expressed a special interest in performing Melfan, Illensan, and Earth-human surgery. Those are the mind tapes it is most likely to need in the future, if it has a future here. Dammit, you could totally wreck Thornnastor's sanity."

"In my opinion no, sir," said O'Mara. "The Tralthan's mind is strong, well balanced, and highly adaptable. Besides, the other-species mind partners, unlike Marrasarah, will not be long-term visitors. There won't be enough time for it to be seriously influenced by them."

Mannen was silent for a long moment, then said, "Right. I'm becoming suspicious about my own sanity, but you've talked me into it. There is one condition."

"Sir?"

"You must be present during the operation," Mannen said firmly, "in case Thornnastor becomes mentally unstable and we need your help in pacifying it, because OR isn't the best place for an outsized and overmuscled surgeon to run amok. Agreed?"

O'Mara hesitated. "I've no medical training."

"We'll be hip deep in medics down there," Mannen said. "What we'll need is someone to treat a disturbed doctor, not the patient. If Thornnastor does go unstable on us, what will you do?"

"Talk to it first and try verbal pacification," O'Mara replied. "If that fails I'll shoot it with an anesthetic dart gun previously concealed in the OR. Can you make sure that the dart is sharp and the anesthetic is strong enough? Tralthans have tough skins and a lot of body mass so we will need, I mean we might need, something that works fast."

"Another one of your simple, direct solutions," Mannen said. "Right, I'll see to it."

"I'd like to thank you, sir," said O'Mara gratefully, "for cooperating in this unusual form of therapy."

"You can do that by giving me back a fully sane and functioning Thornnastor," said Mannen. "I'm almost afraid to ask, Lieutenant, but is there anything else you need from me?"

"Yes, sir," said O'Mara, smiling. "I believe one of the other-species trainees is giving you some cause for concern. You can pick a likely candidate. Its condition is fictional, of course, but an element of hypochondria and the ability to talk about itself for long periods would be an advantage. It would have to be interviewed in its quarters, or in an empty lecture hall or anywhere but the Psychology Department during the hour preceding Thornnastor's op. I will be impressing the three extra mind tapes then and can't afford to have the major walking in and asking awkward questions."

Mannen put his forehead into his hands and spoke to the top of his desk.

"Right," he said. "But please go now before you destroy all my illusions, and confirm my worst fears, about what goes on in the Psychology Department."

O'Mara smiled and left quickly. He had to talk to Thornnastor again and sell it on the multiple-tape idea before it retired for the night. It might take a long time and he as well as the Tralthan might lose a lot of sleep. But that, at least, would cut down on the volume of snoring in the area.

The glass-walled OR was in readiness when Thornnastor and O'Mara arrived outside punctually the next day. As it was primarily an examination of the surgeon's procedure as well as an attempt to rectify serious traumatic damage to the patient, the room was more crowded than usual. The patient was already anesthetized and the other members of the operating team, two Melfans and one Earth-human, were standing by the table to assist, as were, not quite as close, Mannen and a Nidian tutor. Before they entered, O'Mara put a hand against the Tralthan's leathery flank.

"Wait," he said worriedly. "How are you feeling?"

Softly, for a Tralthan, Thornnastor growled, "How should a person with a quadruply split personality feel? I think I'll be all right."

O'Mara nodded and followed it inside; then he moved across the room to stand between Mannen and the other tutor.

"Recorders on?" said Thornnastor calmly. "Very well, I'll begin. This is patient Murrenth, physiological classification DBLF, a shipboard technician in the Kelgian space service. It presented with internal injuries sustained as the result of being trapped briefly by shifting cargo, briefly because fellow crew members were able to rescue it within a few minutes. Initially it was thought that no serious trauma had occurred because the patient, perhaps for psychological reasons including the fact that the accident was partly its own fault, did not report any physical discomfort. Two days later it began losing fur mobility over the back and one side of the body. Its condition was reclassified to DBLF Emergency Three and it was rushed here."

One of the Tralthan's tentacles rose to pull down the scanner attached to the ceiling by a telescoping arm until it was positioned above the operative field. It curled an eye toward the wall-mounted diagnostic screen which was showing a massive enlargement of the scanner image.

"It was discovered that serious trauma had in fact occurred," Thornnastor continued, "but too subtle for detection by the equipment available on the patient's ship. The temporary pressure of the cargo that fell on Murrenth's back and side caused a minor constriction of the blood flow through the capilliary system in those areas. This caused micro-clots to form which reduced the blood supply to the delicate muscles and nerve network controlling fur mobility. The condition has been worsening, an immediate surgical intervention is indicated, and . . ."

"And the prognosis is lousy," Mannen said softly to O'Mara. "I'm afraid this is going to be an examination for surgical technique, not for a successful result."

". . . care must be taken," Thornnastor was saying, "to comb the fur carefully from both sides of the entry-wound position before making the incision. Each individual strand of fur is a delicate part of the body to which it belongs, and the possession of its living and undamaged fur has immense psychological and interpersonal social significance for the being concerned . . ."

What it was not saying, O'Mara knew, was that to any Kelgian even the slightest blemish on their beautiful, silvery body fur or the smallest area of restricted mobility was the ultimate physical disfigurement, one that caused them to withdraw voluntarily from all social contact with their fellows as if they had been old-time Earth-human lepers. The fur motions were a completely involuntary process that could not be halted or modified in any way. This meant that the deep, helpless sympathy and revulsion that a whole Kelgian felt for such a disfigured one could not be hidden either, so that withdrawing from society was the only option short of suicide.

The mind-tape donor, the brilliant and gifted Kelgian surgeon Marrasarah, whose physical beauty had been surpassed only by the brilliance of her mind and warmth of her personality, had been driven to resign a promising career because of fur damage. Almost certainly a similar fate awaited patient Murrenth, so it was no wonder that its Kelgian mind partner had affected Thornnastor's own mind so deeply. In many respects the personalities of the patient and surgeon were the same—and, now that he was so intimately aware of Marrasarah's mind, feelings, and personality, O'Mara was finding it difficult at times to think of her as an "it".

Even though Marrasarah was a living and suffering person in the minds of Thornnastor and O'Mara, it was simply a recording and nothing at all could be done for it. But here and now, if he understood the Tralthan's feelings and motivation correctly, Thornnastor needed to cure Murrenth to stop that awful tragedy from happening again. It was a matter of professional pride but it was also deeply personal. The patient and the mind partner had become one. In its own mind Thornnastor was trying to cure both of them, and if the Murrenth procedure was as unsuccessful as all the medical probabilities insisted it would be, O'Mara hated to think of what it would do to the Tralthan surgeon.

"Field viewer set to fifty magnifications," said Thornnastor calmly. "Stepped-down scalpel and retractor to reduction factor ten. Ready? We will begin . . ."

The magnifier slid forward on its telescoping arm and was interposed between the operative field and two of Thornnastor's dirigible eyes as it picked up a knife whose large handle contained the mechanism which could deliver a cut ranging between a deep, six-inch, surgical slash to an incision so tiny and precise that it could only be seen by a microscope. With this procedure very precise work was possible, O'Mara knew as he turned his attention to the big diagnostic screen on the wall, provided the surgeon had rock steady hands or, in this case, tentacles.

On the screen the individual strands of fur looked like the slim, curving trunks of palm trees that were being bent slowly apart to reveal the heavily wrinkled organic ground surface from which they grew. A blade appeared, looking incredibly massive under the high magnification, and made an incision which cut cleanly between the parted trunks without touching much less damaging a single one of them. It went deeper, revealing the thin rootlets with their individual systems of tiny muscles that gave every hair its mobility, and these it avoided, too.

Like a thick, curving length of cable, one of the blocked capillaries appeared on center screen. A tiny longitudinal incision was made and a fine probe with a thickened tip inserted carefully into the opening. There was very little bleeding, just a few droplets which looked under the high magnification to be the size of footballs.

O'Mara closed his eyes briefly so as to shut out his view of the screen and to remind himself that Thornnastor was working inside a capillary not much thicker than a hair while it tried to find and dissolve a clot without blasting a hole in the affected blood vessel and undoing all its previous, meticulous work.

There were many such blood vessels and many clots. But there was something about the surgeon's work that was not quite right.

"This is microsurgery of a very high order," he said quietly to Mannen, "but I don't recognize the procedure."

"I didn't know you had medical training," said Mannen, then nodded. "Of course, I forgot that you have the Marrasarah mind tape, too. What's wrong with it?"

Thornnastor cleared its breathing passages and made a loud, disapproving sound.

"As the being O'Mara has just observed," it said, "my procedure departs from normal Kelgian practice because I have made a synthesis of the surgical knowledge and experience of the three other mind partners that are available to me. The work is delicate and requires concentration. Apart from the necessary verbal contact between the operating team, I would appreciate absolute silence."

Mannen, the Nidian tutor, and O'Mara maintained a complete and, in his own case, an admiring silence until Thornnastor withdrew, closed, and stood back.

"As you can see," it said, curling one eye toward the wall screen, "the interrupted blood supply to the root muscles has been corrected and the connective nerve network that controls fur movement is intact. But the patient must be massively sedated and its fur rendered motionless until the area has a chance to recover completely from the recently inflicted surgical trauma, and heal."

Suddenly it stamped its two medial feet, a habit of Tralthans who were in the grip of strong emotion, making all the loose equipment in the room rattle.

"Thank you, everyone," it ended. "I believe we have an optimum result."

# CHAPTER 15

As befitted his high position in the hospital's hierarchy, Senior Tutor Mannen occupied the only Earth-human chair while O'Mara and Thornnastor, whose species had no use for furniture, stood before Craythorne's desk. The major's voice was quiet and calm as he spoke, but it was obvious that he was very, very angry.

"Doctors," he said, "I've asked you here principally to apologize for Lieutenant O'Mara's conduct in this case. Normally I encourage initiative in my people, and must therefore bear full responsibility for the results if they make mistakes, but in this case he was, well, overenthusiastic and badly overstepped the mark. I hope you will take it no further and will allow me to deal with it as an internal disciplinary matter?"

"Of course, Major," said Mannen. He smiled suddenly. "But go easy on him."

Craythorne shook his head, looking puzzled; then he spoke to the Tralthan.

"Now that O'Mara has erased the four mind tapes it impressed two days ago," he said, "may I assume that psychologically you are back to normal, Doctor, and there have been no emotional aftereffects?"

"You may not assume that," said Thornnastor. "And while 'doctor' is quite suitable and less verbally cumbersome for normal conversational use, you should know that this morning I was promoted to senior physician."

"Then please accept my congratulations, Senior Physician Thornnastor," said the major, smiling but looking worried. "Where am I wrong? Are you still suffering mental disorientation following the erasure of the mind tapes?"

"There is still some mental disorientation, naturally," the Tralthan replied, "but that is because only the emotionally troublesome Kelgian tape was erased and, with Senior Tutor Mannen's agreement and Lieutenant O'Mara's cooperation, I elected to retain permanently the other three."

"But, but *why?*" said Craythorne, still looking worried. "That was, is, very risky. We have no idea of the mental repercussions that could result. It has never been done before."

"But it will be done again," said Mannen, looking at Thornnastor and O'Mara. "It will be done a great many times."

The major shook his head. "You'll have to explain."

Thornnastor said, "With my mind filled with the memories and personalities of four other-species entities, the effect was as O'Mara foretold. The high degree of concentration required during the operation caused only the medical knowledge of my mind partners to be brought forward and the unwanted emotional material to fade into the background. I was able to call on medical data and operating experience of four top other-species surgeons, and synthesize that material into a radical new procedure. Without the multiple mind partners the operation would not have been successful."

"The senior physician," Mannen joined in, "tells me that it can accommodate its three mind partners very well and looks forward to them being permanent residents. And if Thornnastor can do that, why not others? Naturally, Major, we'll need to consult your department regarding the emotional stability and general suitability of candidates for multiple mind impressions, but you must see where this is leading.

"Up to now," Mannen went on quickly, so as not to give time for the Major to show his ignorance, "our plan was to have a surgeon-in-charge take just the one tape needed to treat his, her, or its other-species patient, then have it erased on completion so that the process could be repeated indefinitely with future cases. But when we have medics available who carry simultaneously the surgical knowledge and experience of several different species, much more is possible.

"Not only will they be able to devise and perform new surgical procedures as did Thornnastor here," the senior tutor went on, his voice rising in quiet excitement, "but they will be able to head original research projects into xenobiology and multi-species medicine. And if we ever find a wrecked ship with injured survivors of a previously unknown species on board, these special doctors, whose minds will be crammed with physiological and medical data on a multiplicity of known life-forms, will be able to advise on treatment with a greatly reduced risk of our well-intentioned tinkering killing the people we will be trying to save. They will be a special group and we'll have to think of a name for them, clinical synthesists, xenobiological diagnosticians, something like that . . ."

Mannen broke off, looking almost ashamed at losing his clinical objectivity to the extent of showing human excitement and pleasure at this new development in the field he loved. He looked at his watch, stood up, and turned away. Thornnastor was already moving toward the door.

"Lectures. I have to go," he said. Then he paused to smile at O'Mara and added, "Major, earlier I suggested that you go easy on the lieutenant. Go very easy on him."

When they had gone, Craythorne nodded toward the vacated chair and said, "Lieutenant, I think you have raised insubordination to the status of a major art form and there are times, like now, when I could find it easy to be nasty to you. But you always wriggle out of trouble by the sneaky expedient of always being right. So . . ." He slapped a pile of folders that were lying on his desk. ". . . I'm giving you a long, boring, routine job which you may like to consider as a punishment. It's the weekly trainee updates for inclusion, if you think there is anything that warrants further investigation, in their psych files. I don't believe you will be able—or maybe I'm hoping that you won't be able—to do anything creatively insubordinate with them. And when you've finished that chore, go to Level One-Eleven and start practicing on the residents what you've been preaching to Mannen and me about the fun aspects of eating meals together and listening to each others' sleeping noises."

Craythorne stopped but continued to look at him without speaking.

"Sir," said O'Mara, to fill the lengthening silence.

"Regarding the Thornnastor business," Craythorne went on, "that was very well done, whether or not you knew what you were doing at the time. In the light of the emotional content, we will not use the Marrasarah tape on anyone again. You disobeyed standing instructions, for the first and only time if you want to remain here, by self-impressing the tape for a few hours before erasing it, right? So the disobedience has been rectified and the incident will not be mentioned again."

As he lifted the pile of folders, O'Mara nodded without speaking. Major Craythorne was a fine man and he didn't want to lie to him and so, in Kelgian fashion, he remained silent. It was true that O'Mara had impressed himself with the Marrasarah mind tape. He just hadn't erased it again.

His punishment took just two hours to complete and while it was routine it was not completely boring unless, O'Mara thought, boredom like beauty lay in the mental eye of the beholder. Each one of the two hundred-odd files contained information on the individual trainees' past and current progress, with notes on lectures attended and the performance of ward duties, and particularly their person-to-person contacts with patients, by the relevant tutors and charge nurses.

In the majority of cases the notes consisted of a hastily scrawled "Progress satisfactory" or "Moving up, but not too fast." One of them, signed by Mannen, said, "Not happy working with Il-lensans, but then who is? Will schedule another protective suit drill in chlorine environment soonest. No psych action required unless trainee's fear increases."

There were two other such entries, both in Mannen's writing. One read, "Creesik (m), MSVK. Initial progress rapid and highly satisfactory but recently has been slowing down to slightly above average. Watching," and the other said, "Neenil (f), MSVK. Initially a very slow starter but now picking up nicely. Keen, seems to have discovered extra motivation, but displays signs of fatigue. Have suggested that it spend a little more of its free time not studying so hard."

Psychiatric action had not been requested on either of the last two cases, but O'Mara had a feeling about them, or maybe it was simply a hope driven by boredom that it would be nice if he could do a little therapeutic tinkering before the trouble, if there was going to be any trouble, could develop. He placed the two files on one side for closer study, telling himself that they both lived on Level One-Eleven and he would be in the neighborhood anyway.

When he returned to them, O'Mara decided that it would be a good idea to learn something about their home environment and physical body requirements before he began a covert, unofficial in-vstigation of their minds. At present all he knew about them was that one was female and the other male, that they were at different levels of training with lectures and ward duties that didn't coincide, and so far as he knew the only thing they had in common was be-longing to the same species. He called up the library computer and aked it to display general information, sociological environment, and medicine as practiced by physiological classification MSVK, the Euril life-form.

His reception on One-Eleven was less hostile than the first one had been. The usual proportion of door IDs were tagged ON DUTY or DO NOT DISTURB, and the people who did answer, with the exception of the Kelgians, showed a combination of politeness and impatience as they listened. That was understandable, because they had probably heard Mannen, Craythorne, or himself saying it already. The sleeping noises coming from a few of the rooms sounded slightly less horrendous, O'Mara thought, but that might be because he was getting used to them.

He found Creesik's door ajar and marked simply ABSENT, but Neenil's was tagged OCCUPIED and was opened at once.

"Trainee Neenil," he began, only to be interrupted by the other's twittering speech.

"Creesik," it said. "I was just leaving."

"Please don't leave on my account," he said, thinking quickly. "I intended to visit each of you. If you will not be inconvenienced, it will be easier for me to speak to both of you at the same time."

"Then come in, O'Mara," said Creesik.

It was the first time he had had more than a glimpse from the corridor entrance into a Euril's living quarters although, in an attempt to show good manners by not staring, he used his peripheral vision to examine the place as another Euril dropped from a perch before the study alcove and screen and hopped forward to meet him.

"I am Neenil," it said, the soft twittering of its voice forming a background to the translated words. "You have our attention."

"Thank you," said O'Mara, still appearing not to look at his surroundings. The walls were covered with pictures of Euril land and seascape, a photograph of what looked like the immediate family flock, and a simple but quietly resplendent framed certificate which, judging from its place of honor above the study console, had originated from an important institution of some kind. Occupying one-quarter of the floor area in one corner was a circular nest standing to about Euril shoulder height, thickly upholstered and with light, padded sheets hanging over one edge. He went on, "If anything, this a social rather than a professional visit. I wanted to let you know what we are hoping to do about the nightly noise pollution."

Creesik cocked its head to one side and said, "Our senior tutor and your Major Craythorne have already discussed this with us, including the unavoidable delays expected in the arrival of the hush-field installations and in replacing the dining-hall furniture. We both formed the impression that these were problems we might have to solve ourselves. Was there anything else you wanted to say?"

"Only to ask if you have any other complaints or problems," said O'Mara, trying to keep the conversation going. "To Earth-humans, yours is a very unusual species. How are you both settling in here, generally?"

Cocking its head again, Creesik said, "If you are wondering why and how a species with three legs and no hands is able to perform surgery, you won't be the first to ask. We use our beaks rather than our nonexistent digits. What precisely did you want to know?"

In its condescending fashion the library computer had given him all that a nonspecialist layman enquirer needed to know about Euril evolution and history, couched in terms that had reminded him of his lessons in elementary school. The species no longer had the ability to fly because they had long since rid themselves in many subtle and deadly ways of the many-limbed and clawed predators from whom flight had been their only escape. Using their long, flexible beaks and precisely controlled neck muscles, they became tool users and ultimately developed the technologically advanced civilization that enabled them to travel to the stars. They had done it by using their brains and their beaks. In the area of surgery, they used a range of hollow, conelike instruments fitted to their beaks, and the rapid, pecking procedures they had developed were unequaled when speedy surgery was required. Eurils did everything, well, practically everything, including talk, with their mouths.

Before O'Mara could reveal that he wasn't entirely ignorant, Neenil made a low, twittering sound that did not translate into words and said, "Speaking personally, I am content and completely happy here."

*An enthusiastic response if I ever heard one,* O'Mara thought, and wondered if his sudden smile would mean anything to them. He said, "Your contentment is reflected in your work. The senior tutor is well pleased with your recent progress and, in my capacity as a psychologist, I'm especially glad that contentment is the reason."

"But the senior tutor," said Creesik sharply, "is not pleased with my progress. Is that why you're here?"

There was unnecessary anger surfacing here, O'Mara thought, and perhaps a little guilt. He tried to avoid a lie by hiding behind the literal truth. "Your progress remains satisfactory, and I haven't been asked to interview you. In your weekly reports, however, Dr. Mannen expresses a minor concern regarding the symptoms of fatigue or lassitude you have been displaying recently. That's all."

"So it's just you who wants to know the reason for this minor, unimportant, and non-life-threatening debility?" said Creesik. Its neck feathers were practically standing on end and it was jumping up and down on its thin, birdlike limbs. This was the first time, O'Mara thought, that he had ever seen a person who was literally hopping mad. It went on angrily, "Why are you people always so concerned about sex?"

# CHAPTER 16

There was an awkward silence while O'Mara tried to find the right words to extricate himself from this delicate situation without giving further offense. While deliberately not looking around the room he had noticed the rumpled nest and suspected that the two of them were an item, but he would certainly not have mentioned it. Suddenly Neenil made another soft twittering sound and in an obvious attempt to lighten the situation, it said, "Psychologists are always concerned about sex. This holds true on Euril, and probably on every civilized world throughout the Galactic Federation."

O'Mara had never kissed another person in his life and, looking at that long, flexible, wrinkled beak with its tiny, pointed teeth, he wasn't going to do it now. But he felt so grateful to Neenil for giving him an excuse to continue the conversation that for a moment he was tempted.

"I had not intended to discuss sex," he said, looking at Neenil, "but it seems that it is expected of me. This being so, I would say that the activity has had a very beneficial effect on your work. Why exactly this should be is for you to say, but only if you wish to discuss what is, after all, a private and personal matter."

He looked at Creeşik and went on, "This also explains the minor reduction of physical and mental effort you have displayed. In this situation, which involves a new relationship with an unusually attractive partner . . ." O'Mara couldn't see any physical difference between the two of them, but he wanted to give Neenil the benefit of the doubt. ". . . an initial period of, let us say, overenthusiasm is normal with, of course, a consequent degree of physical debilitation. And there would be times when the minds concerned find difficulty in concentrating on anyone or anything else. But in time this degree of urgency will diminish, the process will stabilize and when, or if, longer-term plans are made . . ."

Creesik had stopped hopping and its neck feathers were lying flat again. It said, "O'Mara, have you a lot of experience in this area?"

"No," O'Mara replied, "but I've studied a lot of factual and fictional material on the subject. My knowledge is purely theoretical."

There seemed to be a gleam of impish humor in Neenil's tiny eyes as it joined in, "That is difficult to believe. My own factual knowledge of DBDG anatomy tells me that you are unusually large and well muscled, and singularly lacking in unsightly, wobbly slabs of adipose tissue, for a male of your species. I'm not able to judge the beauty or otherwise of your facial features. But then . . ." It made another low, twittering sound that did not translate and cocked its head to look briefly at Creesik. ". . . beautiful male facial features are not the prime consideration. Surely there is or has been a female DBDG on the staff who has—"

"No!" said O'Mara, more loudly than he had intended. In a quieter tone he added defensively, "As you know, the type of work I do doesn't endear me to people, and my duties rarely allow me enough time to seek female companionship."

"From my knowledge of DBDG physiology," said Creesik, "I would say that the recent change in O'Mara's facial skin coloration—bearing in mind that it has not indulged in any physical activity that would elevate its blood pressure—is indicative of embarrassment. Stop teasing it, dear."

"Nonsense," said Neenil. "Psychologists are never embarrassed talking about sex. We were reticent at first because it is a private thing, but not embarrassed. I don't mind O'Mara knowing, if it hasn't already guessed, that the improvement in my work is due to my wanting us to qualify together. With Sector General qualifications in multi-species surgery there isn't a medical establishment in the Federation who wouldn't hop at the chance to get us, and if you wanted to stay here I would, too, and . . ."

". . . we would be life-mates and warm your eggs together," Creesik ended for it, "whatever happened."

O'Mara was glad that the two love-birds (and he was not thinking of the word in any derogatory fashion) were talking to each other and letting him escape further embarrassment. But his relief was premature.

"O'Mara," said Neenil, "I don't understand why you are denying yourself such a great pleasure, satisfaction, and emotional comfort. But you must know this from past experience . . ."

"No," O'Mara broke in, then cursed himself for not remaining silent, Kelgian fashion. What was making him want to tell these people the truth?

There was a moment's silence while they both cocked their heads to one side and stared at him. Creesik spoke first.

"No wonder," it said, "you're mad enough to be a psychologist."

"Don't joke about it, Creesik," said Neenil. "This is very serious. O'Mara, are you saying that you have never wanted, never felt the need to love another person in your entire adult life?"

"I didn't say that," said O'Mara, cursing himself again for telling the exact truth. Why the hell was he doing it? There was no weight on his conscience, nothing to feel guilty about, just the sudden surfacing of anger mixed with his helpless, hopeless feeling of sadness.

Neenil made a soft, sympathetic twittering sound, then said, "Have you loved someone in the past but the love was not returned?"

"No," said O'Mara.

"Are your feelings for someone of the present," Neenil persisted, "but you have not spoken of them so that the entity concerned doesn't as yet know what you feel?"

"Yes," he said.

"O'Mara," said Neenil, "you must speak to this female. Whether the answer is good or bad for you, you must speak your mind to her. If the answer is bad, well, among my species unrequited love is a serious condition but it is rarely fatal . . ."

"Now who's making a joke?" said Creesik.

"I'm being serious." Neenil went on, "Speak of what is in your mind, O'Mara. Then, at least, you will know what this person feels about you and be able to allow your emotional life, perhaps both of your emotional lives, to go on from there."

"This person," said O'Mara, "doesn't even know I exist and, and lives halfway across the galaxy."

He shook his head in self-irritation. This was getting way out of control. The things he was saying he had never believed that he would ever tell to another soul, and most certainly not to Craythorne, who would probably fire him on the spot. But here he was talking about it, admittedly in the most general terms and without mentioning names or details, to a pair of enamored Eurils. He had to end this quickly and get away from here.

"I'm sorry," he said. "This was to be a social visit. I came to talk to you, but not about something that I've never spoken of to any other person. As a psychologist, I can't understand why I'm talking to you about it now. Perhaps I'm feeling envious over what you two have and I haven't . . ."

Neenil and Creesik were twittering again. It had a sympathetic sound. Their heads were cocked sideways and they were looking at each other.

He looked at Creesik and went on, ". . . but no matter, I called at an inconvenient time and I'll go now. There is no reason for you to leave."

"You show great sensitivity, and delicacy, O'Mara," said Creesik, "but there is a reason to leave. If I stayed, neither of us would be able to finish our study assignments."

It hopped toward the door. As he turned to follow, Neenil spoke again.

"This is not right, O'Mara," it said. "You must search for and find this being, and speak your mind to it. Promise me."

O'Mara left without replying because he could not promise the impossible and he wanted to avoid hurting the other's feelings with a negative reply. Neenil was coming across as a particularly nice and currently very happy person who in its present emotional state wished everyone else to be as happy as it was. Sadly, silently, and enviously he wished it and its partner joy.

He thought about the Euril conversation off and on during the next four days when the major and he were kept too busy sorting out minor other-species problems to do anything but nod at each other in passing. Once, when he was alone in the department, he did some serious thanking about them. The hospital grapevine, a fast-reacting plant with its nerve and speech centers in the dining hall, had not given the smallest twitch or whisper of gossip about him and his mysterious unrequited love, so obviously the Euril couple weren't the kind of people who gossiped. He hadn't seen them again but his liking for them was increasing.

Providing Creesik remained in Sector General as well, he thought Neenil would make a good therapist. He would bear that in mind in case his chief ever mentioned needing another assistant. As if on cue, Craythorne hurried through the department and waved him toward the inner office.

"Sit down and relax, Lieutenant," he said, smiling. "You aren't in any trouble, so far as I know. We've a lot of things to talk about but none of them are urgent." He looked at O'Mara for a moment. "Unless that expression you're wearing means that you have a more urgent problem to discuss?"

"This isn't urgent, either, sir," he replied. "But it's something you might want to think about."

"Go on, Lieutenant."

"There is no necessity at this stage to mention individuals and species," said O'Mara carefully, "but while I was talking to some of the people on Level One-Eleven it became apparent that pairing-off was taking place. Normally there would be nothing to interest the department in that, but in the situation here ..."

"In the situation on One-Eleven," said Craythorne dryly, "the trainees will be glad that some of the others are going to bed without making sleeping noises. Sorry, O'Mara, my jokes are never funny. Seriously, are you worried about an impending population explosion?"

"No, sir," said O'Mara, "not immediately. But the trainees who qualify for permanent staff positions here, and who become what the Kelgians call life-mates, will want to have families. We would be in serious trouble with their home-planet authorities, not to mention the Federation Primary Rule, for infringing their rights. When the hospital is up and running for a few years, it's something we'll have to think about."

The major nodded. "You're right. It won't happen tomorrow, I sincerely hope. You have a word with Mannen about it. He likes talking to you, he says, because you don't take as long as I do to get to the point. Tell him that, if and when, to tell us which other-species obstetricians we need to approach for mind tapes." He laughed quietly and went on, "After all, the hospital's first patient was an infant Hudlar, as you very well know. Was there anything else you wanted to say?"

"No, sir."

"Good," said Craythorne. "Now we can discuss a less long-term problem. Six months from now the real exotics will begin to arrive: SNLUs, TLTUs, VTXMs, people like that. Building accommodation for them will be a Maintenance problem, naturally, and they'll be calling in same-species environmental engineers, and the Telfi ward will become part of the main power reactor. How exactly we're going to treat the emotional difficulties of beings who breathe high-pressure superheated steam, or methane crystalline life-forms who live close to absolute zero, or gestalt entities who absorb hard radiation, I'm unable to say right now, but we'll do our best. It will mean us putting in a lot of time on the library computer and, of course, getting more departmental help."

Craythorne paused. O'Mara remained silent.

"Don't worry, Lieutenant," the major went on. "The help in question is Earth-human, a retired Monitor Corps officer who volunteered himself for the position. He's totally unlike you because he's old, frail, and gentle, I'm told, except during philosophical arguments. He'll be arriving two weeks from now."

"I'll be looking forward to meeting him then," said O'Mara with an obvious lack of enthusiasm.

Craythorne shook his head. "You won't be meeting him then, because, Lieutenant, you won't be here."

O'Mara stared hard at the major, not speaking. He had thought that he was improving, losing some of the rough edges to his manner when dealing with people, but apparently he was still guilty of wearing his heavy boots and an old, frail, gentle ex-Monitor Corps officer was replacing him. Craythorne returned his stare without dropping his eyes, plainly reading the bitter disappointment on O'Mara's face; then he shook his head again.

"Don't jump to conclusions, Lieutenant," he said. "You've worked very hard during these past two years with the department, but you're beginning to show signs of stress. I don't know what, precisely, is troubling your mind, and I know you would never admit to any weakness much less tell your superior officer if there was anything bothering you, but something most definitely is. This is the best opportunity you'll have for a while to get away from this place, so I want you to relax, rest, or at least do something strenuously different for a while, and sort things out for yourself. You have a lot of leave owing. Take it."

O'Mara had not realized that he was holding his breath until it came out in a long sigh of relief. He said, "Thank you, sir. But I've no family or planetside friends. There's nowhere I want to go and nothing else I want to do."

The major frowned. "Lieutenant," he said, "that answer falls into the grey area between a chronic lack of imagination and manic dedication to duty. As a psychologist I am prescribing a six-week change of scene, and as your superior officer I am making it an order. Go anywhere you like, but go." "

O'Mara spent the rest of the day tidying up clerical loose ends, speaking to the transport officer about the availability of outgoing flights, and trying to make up his mind where he wanted to go. But he kept thinking back to Neenil and the Euril's last, concerned words to him.

"You must search for and find this being," it had said. "Speak your mind to it."

# CHAPTER 17

He had known, although he had never really expected to make use of the knowledge, that since he was a Monitor Corps officer on space service no commercial vessel (provided it had a species-suitable berth free and it was going in the right direction) could refuse to take him as a passenger. There was no restriction regarding destinations or the number of ship transfers he could make, but if he wanted to go fast and far it was best to stick to the busy commercial routes serving the long-established star-traveling cultures of Traltha, Orligia, Kelgia, and Earth. He was free to visit a more out-of-the-way planet or colony world if he wished, but that could mean spending a large proportion of his leave waiting for a suitable connection.

The Monitor Corps supply vessel *Trosshannon* plied the three-cornered route between Nidia, Melf, and Sector General. As the initial letter of its name implied, it had been built on the heavy-gravity world of Traltha, where they built starships that were renowned throughout the Federation for their structural strength and dependability. It was said that on Traltha even the earthmoving machinery was put together by watchmakers. *Trosshannon* listed accommodation with environmental support for five physiological classifications: Tralthan FGLIs, Melfan ELNTs, Hudlar FROBs, Kelgian DBLFs, and DBDGs like or unlike himself who were expected to use the same cabin type even though it was a tight squeeze for Orligians and the furniture was on the large size for Nidians, who considered themselves tall if they made it to more than a meter.

He met the eight-man, Earth-human crew, who were all Monitor Corps personnel, only at mealtimes. They were friendly enough but they made it clear that they were very busy and, other than at meals, they preferred him not to get underfoot. O'Mara spent most of that four-day trip in his quarters, which was exactly what he wanted to do. But Craythorne had been right about him being tired. He was surprised at how much of the time he spent sleeping.

O'Mara was feeling more relaxed than he had been for a long time when *Trosshannon* dropped into the Retlin transport complex on the outskirts of Nidia's planetary capital whose name it bore. It was the largest space, air, and surface communication facility in the Federation as well as, from the point of view of the local families with young children who thronged the public viewing area, its most popular other-species zoo. As the moving walkway took him through the disembarking tunnel toward the main concourse, it felt strange to be the focus of so many curious eyes and excited, barking conversations and realize that to the many hundreds of tiny, red-furred beings staring at him he was just another strange extraterrestrial visitor.

Even though he was carrying all his belongings in a backpack so that there was no necessity for him to go though baggage claim, and Retlin was also reputed to be the most well-organized and well-appointed transport terminal on all of the civilized worlds, it was still easy for a strange visitor regardless of its species to get lost. An enormous, hairy Orligian wearing a weapons harness suggesting that it might be a security guard gave him directions.

The information facility comprised a long line of screened cubicles, each one bearing a stylized diagram representing the various star-traveling races that made up the Galactic Federation, sized and furnished to suit the physical requirements of the user. He found one bearing the Earth-human symbol, and went inside to find a viewscreen displaying a plan view of the complex interior covering the facing wall, with a winking blue location light showing his present position and another that could be moved to the area where he wanted to go, and flashing guidelines to help him get there. Except for the comfortable, Earth-human chair—in Sector General people were not encouraged to sit and browse—it was similar to the information screens used on every level of the hospital.

He was able to find the Monitor Corps' Personnel-in-Transit office without difficulty. Its wall decorations ran heavily to pictures of service vessels ranging from tiny couriers through long-range survey cruisers up to the mighty Emperor-class capital ships. With a single exception, its six reception desk consoles were being manned by people who weren't men, but he chose that one because the others were busy. As he approached the empty position, a graying NCO wearing full uniform so clean and crisp that it reminded him of Craythorne on a ceremonial occasion looked up. The other's eyes rested briefly on O'Mara's coveralls and his beret tightly folded under the right shoulder strap, which meant that neither of them had to waste time saluting; then he gave a friendly nod.

"Sir?" he said.

O'Mara gave his name and service ID code and said, "I arrived within the past hour on *Trosshannon* and would like a berth on anything you have going to Traltha, Melf, Kelgia, or Earth. The destination isn't important but the stopover time is. I don't want to spend too much of my leave on Nidia."

"Nidian low ceilings give me trouble, too," the other said, smiling, "but if you need to stay here for a while, there's always the

Earth-human officers' quarters on the base. They're very comfortable."

"Thank you," said O'Mara, returning the smile and looking pointedly at the other's impeccable uniform, "but on Nidia Base I wouldn't feel that I was on leave. Have you anything going anywhere soon?"

"I know what you mean," said the NCO. "Give me a moment to check, sir."

On the base, O'Mara thought as the other began tapping keys, the uniform dress regulations would be less relaxed, and there would be a lot more saluting and fellow officers displaying too much friendly curiosity about his background. He was technically an officer but nobody, himself included, had ever considered him to be a gentleman. There could be trouble if their curiosity became too persistent. O'Mara thought that he would rather squeeze himself into a room in one of the local Nidian hotels.

"You're in luck, sir," said the other suddenly, and hesitated. "Well, you might be in luck. How about *Kreskhallar*, Melfan registry, a medium-sized passenger vessel with a mixed-species crew and with accommodation for warm-blooded oxygen-breathers, leaving from Dock Thirty-Seven just three and a half hours from now. It operates a continuous, round-trip, cut-price sightseeing tour of the big five—Melf, Earth, Traltha, Kelgia, Nidia, and back to Melf. Currently the passengers are mostly Kelgian on some kind of star-traveling literary convention, it says here, with other-species passengers joining and leaving at their home planets. The luxury rating isn't high, sir, only two stars, and with all those DBLFs . . ."

"Thank you," O'Mara broke in, "I'll take it."

The NCO looked concerned. He said, "Sir, if you're not used to them, Kelgians can be a bit hard to take even one at a time. Before I book you in, are you sure about this?"

O'Mara nodded. "Go ahead, Sergeant," he said, "I'm used to working with Kelgians."

"You are?" said the other, giving him another close but unob-
strusive visual examination as he tapped keys. Plainly his curiosity
got the better of him because he went on, "If you don't mind me
asking, sir, what ship?"

"No ship," he said. "Sector General."

"Oh," said the sergeant, looking impressed. He was still sitting
at his console but somehow he gave the impression that he was
standing at attention as he added, "Enjoy your leave, sir."

As he had no idea what the food would be like on a two-star
passenger vessel, or how long it would be before they served it,
O'Mara decided to play safe by refueling in one of the complex's
multi-species restaurants. The place reminded him of the hospital's
main dining hall, but with the addition of wall murals showing Nidian land- and seascapes, and loud background music whose planet
of origin he did not recognize but which was terrible. It had a discordant, urgent beat that, he decided, was intended to make the
diners eat faster to escape from it. Out of sheer contrariness he ate
slowly, blocking the music from his mind while he tried to think
about what he could do with himself over the next six weeks, until
it was time to board.

It was *Kreskhallar*'s passenger liaison officer, Larragh-Yal, an
obviously overworked or perhaps just overwrought Nidian, who
welcomed him aboard, wished him a pleasant voyage, and gave him
directions to his cabin in a voice which, even through the translator, suggested that its mind was on other things. Probably, he
thought wryly, the shipload of Kelgians. He was given a locator that
would tell him how to get to the dining and recreation rooms, the
observation deck, and the other passenger services, and asked if he
had any special requirements.

"Only peace and quiet," said O'Mara. "I'll be staying in my
cabin most of the time."

"With this bunch of furry sword-and-sorcery fanatics we have
on board," it said, sounding relieved that he might turn out to be
one of that rare breed, a minimum-maintenance passenger, "I don't

blame you, Lieutenant. But if you should need anything, the locator card will find me. I, ah, expect you already know that the Monitor Corps will reimburse our company for your travel fare, basic cabin accommodation, food, and a moderate quantity of liquid refreshment. Anything else you will have to pay for yourself."

O'Mara nodded. "There will be nothing else."

"I don't want to sound mean, Lieutenant," the other went on, "nor do I have to stick too closely to the regulations in your case. After all, you're the only Monitor Corps officer on the ship. Your presence would raise the morale of our security people as well as having a steadying influence on some of the passengers."

"Larragh-Yal," said O'Mara firmly, "I'm on leave."

"Of course, sir," said the other. "But a sheathed weapon is still a deterrent."

His cabin was about half the size of his quarters at the hospital, but comfortable if one only wanted to sleep rather than stay there most of the time. There were a viewscreen and a menu of multi-species entertainment tapes that looked old and tired even by Sector General standards, but the amenities did not include a food dispenser. If he wanted to eat alone he would have to order cabin service. The extra cost didn't worry him, but the type of person he had once been did not feel happy with the idea of another intelligent entity becoming his servant for however short a time, nor did he know how an officer was expected to behave in that situation. He would feel awkward and embarrassed by the whole business.

The alternative was to use the ship's dining room and meet people, some of whom, Larragh-Yal had implied, might not be too happy to meet him.

The whole idea was ridiculous. He had been working so long with Monitor Corps specialists—and he had even become one himself—that he had almost forgotten that the force's primary function was the maintenance of the Pax Galactica, a duty it had performed so well over the past century since its formation that it had been given other jobs to do. Its vast, Emperor-class capital ships, each one capable of wrecking a planet although none of them ever had, were on standby for disaster-relief or colonization-support operations, because a vessel that could level a whole country could clear and till an awful lot of fallow land for settlers. The thousands of lesser ships, the light and heavy cruisers, transports and small communications vessels, while still retaining their weaponry and their highly trained and disciplined multi-species crews, practiced the arts of peace rather than war—although, on the rare occasions when widespread violence occurred which posed a threat to Federation stability, no matter how many ships and land forces had to be deployed or how much firepower was required to regulate the situation, it was always referred to as a police action. But usually the violence and the lawbreakers were stopped before it got that far, by infiltration, subversion, and other nonviolent dirty tricks. O'Mara had heard that the specialist Corps psychologists who now handled the first-contact situations had been nasty, devious, and quite brilliant in that form of activity, and he wondered if the polished and urbane Major Craythorne had ever had a hand in stopping a war or, he corrected himself, a riot that required police action on a planetary scale.

As the Galactic Federation's executive and law-enforcement arm, the Monitor Corps had rendered redundant the large, national armies that once had fought each other on the member worlds, and taken over as the galaxy's peacekeeper. In essence, regardless of the wide range of specialist duties the Corpsmen now performed, each and every one was regarded as a policeman, a form of life that was never supposed to be off-duty even when on leave. If, as Larragh-Yal had said, there were a few potential troublemakers among the passengers, they were people he could not help meeting when he went to the dining room or anywhere else on the ship, and they might not be happy with the idea of what they thought was a policeman mixing with them and trying to spoil their fun. O'Mara sighed and began to unpack.

He was finished by the time the launch warning and thirty-second countdown was relayed over the ships's PA system, and he watched through the cabin's direct-vision port as Retlin Complex dropped away and the city proper and then more and more of the surrounding countryside crawled into his field of view. There had been no sensation of motion in spite of the high takeoff acceleration; the old vessel's gravity compensators, at least, were working. He had been taken to space construction sites on ships where they hadn't been, and traveling with a bunch of spacesick and regurgitating other-species workmates was not an experience he wanted to repeat. The planetary surface shrank until Nidia filled the viewport. He continued to watch it, telling himself that the ship was simply a scaled-down Sector General without doctors and he shouldn't worry about it, until they were at jump distance and suddenly there was nothing to see but the flickering grey fog of hyperspace.

Shortly afterward the PA cleared its throat and said, "For the information of passengers who have come aboard at Nidia, the first Meal of Welcome for the next leg of our tour will be served in the dining room in three standard hours' time. As you probably already know, it has become a tradition that all passengers, except for members of those species who do not customarily use body coverings or decorations, should wear formal dress for this occasion. Thank you for your attention."

O'Mara was feeling hungry again. In three hours' time he would be starving.

He dressed in full uniform, the first time he had done so since Sergeant Wenalont had fitted him with it, and feeling safe in the knowledge that as the only Monitor on board he would have to neither give nor return salutes, but to be doubly sure he folded his beret under the shoulder tab. As he stared at himself in the cabin mirror he thought that he looked well, very well, and remembered some of the other things the technical sergeant and tailor had said to him. He wondered if the passenger list included any young, unattached Earth-human females, then sadly put the thought out of his mind. For him a shipboard romance was not an option.

He was a Corps psychologist, O'Mara reminded himself as he stared at his image, but he had to admit that he looked like everybody's idea of a hefty, scowling policeman.

# CHAPTER 18

The room had provision for seating three hundred diners, he saw from the entrance, and even though there were only about two hundred and fifty passengers present, there were no single or empty tables. Instead there were rows of long, twenty-place tables with species-suitable furniture that could be moved around if different physiological classifications wanted to eat and talk together, which many of them were doing. The Orligian headwaiter—or, since it was fully dressed, possibly headwaitress—came forward to lead him to an unoccupied space at a table.

It was probably ship regulation dress, but he thought the black trousers and the hairy head and hands projecting from the neck and cuffs of the stiff, white tunic made it look ridiculous as well as feel very uncomfortable because Orligians usually wore nothing but a light harness that allowed the air to penetrate their fur and cool their bodies.

He was shown to a table containing fourteen Kelgian passengers, a Nidian, two Melfans, and one from Earth, and, inevitably, given the place opposite the Earth-human female.

She was dark-haired, young, and slim, and wore the minimum of jewelry on her head and ears and on the front of her high-collared, formal dress, which fitted her like a thin coat of black paint. Back at the hospital the Earth-human nurses had taken to wearing their whites very tight because, they insisted, it aided them in making fast changes into their other-species environmental protection suits, even though the style did not suit some of them. With this one it did.

O'Mara gave her a brief nod and did the same to the few other-species diners who had turned to look at him, then sat down quickly and fixed his eyes on the menu display. Doubtless Craythorne would have said and done something different, but he just wanted to eat and not talk. That was not to be.

"Good evening, Lieutenant," she said pleasantly. "I'm afraid it's a fixed menu on the first night out, and for the rest of the time too, as a matter of fact, although the Earth-human food they serve is usually quite good. If you don't like it or have any special preferences, you'll just have to starve."

"I am starving," said O'Mara, looking up at her, "and I've no special preferences. Food is just fuel."

The Kelgian in the seat beside him spiked its fur in shock and said, "A culinary barbarian! But what else can one expect of a large, over-muscled carnivore. Probably a messy eater, too."

The young woman looked suddenly concerned. She said quickly, "Lieutenant, please don't feel offended, Kelgians always say . . ."

". . . exactly what they feel, ma'am," O'Mara finished for her. He tried to smile, an exercise to which his facial muscles were long unused, then glanced toward the Kelgian and added, "I don't have mobile fur to show you how I feel, friend, but right now I am feeling very hungry but not, I think, hungry enough to eat you."

"There is doubt in your mind?" said the other.

Before O'Mara could reply there was a quiet, triple chime that came from somewhere inside their table, the place panel in front of him slid aside, and the first course rose into sight.

"Saved by the bell," said the Kelgian as it bent its over its own platter.

O'Mara didn't have to speak again until the meal was finished, by which time he was pleasantly distended and feeling well disposed toward everyone in general but not, he told himself firmly, toward anyone in particular.

"You're looking much happier, Lieutenant," said the young woman. "What do you think of the ship's food now?"

"It's still only fuel," said O'Mara, "but premium grade."

"That is a very large and energy-hungry body you have there," she said. "But I'd say, even before we get to see you in a swimsuit, that you are a heavy energy user as well because you don't seem to store any of it as fat. Do you like to swim?"

"The water restrictions on space service don't allow it," he replied. "I can't swim."

"Then I'd be happy to teach you," she said, "just for the company. It isn't a big pool, but the Kelgians, who make up most of the passenger list, don't like getting their fur wet and the Melfans just sink and crawl about on the bottom so they say they might as well stay in air. We're the only Earth-humans on board and will have the place to ourselves most of the time. There wouldn't be many other-species onlookers to embarrass you if you didn't do well at first. I've never taught anyone to swim before so it might be fun. Are you called anything else besides Lieutenant, Lieutenant?"

"O'Mara," he said. "But about the pool, I'm not sure that I could . . ."

"Joan," she said.

"Kledenth," said the Kelgian beside him, "if anyone is interested."

"I don't want to sound pushy," she continued, "but believe it or not, you're the first Earth-human we've had on this trip and I'm dying to talk with someone who doesn't need a translator. And of course you could swim, or at least stay afloat. If you take a deep breath and don't quite empty your lungs, you won't sink, and if you did get into trouble, I'd be there to grab you and hold your head above water. All you really need to swim is a bit of confidence."

O'Mara didn't reply.

"Alternatively," she went on, "there's the exercise machinery if you want to get hot and sweaty, unless you prefer playing table games like chess or scremman. Or there's the observation gallery, where you can guzzle umpteen varieties of different other-planetary booze until you begin to see things crawling about in hyperspace outside. Which reminds me, do you know what Chorrantir, our only Tralthan passenger, said about alcoholics on its home world? It said that eventually they begin seeing pink Earth-humans."

"Oh, God," he said, and smiled in spite of himself.

"Come on, Lieutenant O'Mara," Joan persisted. "That uniform looks good on you, but everybody on the ship knows by now that we have a Monitor on board, so you should relax and take it off. What do you say?"

"This conversation," said Kledenth suddenly, "is much more interesting than the endless talking from my friends down the table about other-world legends and the heroic, or sometimes utterly reprehensible, figures who populate them. To some of these people it has become a religion rather than a hobby. Well, what do you say, O'Mara?"

"Nothing," he said uncomfortably. "I'm still thinking about it."

"But there's nothing to think about," Kledenth went on, its fur rippling in small, uneven waves. "I know that you Earth-humans don't have our ability to outwardly express inner feelings without ambiguity but, even to me, in this situation the bare words are more than adequate. The female concerned is young and probably physically attractive to you—although as a Kelgian I consider it to be an unsightly life-form whose wobbly chest lumps give it a ridiculous, top-heavy look—and plainly feeling bored and possibly sexually frustrated because she was the only member of her species among the passengers. Now a same-species male has come among us and the situation has changed for the better. Again I cannot speak with authority, O'Mara, but presumably you, too, are beautiful or have other male attributes which she finds attractive. . . ."

O'Mara felt his face growing warm. He tried to halt the other with an upraised hand, but either it didn't know the significance of the gesture or was simply ignoring it.

". . . To me it is clear," Keldenth went on, "that this invitation to widen your experience by learning to swim will, I understand, require you to divest yourselves of all or most of those ridiculous body coverings, and place you in a situation of close physical intimacy which is also, if my understanding of Earth-human sexual practices is correct, the usual prelude to mating. I can foresee you having an interesting and enjoyable voyage. So what *do* you say, O'Mara?"

He looked away from Kledenth's narrow, cone-shaped head with its tiny, bright eyes and the rippling neck fur and toward Joan, trying to find the right words to apologize for the embarrassment that the other must have been causing her. But she was staring intently at him, half-smiling and plainly not at all embarrassed but enjoying his obvious discomfort.

"I'm sorry, Lieutenant O'Mara," she said, "but Kledenth is quite right. After spending six weeks with a shipload of Kelgians, their habit of straight talking begins to rub off, so I'm beginning to say exactly what I feel. But it is wrong in thinking that I'm sexually frustrated. It's same-species conversation and a pool partner I need, not sex. At the risk of sounding repetitious, what do you say?"

O'Mara looked at her but he couldn't say anything. Suddenly she looked mortified.

"I know it isn't usual with space service officers," she said, "but have you got a wife already, or a serious woman-friend somewhere?"

He could easily have lied his way out of trouble, but in Kelgian fashion she was being completely honest and forthright, and to Kelgians one always told the truth.

"No," he said.

"Then I don't understand why you won't . . ." Joan began, then stopped.

For a long moment she stared at him while her face slowly deepened in color. In the light of the preceding conversation, O'Mara would not have been surprised at anything she said or did, but he had never expected to see her blush.

"Looking closely at you," she continued, doing just that as her eyes moved from his chest and arms that filled the large uniform to the still young but lived-in face that stared out of his shaving mirror every morning, "I find this very difficult to believe, and I don't want to give offense, but have I made a serious mistake? Do you not find my company attractive because I'm, well, the wrong gender?"

"No," said O'Mara seriously, "the wrong species."

She stared at him openmouthed and aghast.

Kledenth said, "Are you getting therapy for it?"

Slowly she began to laugh, loudly and long. O'Mara stared at her without changing his expression until the laughter subsided into a broad smile.

"You sounded so, so *serious* when you said that," she said, "and you look so dour and unapproachable that I never suspected that you could have a sense of humor. But don't ever make a joke like that in the pool or you'll be the one responsible for drowning *me*."

In the event, neither of them drowned, although the enthusiasm she displayed while making sure he stayed afloat made the process feel like a bout of mixed wrestling. And while they were sitting on loungers at the edge of the pool before or after a swimming lesson it was worse, or better, because she could see that he was attracted to her. She kept telling him to relax, to be less serious about everything and to remember that he was, after all, on leave. It was obvious that he was becoming a challenge to her. But he wasn't playing hard to get, just feeling too embarrassed and uncertain about himself to play at all. He kept trying to find excuses to return to his cabin to avoid being alone at the pool with her for too long.

He was, after all, only human.

In the dining room, on the recreation deck, and in the big observation lounge, where there would be nothing to look at but each other until *Kreskhallar* emerged from hyperspace, the soft assault continued although at times it became less frontal. In the lounge there was nothing to do but talk, usually about and often with the other passengers, and drink various other-world concoctions that were intended to lower his resistance and/or remove his inhibitions, which they didn't. She said very little about herself other than that she had recently graduated top of her year—she didn't mention her specialty—and that to celebrate her parents had paid for this five-world, star-traveling convention that would enable her to visit worlds she was never likely to see otherwise while indulging her hobby among people of like mind.

O'Mara told her even less about himself, because the uniform, which he had taken to wearing on every social occasion like a suit of green armor, told her what he did in real life.

But there was one evening, when the ship was ten hours out of Traltha's planetary capital, Naorthant, and the stars and myriad moons of the Tralthan system had been shining into the darkened observation lounge, when he had returned alone to his cabin with his resistance very low indeed.

Angrily he wondered why he was acting like some stupid knight errant from the legends that the passengers discussed endlessly among themselves. What was he trying to prove? She was an intelligent and very desirable young women, so much so that he couldn't understand why she had any time for a coarse, ugly person like himself at all. And there was no way that it could become a permanent commitment, because it would end when *Kreskhallar* returned her to Earth in four weeks' time. Nobody in Sector General would ever know about it, whatever "it" turned out to be, and if they did find out, neither Craythorne nor anyone else would care. He was on leave, after all, and he had been told by his chief to relax and enjoy himself.

He wasn't being unfaithful, he told himself again and again as he tossed sleepless in his bunk while in the darkness of the cabin pictures formed of Joan wearing even less than she had worn in the pool. It was utterly stupid, probably even insane, to feel that he was being unfaithful to someone who didn't even know he was alive.

# CHAPTER 19

**H**is idea of casual dress would have been a clean set of Monitor green coveralls with the insignia removed, but Joan would have none of that. Instead she insisted that he dress like a tourist for the sightseeing trips of Traltha's famed beauty spots and, inwardly kicking and screaming, he was dragged into the Earth-human section of the spaceport's shopping mall, where she became a sartorial tyrant regarding his wardrobe. He had never been the kind of person who merged into the background, O'Mara thought ruefully, but the result was so loud and garish that he was sure people would be able to hear as well as see him coming.

Traltha was a heavy planet pulling two-plus Earth Gs which meant that, except when sleeping or resting flat, they were required to wear gravity-nullifier harnesses at all times. O'Mara could have stood upright and moved about without one, but the others did not have his experience on space construction sites and could have fallen over and broken something and he would, after all, merely have been showing off.

The first time Joan appeared wearing hers she remarked that

the antigravity harness could easily have doubled as a medieval Earth chastity belt.

On the atmosphere flights to justly famous Dunelton Gorge and the beautiful Bay of Trammith, and during the two-day stopovers for sightseeing, they traveled, talked, seriously and otherwise, and had all their meals together, but O'Mara had the feeling that a little distance was beginning to grow between them. By then he had learned how to swim well enough to try doing it from the gently sloping golden beach that fringed the bay, accompanied, naturally, by his shapely lifeguard. But their tour guide forbade all swimming, pointing out that Trammith was a nature preserve sparsely populated by a rare and protected species of sea predators who didn't care what or who they ate, so there was no close physical contact with her either in or out of the water.

Had she simply given up on him, he wondered, because he had refused to take the many chances she had given him and was backing off while she still had some pride left? Or, now that he no longer wore uniform and was beginning to show more interest in her, was she trying to encourage him further by playing hard to get?

Only a nasty, devious-minded psychologist, he told himself, would have a thought like that.

He couldn't believe that someone with his unfriendly personality could get into a situation like this. As soon as they returned to Naorthant spaceport he could simply detach himself from it by going to the Monitor office and boarding the next available ship going somewhere, anywhere, else. But that would be a stupid as well as a cowardly thing to do because, he was beginning to realize, he had been having a very enjoyable if recently a frustrating time on *Kreskhallar*. So whatever way the situation developed, he told himself firmly, it wouldn't be all bad.

Early on the first night out they were on the recreation deck looking out at the stars and blue-green, mottled image of Traltha shrinking astern while they argued about the Arthurian legend of ancient Earth.

". . . This is another one of your legends that I've never understood," Kledenth was saying. "You had an aging, wise, and enlightened king who, because of the pressures of maintaining order in its country, neglected the physical and emotional needs of its much younger life-mate and queen, who in turn became so emotionally involved with its younger and physically more attractive bodyguard that it ignored the promises of fidelity it had already made and ultimately an unlawful mating for pleasure took place. As a result the once stable and prospering kingdom disintegrated and everybody died, or lived unhappily ever after. I read the story and watched some of the dramatizations, but I still can't understand why the king allowed it to happen. Was it as wise as you say, unable to communicate its emotions, blind, or just plain stupid? I think it's a bad story that doesn't deserve to be told."

"The point is," said Joan, "that it's a bad, sad story that could have been good. I don't mind if the characters have to suffer provided there is a happy ending. But if people could read the signals correctly, there would be a happy ending without anyone having to suffer."

She looked at O'Mara and quickly looked away again.

"If it had happened on Kelgia," said Kledenth, "both the queen's and the bodyguard's fur would have warned the king of what was happening right from the beginning. It could have paid more attention to its young life-mate or got rid of the bodygard, nonviolently since it liked them both. And speaking of emotional signals, O'Mara, are you still misreading or just ignoring yours?"

"My favorite character in that story is Merlin," said O'Mara, trying to move the conversation onto safer ground, "the magician who went through time in reverse and met the elderly king long before meeting Arthur as a boy. Merlin has never been given the attention he deserves, and even though time travel in either direction is impossible . . ."

"There speaks the typical hardheaded technocrat," Joan said softly. "Is there no room in your mind for magic?"

"As a child I had plenty of room there for magic," said O'Mara, "but only while reading or, as now, talking about the story. Centuries ago it was the technocrats who formed groups and came together as you people are doing now, but they did it to discuss and write and dream about the effects of future advances in science. Now it has all happened. We have star travel, frequent contact and commerce with other-species sapients, antigravity, advanced medicine, everything, and so there is very little room left to us for scientific dreaming. Yet on every civilized planet there are individuals or groups who spend their spare time thinking about, writing about, or discussing the magic and legends of their pasts. Magic is all we have left."

There was a moment of silence that was broken by Joan. "So you are a closet fantasy fan," she said. "O'Mara, you're a strange and very interesting man, as well as being a waste of a valuable natural resource, with muscles."

Kledenth rippled its fur and said, "O'Mara, normally I would tell you exactly what I think and feel about this situation, and you. But I have been studying a tourist book about polite and nonoffensive conversational usage and wish to practice it before we visit Earth. I think your insensitive behavior toward this female makes me conclude that you are mentally disadvantaged, visually impaired, and that your parents were unmarried."

Before O'Mara could think of a suitably polite response he felt the instant of vertigo that marked their insertion into hyperspace followed by a momentary unsteadiness in the deck underfoot. The artificial-gravity system, he guessed, had made a less than smooth transition during the changeover from compensating for the five-G thrust of the main engines to the weightlessness of hyperspace. Right now the officer responsible would be having harsh words said to him, her, or it by the captain. Even minor fluctuations in the artificial G could cause nausea in some life-forms and spacesickness on a modern interstellar passenger vessel was just not supposed to happen. Apparently the others hadn't noticed anything.

"Well, there's nothing more to see here," said Joan. She tried to encircle his upper arm gently with her long, delicate fingers and pull him away from the viewing panel. "Let's go for another swimming lesson. I haven't shown you everything yet."

# CHAPTER 20

Their single Tralthan passenger had completed its round-trip tour and left the ship on its home world, where two others, who as honeymooners were no longer single in either sense of the word, had come aboard. As yet they had shown no interest in other-species legends or in anything but each other apart from galloping ponderously up and down the sloping ramp on one side of the pool.

"Theoretically," said O'Mara, "it is possible for two Earth-humans and a pair of overenthusiastic Tralthans to swim together, but ..."

"We'd be mad in the head to try it," Joan finished for him. Laughing, she added, "Am I right in thinking that you dislike the water, Kledenth?"

"You're wrong," said the Kelgian, ruffling its fur. "I intensely hate, detest, and abhor the water. Let's move over to the lounger beside the direct-vision panel. There's nothing to see, but at least we'll be out of range of the liquid fallout."

They picked their way between the multi-species exercising

and gaming equipment that filled the remainder of the recreation deck area. Apart from the swimmers, two Nidians playing something fast and complicated that involved knocking two tiny white balls between them, and a Melfan who was lying reading on something that resembled a surrealistic wastepaper basket, they had the place to themselves. Kledenth curled itself into a thick, furry S on a nearby mattress while Joan and O'Mara stretched out on loungers.

With nothing but grey hyperspace showing beyond the big direct-vision panel, they lay watching the two Tralthans charging in and out of the pool and slapping at the water with their total of eight tentacles while making untranslatable noises to each other that sounded like hysterical foghorns. Every few seconds they were hidden by clouds of self-created spray.

"Extroverts," said Kledenth.

Joan laughed suddenly and said, "Now, there is a life-form that really enjoys swimming."

"Not so," said O'Mara, watching them and trying not to allow the concern he was feeling from reaching his voice. "They love playing in water and they're safe so long as their breathing orifices aren't below the surface for more than a few minutes. But their body density is too great for them to be able to stay afloat even with the aid of maximum muscular effort. Those two are being very foolish."

"Lieutenant O'Mara," she said, wriggling her slender body into a more comfortable position on the lounger in a way that immediately upped his blood pressure, "I bow to your superior knowledge of nonswimming Tralthans. But they can't go on not swimming and expending energy at that rate for much longer, and then it will be our turn to make fools of ourselves. . . . What the hell!"

Slowly their loungers were tipping sideways as if trying to roll their bodies onto the deck, which had developed a gentle slope in the same direction. Water spilled over the nearest edge of the pool and rolled in a six-inch tidal wave toward them, breaking against the deck supports of intervening equipment as it came. Suddenly the deck tilted in the opposite direction, and the miniature tidal wave gurgled to a stop and began flowing back into the pool as the deck and their loungers became level again. The Tralthans were still creating so much turbulence that they apparently hadn't noticed anything.

Again O'Mara felt the instant of vertigo characteristic of reemergence into normal space. He didn't have to look at the direct-vision panel to know that it was again showing the stars and that, even though they had been traveling for only a short time in the hyperdimension, the Traltha system had been left far astern. A few seconds later the lounger padding pushed him gently into the air as they went weightless.

This was not a normal occurrence, he knew, particularly on a passenger vessel. Plainly *Kreskhallar* was having problems, perhaps serious ones. Joan was looking frightened and Kledenth's fur was agitated.

"There's nothing to worry about," he said, knowing that he was lying reassuringly to one Earth-person even though there was a Kelgian present who would accept it as the truth. "Is this your first experience of weightlessness? It looks as if the artificial gravity is on the blink, so just hold on to something solid until ..."

He broke off as the ship's public-address system cleared its throat.

"This is your captain," it said. "Please remain calm. A minor malfunction has occurred in our artificial-gravity system. There is no danger to the ship and the period of weightlessness is a temporary inconvenience for which I can only apologize. Will all passengers currently occupying their cabins please remain in them until further notice. Those in other parts of the ship, particularly if they are in large, open areas such as the recreation deck, must return to their cabins as soon as possible. Anyone who lacks experience in weightless or low-G maneuvering should request assistance from a crew member, or from a fellow passenger with the necessary ability to assist you to your quarters. ..."

He was aware of sideways motion, so gentle and gradual that he wasn't surprised that the others hadn't noticed it.

"As you will already have seen if you are close to a direct-vision port," the captain continued, "we have returned to normal space, where we are able to apply lateral spin to the ship so that centrifugal force in the cabin areas inboard of the outer hull will replace the artificial gravity for the time necessary to repair the . . ."

"You may take me to my cabin, Lieutenant O'Mara," Joan broke in, holding onto her lounger with one hand and grabbing O'Mara's wrist with the other. "The captain just made that an order."

"No!" said O'Mara loudly, pulling his arm away and looking all around the big room for the nearest communicator. He spotted it about twenty meters away on the far side of the direct-vision panel. It had been years since he'd worked in gravity-free conditions, he thought as he grasped the sides of the lounger, drew his knees up until his feet were between his hands and prepared to make a weightless jump, but it was an ability that one never forgot.

"Dammit," said Joan, her face red with anger and embarrassment, "you didn't have to be so bloody *definite* about it!"

"I was talking to that stupid captain, not you," O'Mara said angrily. He launched himself carefully in the direction of the communicator and continued speaking quickly as he moved. "Listen to me, carefully. You and Kledenth get out of here. Push off from the loungers, gently, and aim where you need to go or you'll spin and lose orientation. Or do it in stages by pulling yourselves along or pushing against intervening fixed equipment to the nearest side wall and then around to the entrance. On no account take a shortcut across the deck or ceiling or go anywhere near the pool. Tell that Nidian and the two Melfans to do the same, and the Tralthans if you can make them hear you. Water is dangerous stuff in the weightless condition because it falls apart into . . . Just listen while I'm on the communicator, I don't have time to explain twice."

He landed neatly on his hands and knees beside the unit, steadied himself, and jabbed the attention button. The screen lit with the image of the ship's crest and a cool, translated voice said that the call would be dealt with as soon as possible and to please wait. He looked around quickly.

Joan was relaying his instructions to the other passengers while trying to help Kledenth, but the public-address system and the Tralthans were making so much noise that her voice lacked the necessary volume and authority to get results. So far as he could see, nobody had moved from their original positions. He jabbed the button again.

The captain was saying, ". . . We will increase our spin until the centrifugal force inboard of the outer hull matches the gravity pull of one standard Earth G although, until the artificial-gravity system is returned, the outer cabin wall will be the floor. Once again we apologize for this temporary inconvenience. That is all."

O'Mara swore again and this time he kept his thumb on the button. Behind him he could see the water slowly rising above the sides of the pool and, its edges still held by the cohesion of surface tension, begin to roll down on them like a vast gob of clear syrup. Suddenly bulges and ripples caused by movements of the Tralthans appeared all over the slow-moving, transparent mass. Great, uneven lumps grew out of the surface like fat, shapeless arms that broke free and moved like monstrous, slow-moving amoebas toward the inner hull. The Tralthan noise was beginning to sound frightened, the flailing of their tentacles agitated rather than playful.

He noticed the other button then, the yellow one with the transparent cover and the warning sign, and swore again. This time it was at his own stupidity for not remembering that, on the older Melfan-built civilian vessels, yellow was the color denoting urgency rather than red. He flipped up the cover so hard that it came away in his hand and stabbed at the button as if it was a mortal enemy.

A boney, Melfan head appeared. The eyes stared at him for an instant; then an impatient, translated voice said, "Passengers are not allowed to use this channel unless there is . . ."

"An emergency, I know," he broke in. "O'Mara, Monitor Corps, on the recreation deck. Please connect me with your captain. I must speak to him, her, or it at once. Meanwhile, cancel the order to spin the ship. Do that now."

"Sir, you have no operational authority on this civilian vessel," the other replied angrily. "And the captain is busy right now."

"Then I'll talk to one of the responsible ship's officers," said O'Mara. "Presumably that means you?"

The exoskeletal features were incapable of changing color or registering emotion, but he could hear the Melfan's pincers opening and closing with a sound like castanets. He moved to the side of the screen to give the other a clearer view of what was happening in the room, then continued speaking.

"The weightlessness and now the increasing spin are combining to empty the swimming pool," he said, forcing himself to speak slowly and clearly. "Unless the spin, and the buildup of centrifugal force, is checked right now, within a few minutes, at the present rate of descent, many tons of water will fall against the inner hull. The hull structure will take it, but can the seals of the direct-vision panel?"

"The seals can take it," said the Melfan, and added, "Well, probably."

"With the falling water," O'Mara went on, "will be the weight of two adult Tralthan swimmers. Can they take that, too?"

"Negative," said the officer, swiveling its head to look offscreen. "Captain! Emergency Blue Three. Risk of imminent hull breach on the rec deck. I'm putting the image on your repeater screen. Kill the spin and return to weightless conditions, *now!*"

"No," said O'Mara sharply. "We need a little weight here, no more than one-eighth G, to allow the water to stabilize so we can rescue the swimmers and nonaquatics. Weightless it will be scattered in liquid lumps all over the place with no stable surface to swim to. In those conditions people can panic and drown."

He stopped as the Melfan's face was replaced by the hairy, Orligian features of the captain.

"Understood, Lieutenant," it growled through its translator. "No more than one-eighth G. You've got it. I'm sending the ship's medic, Dr. Sennelt, to you. It's all I can spare right now. Keep this vision channel open so's we can see what's happening . . ."

Before the other had finished speaking, O'Mara had launched himself toward the tangled bodies of Joan and Kledenth.

The Kelgian was trying to wrap itself around Joan, who was trying desperately to push both of them sideways to escape the slowly falling mass of water that was now only a few meters above them. But neither of them were in contact with anything solid, so they were just rotating untidily around their common center of gravity. O'Mara landed on the nearest lounger, wrapped his lower legs around it, grabbed Joan firmly by the wrists, and pulled her free. Then he transferred his grip to her upper arms.

"Listen to me," he said urgently. "There's no time to get both of you to the side wall. You've got to jump straight up, as hard as you can, in a vertical dive through the water." He glanced upward at the struggling, shadowy bodies of the Tralthans and added, "No, angle your dive to the right or you'll hit those two. Dive fast and cleanly, like you always do. You might hit turbulence, air pockets, places where there's nothing but bubbles that you can't see through. Keep going, don't stop to breathe or you could disorientate and drown, until your momentum takes you through to clear air and beyond to the entrance wall. Did you understand that? Now, hyperventilate for a few seconds, then go!"

She nodded and swore, still struggling to pull free of the panicking Kledenth. O'Mara knew exactly where to grab a male Kelgian to make it let go. He gripped her by the upper thighs, steadied her feet against the deck, and said, "Don't worry, I'll take care of Kledenth. *Go!*"

O'Mara wrapped both arms around the Kelgian's middle, looked up quickly then sideways toward the wall. The lower surface of the water was rippling and growing enormous blisters that bulged downward less than two meters and about ten seconds distant in space and time. They might just make it to the side wall before the watery mass landed on them. Kledenth saw it, too, and began making high-pitched, terrified sounds. Just as he was about to kick away from the lounger framework on a path that would take them laterally along the deck, it tried to wriggle out of his arms.

"You'll be all right," he said. "Hold still, dammit!"

But instead of holding still, Kledenth's body went into a panic convulsion and suddenly O'Mara's face was buried in rippling fur. One foot slipped from the lounger frame just as he jumped. Instead of flying toward the side wall they spun together into the deck. He had barely time to fill his lungs before the water was all around them.

Through the fog of air bubbles escaping from Kledenth's fur he saw the dark, indistinct shape of one of the Tralthans falling slowly down on them. Desperately he felt around with his free hand in the opaque turbulence for the lounger frame, found it, and, bending at the knees and changing to a two-handed grip on the Kelgian's frantically wriggling body, he planted his feet against the frame and prepared to kick out hard. But too late.

The Tralthan's massive body landed on them, pinning O'Mara's feet and the Kledenth's lower body to the deck. There was a sudden, bright explosion of bubbles as the sudden pressure from the Tralthan's body pushed all the air out of the Kelgian's lungs. He fought the instinctive urge to grasp with the pain in his feet and fought instead to keep as much air as possible in his own lungs.

He was going to need it.

# CHAPTER 21

O'Mara released his grip on Kledenth and quickly bent double to get his hands under the Tralthan's massive body. It was unconscious and unable to help him. In normal conditions it would have been impossible to lift it but, supported as it was by the water and with less than a quarter G acting on it, he should be able to roll the dead weight off his feet and the Kelgian's trapped lower body.

The Tralthan's body had lost three-quarters of its weight, but it still possessed all of its inertia. He gripped it solidly at the roots of two of its four tentacles and strained upward until he felt as if his arms would tear off at the shoulders. Slowly it began to move and just as slowly kept on moving. Suddenly his feet were free and so was the trapped Kelgian. But he had used too much of his available oxygen. The turbulence had settled and the water was no longer clouded by bubbles, but large, throbbing patches of blackness were keeping him from seeing clearly and he felt as if the Tralthan beside them were sitting on his chest. He wrapped his arms around Kledenth's middle again, felt for the deck surface with his feet. The stale air in his lungs burst out in an explosion of bubbles as he used the last of the strength in his leaden legs to jump straight up.

He was startled at how soon they broke surface and, gasping desperately for air as he looked around, he immediately saw why. The captain had remotely opened the airtight doors at each side of the room. Presently they were under the surface and the pool water was gurgling through the openings into two large, adjoining storerooms. The surface was still puckered with tiny, steep-sided, lowgravity wavelets, but the level was dropping rapidly. Suddenly his feet were in contact with the deck and he was able to hold Kledenth's head clear of the water.

The upper body of one of the Tralthan swimmers was emerging slowly from the water. It was choking and gasping and obviously in great emotional distress as it slapped at the water with its tentacles in a desperate effort to find its life-mate, who was still under the surface, but he knew that it would be fine as soon as it cleared its air passages. High above him the Melfan and the Nidian passengers were holding on to fixed equipment near the entrance and Joan was doing the same about five meters distant. He was about to call to her when a Melfan wearing an antigravity harness and with a caduceus on its crew insignia appeared in the entrance and came swooping down toward them. Dr. Sennelt had arrived.

"Doctor," he said urgently. "This is passenger Kledenth, Kelgian, non-aquatic, immersed and unconscious for two plus minutes with emptied lungs. Will you be careful to check for . . ."

"Don't worry, sir," said the medic as it cradled Kledenth's limp body in its triple-jointed forward limbs. "I'll take over from here. How about you, Lieutenant?"

O'Mara shook his head. "I'm all right," he said impatiently. "But there could be internal trauma as a result of it being rolled on by a drowning Tralthan, who is still underwater, lying on its side and unconscious."

"That could be very serious," said Dr. Sennelt as it tapped buttons on its antigravity harness and the limp body of Kledenth and it began rising toward the entrance, "but there's nothing much I can do right now without special equipment to lift it upright and out of the water. I'll have a team with a Tralthan-sized antigravity pallet here in ten minutes and be back myself to supervise."

"That could be too late . . ." O'Mara broke in.

"Meanwhile," Sennelt called back as it rose to the entrance, "I'm taking Kledenth to sickbay."

O'Mara swore, not quite under his breath, looked at Joan, who was still clinging to the furniture above him, and said urgently, "Joan, would you climb down here, carefully but quickly please? I need your help." He swung around to the other Tralthan, who was still gasping and spluttering but no longer seemed distressed, and pointed at its unconscious life-mate, whose flank and one side of its head were coming into view above the subsiding water level.

"You'll be all right in a few minutes," he said quickly, "but right now I need you to help lift your life-mate onto its feet and hold it there. You know how important that is for your particular lifeform. Move around to this side. Slide your forward tentacles under it, just here and here. Now lift! That's it. But hold it steady; it's wobbling all over the place."

With the two storerooms filled and nowhere else for it to go, the water level was no longer dropping. Only the Tralthan's six stubby legs and underside were submerged now. O'Mara took a deep breath, hunkered down underwater, and, one by one, tried to pull the legs laterally outward as far as they would go in an attempt to give the body more vertical stability. It was the most intensive period of hard work that he had ever done and, he knew, if he hadn't already been underwater he would have been sweating like a pig. When it was over and he surfaced gasping, Joan was beside him.

"How can I help?" she said calmly.

"With artificial respiration . . ." O'Mara began, but had to stop for a moment to catch his breath. Then he pointed to one of the Tralthan's gills before going on quickly, "With their general physical structure and breathing orifices like those—they have four of them—you can understand that they can't give each other mouth-to-mouth resuscitation. But we can. It's done by first filling our lungs, pressing our lips tightly around the gill opening, and blowing the air in hard. Wait for a count of three, then suck to remove some of the liquid content of the lung, spit out, and repeat the process as regularly and as quickly as you can. I'll show you."

He demonstrated briefly then looked at her. "You got that?"

Joan made a face and said, "Yes, but I'm not sure I want it. But oh, well, I did offer."

Hesitating at first but soon getting into the rhythm, she joined O'Mara in blowing hard, sucking, and spitting out. Only once did she stop to look at him and wipe her lips with the back of her hand.

"Yuk," she said with feeling. "That stuff smells and tastes *awful!* Are you sure I'm blowing and sucking at the right body orifice?"

"Trust me," said O'Mara.

They continued working for perhaps a minute while the other Tralthan silently held its life-mate upright. It had stopped asking them if they knew what they were doing. He became aware that their patient's legs were beginning to stiffen and its four tentacles, which had been hanging limply at it sides, were beginning to twitch.

"Quickly, back off!" he said urgently. "It's coming to."

Suddenly the unconscious Tralthan came alive again, stamping its feet and thrashing around with its tentacles while water, bubbles, and mucus jetted from its gills, until the comforting words and encircling tentacles of its life-mate made it settle down. Joan laughed quietly.

"I think we did it," said O'Mara.

"Yes," said Joan, raising a fist in triumph as she looked at him. "And would you believe that was my first time for giving mouth-to-mouth?"

Before he could reply, Dr. Sennelt, followed by two other crew members guiding a wide antigravity pallet, dropped down beside them.

"And that's the first time I've ever seen Earth-humans do it to a Tralthan," said Sennelt, clicking a pincer in appreciation. "Very nice work, people. But now we have to move you into the corridor. The Tralthans first, one at a time, then you two can share the pallet for the final trip. The captain is about to . . ."

"This is the captain," broke in a voice on the PA. "I am pleased to tell you that the artificial-gravity system on the recreation deck is again functional and will be gradually restored to normal pull within the next fifteen minutes. Passengers are requested to stay clear of the area for three hours to enable us to mop up and replace damaged equipment. No injuries have been reported and we are returning to hyperspace as I speak. Once again, my apologies for any inconvenience caused. That is all."

While the first Tralthan was being loaded onto the antigravity pallet and moved up to the corridor, Joan stood waist deep in the water looking up at him intently without speaking. Usually she had plenty to say, and her expression and uncharacteristic silence were disconcerting. He felt an awkward question coming on that he would rather not answer.

"That Tralthan resuscitation technique saved its life," she said. "You saved its life. Where did you learn to do that?"

"I meet lots of different species on space establishments," he replied, telling the truth if not all of it, "and one picks up things. It was simply a bit of other-species first aid. But you did well, really well. It was an unpleasant thing to have to do, but you did it like a professional. You said this was a trip to celebrate your graduation. Was it from medical school?"

"No," said Joan. She looked uncomfortable for a moment, then added, "All right, yes. Technically, that is. I've just qualified as a vet."

"I see," said O'Mara very seriously. "Then you were already accustomed to treating other species, even though the life-forms concerned are not usually sapient. And remember, it was we, not me, who saved its life."

Before she could reply, the pallet returned from taking the second Tralthan to the corridor and the Orligian crew member guiding it growled politely at them to climb aboard. Their silence continued after they disembarked in the corridor and the transparent door of the recreation deck hissed shut behind them.

Gradually the walls of the corridor moved into the vertical again and the floor was down again, as was that of the recreation deck. Through the transparent door they watched the water roll from the opposite wall and pour out of the two storage compartments to slosh about the floor until it found its way back into the swimming pool. Apart from the items of furniture that had been demolished by the slowly falling Tralthans and a few puddles here and there, the place had returned to normal. Suddenly a nearby public-address speaker cleared it throat.

"This is the captain speaking," it said. "Would the Earth-human passenger Kelleher and Monitor Corps Lieutenant O'Mara oblige me by coming to the control deck at hour twenty-one hundred this evening. Thank you."

"O'Mara," said Joan, smiling, "the captain is going to thank us officially, and maybe even give you a medal. And so it should."

She looked at him with sudden concern and went on, "But I'm not sure about the medal. There was a while back there when you seemed to be giving the captain orders. Senior ship's officers can be a bit stuffy about insubordination, even from a passenger. Still, maybe it will just say nice, pompous things to you and allow you to travel free on this trip."

"As a Corps officer in the space service," he said, "I travel free anyway. The thanks or medals aren't important right now. It's Kledenth that I'm worried about. Having a Tralthan land on it, even a quarter-weight one, could cause serious injury . . ."

He broke off as Dr. Sennelt appeared suddenly behind them. It said, "Passenger Kledenth is doing fine, sir. We've pumped out its lungs, are in the process of drying out its fur, and have given it a head-to-tail internal scan with optimum results. As a precaution we have placed it on continuous monitor observation, so it is unable to receive visitors at present. But please believe me, you have nothing to worry about. The Tralthan you resuscitated also said that it is fine and insisted that it requires no treatment other than the ministrations of its new life-mate. It elected to return to their cabin, presumably to rest. But it's you two who concern me now. Are you sure you're feeling all right? Have you any respiratory difficulties? Or delayed shock? Would anyone want to visit sickbay for a checkup?"

They shook their heads.

"Among Earth-humans," said the doctor, "I'm told that particular form of head gesture indicates a negative response. Good. The captain will speak to you after dinner, but before I leave you I would like to express my own personal thanks for what you've done. A passenger terminating during a pleasure cruise, whether through age, injury, or a stupid accident as this could have been, is a bad thing. It is bad in itself and, it shames me even to mention this, very bad for the future prospects of the small, independent, and, well, economically run spaceline to which *Kreskhallar* belongs. So we have to thank you for more than you perhaps realize. But now I have a long accident report to write."

"Before you go, Doctor," said O'Mara quickly, "I'm still worried about Kledenth. I'd be grateful if you could let me know of any change in its condition, however small."

As Sennelt turned to go it said, "I would be pleased to do that for you, sir."

A few minutes after it left them the door of the recreation deck hissed open to allow four mixed-species cleaning and repair personnel with their robots to go inside. O'Mara had never derived much pleasure from watching other people work and, it seemed, neither had Joan because she was looking only at him. Before she could say anything, he pretended to shiver.

"The corridor air-conditioning is a bit low," he said, smiling. "If you'll excuse me, I'll go and dress for dinner."

# CHAPTER 22

A few of the Kelgians at their table noticed the absence of Kledenth and talked about it and the artificial-gravity failure, but only among themselves. Plainly the news of the recreation-deck incident was not yet common knowledge, and O'Mara didn't want to talk about it, either. In fact, except for the occasional polite monosyllable, he was refusing to talk about anything. Joan was beginning to look annoyed with him. Then suddenly she stared over his shoulders and smiled.

"If you're still worrying about Kledenth," she said, "you can stop right now."

He twisted around in his chair to see Dr. Sennelt and Kledenth picking their way between the tables toward them. The Kelgian undulated forward quickly and curled its body into its seat. It was the doctor who spoke first.

"You wanted me to tell you how my casualty was progressing, Lieutenant," it said, "so I decided to show you instead. Kledenth is physically mobile and says that it is feeling well, but hungry. Clinically these are very good signs. It has absolutely nothing to worry about."

It clicked a pincer in farewell and turned away.

Joan was still smiling, but not O'Mara. He was relieved, but at the same time he was inclined to distrust a well-meaning but overoptimistic ship's doctor who could have only limited physiological knowledge and experience where an other-species patient was concerned. Similar thoughts must have been going through Joan's mind.

"It's great to have you back," she said. "But how are you really feeling?"

"How d'you think I'm feeling?" Kledenth replied in its ungracious Kelgian fashion. "I was sat on by a Tralthan, nearly drowned, my fur got wet all over and stuck to me for hours. It was a horrible sensation, like I'd suddenly lost the ability to communicate feelings. I'm feeling terrible, but all right. Kelgians don't have much bone structure, except in the head, so we're inclined to squish and bounce back instead of breaking up. Your concern is appreciated."

O'Mara still wasn't satisfied. He said, "Are you sure there are no symptoms of—"

"Lieutenant," Kledenth broke in. "You're beginning to sound like Dr. Sennelt, who told me that you probably saved my life. For that favor I feel grateful, more grateful than I can say in simple, unsupported words to a being who is unable to read my fur. But this great favor I shall totally discount if you cause me to die of starvation. I need to eat, O'Mara, not talk."

Both Earth-humans laughed and O'Mara found conversation easier as they continued the meal. Even Kledenth was talking as well as eating, but mostly to its same-species friends farther up the table. But his attention kept drifting from Joan to the animated fur of the Kelgian beside him. He thought she hadn't noticed until she leaned suddenly toward him.

"O'Mara," she said quietly, "what the hell is bothering you?"

He forced a laugh that sounded hollow even to himself and said, "You mean, apart from you?"

She shook her head impatiently. "Unfortunately," she said, "I don't bother you, at least not very much. You've hardly taken your eyes off Kledenth since it arrived. Why?"

He hesitated and tried to choose words which would sound neither egocentric nor too critical of the ship doctor's ability, which, he felt sure, would in ordinary circumstances have been adequate. O'Mara was a layman, after all, and not supposed to know anything about the subject. But he did know a lot about Kelgian physiology, every bit as much as his mind partner and top medical specialist knew, and he would be in serious trouble if he told anyone else how he knew it, because the Marrasarah mind tape should have been erased. The trouble was that when a Kelgian was apparently sharing his mind, it was very difficult to lie.

"Sennelt is a good enough doctor," he said. "What worries me is that it might not know enough about Kelgian anatomy."

"And you do?"

"Yes," he said.

She frowned at him for a moment, then said seriously, "Apart from a few hints about space construction work, for which you certainly have the muscles, you've been reticent about what exactly it is that you do. Are you a medic, or were you once a medic, but for some reason want to hide that fact?"

He shook his head. "I have no formal medical qualifications."

"But you think you know enough about other-species first aid," she went on, "to second-guess the ship's medical officer? What the hell do you do, exactly?"

O'Mara wished again that there weren't a truth-telling Kelgian influencing so much of his mind.

"I'm a psychologist," he said.

She sat back suddenly in her chair, her face reddening with anger and embarrassment. After a moment she said, "And in the way of psychologists, you have been calmly and clinically observing my behavior while I was trying to, to make a fool of myself over you?"

O'Mara shook his head and held her eyes for a long moment, then said quietly, "I was observing myself, not very calmly nor clinically, trying not to make a fool of myself over you."

She continued to stare at him without speaking, but her angry color was slowly returning to normal.

Apologetically, he went on, "I should have told you, I suppose. But I'm on leave and, well, nobody needed to know." He smiled. "If it helps you feel any better about it, I'm an other-species psychologist."

"An other-species . . . ?" she began, then laughed quietly. "I think that makes me feel worse! But it explains your concern for Kledenth. Are you diagnosing a condition Sennelt missed purely from behavioral observation?"

"Not entirely," he replied, still telling the truth but not all of it. "In my job I've met, talked with, and come to know many Kelgians, one in particular very well, and I know how they feel and think. Kledenth may not yet be aware that there is anything wrong with it, but there is."

Joan's anger and embarrassment had been replaced by interest now. She said, "If I understand you correctly, the compression of its body when the Tralthan fell on it, and the subsequent near-drowning, have caused a delayed-action but potentially severe emotional trauma. Are you trying to avoid or relieve this condition by tinkering with its mind?"

O'Mara shook his head. "Unfortunately," he said very seriously, "Kledenth's condition is purely physical. If left untreated the emotional problems will surely follow."

"Then I don't understand you," said Joan. "Explain it to me."

He didn't want to explain, because that would lead to telling her all about the mind-tape trials and virtually everything else about himself, but neither did he want to lie to her. He was saved from having to make the decision by Kledenth turning suddenly to rejoin the conversation.

"I thought I heard talking about me," it said. "Is it more interesting and important than the things these others are saying?"

"Probably not as interesting," O'Mara replied, slipping automatically into direct, Kelgian speech mode, "but certainly more important. Have you retold your adventure often enough, and heard enough praise and sympathy from your friends, to give us your undivided attention?"

Kledenth's fur rose into irritated spikes, but Joan spoke before it could reply. Plainly she was happier with the more tactful and gentle approach.

"We were worried," she said, "in case you are not as well as Dr. Sennelt thinks you are. We think there may be aftereffects. To reassure us, the lieutenant wishes to ask you a few questions."

"More than a few," said O'Mara.

A new pattern of ripples disturbed Kledenth's fur. It turned its attention from Joan and brought its small, cone-shaped head to within a few inches of O'Mara's face and said, "Then ask them."

"Right," said O'Mara. "Your medial body and legs were pressed between the drowning Tralthan and the deck for a period of four-plus minutes before you were freed. Are you aware of any discomfort in these limbs, or from the muscles that operate them, or from the tegument overlaying those areas to which the fur is attached? Have you noticed any impairment of movement or lack of sensation in these limbs? Any feelings of surface pain, or tingling or any other unusual sensations from other parts of the body not directly affected by the temporary constriction? I realize that the recent nature of the incident and the associated emotional trauma means that there will be a psychological component in your relating of the symptoms. I shall make allowances for any emotional coloration, so be as objective or subjective as you wish. Speak."

Joan was frowning again. "O'Mara, aren't you being a little insensitive . . . ?" she began, but Kledenth cut her off.

"I am aware of many aches and pains," it said. "They may be subjective but from inside they feel as objective as hell. The doctor didn't ask as many questions as this. What's wrong? You're beginning to frighten me."

He could see that growing fear, or rather the memories and clinical experience of the top Kelgian surgeon in his mind enabled him to see and read it from the tight, uneven pattern of ripples that were agitating Kledenth's fur.

"Fear," he said, "is a temporary condition which disappears when the cause and uncertainty associated with it is understood and removed. Your condition may or may not be temporary, that is what I'm trying to establish. What exactly did Sennelt say and, more important, do to you?"

"It said a lot," the Kelgian replied, "mostly reassuring things and advice about taking it easy for a few days and not worrying. It went over me with one of those portable scanner things, then suspended me in null-G while it used a hot-air fan to dry my fur. It made me walk around sickbay and watched until I told it I felt hungry, then it brought me here. What else did you expect it to do?"

O'Mara paused for a moment, thinking about the limited facilities and, comparatively, nonspecialized and even more limited experience of a ship's medic who was expected to know only a very little about everything. Sennelt was a good enough doctor, but *Kreskhallar* wasn't Sector General.

"In the circumstances," O'Mara replied, "nothing else. Before or during the drying of your fur did Sennelt spray it with any surface medication, conditioner, or similar substance?"

"No," said Kledenth. "I wouldn't allow it. My fur needs no such enhancements."

"I can see that," said O'Mara. "It is remarkably beautiful and expressive fur. But when you arrived with Sennelt and during the initial conversation with your friends, I noticed a slowing in its overall mobility compared to my earlier observations of you. The fur's reduced response time to vocal and emotional stimuli is minor and could be due simply to delayed shock or associated psychological factors stemming from your accident, but I'm not entirely satisfied with Sennelt's prognosis and I intend—"

"You think there's something wrong with my *fur!*" Kledenth broke in, its fur standing out in spikes of fear and anger. "But, but what do you know, you're only a bloody policeman! And if you happen to be right, what can you do about it? O'Mara, you shouldn't frighten me with talk like this."

Everyone else at the table had stopped talking to watch, and the fur on the other Kelgian diners was twitching in sympathy with Kledenth's distress. Even Joan, who was unable to read fur, had sensed Kledenth's feelings and was staring furiously at him. O'Mara raised a hand quickly before she could speak, knowing that she would consider the gesture ill-mannered, but he needed a moment to regain control. For the past few minutes his mind partner had almost taken over.

He knew that the feeling was purely subjective because the mind tape impressed only the donor's memories. But those memories had included personal experience with dysfunctional fur that it would not have wanted any other member of its species to share. But now it was time to stop thinking and talking like a Kelgian and to say some kindly, reassuring Earth-human words to the badly frightened Kledenth, even though he knew that the reassurance he would give would be less than honest.

"Right now I don't know what I can do for you," said O'Mara, "but I promise to do something. In a short time Joan and I will be talking to the captain, who considers that it owes us a favor. I shall ask it for a long consultation with Dr. Sennelt, during which I shall ask for answers to the questions that are troubling us both. It is possible that my worries are without foundation and the doctor will be able to set my mind at rest when, naturally, I shall pass the good news to you without delay. But until then try not to worry because there may not be anything to worry about."

Kledenth said a word that their translators had not been programmed to handle and its fur began to settle into normal levels of mobility. But before it could go on, the other Kelgians at the table began asking it more questions about what might be wrong and it was suddenly too busy to talk to him. Joan was still looking unfriendly rather than angry. She didn't speak to him either until they were in the corridor on the way to their appointment with the captain. It was probably subjective, he thought, but it felt as if the air-conditioning temperature had been reduced by quite a few degrees.

She said, "You were unnecessarily rough on Kledenth, especially for someone who might not know what he's talking about. Earlier you told me that you weren't a medic. But you weren't talking first aid back there. Is there something you're keeping to yourself, and are you going to tell me about it?"

"No," said O'Mara.

"Then all I can say," she said coldly, "is that if you were a doctor, or maybe a medical student who couldn't pass the finals, then they certainly failed you on your bedside manner."

# CHAPTER 23

The invitation to visit *Kreskhallar*'s control deck was a courtesy rarely extended to mere passengers, because it was there that the shipboard god, who was also known to lesser mortals as Captain Grulya-Mar, dwelt and had its august being. For a great, hairy, and bearlike Orligian, it was gracious, unsparing in its compliments and thanks, pompous and condescending. The condescension was probably due to its thinking that this was their first time to see a starship's control deck, but it didn't stop talking long enough for O'Mara to tell it that it was only half right.

He could see that Joan was tremendously pleased and impressed and was paying rapt attention to everything Grulya-Mar said or showed them, but he wasn't sure that he could respect a captain who omitted to introduce its mixed-species fellow officers by name while acting as if they were part of the ship's equipment he was pointing out. As the brief tour neared its end, the other's gracious manner became increasingly diluted with impatience.

"I hope you have enjoyed this visit to my control center," it said, "but now there are operational matters I must attend to. Once again, my sincere and personal thanks, and those of my tour operator, for your quick thinking and assessment of the situation on the recreation deck, Lieutenant, and to both of you for your prompt and concerted action in what followed. You may well have saved two lives, Sennelt tells me, and you have certainly preserved the unblemished safety record of my ship."

Joan, looking pleased and embarrassed, gave a final look around the control deck and said, "We were pleased to help. Thank you, Captain, for your time and courtesy."

"It was a pleasure," said Grulya-Mar, "but as I've already said, the thanks are due entirely to you two, and if there is any favor, anything at all within my power, that I or any of my officers can do for you, you have only to ask."

Joan began turning away, but stopped when she saw that O'Mara had remained still and facing the captain. He said, "Sir, there is something I would like you to do, and it isn't a small, shipboard favor."

The captain hesitated. There was too much facial hair for him to read its expression but its eyes had a wary look as it said, "What exactly do you want me to do for you, Lieutenant?"

"For myself, nothing," O'Mara replied. "The favor is for passenger Kledenth. I strongly suspect that its injuries require urgent specialist attention in a same-species hospital. I respectfully request that *Kreskhallar* divert to Kelgia without delay."

"Impossible!" Grulya-Mar burst out. "Our next scheduled world is Melf, where our present Melfan passengers will be leaving us and new ones coming on board. My medical officer has examined Kledenth and reported it to be uninjured and in excellent health."

"It will not remain that way for long," said O'Mara.

"Your request is utterly preposterous," said the other angrily.

"If you mention your suspicions to passenger Kledenth, you will only cause it unnecessary emotional distress. Sennelt is the expert in this field. Or have you medical qualifications that you haven't mentioned to us?"

O'Mara shook his head, then said carefully, "I have no formal medical training, but in my work I've come to know many Kelgians well . . ." *Especially the one who is presently sharing my mind,* he thought dryly, and knew that what he was about to say was the absolute truth. ". . . and have picked up medical information of a kind that is not available to Dr. Sennelt."

"In your work where?" said the other sharply.

"At Sector General," said O'Mara.

There was a moment's silence. He was aware of the captain's organic ship's equipment turning away from their control consoles to look at him. Joan was staring at him, too, looking impressed but puzzled. There were very few sapient beings in the Galactic Federation who were unaware of Sector General and what it stood for, and even the angry bristling of the captain's fur was beginning slowly to subside.

"I see," said Grulya-Mar finally, returning to his pompous, condescending manner. "However, you yourself have admitted that you've no qualifications so that the medical information or hearsay that you have picked up, even in the galaxy's most advanced multi-species hospital, is irrelevant. I will not alter my flight schedule, Lieutenant O'Mara, but I will compromise to this extent. Out of gratitude for the good work you did on the recreation deck, and to relieve the obvious if mistaken concern you feel for this Kelgian passenger, I shall instruct my medical officer to reexamine it in your presence in order to provide you with further reassurance. But only if you yourself can convince Kledenth of the necessity for the reexamination and to accompany you to sickbay."

It raised a large, hairy hand and added, "You have my permission to go."

When they were back in the corridor leading to the passenger section, Joan said, "You're a very reticent man, O'Mara. Why didn't you tell me you were from Sector General? I've got a million questions I want to ask about that place, especially from somebody who knows the answers firsthand, and I'm sure the other passengers feel the same way."

"Maybe that's the reason," he said dryly. "But I'll answer some of your questions while we're finding Kledenth and bringing it back with us to sickbay. If you don't mind, I need you there, too. But persuading it to submit to another examination won't be easy."

"I don't mind," she said. "In fact, I'm looking forward to having a ringside seat at this three-cornered medical battle, because neither Kledenth nor Sennelt will be pleased with you." She smiled suddenly and added, "But don't worry about your powers of persuasion. A multi-species psychologist from Sector General should be able to talk anybody into doing anything."

It took nearly two hours of intense conversation to convince Kledenth to return to the sickbay, and then it did so only because O'Mara had made it afraid again. Where he was concerned its manner was completely hostile, with Joan it was neutral, and toward Sennelt its fur was reflecting a desperate pleading that the doctor would be able to prove beyond a shadow of O'Mara's doubts that it was all right.

As it spoke the Melfan's voice was clinically calm but the pincers that were not engaged in moving the scanner over Kledenth's lower body were clicking angrily.

It said, "As you can see, if you are capable of reading this deep-scan image, the earlier compression effects have cleared and there is no interruption of the blood supply between the hearts, lungs, brain, and the major ambulatory muscles serving the legs and forward manipulators. The areas of subdermal contusion affecting the local capillary and nerve networks that you and, since you talked to it, passenger Kledenth are worried about is minor bruising and transitory. There is no justification for thinking otherwise unless, for some obscure psychological reason, you are trying to justify yourself."

O'Mara took a firm hold on his temper, then reached forward to take an even tighter grip on the scanner, knowing that in a tug-of-war between the Melfan's pincers and his Earth-human hands there would be no contest.

"May I borrow this for a moment," he said, making a verbal pretense at politeness. He ran the scanner slowly over the area of bruising while closely studying the visual display before going on. "The general contusions are disguising the fact that the blood flow in the capillary network that supplies the tiny, individual muscles that control each strand of fur has been reduced. No gross, traumatic damage is apparent, but the stagnant blood is not clearing fast enough and the micromusculature is being slowly starved of nutrients. The condition is so gradual that there are no marked symptoms, and it is quite understandable that a nonspecialist like yourself would miss them. But the condition is irreversible and, if it isn't dealt with urgently, complete necrosis of the muscles controlling the fur is at most a few days off. Doctor, will you look again at the . . . ?"

"No," said Sennelt firmly. "There is nothing new or dangerous to see that would cause me to influence the captain into altering course. And let me remind you, Lieutenant, you are needlessly worrying the patient."

"I am very worried," said Kledenth suddenly. "If I ask, would the captain change course for me?"

"At least you're admitting that it's a patient," said O'Mara angrily, before Sennelt could reply, "which implies that you think there just might be something wrong with it." He turned suddenly to Joan and went on, "Please, you have a look at this area and tell me what you think. I'll focus the scanner for you so you can . . ."

He broke off as the doctor began clicking, loudly and continuously like an overloaded radiation counter. When it spoke its sarcasm was apparent even through their translators. "Does every passenger on this damned ship think it's a medic? Well, given that we are not going to divert to Kelgia, what would you two would-be doctors consider an acceptable second form of treatment?"

Joan, unknown to the Melfan doctor, was far from being a medical ignoramus. Her face was reddening with anger and embarrassment, but before she could protest, O'Mara shook his head warningly at her. In its present mood Sennelt was likely to be even more sarcastic about a newly qualified veterinary surgeon. He strove for calmness and clinical objectivity.

"I would suggest massive bed rest with heavy sedation," he said, "in the hope that the reduced blood supply to the area will be enough to maintain the resting muscles. There should be round-the-clock monitoring and, as the condition worsens to the point where both the patient and medical officer become aware of it, emotional support of a verbal nature will be helpful until . . ."

"I need some of your verbal support right now," sajd Kledenth.

"Enough!" said the doctor. "Frankly, Lieutenant, your behavior in this matter is incredibly insensitive and completely irresponsible. In spite of what you've done for us earlier, I intend to report this to the Monitor Corps authorities at our next port of call. As for your suggested line of treatment, passenger Kledenth may take massive rest here or in its own cabin, or indulge in violent exercise on the recreation deck, as and when it chooses. There will be no medical monitor or massive sedation because in my"—it laid heavy stress on the word—"*professional* opinion they are totally unnecessary. As for emotional support, that it deserves. I strongly suggest that you talk to it while it rests here, for as long as it takes for you to negate the emotional trauma you have caused. And if passenger Kledenth tires of listening to you, which it may well do since this is your sleeping period, it has my permission to return to its cabin and subsequently resume normal passenger activities at any time no matter what you say to it.

"I will leave you now," it ended, "before I use language not befitting a ship's officer."

The sickbay door hissed shut behind it and the clicking sound of its feet diminished as it moved down the corridor. Joan looked at Kledenth's agitated fur and then at its face.

"I'm sorry," she said. "All I can do is talk to you, but I won't know what to say because I don't know what I'm talking about. Lieutenant, as an other-species psychologist can you think of anything appropriate to say or do?"

O'Mara was walking quickly around the room, staring through transparent doors into the medicine and instrument cabinets. A few of them were locked, but the fastenings were less than robust and were easy to force open. He didn't answer until he had rejoined them.

"I have a lot to say and more to do," he replied briskly, "but I'll need the agreement and help of both of you. First I want you to pay close attention to what I'm saying, and while I'm talking I want you"—he looked intently at Joan—"to run that scanner over the affected area so I can explain what you will be seeing. . . ."

O'Mara described a condition that was encountered rarely among Kelgians, and then usually in the very young, and a procedure to relieve it that was simple, radical, and not without risk. The alternative to not having the operation was progressive and irreversible paralysis of the medial body fur. It was his own voice he was using, but the calm authority and certainty of his manner was based on the specialist knowledge and clinical experience of the donor of his mind tape. As he finished his step-by-step description of the indicated procedure, he knew from the way Kledenth's fur was reacting and Joan was looking at him that there was a yawning credibility gap opening between them. Even before she spoke he knew that he would have to end by telling them the truth. All of it.

"Lieutenant," she said, "you certainly sound as if you know what you're talking about, but *how* do you know? This, as I've told you before, isn't the kind of stuff you picked up in a first-aid lecture."

"You don't know what this means, O'Mara," Kledenth said, its fur rising in stiff, agitated spikes, "because you are not a Kelgian."

"Believe me, I do know," said O'Mara. He took a few seconds to remind himself of how stupid he was being, because if either of them told anyone else of what he was about to say and do, he would be out of Sector General and the Monitor Corps within days and probably find himself sentenced to an indefinite stay in one of the Federation's psychiatric-adjustment facilities. But that was a risk that neither he nor his mind partner considered important compared with the fate that might lie ahead for Kledenth. He took a deep breath and began to speak.

He told them briefly about his work in Sector General and, without mentioning Thornnastor or the tape donor by name, the psychological investigation that had led to him impressing himself with the Marrasarah tape, which, although it was completely against regulations, he still carried. The memory-transfer technique was not widely known, he explained, because single-species, planet-based hospitals had no interest in it unless one of their senior staff became so eminent in the field that it was invited by the Galactic Medical Council to be a mind donor.

". . . It is the complete memories and experience of just such a person that I carry in my mind now," O'Mara went on. "In its time it was reputed to be the most able specialist in thoracic surgery on Kelgia. That is why you have to trust and accept everything I tell you."

Joan was staring at him intently, her expression reflecting a strange mixture of wonder, excitement, and concern, while Kledenth's fur was a mass of silvery spikes. It was the Kelgian who spoke first.

"So your mind is partly Kelgian," it said. "I wondered why you talked straight like one of us. But if half my fur is going to lose mobility like you say, what are *you* going to do about it?"

Without replying, O'Mara turned away and walked quickly to the medicine cabinets, where he began filling a tray with the instruments, anesthetic, and medication that would be required. He himself had no idea of what he was doing, but his mind partner knew exactly what was needed. The instruments were designed for Sennelt's use, but Earth-human digits were acknowledged to be the most adaptable and efficient manipulatory appendages in the Federation.

"Oh, God," said Joan in a frightened voice when he returned with the filled tray, "he's, he's going to operate on you."

O'Mara shook his head firmly. He held out his hands to her at waist level. and rotated them slowly to show the thick, blunt fingers and the palms which, in spite of his recent elevation to the status of officer and gentleman, still bore the calluses of his years in space construction.

"These are not the hands of a surgeon . . ." he said.

He bent forward quickly, took her hands gently but firmly in his, and lifted them up. They lay cupped in his roughened palms, slender, beautiful, and strong, as if fashioned in warm and living porcelain.

". . . but these are."

She shook her head, looking suddenly frightened, but she didn't pull her hands away. He gave them a reassuring squeeze.

"Please listen to me," he said, "because I'm being very serious. You are used to operating on small life-forms, which means that at times the procedure requires fine work in a severely restricted operative field. The fact that your patients are nonsapient is irrelevant. You now understand the clinical problem and the necessity for immediate surgery if Kledenth is not to be condemned to a future that, for any Kelgian, is too terrible to contemplate. The procedure, although considered radical, is fairly straightforward. You have the necessary surgical skills and I shall be guiding your hands at every stage. Please."

"Yes, Earth-person Joan," said Kledenth, "please do it."

He was beginning to realize that her hands, like the rest of her well-formed body, were really beautiful. Even when she was being subjected to the present severe emotional stress, they weren't shaking a bit.

# CHAPTER 24

O'Mara sat as comfortably as it was possible to be in Sennelt's Melfan chair, watching the tiny dream-stirrings of Kledenth's fur as it slept off the anesthetic while he tried to calculate the exact amount of trouble he could expect. But of one thing he was sure: the trouble would involve himself and nobody else.

Before Joan, at his insistence, had returned to her cabin to get some sleep before breakfast, which was only three hours away, they had come to an agreement about the operation. She had performed it, her technique had been flawless, and the prognosis was favorable, but so far as outsiders were concerned she had not even been there. It was O'Mara who had done all the work, would bear the entire responsibility for and take all the blame or, if there was any, the credit for what could be regarded as an irresponsible and unlawful surgical assault on a defenseless patient. The patient, who was incapable of telling a lie, had promised to exercise the Kelgian option of saying nothing at all to anyone about the incident.

No matter what happened to himself, O'Mara was pleased that the not so innocent bystander would not be involved even though he, personally, was beginning to wish that he could be closely involved with her. He sighed, checked the audible warning on the monitors they had attached to Kledenth, then wriggled into a less uncomfortable position on the Melfan chair and tried to sleep.

But the inside of his closed eyelids were slowly becoming a three-dimensional viewscreen displaying pictures of Joan. He watched again the delicate precision of her technique as she worked on Kledenth, and saw her as she pointed out the scenery and talked animatedly about the beauties of the Dunelton Gorge, and in formal dress at dinner. But mostly the pictures, bright and sharp and tactile, were of her teaching him to swim in the pool. Some of the things she was saying and doing were not as he remembered them, and as a psychologist he could recognize the beginning of a wish-fulfillment dream when he saw one. But before it could end as all such dreams end, he was awakened by the steady clicking of Melfan feet moving along the corridor.

Sennelt entered and stopped as if surprised to see anyone there. Then it hurried across the room to the sleeping Kledenth and saw the dressing that was covering the operation site. It looked at O'Mara for a moment and used words that his translator refused to accept, then jabbed keys on the room's communicator.

"Captain," it said urgently. "Medical emergency in sickbay. I need you here at once. Lieutenant O'Mara is involved. Bring security backup."

Grulya-Mar arrived within three minutes, accompanied by two security officers who, like itself, were large, muscular, and unarmed Orligians. They watched O'Mara intently without moving or speaking, which wasn't surprising because Dr. Sennelt was plying its scanner and doing all the talking and beginning to repeat itself.

". . . As I said, sir," it went on without looking up from the scanner, "this could be a very serious, perhaps even a tragic situation. Lieutenant O'Mara, unlawfully and on its own initiative, has performed an operation on passenger Kledenth. I don't know what exactly it has done or was trying to do, but the surgical procedure was invasive. My knowledge of Kelgian physiology is minimal, normally I only have to contend with other-species minor accidents and abrasions, but in this case serious and potentially lethal damage could have been done. A nonmedic performing surgery, even if it talked the passenger into giving its permission, doesn't bear thinking about. . . ."

"Your recommendations, Doctor?" the captain broke in.

Sennelt put down its scanner and said, "The patient should remain in deep sedation so as to reduce the body movements which might otherwise cause adverse postoperative effects. Continuous round-the-clock monitoring should be maintained until specialist treatment is available in an own-species hospital. That means, sir, in the best interests of passenger Kledenth you must divert to Kelgia with minimum delay."

Grulya-Mar hesitated for less than three seconds before it moved quickly to the communicator. The screen lit up with the head and shoulders of a Nidian.

"Astrogation," it said.

"Recompute and lay in a course for Kelgia," said the captain. "Do it now. Off."

Grulya-Mar turned then to join the others in staring silently at O'Mara, who stared back at them for as long as he could before breaking the silence.

"Sedation, massive rest, and specialist attention on its home planet," he said quietly, "was all I wanted you to do for it in the first place. I'm pleased that Dr. Sennelt agrees with me."

The medic didn't respond. Its pincers were snapping open and closed while its entire body quivered as if it was about to have some kind of fit. O'Mara wondered what the lead-up to a cardiovascular incident would look like in an exoskeletal life-form whose face could never change color. He turned his attention to the two Orligian security officers and added, "Now what?"

Like Grulya-Mar, they were large, heavily built, and at least ten inches taller than he was. He knew that he could take one of them and almost certainly both, because space construction was a tough school and he had had barefisted disputes with members of their species many times. But if the captain joined in as well, all four of them would be sharing the sickbay with Kledenth.

A fight like that could never be concealed from the passengers or Grulya-Mar's superiors. Their star-tour operation would suffer, and so would the professional futures of the officers concerned. Besides, when Major Craythorne got to hear about it he would certainly not be pleased. O'Mara wasn't pleased at the thought himself, because he had hoped that the bad old days of gaining respect solely by the use of his fists were long gone. But he was feeling bad over the trouble he was in, and even though he and his mind partner had had no choice but to operate on Kledenth, he hoped these hairy heavies wouldn't push him too far. Similar thoughts must have been going through Grulya-Mar's mind.

"Since you cannot leave the ship," it said in a voice of quiet fury, "and even though your mental stability may be in question, I see no reason why you should be forcibly restrained. At the same time it is in both our interests that the Kledenth incident be kept from the other passengers until we reach Kelgia and the full extent of the damage you have done is assessed by their medical authorities, after which you will leave my ship to await the indicated legal proceedings and disciplinary measures that will be taken by your superiors. Until that time you will confine yourself to your cabin and make no further use of the recreation-deck facilities or dining room. Is this agreeable to you?"

"Yes," he said.

While the captain had been talking, the two security officers had been edging closer in the expectation of imminent violence. They relaxed visibly and backed away again, leaving him a clear path to the door.

"Please leave now," said Grulya-Mar.

O'Mara nodded, but paused when he was halfway to the entrance.

"May I be allowed communicator contact with sickbay," he said, "so that I can check on the progress of the patient?"

The captain gave an untranslatable growl and the hair bristled all over its body, but it was Sennelt, who was plainly anxious to maintain the peace, who replied.

"You may contact me here at any time, Lieutenant," it said, then added with heavy sarcasm, "although I will not promise to take your medical advice regarding the patient's treatment."

He was in his cabin only a few minutes when a Nidian steward arrived to leave a breakfast tray, explaining that it contained the type and amount of Earth-human food that O'Mara usually consumed, but if he wanted something different to eat in future or if there were any card or board games or puzzles that might help him to pass the time, the lieutenant had only to ask. Plainly, he thought wryly, the captain was doing all it could to keep the ship's madman pacified. But the characteristic heavy breathing and snuffling sounds from outside the door told him that Orligian security guards had been posted outside his door. He shifted the contents of the tray without really tasting it, then threw himself onto his bunk to think dark thoughts about his uncertain and probably unhappy future.

It was about an hour later that a quiet knocking on the door brought his mind back to the here and now. Thinking it was the steward returning for the breakfast tray he growled, "Come in."

It was Joan.

She was wearing an incredibly abbreviated white swimsuit and sandals with the incandescently patterned towel she had bought on Traltha draped around her shoulders. He began swinging his feet to the floor, but she moved forward quickly, placed a small, firm hand on his chest, and pushed him back into his bunk.

"Stay there," she said. "You didn't get any sleep last night, remember. How is our patient and, more important, how are you?"

"I don't know," said O'Mara, "twice."

She gave a small frown of concern, turned away, and sat down in the only chair. The cabin was so small that she was still disturbingly close.

"Seriously," she said, "what is going to happen to you as a result of this Kledenth business? Will it be bad?"

O'Mara tried to smile. "Same answer," he said.

She continued staring at him, her expression reflecting puzzlement and concern. For the first time since he had come aboard over two weeks earlier, she wasn't actively trying to attract him, and for some strange reason that was making the attraction stronger. He wanted to look away from her steady, brown eyes, but he could not look anywhere else without feeling even more disturbed and possibly giving offense.

"All right," he said finally. "Depending on whether or not Kledenth's op was successful, and in diminishing order of importance, I could be kicked out of the Monitor Corps, I could be prosecuted for pretending to be a doctor, sent for psychological reconstruction because I believed I was a doctor." He forced a laugh. "Or maybe all three at once."

She shook her head. "I don't understand you, O'Mara," she said. "You're throwing your whole career away because of a Kelgian you thought was sick."

"No," he corrected her quietly. "I *knew* it was sick."

"So you knew or thought you knew or maybe firmly believed that it was sick," she continued, "enough to talk me into operating on it. I still don't believe I did that. It was something I've always dreamed of doing, of using my skill to save the life, not of someone's pet but of a fully sapient being. I've no wish to repeat the experience, it carries too much responsibility, but you talked me through it. I think it was successful because you guided my hands at every stage and you seemed to know what had to be done. But *I* did it, not you, and it's not fair that you should take all the blame when you didn't even lay a bloody knife on the patient!"

"You did the real work," he said, "all of it with your own hands. They are very nice hands, sensitive, precise, lovely hands that did what they had to once you knew what that was. But as I said before, you will take none of the credit, now or ever, or you'll be in worse trouble with the medical authorities than I am, and you must take none of the blame, either. Kledenth owes you an awful lot for saving its fur, but it has promised not to mention the op to anyone, on the ship or at home, and I've told it not to thank you verbally in case it is overheard and you land in trouble, too. Talking about it won't help either of us, so you won't be able to tell anyone, ever, unless possibly your grandchildren."

"I can live with that," she said, "but there must be something I can do." She looked down at her hands suddenly and smiled. "Do you realize that is the first compliment you've ever paid me, and then it was only to my hands. Isn't there anything else nice about me that you can compliment?"

O'Mara kept his eyes firmly on her face so as to avoid staring at the other nice things about her, but he couldn't do anything about his peripheral vision. Neither could he trust himself to speak.

"A gentleman would invent a few," she said. Apparently changing the subject, she went on, "When you didn't show at breakfast I came to see how you were, and to ask if you wanted to go to the pool. As an amateur, one-species psychologist I wanted to take your mind off your troubles and generally help you to relax. But that pair of grizzly bears outside said you were confined to quarters. I asked again nicely and tried very hard to make them change their minds . . ." She smiled and shook her head. ". . . but I guess I'm just not their type."

"That much is true," said O'Mara, laughing in spite of himself. "But after yesterday I didn't think I needed any more swimming lessons. You taught me very well, and the way you handled that Tralthan resuscitation was first-class."

"Two more compliments," she said in mock disbelief. "O'Mara, I'll make a gentleman of you yet. But there's something else I've wanted to show you for several days now. We won't need the pool."

She stood up slowly and dropped her towel onto the chair before she moved to the edge of his bunk to bend over him. It was no longer possible to look only at her eyes and, he thought, in that swimsuit there wasn't very much more that she could show him. He pushed himself up onto his elbows so that her nose bumped gently against his forehead. Her fingers brushed like warm feathers along the bristles at the side of his unshaven face and jaw; then they moved gently to the back of his neck. Her eyes were only a few inches from his. He felt her breath on his face as she spoke quietly.

"Just relax," she said seriously. "For this lesson I'll begin by demonstrating a little same-species mouth-to-mouth."

The demonstrations with many variations continued at every possible opportunity until *Kreskhallar* landed at Kelgia's main spaceport. During those three days they didn't even mention their worries about Kledenth to each other, and O'Mara, although he could not be completely honest with her, felt more relaxed and happier than he had ever remembered being in his entire life and, Joan told him several times, so did she. Their worries surfaced again as they stood at the cabin's viewpoint staring down at the tiny shape of the ambulance that was taking Kledenth to hospital, but another four hours passed before the communicator lit to show the bony features of Dr. Sennelt.

"Lieutenant O'Mara," it said, "please come to the captain's cabin at once. Your security guard will escort you there."

"I want to go with you," said Joan pleadingly. "I won't say anything or take any of the blame but, but I want to know right away what they're going to do to you. O'Mara, please."

He looked at her steadily for a moment, then he nodded and followed her into the corridor. The guards made no comment about Joan accompanying him to the captain's large, well-appointed cabin, and O'Mara spoke before Grulya-Mar had a chance to object to her presence.

"As you know, sir," he said quickly, nodding toward Joan, "this passenger's help was invaluable during the swimming-pool incident, and I have kept her fully informed about the subsequent developments. Be assured, that information and anything else you tell me now will not be discussed beyond this room. What have you to say to me, Captain?"

Grulya-Mar nodded at Joan before returning its full attention to O'Mara, but for a long moment it said nothing. Joan, who was looking increasingly apprehensive as the seconds dragged past, gripped his arm tightly. Finally the captain made the disgusting, guttural sound that Orligians make when clearing the throat.

"I must begin by apologizing," said Grulya-Mar. "We have just received a signal from the hospital saying that the operation you performed on passenger Kledenth was radical—it has been done only a few times in their recorded medical history—impressive, and most of all, timely. Had it not been performed within a few hours of the compression injury being sustained, they say, Kledenth would have lost fur mobility and been disfigured for life. Against the doctor's medical advice and my opposition you insisted that you knew best, and you did, because we have been assured that the patient is well and, barring future accidents, will continue so for the indefinite future. Dr. Sennelt and I apologize for misjudging you, and we thank you again for the good work done by both of you on the recreation deck . . ."

Joan was smiling broadly. Her grip on his arm tightened, in relief now instead of apprehension.

". . . but we are faced with a problem," the captain went on, "because the Kelgian doctors wish to thank you officially for . . ."

"No," said O'Mara firmly. "If it came out that an unqualified nonmedic who happens to have a good memory for clinical detail had done the work, I would be in serious trouble. You know that. May I make a suggestion?"

"Please do," said the captain.

O'Mara looked apologetically at Joan, who nodded happily at him before he went on, "Officially I am a passenger who took no part in this. The only medically qualified person on the ship is Dr. Sennelt. Let it take the credit. The Kelgians would find that much easier to believe than the truth."

"But I don't deserve . . ." the doctor began. Grulya-Mar cut it off with a raised hand.

"Thank you, Lieutenant O'Mara," said the captain. "That solution satisfies everyone's needs. As this was an unscheduled stop for a medical emergency, we will leave again within the hour and so avoid the possibility of the Kelgians wanting to meet and ask embarrassing clinical questions that my medical officer is not equipped to answer. When we return for our scheduled stopover in ten days' time it will be old news, but if they still want to meet Dr. Sennelt it will be regrettably confined to its quarters with an incapacitating and non-life-threatening condition that precludes its having visitors. The secret of what happened here will be kept because it is in everyone concerned's best interest to do so. But there is another matter, Lieutenant.

"I realize that I sound ungrateful," the captain went on, "but in addition to the possibility of you talking about this matter to your friend at the wrong time and perhaps being overheard, your continued presence on this ship would be a constant reminder and an embarrassment to my medical officer and myself. A few minutes ago we received a signal from passenger Kledenth's family inviting you to stay with them whenever you are on Kelgia. They say that they owe both of you an obligation beyond discharge. You just have time to pack your personal belongings and leave before *Kreskhallar* takes off. O'Mara, I do not want to see or speak to you again."

O'Mara felt Joan's grip tighten on his arm again, and he spoke quickly to head off her impending eruption. He looked steadily at the two officers and said, "You *are* being ungrateful, but no matter. My leave is nearing its end and I plan to do a little traveling on Kel-

gia for a few days before returning to Sector General. I will not see
or talk to you again, either, which will be a considerable negative
pleasure. I'll leave you, now."

Joan's farewell at the mouth of the boarding tube was warm
and sad but not tearful. She didn't offer to stay with him during his
final few days on Kelgia, because she had to resume her own life
when the ship put in to Earth. But her arms were wrapped tightly
around his waist and she didn't seem able to let go. Neither did she
seem able to stop talking.

"...I don't know what I expected on this voyage," she was saying, "except to meet a lot of extraterrestrials and talk about their legends and, if I was really lucky, meet somebody interesting of my
own species. Well, I did all those things, and more that I wouldn't
have believed possible for me. It feels as if we created a legend of our
very own. I'll never forget this. Or you."

Two Nidian crew members were waiting nearby, impatient to
remove the boarding tube. He detached her arms gently and said,
"Nor I you. But I have to go."

Reluctantly she stood back and looked up into his face. Her expression very serious, she said, "You are a strange person, O'Mara,
a big, strong, ugly, caring, and, and a very gentle man that I would
like to know better. There will be other leaves, and you know
where I live. Or maybe Kledenth's people will let us meet halfway
on Kelgia."

She stood on her toes and kissed him briefly but with feeling,
and added, "As I remember it, I'm good at meeting you halfway."

On his return to Sector General he reported at once to the department. Major Craythorne looked up and smiled as O'Mara entered
the chief psychologist's office. He regarded O'Mara's face intently
for a moment.

"You look well," he said, "relaxed and rested. How did you
spend your leave?"

"I traveled a lot," O'Mara replied seriously, "did some sight-seeing, visited with a friend, had a whirlwind shipboard romance. You know, the usual kind of thing."

Craythorne raised his eyebrows, then laughed quietly.

"And you seem to have found a sense of humor too," he said. "For the next job I have for you, you'll need it."

# CHAPTER 25

Over the next twelve years O'Mara settled into the abnormal routine that was considered normal for a member of the Other-Species Psychology Department. The early operational problems of the hospital had been solved; the medical and maintenance staff, regardless of species, had learned and accepted each other's alien ways and were living together in often noisy accord. He was allowed to work with little or no supervision because, as Craythorne was fond of telling him, it was better for the major's peace of mind to simply point him at a problem and take his report on its final resolution without having to worry himself sick about the unorthodox things O'Mara did in between. In that time he took many periods of leave as soon as they became due, traveling to wherever the available transport took him but always ending up on the same destination planet. His chief didn't ask how he spent his leaves because, from the observed beneficial psychological results, Craythorne thought he knew. But on his return from his most recent one, O'Mara thought Craythorne looked almost ill at ease, which was strange behavior indeed for the major.

"Sit down, Lieutenant," Craythorne said in the manner of one who is working around to a subject gradually. "During your absence the department managed to function without you but, needless to say, I'm very glad to have you back."

"Sir," said O'Mara, "are you trying to find a gentle way of telling me some bad news?"

"Remind me never to play poker with you, Lieutenant," said Craythorne with a smile that looked disquietingly sympathetic. "The news is good and bad, depending on our points of view. I'm leaving the hospital."

O'Mara didn't speak and he tried not to think until he had enough information to know what to think about.

"In many ways I'm reluctant to go," Craythorne went on, "but in the Corps one goes where one is told. Besides, it will mean a significant promotion for me in that it involves my taking complete responsibility for the psychological assessment of other-species recruits from the whole of Sector Ten. I could be a full fleet commander, administrative of course, in three years."

"Congratulations," said O'Mara, meaning it but waiting for the bad news.

"Thank you," said Craythorne. After a moment he went on, "We both know that the work of the department cannot be done effectively by Padre Carmody and yourself, so a new Earth-human psychologist called Braithwaite will be joining the staff. I've seen his psych file and had no hesitation about giving him the position. Admittedly he is a little green where other-species therapy is concerned, his personality is pleasant if a little serious, he is intelligent, adaptable, enthusiastic about the job, and, like myself . . ." He smiled. ". . . very well-mannered and impeccable regarding his uniform. I'm sure you'll be comfortable with him and will soon be able to show him the ropes and settle him in very quickly."

"I understand," said O'Mara stiffly.

The major smiled again and said, "What exactly do you think you understand?"

"I understand that I am to wet-nurse a keen young career officer until he is in a position to give me and everyone else orders in such a way that he sounds as if he knows what he's talking about. Sir."

"And you wouldn't feel comfortable," said Craythorne, "in the role of a stern but kindly father figure? Frankly, O'Mara, neither would I, but that is what you'll have to do. But that isn't all I want you to do."

"First," Craythorne went on, "a staff of three psychologists—and I'm including the padre because in many respects he is a more effective hands-on psychologist than either of us—are barely enough to operate this department. But that is all we're allowed right now and that is why, in addition to dealing with the work piled on your desk in the outer office, you and the padre must bring the new man up to speed as quickly as possible. Before I leave, I'd also like you to learn to wear your uniform, if not with pride, then at least as if you hadn't thrown it on as an afterthought. And while you're doing that, I'd like you to lose that habit of speaking with almost Kelgian honesty in your conversations with members of the senior medical staff, because I won't be here to apologize for you or act as a diplomatic buffer. So, just to keep me from worrying myself sick about you when I'm in far-off Sector Ten, will you do that?"

"I'll try, sir," said O'Mara in a voice totally lacking in self-certainty.

"Good," said Craythorne. "Until I leave, in three days' time, I'll be too busy tying up administrative loose ends and saying good-bye to our colleagues and, at times, past patients to spend much time helping you in the department." He grinned suddenly. "Meanwhile I want you to move your paperwork in here and start using my desk. The sooner people get used to the idea that you are the new chief psychologist the better. Your mouth is open."

O'Mara closed it without speaking. He was too surprised and pleased to have anything to say.

Craythorne stood up, leaned across his desk, shook his hand

firmly, and said, "I know how you hate these embarrassing formalities, but this is probably the last chance I'll have to tell you exactly what I think of you, which is a lot. My warmest congratulations, O'Mara. The promotion is well deserved and, when the Corps submitted a list of several other possible candidates, the hospital's seniors would accept nobody but you. . . ."

He walked around his desk, still shaking O'Mara's hand and letting go of it only to point at his vacant chair.

"Sit down," he ended, "while it's still warm."

The biggest problem during the first few weeks following Major Craythorne's departure and the installation of Lieutenant Braithwaite was remembering that he was supposed to sit in that chair instead of being sent all over the hospital to talk to and assess troubled staff members who just might become the department's patients. Now Lieutenant O'Mara wasn't sent to deal with them because, unless they were biting their tails or otherwise throwing emotional fits all over their wards, they had to make appointments to see the newly promoted Major O'Mara. A large part of the problem was convincing himself that he was now Sector General's chief psychologist and acting the part because he just could not learn, never in a thousand years, to behave like his predecessor.

O'Mara had tried very hard. He had forced himself to smile at people more often, a strange and uncomfortable process for facial muscles unused to that form of exercise, and he felt sure that anyone capable of reading his expression would think that he was projecting the worst kind of insincerity, that of trying to act like the diplomat he most definitely was not, or that he was unsure of himself, unhappy with his new responsibility, or, worst of all, that he was unable to do his job. That was not so. He was fully capable of doing the job, provided he could do it his own way.

Trying to say one thing while meaning another had never come easy to him, and with the totally open and honest personality of Marrasarah sharing his mind, diplomacy was next to impossible. The people in the hospital, regardless of their species, social graces, or the kind of personal feelings they held toward him, would have to be told that. Fortunately, O'Mara thought as he summoned his staff to the inner office, he no longer had to tell them in person.

He looked up at them through lowered brows as they filed in to stand in front of his desk, the frail, old, and gentle Padre Lioren and the eager, fresh-faced, and impeccably uniformed Braithwaite, who constantly reminded O'Mara of his former chief except that the lieutenant had more and darker hair. Presumably their consciences were clear, because neither of them looked ill at ease, just warily expectant. In Other-Species Psychology one learned to expect the worst.

"Relax," he said, "I am about to impart information, not add to your workload. And stand. You won't be here long enough to warrant the expenditure of energy sitting down and getting up again."

He placed his hard, callused hands flat on the desk for a moment before looking up, then went on, "As a person my predecessor, Major Craythorne, was known throughout the hospital as a kind, gentle, and very approachable man. I am none of those things. For the past few weeks since he left us I have been trying to emulate him and, judging by the reactions I had to this new, soft-spoken, and polite O'Mara, totally without success. So I've decided to stop trying.

"I shall, of course," he went on, "continue to treat my share of the patients, or rather the emotionally distressed doctors, nurses, and maintenance personnel who may become our patients, as and when necessary. These cases I shall handle with the degree of sensitivity and expertise required. I am, as you know, very good at this job. But I shall not, repeat not, try to be nice to people, regardless of their species or rank, unless I consider their particular condition warrants a soft approach. The old, nasty O'Mara is back. Is that understood?"

The padre nodded and said, "Good." Braithwaite's nod was more hesitant. As the new boy he hadn't had the opportunity of meeting the old, nasty O'Mara and was worrying about what the future might hold.

"Since I have the rank," he went on, "it seems a pity not to abuse it. My behavior toward patients will be as their conditions warrant. With the medical and maintenance staff, my friends if any, working colleagues, and those others I consider to be mentally healthy or at least quasi-normal, I reserve the right to relax and be my nasty, sarcastic, infuriating self.

"I know how much work you have out there waiting for attention," he added. "Standing there gaping at me isn't getting it done."

As they were leaving, O'Mara overheard the padre saying softly, "Relax, Lieutenant, he thinks we're quasi-normal. Don't you know a professional compliment when you hear one?"

O'Mara continued paying the same form of professional compliment and, thanks to the padre and Braithwaite talking freely about their chief, the people with whom he came into contact became more relaxed and even pleased in inverse proportion to his degree of nastiness. His subordinates had done a good job of convincing everyone that, psychologically speaking, black was white. Only the seriously distressed personnel got as far as his inner office, his staff were fond of telling each other when he was within earshot, because the less troubled people preferred to trust themselves to the friendlier padre or Braithwaite—if they didn't have second thoughts and decide to solve their problems themselves. Which was fine by O'Mara, because he had always held that in the long term self-help was the best kind.

As the weeks and months passed into years, O'Mara grew accustomed to his new rank, mostly by completely ignoring it and treating the higher and lower ranks as if they were the same. He saved the increased salary and duly took all of the leave to which a major was entitled, although sometimes he returned saddened and angry rather than relaxed. But Iron Man O'Mara, as rumor had it, was capable of suffering nothing less than metal fatigue, so he was not supposed to have emotional problems. If anyone out of polite curiosity asked where he had been or whether or not he had enjoyed himself there, he told them nothing in such a way that they never asked him again.

But there were times when he could not be impolite even with those people he admired and thought of as the closest thing he had to friends. Thornnastor—who had been appointed diagnostician-in-charge of Pathology, although it preferred to keep its subjects alive and advise on their cure rather than dissect them post-mortem—had many problems. They were not its own because, in spite of its mind carrying six different other-species Educator tapes, it was the most intelligent and emotionally stable entity in the hospital. But it had to discuss the emotional upsets, interstaff conflicts, and possible xenophobic reactions within its department's widening sphere of influence, as well as requesting psychiatric support with patients whose conditions included a psychological component. And there was Senior Tutor Mannen (whose other-species students insisted that he and his dog had a symbiotic relationship), who worried continually about the mental health and professional future of his charges. Mannen was especially concerned, as was O'Mara himself, about a male and a female Earth-human, both of whom were exemplary students with bright futures in other-species medicine ahead of them. It was small consolation that the trouble they might cause themselves, their colleagues, and the succession of less brilliant superiors they would encounter on their climb to medical eminence would not be their own fault.

Mannen did not want him to tinker with two such strong, healthy, and well-integrated minds even if he'd had the right to do so, and when, at the senior tutor's insistence, O'Mara interviewed them in depth, neither did he. Some personalities were better left as they were. But the situation with them would have to be closely monitored and, indirectly, controlled.

He had few ethical qualms about exerting influence of a nonpsychological type on them through the deliberate manipulation of their duty schedules. It was, after all, for their own good.

With the best will in the world—and he would admit only to himself that he liked and admired both of them very much—he would have to see to it that for the time being trainees Murchison and Conway were kept apart.

# CHAPTER 26

**M**urchison had created a precedent and delighted Senior Tutor Mannen by being appointed charge nurse of Ward Thirty-Nine, the mixed Melfan, Kelgian, and Nidian surgical recovery unit, immediately upon graduation from trainee status. There she asked nothing of her nursing staff that she wasn't able and willing to do herself, and she led her team politely, firmly, and with absolute fairness from in front. On O'Mara's recommendation, delivered via Mannen, she was given increased responsibility for certain problem patients who were not responding to orthodox lines of treatment. As a result, her ability to observe, analyze, synthesize, and diagnose from the often sparse available data brought her work, as O'Mara knew it would, to the attention of Thornnastor, who said that she was performing original work of a quality not expected of a member of the nursing staff and, if she was willing, her talents could be more gainfully employed in its own department as a junior pathologist. Murchison, as her psych file said she would, was happy to transfer up and across the ladder of promotion, because original xenobiological research was the kind of work she had always wanted to do.

She allowed herself no distractions because, she had told Mannen pleasantly but firmly, she had no time to waste on socializing with its risk of her becoming emotionally involved with a male member of her species. This complete dedication to her career pleased the senior tutor very much, but not her Earth-human male colleagues, who were fond of admitting to everyone including O'Mara that, so far as they were concerned, she was the only person in the hospital that they found impossible to regard with anything resembling clinical detachment. Every one of them had attempted vainly to conquer and exploit what they considered to be one of the hospital's most desirable natural resources, only to be rejected firmly and with such good humor that their feelings of desire never turned to dislike.

But unrequited love, as O'Mara knew from long experience, was rarely a life- or sanity-threatening condition.

The younger Conway, he remembered, had been the only Earth-human male on the junior staff who had not shown, or had done a good job of concealing, his feelings for her during the first few occasions when they made professional contact. It wasn't that he was antisocial, anything but; it was simply that he honestly preferred making friends with other-species staff. He had told O'Mara during the initial interview that his life's ambition was to practice medicine in a multi-species hospital, he had succeeded in gaining entry to the biggest and best in the galaxy, and a serious romantic relationship would be an unwanted distraction from his studies. Normally an Earth-human person who preferred socializing with Tralthans, Melfans, and the other even more alien patients and staff members would have been a matter for psychiatric concern, but in Sector General such an abnormality was a distinct advantage.

The psych profiles of Murchison and young Conway, he remembered, had been so alike that if the old adage about opposites attracting and likes repelling had held true they should never have become an item. But O'Mara had taken such a fatherly interest in them fulfilling their future potential that he had shamelessly tinkered, not with their minds, but with their single and later their joint work assignments. He had been deliberately hard on them by forcing them to make clinical adaptations and decisions and to take responsibility far above their nominal rank. And what he hadn't done to them fate had—in the shape of the Etlan War and a succession of combined rescue and first-contact missions on the special ambulance ship *Rhabwar*—testing them not quite to destruction until they were really good, separately and together. At all times he had remained as sarcastic and nasty toward them as ever. But he wondered if they would ever realize how much he liked them as people and how intensely proud he was of the fact that Murchison, still so maturely beautiful that Earth-human males looked after her when she passed, was now in line to succeed Thornnastor as head of Pathology, while the brilliant young Conway, no longer quite so young, was the diagnostician-in-charge of Other-Species Surgery, and that he felt especially pleased that they were now life-mates.

With the exception of two other beings, one of whom would never visit Sector General in person and the other of whom would not talk to anyone other than himself about it, O'Mara was able to conceal those feelings. He shook his head abruptly in self-irritation at his increasing tendency to spend so much of his mental life in the past, looked at his watch, and prepared once again to have all his feelings read like an open book.

When Senior Physician Prilicla entered the office a few moments later, O'Mara pointed at the item of furniture resembling a surrealistic wastepaper basket, which the Cinrusskin empath found most comfortable, then said gruffly, "Well, little friend, how am I feeling?"

Prilicla made a musical trilling sound that did not translate because it was the Cinrusskin's equivalent of laughter, and said, "You know your feelings, friend O'Mara, as do I, so there isn't much sense in either of us listing them aloud. I assume the question is partly rhetorical. The other part may have something to do with your feelings of general anxiety coupled with the emotional tension characteristic of a mind that is about to make a suggestion that may not be well received. I'm an empath, remember, not a telepath."

"Sometimes I wonder about that," said O'Mara quietly.

"Observation and deduction," it went on, "even without the ability to read emotions, can amount to the same thing, as you would know if you played poker. I know what you feel, not what you think, so if you are forcing yourself to impart bad news, you'll have to tell me exactly what you are thinking."

O'Mara sighed. "You are a psychiatrist's psychiatrist," he said, "in addition to everything else."

For a moment the other's fragile, insectile body trembled in response to his emotional radiation, but it waited in silence for him to speak. O'Mara lengthened the silence while he tried to choose the right words to break it.

"Little friend," he said finally, "I intended the purpose of this meeting to be a discussion of possibilities and a request for help rather than to give you another work assignment. You may know that my time at Sector General is limited, and that I will be leaving as soon as I have chosen and installed my successor, who will be both the hospital's administrator and its chief psychologist. The choice will be difficult."

Prilicla opened its iridescent wings and shook them out before refolding them tightly against its body again. It remained silent.

He went on, "All of the people I have in mind, the outsider as well as those already on the staff, are good. I could leave now knowing that any of them would do an adequate job. But I want to know more than my own insight and experience can tell me about the successful applicant's inner feelings. Frankly, I feel possessive. For a very long time the psychological health of this place has been my baby, the only one I have, or will ever have, and I don't want to hand it over to a parent who is merely adequate. That's why I feel it necessary, if you agree, that you monitor the feelings of all the applicants and report them to me so as to guide me in my final choice."

"I know your feelings, friend O'Mara, and those of every other source of emotional radiation whether it is large and strong, simple, complex, weak, or even nonsapient. They cannot be concealed from me, but that doesn't mean that I will impart them to a third party if the ethic governing privileged information is involved; otherwise I will be pleased to advise you. But you rarely take advice. Since I detected the presence of your Kelgian mind partner and you reluctantly confided the details to me, my advice has been that its continued occupancy of your mind has caused you as much emotional disruption as contentment over the years and that you should have it erased. I feel its presence still affecting you."

"It is," said O'Mara, "but we both know that the Marrasarah business is not the strongest feeling in my mind, and that you are trying to change the subject."

"Naturally," said Prilicla, its body trembling slightly, "because I feel you nerving yourself to say something that you believe I will find unpleasant. Be direct like your Kelgian mind partner and tell me what it is."

"Right," said O'Mara. "But first I want to talk about you, little friend, before I talk to you. Think back to the time you first came here, for a probationary period because neither of us believed that an empath with your degree of sensitivity could survive here for long. In Sector General people in large numbers suffer physical trauma, fear, and emotional uncertainty. That is an accepted fact of hospital life. To an emotion-sensitive like you it must have been, and probably still is, hell. The therapeutic help I was able to give you in the early days was minimal. But against all the odds you did survive. Not only that, you assumed extra surgical responsibilities and remained effective and mentally stable during the processing of the hundreds of extra casualties that resulted from the Etlan War. When you were promoted to senior physician and took over medical charge of *Rhabwar*, you and your hypersensitive empathy climbed about in shifting ship wreckage and disaster areas so you could point out the dead from the dying inside their spacesuits and very often save the latter's lives. And now, well, you don't need to use telepathy or empathy or anything but your tiny ear slits to know that . . ."

He broke off for a moment to smile, then went on, "Of course it's only a rumor that you will shortly be promoted to full diagnostician, but I can unofficially confirm it."

The empath's pipestem limbs trembled faintly as it said, "Friend O'Mara, you are heaping me with high professional praise that I know is sincere. It should be making me feel good but it isn't. Why are you emoting so much anxiety?"

O'Mara shook his head and said, "Before I answer that I want to talk about myself, briefly, you'll be glad to hear. Since I started in this job over thirty years ago, without any formal qualifications and with an enormous chip on my shoulder, I deliberately refrained from trying to be friendly. Most of the people think they know the reason, that I'm a self-confessed, thoroughly nasty person who saves his professional sympathy only for the most troubled patients. But only you, little friend, with your damned empathy were able to piece together the complete truth.

"It has been a fact long hallowed by hospital tradition," he went on, "that the chief psychologist be an uncouth, nasty, sarcastic, completely undiplomatic, and thoroughly unlikable person. But it is not an immutable law of nature. We should consider the appointment of an entirely different personality type, one who is well-mannered and diplomatic because he, she, or it always says the right thing, one who is sensitive to the feelings of others but who, when necessary, can politely be very tough. In short, one whom everyone loves rather than loves to hate. That kind of person would be ideal both as administrator and chief psychologist, wouldn't you agree?"

Prilicla had begun to tremble again. "Other than among your own staff," it said, "where would you find such a paragon?"

"I might be looking at it," said O'Mara.

The empath began shaking so hard that it threatened to fall out of its chair. "Now I know the reason for your anxiety, friend O'Mara, because you're expecting me to refuse, which I do. I'm not a psychologist, I'm a doctor who is soon, according to you, to become a diagnostician and the carrier of many other-species mind tapes. Half the time I'll be so confused I won't know who or what I am. At the risk of sounding impolite, friend O'Mara, I think you're mad. The answer is no."

O'Mara smiled. "The new appointment calls for medical as well as psychological qualifications. What better experience could an administrator have than to be a diagnostician with inside knowledge of the workings of many other-species minds, or a chief psychologist who is able to detect the deeply buried emotional problems that cause the minds of its patients to go wrong? That's why I'd like you to consider offering yourself as a candidate. Personally, I think Administrator and Diagnostician-in-Charge of Psychology Prilicla would have a nice ring to it. Stop shaking and listen.

"Any one of my present staff could make a pretty good stab at the job," he continued, "as could Cerdal, who is very highly thought of, not least by itself. If you refuse it, one of them will succeed. But mostly they are followers rather than leaders, gifted but reluctant to take final responsibility. They are perfect subordinates who will be pleased to take the day-to-day running of the department off your hands so that you will have maximum time available for administrative work and the really serious patients. There will be no bad feelings from any of them, except possibly from Cerdal if it chooses to stay, because you they really like. Relax, there's no need to give me your answer right now."

Prilicla stood up. It said, "I can give you my answer now. It is no."

"Please, little friend," said O'Mara, "take time to think about it."

The empath clicked across the office floor on shaking Cinrusskin legs, then paused inside the door to make a soft, trilling sound.

"Don't forget to say something nasty to me as I leave, friend O'Mara," it said, "just so you can remain in character."

# CHAPTER 27

Lieutenant Braithwaite kept his eyes firmly on the remains of a large helping of synthetic steak, roasted potato slices, and mushrooms that no longer filled his plate, thanking the DNA he had inherited from his parents, which enabled him to indulge in the pleasures of overeating without suffering the penalty of becoming overweight, so that his enjoyment would not be spoiled by the sight of what Cerdal was eating. Because of the high level of background noise in the dining hall, they had to raise their voices to be heard, but their strong feeling of mutual irritation was making it very easy for them to shout at each other between the periods of angry silence.

"Dr. Cerdal, we are competing for the same job," Braithwaite said after one of them, "but that doesn't mean we have to dislike each other now or when one of us, or perhaps neither of us, is successful. But lately you have been displaying signs of a growing personal hostility toward me. Why?"

"It's not only you," said Cerdal without looking up, "but you are particularly irritating with your continual advice that is nothing but thinly veiled criticism. You gave me a patient who is visually loathsome, unfriendly, and has now refused even to speak to me. Tunneckis is, is impossible. I've spent days on end with it since it came out of surgery. You gave me the assignment knowing that I would fail, fail both to provide therapy for a stupid, uncooperative patient and to impress O'Mara with my fitness for its position. You and the others have shown me that strangers are not welcome here."

"That's ridiculous," said Braithwaite. "We're all strangers here, and some of us are a lot stranger than others, at least until we get to know each other. Lioren, Cha Thrat, or I could have taken the case, but you said that you had never before treated a telepath and it would be a challenge. You specifically asked for the assignment. I decided to give it to you."

"But without obtaining your superior's permission?" said Cerdal. "It was solely your own decision, correct?"

"Yes," Braithwaite replied. He hesitated for a moment before going on, "As the new administrator, O'Mara has nondepartmental business to attend to at present. You know this. He instructed me to take full responsibility for such assignment decisions, which I did. Would you like to be relieved of the Tunneckis case?"

Cerdal looked up from its plate to stare at him for a moment; then it said, "Is that what you want, Braithwaite, to see me fail? But no matter. Following several days of attempted therapy I've come to regard the patient as a stupid, obdurate, disrespectful, personally repulsive, and worthless being who should not have so much of my time wasted on it. If O'Mara had given me the assignment, he would have wanted me to fail, too, just like the rest of you. And don't waste my time or insult my intelligence with your lying, Earth-human protestations of innocence. And now I expect you'll run as fast as those long, misshapen Earth-human legs will carry you to tell your chief exactly what I said with, I've no doubt, a few embellishments?"

Braithwaite felt his face reddening. He opened his mouth to speak, then brought his teeth together again with an audible click as he tried to impose calm on himself. In an angry Kelgian such a conversational exchange might have been excusable, but his first assessment of Cerdal was that it was a cool, self-assured, smooth-talking diplomat who was in complete control of its emotions. That impression had been shared by everyone else in the department during the job interview. So what he was seeing here was a serious, completely uncharacteristic, and potentially dangerous change in behavior which was verging on outright paranoia and possibly xenophobia. It was his duty to report such sudden and uncharacteristic personality changes to O'Mara. But he didn't want to do that until he could also include the reason behind it.

"Doctor," he said quietly, "are you feeling all right?"

Cerdal didn't answer; instead it left the table without excusing itself.

He couldn't approach Tunneckis directly for information, Braithwaite thought as he finished his meal, because it was Cerdal's patient and that, in the other's present touchy state of mind, would cause even more offense. But as a psychologist, O'Mara was constantly reminding him, indirection was the most well-used tool of his trade. Besides, it was information on Cerdal and not its patient that he needed, and that could be more easily obtained through a third party.

Culcheth was the Kelgian charge nurse on the mixed-species surgical recovery ward which included, at a distance sufficient to minimize the telepathic radiation of the other patients, the isolation chamber that housed Tunneckis. Because Culcheth was a Kelgian, Braithwaite would not have to waste time on misdirection or making tangential approaches.

"Charge Nurse, how is patient Tunneckis doing?" said Braithwaite. "This isn't a visit, I just wanted to know your feelings regarding the patient. Is it friendly, cooperative?"

"Patient Tunneckis is doing as well as can be expected," Culcheth replied, its fur spiking in irritation, "but neither of the diagnosticians will tell me what their expectations are. It cooperates because it has no choice. It is not friendly and I will say no more about it."

The other couldn't lie but it could refuse to speak. Braithwaite tried again.

"Our new psychologist has been attempting to treat it," he said. "What do you think about Dr. Cerdal?"

Culcheth's fur became even more agitated. "That, that organic black hole," it said. "Its fur doesn't move and it's disgusting and its eyes . . . It's like a nightmare I used to have as a child when—"

"But surely," Braithwaite broke in, "you've grown out of child-ish nightmares? Especially in a place like this where you meet and work with them every day?"

"I still don't like it," said Culcheth. "Neither do my nursing staff. We won't be happy until both Tunneckis and Cerdal leave the hospital."

The charge nurse would say no more, and when he persisted with the questioning it became personally abusive. Kelgians always said what they thought, but this one, he was beginning to realize, wasn't thinking straight.

O'Mara was spending a few hours in the luxurious administrator's office when Braithwaite arrived looking cool and impeccable but more worried than usual.

"As I remember," he said, pointing to the nearest chair, "you were supposed to handle your own problems for a while. If you've come up against one you can't solve, for your sake I hope it's seri-ous. Briefly, what is it?"

"I think it's very serious, sir," said the lieutenant, "but I can't be brief."

"Try," said O'Mara.

"Sir," said Braithwaite, "we are all aware that you have intro-duced an element of competitiveness among the candidates for your job. That being so, I must first assure you that in no way have I tried to place Cerdal in a situation beyond its level of competence, or undermine its position in any way that would make it look bad and so eliminate it from the competition. I wouldn't be comfortable doing that and with respect, sir, I'm not sure I want your job that much."

"So Cerdal is the problem," said O'Mara. "Are you still trying to solve it?"

The lieutenant nodded. "I feel sure that Cerdal is showing increasing signs of emotional disturbance," he said. "Over the past few days it has displayed sudden and marked changes in personality and behavior, but that may be only a small part of a greater problem, the part that came to my attention first. I now have reasons to believe that a surgical post-op patient called Tunneckis, currently in recovery and in need of psychological suppport, may also be involved as well as a presently unknown number of other-species medical staff. I'm also aware of a subjective change in my own personality. Without being overtly insubordinate, I no longer feel quite so frightened of or even respectful toward those in authority, including yourself, sir."

"Lieutenant," said O'Mara dryly, "I've been hoping for years to hear you say that. Go on."

"Sir?" said the other, looking puzzled, then went on, "I'm still trying, or maybe just hoping, to solve this problem by myself, but I will need the cooperation of senior department heads, certain members of their medical staff, and maybe their technical-support and maintenance personnel as well. I don't have the rank to request the kind of help I need but you do, which is why I'm here. But frankly, sir, I'm not sure myself what is going on except that—"

O'Mara held up a hand. "Whose help do you need?"

"Initially," Braithwaite replied promptly, "Diagnosticians Thornnastor and Conway, because I don't think that ordinary minds will be able to solve this problem. If there is a problem, that is, and it isn't simply a case of me scaring myself unnecessarily. And Senior Physician Prilicla will be needed for a precise analysis of the emotional radiation of the people involved, and you, of course, for your other-species psychiatric experience. Depending on developments there may be others."

"Is that all?" said O'Mara with heavy sarcasm. "Are you quite sure it's Cerdal and not yourself who's emotionally disturbed?"

"Sir," said Braithwaite, "this matter is serious. And it may be urgent."

O'Mara continued to stare at Braithwaite's face for a moment, while the other stared unblinkingly at his, which was very unusual behavior for the lieutenant. "Tell me exactly what help you need, begining with mine."

Braithwaite gave a relieved sigh, then went on quickly, "First I'd like you to open Cerdal's psych profile to me, or better yet, discuss its contents. From its initial job interview and during a few later conversations with it, I formed the opinion that it was a stable, well-integrated, if a trifle self-important, personality . . ."

"You mean bigheaded," said O'Mara.

". . . who would have no difficulty adapting to the multiplicity of life-forms we have here," the other went on. "Over the past few days, since I assigned patient Tunneckis to it at its own request, Cerdal has displayed a marked change in its professional and social behavior, and there are clear indications of a worsening case of xenophobia. This behavior seems to me to be totally uncharacteristic in the entity I thought I knew. I made discreet inquiries and discovered that the people with whom it had had recent contact also noticed a change for the worse in its behavior, so much so that some of them have come to dislike it so much that they can barely bring themselves to speak to it anymore, and they, too, are exhibiting xenophobic behavior, of a lower intensity.

"I know that a mental abnormality isn't contagious," Braithwaite went on quickly, "whether it stems from patient Tunneckis or

Dr. Cerdal. But Tunneckis is the one common factor in all this because Cerdal, and to a lesser extent the people associated with the
patient's post-op medical care, are the only ones affected. Ridiculous as the idea sounds, the mental-contagion theory has to be
eliminated from the investigation before I clutch at some other stupid straw."

The lieutenant took a deep breath and continued, "There
could be a simple explanation for this behavior if Tunneckis bears
a physical resemblance to something or someone in its past life
about which Cerdal has a deeply buried phobia or if, during the
course of Cerdal's therapy, the patient has revealed something
about itself that triggered this extreme phobic reaction. That's why
I wanted to look at its psych profile."

O'Mara nodded, tapped keys on his console, then swung the
screen around so that they both could read it.

"Move closer, Lieutenant," he said, "and be my guest."

Without appearing to do so, he was studying the information
on the screen as intently as Braithwaite was doing. When they were
finished the other sighed, sat back, and shook his head. O'Mara allowed a little sympathy to enter his voice.

"Sorry, Lieutenant," he said, "this is the profile of a person
who is in all respects sane, well-adjusted, and completely lacking in
xenophobic tendencies."

Braithwaite shook his head again, stubbornly. "But, sir, that
isn't the profile of Cerdal as it is now. That's why I need Prilicla to
do an emotional-radiation reading on everyone concerned, beginning with Cerdal and Tunneckis. And I want to know the details of
what was done to the patient and, if there was any chance that the
procedure was likely to cause more than the simple post-op depression, why we weren't told about it. I've learned that the procedure involved some very delicate work and that Thornnastor and
Conway insisted on doing it themselves. I feel sure something is
badly wrong here, but I don't know what exactly. Our two top

diagnosticians are in the habit of coming up with answers to some very strange questions and maybe they'll do it again, if only it is to tell me that I'm making a fool of myself . . ."

He hesitated and for a moment the old, self-effacing Braithwaite returned as he added, ". . . which I probably am."

"Possibly you are, Lieutenant, not probably," said O'Mara. He swung the screen around to face him again, hit the communications key for the outer office, and went on briskly, "Get Thornnastor, Conway, and Prilicla up here at once. . . . No, hold while I rephrase that. . . ." In an undertone to Braithwaite he said, "Dammit, Lieutenant, I keep forgetting my new eminence and the need for politeness and fake humility that is supposed to go with the job." In a conversational tone he resumed, "Please locate and contact Diagnosticians Thornnastor and Conway and Senior Physician Prilicla, give them my compliments and tell them that their presence is required urgently in Administrator O'Mara's office."

Braithwaite smiled. "Sir," he said, "I couldn't have worded that better myself."

O'Mara ignored the compliment and added, "You stay where you are, Lieutenant. I don't want to sound like a fool to those three by relaying your suspicions to them secondhand. I know you don't know what is going on, but before they arrive I want you to tell me what the hell you *think* is going on."

# CHAPTER 28

The world was known as Kerm in the language of its inhabitants, which was their spoken and written word for "world." They didn't often use those forms of communication, but their telepathic range was restricted to their own-planet species and did not extend to joining with the minds of the members of the star-traveling other-worlders who made contact with them, including those of the Monitor Corps who asked and were granted permission to establish a cultural-study facility on their planet. While agreeing to its presence, they insisted that it be sited in an uninhabited area because, regardless of the species concerned, they received the closer-range thoughts of its personnel as a constant and distressing barrage of mental static. As a result the base was maintained in a state of voluntary mental quarantine and all messages between them were exchanged via sound or vision communicators.

Physiologically the Kermi were classification VBGM, the V prefix indicating the telepathic faculty in an otherwise unexceptional warm-blooded oxygen-breathing life-form. Their body mass was similar to that of an average Earth-human but that, apart from a high degree of intelligence, was all that they had in common. Visually they resembled large, dark-brown slugs whose means of locomotion was a wide apron of muscle attached to the underside rather than legs. A cluster of three short tentacles, each terminating in four digits, grew from the tops of their heads. They were totally lacking in natural weapons of attack or defense.

The species had climbed to the top of the evolutionary tree by using their telepathic faculty alone, either to avoid danger or to cause the danger, in the shape of natural enemies, to avoid them. Too weak to fight and too slow to run, they learned how to control the minds of any predators who posed an imminent threat to either turn the predators against one another or to disappear from the attackers' mental and sensory map. In time they widened the process by making use of these lesser life-forms to work for them and to maintain a balanced planetary ecology of flora and fauna and, ultimately, to give their nonsapient brothers who had helped them to develop their present civilization the protection they had earned and deserved.

There was a moment's silence in the room while Diagnostician Conway, who had been giving the potted history of the Kerma culture, paused to look around at O'Mara, Braithwaite, Thornnastor, Prilicla, and back to O'Mara. When he went on there was a hint of embarrassment in his tone.

"Medical science on Kerm is pretty basic," he said, "and when a life-threatening condition arises with no possibility of a cure, there is nothing much that their doctors can do beyond giving mental solace. In a telepathic culture, remember, there can be no secrets between doctor and patient and this includes not only the bad news but the complete sharing of the associated pain. In this they are like the Telfi VTXMs and, like them, the being who is terminating will voluntarily withdraw itself and its mental and physical pain beyond the telepathic range of its friends so that they will not share its dying anguish.

"When the ranking Monitor Corps officer on Kerm base heard of the Tunneckis case," Conway continued, "it offered the facilities of Sector General. The patient was fully acquainted with the risks plus the fact that we would be learning as we went along instead of knowing what we were doing from the start. This did not matter to Tunneckis and it asked me to proceed. The patient's condition was extremely serious although it was and is not life-threatening, but then neither is that of a Kelgian with dead fur. In the event, the operation was clinically unsatisfactory and Tunneckis now requires psychiatric support."

In its open, bowl-shaped relaxer Prilicla's limbs began trembling in response to a strong source of emotional radiation in the room. Thornnastor cleared its throats with a sound like a hoarse foghorn.

"Administrator," it said, "Conway is being too hard on itself. It, or more accurately we, were operating in completely unknown surgical territory. There was no background anatomical or metabolic knowledge available at all. For religious and ecological reasons the Kermi will not allow strangers to interfere physically with the bodies of their dead or even to investigate those of their nonsapient brothers although in time, when the cultural contact with them widens, this situation may change. As it is, we had to learn what we could while the surgical procedure was in progress. This was not an ideal situation for the surgeon-in-charge."

"I know all that," Conway joined in again, "but I think I still made a mess of it, O'Mara, and ended up handing your department a seriously distressed ex-patient to salvage what you can of its mind. Originally the patient had nothing more to lose and I considered the risks acceptable."

The trembling of Prilicla's limbs increased for a moment, then subsided as Conway regained control of his emotional radiation and went on, "But why are you interested in the details of our surgical foul-up when it's the mental fallout that should concern you? I'm far from happy about this result because frankly I didn't know what the hell I was doing."

O'Mara looked at Braithwaite for a moment and said, "This is your case, Lieutenant."

Braithwaite took a deep breath and managed to sound respectful as he said, "Sir, it's because I don't know what the hell I'm doing, either, that I asked for you people. I'm hoping that something in the overall clinical picture, I don't know what, might suggest a line of investigation."

"And if you don't know what you're looking for," said Conway, "you have to look at everything. Right?"

Before Braithwaite had finished nodding, Conway was on his feet and moving quickly toward the big wall screen facing O'Mara's desk. He tapped keys and the greatly enlarged features of a Nidian appeared.

"Medical records," it growled.

"Patient Tunneckis," said Conway briskly. "Planet of origin, Kerm. Cranial surgery, unique procedure, surgeon-in-charge Diagnostician Conway with Diagnostician Thornnastor and Senior Physician Prilicla assisting, location OR One-Twelve. Run the complete op without edits from anesthetic to the transfer to Recovery. Go."

"Sir," said the Nidian. "This one is flagged by you as restricted. It is marked for the information of the participating OR staff only, and on no account is it to be used for teaching purposes or general public viewing. Do you wish to amend this instruction?"

"Obviously," said Conway. "But I want one screening only to this location, please. Run it now."

The big screen was suddenly filled with the sharp, bright image of OR One-Twelve, in which patient Tunneckis was held rigid by tight body restraints. A shaped block was further immobilizing its head while serving as a rigid support for the fixed-focus scanner that was centered above its closed eyes. A short length of the narrow, hollow tubing that would guide the instrument probe projected from one ear, and a two-sided viewscreen was suspended above the operative area at a height convenient to the surgeons' eyes. Just below the screen on Conway's side there was a small, rigidly mounted set of controls for the remotely controlled probe instruments. Thornnastor and Conway were bending over the patient and Prilicla was maintaining stable hovering flight close above it.

"This patient," said the image of Conway, with the briefest of glances toward the recording equipment, "was the single occupant in a self-controlled groundcar which sustained an accidental lightning strike. The safety systems functioned to earth the charge through the vehicle's outer shell so that the patient apparently escaped without injury. Within a few hours of the accident, however, the patient reported an increasing impairment of its telepathic faculty which within five days culminated in it becoming telepathically deaf and dumb. Surgical intervention to relieve a dysfunction in the telepathic faculty is beyond the medical science of its home planet or, for that matter, any other world in the Federation, and we were asked to help. Is the patient ready?"

"Yes, friend Conway," said Prilicla. "The level of emotional radiation is characteristic of a deeply unconscious patient."

As Conway nodded, the picture on the big wall screen split to show two images. One was a close-up of the patient's head and Conway's fingers gently inserting the tube into Tunneckis's ear cavity, while the other showed the magnified deep scanner image of the operation site.

"Rather than open the cranium and hack a path to the trouble spot through brain tissue of whose sensory functions we are entirely ignorant," Conway went on, "we will approach as closely as possible to the operative field via an existing channel, in this instance through one of the two ear openings. Aural rather than telepathic deafness may result on that side, but probably not, because we can rebuild the inner-ear structure much more easily than the job we are attempting now. Increase to six magnifications. I'm going in...."

Conway's fingers were gently moving the thin, hollow tube inside the ear, but his eyes were on the magnified image, where it seemed as if a length of heavy piping with rounded edges was being forced in a series of jerks and pauses deeper into a narrowing, fleshy tunnel.

"That's as close as we'll get to the site without risking serious damage," said Conway finally. "Now we'll move in with the fine stuff."

A cluster of cables that looked fine even under the high magnification was threaded into the hollow tube and moved forward to its inner end. They included a tiny but intense light source, an all-around visual sensor, and various cutting and sampling tools whose blades and bearings verged on the microscopic. The cable strands emanated from a flat, transparent box with a pair of metallic operating gauntlets inside it. Slowly and carefully Conway moved his fingers from around the fine strands of cable and slipped his hands into the box and the gloves.

"Magnification two hundred," said Conway. "Instrument motion reduction down one-five percent."

Even the tiny movements of his hands and fingers, rendered incredibly minute by the reduction mechanism, looked like the awkward, barely coordinated motions of a twitching convulsive.

"Motion stepdown to one-fifty," he said.

On the screen the movements of the strand with the cutting head at its tip became smoother and more assured as it burrowed a path through the inner ear membrane and into the tissue beyond. It was closely followed into the narrow, fleshy tunnel it was creating by the light source, the vision pickup, and the instruments that would gather tissue and fluid samples for analysis. The tiny tunnel was beginning to look crowded.

"There is some collateral tissue damage," said Thornnastor.

"The reduced size of the instruments has rendered it minimal, and allowable."

"This is new territory," said Conway quietly. "We don't know what is allowable. Ah, we're in."

The split-screen images from the external scanner and of Conway's hands in the reduction gauntlets was replaced by the tremendously magnified view from the internal vision pickup that was moving through what appeared to be a series of interconnecting, submerged caverns. In the strong light their convoluted walls showed pink with patches of yellow and they were covered with plantlike growths whose tight clusters of slender stems were topped by single, crystalline flowers that were pale blue or red verging on black. The majority of the stems were headless and on the few that weren't the crystals looked deformed or damaged. Pieces of crystalline debris stirred in the eddies created by the motion of the invading instruments.

"I'll need a specimen of the fluid for analysis," said Thornnastor. "Also samples of that floating debris, which appears to be fragmented crystalline material, and a few complete crystals if you can detach them from their stalks. I'll need stalk samples as well, complete with their crystal flowers."

"Right," said Conway. "Increase the magnification to two hundred."

A tiny amount of the fluid which included the debris was withdrawn. Then the cutter and grabs, looking like gigantic earthmoving machinery under the high magnification, moved in to harvest the required stalks and crystals.

"I have enough for the analyzer, now," said Thornnastor. "But the fluid is something more than a simple saline solution. This will take a little time."

"I feel your concern, friend Conway," Prilicla's voice joined in, "but it is unnecessary. There is no change in the patient's emotional status even at the subconscious level, which is the most accurate guide to anything going wrong. The invasive procedure is so delicate that I doubt that it would have felt anything even if it had been fully conscious."

There was a faint, rustling sound that might have been Conway sighing with relief, and then he said, "Thank you for the reassurance, little friend, you must have felt I needed it. But what we're seeing here is an organic telepathic transmitter and receiver that is damaged and inoperative. Dammit, in primary-school science class I couldn't even build a homemade radio that worked."

It was Thornnastor who looked up with one eye from its analyzer to break the lengthening silence.

"This is interesting," it said. "The fluid is a complex of metallic salts, predominantly copper, with a large number of other minerals in trace quantities that have yet to be identified. It seems that the crystals, which are very faintly radioactive, grow within the fluid and attach themselves to the clusters of stalks only when they are fully formed. Apart from providing cup-shaped attachment points at their tips and serving as a protective sheath for the connective nerve pathway to the central brain, they are merely the supports for their individual crystals.

"We can reproduce the fluid," it went on, "and seed it with fragments of the damaged crystals and regrow and reirradiate them. Pathologist Murchison is standing by in the lab and it tells me that the crystals form so quickly that it should be able to complete the process in just over an hour. This would give us enough time for lunch."

"What?" said Conway.

"Friend Thornnastor is a massive and energy-hungry lifeform," said Prilicla, "but it is simply making a pleasantry aimed at reducing emotional tension."

The image showing the site of Tunneckis's telepathic faculty remained steady on the wall screen, but the conversation of the operating team discussing it became so densely technical that O'Mara

found it difficult to follow even with both his minds. He was glad
when the regrown crystals in their growth medium arrived and
were injected slowly into the cerebral fluid.

It was obvious even to O'Mara that there were problems.

The newly introduced crystals refused to attach themselves to
stalks. Conway stepped up the magnification several times and,
sweating in his effort to make minimal movements, tried to use his
microinstruments to nudge and hold them together, in vain. The
emotional radiation in the room was so intense that Prilicla, trembling in every limb, was forced to land. Finally Conway shook his
head, regained enough control over his feelings for the empath to
stop trembling, and looked up.

"The receptor cups on the stalks appear to fit the new crystals,"
he said calmly, "which means that either the reproduction of the
new crystals or the fluid in which they were grown was at fault, or
both, so that they are either rejecting or temporarily ignoring the
stalks. I'm hoping, in fact I'm being hopelessly optimistic, that it is
the latter and that the joining process simply requires more time.
That being the case, and unless anyone has any other ideas, I suggest we withdraw at once in the hope that the patient, as so many
of them do, proceeds to heal itself."

There was total silence in O'Mara's office as Conway switched
off the wall screen before turning to face them again.

"The rest of this is simply the op debriefing and my general instructions to the medical staff of the recuperation ward," he went
on, "and frankly I dislike listening to myself making excuses. Patient
Tunneckis did not recover. In addition it has become emotionally
disturbed to the stage where psychiatric assistance was requested.
It's gratifying to belong to a hospital with the reputation of doing
the medically impossible, but, regrettably, we can't do it all the time.
Patient Tunneckis, I'm afraid, remains as it was, telepathically deaf
and dumb."

Conway silently resumed his seat and the silence lengthened.

Thornnastor and Prilicla joined the others in saying nothing. O'Mara was totally surprised and very pleased when it was the usually quiet and self-effacing Lieutenant Braithwaite who broke the silence.

"Diagnostician Conway," he said politely, "I completely disagree."

# CHAPTER 29

Conway, Thornnastor, Prilicla, and O'Mara turned their total of ten eyes on the lieutenant, who kept his fixed unwaveringly on Conway. He spoke again before the other could react.

"There is evidence to suggest," Braithwaite continued, respectfully but firmly, "that your patient is making some form of projective telepathic contact with the members of several different species, specifically those belonging to the medical staff who have been or are attending it. So far as I can gather from their reported conversations with the patient, Tunneckis and they are completely unaware of what is happening."

Conway looked quickly toward O'Mara, then back to Braithwaite. He smiled and said, "Has your chief made you aware of the brain-itch phenomenon, Lieutenant? It's very rare, but I've experienced it a few times myself around telepaths. It's a temporary irritation, not a physical or mental health risk."

Braithwaite nodded. "I'm aware of it, sir. It occurs when a member of a species who is not normally telepathic but whose distant ancestors possessed the gene for a telepathic faculty, and evolved speech and hearing instead, encounters a transmission that its long-atrophied receiver cannot process. The result, if they feel anything at all, is an unlocalized itching deep inside both ears. Occasionally, as happened with you, a complete telepathic mind-picture is received which fades within seconds. The effect with Tunneckis is more insidious and, I believe, dangerous.

"Since you took part in the operation," he went on, looking briefly toward Prilicla and Thornnastor, "are any of you aware of uncharacteristic changes in your behavior or thought patterns, however small? Do any of you find yourselves feeling unusual levels of irritation toward other-species colleagues or subordinate staff? Are you worried about what they might do to you someday? Do you find yourselves wishing you had own-species assistants rather than a bunch of weird aliens who . . ."

"Dammit, Lieutenant," Conway broke in, his face deepening in color, "are you suggesting xenophobic behavior in people like *us*?"

"In people with your wide, other-species experience and length of hospital service," Braithwaite replied calmly, "xenophobia is unlikely. But it is a possibility that must be considered."

Before Conway could respond, Prilicla said, "Friend Braithwaite, the five sources of emotional radiation in this room give no indications of xenophobia, either now or in the past. You are now feeling relief. Why is that?"

"Because," said the lieutenant, "I thought you might have been infected, contaminated, influenced, whatever is the proper word to describe a telepathic contagion, by Tunneckis during the operation, as was our Dr. Cerdal while practicing its therapy. Obviously this did not happen. Perhaps the duration of exposure is a factor, which would explain why it is Dr. Cerdal—who as its therapist is frequently in attendance—is the person most strongly affected at present. The symptoms of the nursing staff, who have more important things to do than talk for long periods with the patient, are less obvious."

"Dr. Cerdal," said O'Mara before anyone could ask who it was, "is an able psychologist and one of the contenders for my job, although becoming one of my department's patients is an unusual way of impressing me."

Conway smiled and Thornnastor stamped one of its medial feet in polite appreciation of O'Mara's attempt to lighten the atmosphere, but Prilicla was shaking again. It was the slow, irregular tremor the Cinrusskin made when it was nerving itself to say something which might give rise to an unpleasant emotional reaction which its empathy would cause it to share.

"Friend Braithwaite," it said hesitantly, "have you considered the possibility that friend Cerdal's problem may be self-generated? That the emotional pressures of competing for the top job, in surroundings which to it must seem very strange and perhaps frightening, have uncovered an unsuspected flaw in its normally well-integrated personality? And that your xenophobia theory, with apologies, is all wrong?"

"I've considered that possibility, Dr. Prilicla," said the lieutenant, "and discarded it. But I would be very relieved and pleased if any of you can prove me all wrong."

Prilicla made the musical trilling sound that was Cinrusskin laughter and said, "Then I would take great pleasure in relieving and pleasing you, friend Braithwaite. How, precisely, can I prove you wrong?"

The lieutenant told Prilicla, followed by Conway and Thornnastor, what he wanted done. In the presence of three of the most senior medical staff in the hospital his manner was respectful, O'Mara was pleased to see, but without the slightest trace of subservience. He remained silent for several minutes after the three medics had left the office.

"You may not know exactly what you're doing, Lieutenant," he said finally, "but you seem to be doing it very well. And now, after ordering the top medical brass around for the past ten minutes, presumably you have a job for me?"

"I would appreciate any help and advice you could give me,

sir," said Braithwaite. "Or instructions. If it is convenient I'd like us both to talk to Tunneckis's ward staff."

"Suppose," said O'Mara, "I were to tell you, less tactfully than Prilicla, that you're all wrong and advise you to cease and desist your present line of investigation forthwith, what then?"

"In certain circumstances," Braithwaite replied, calmly ducking the question, "negative advice can be helpful."

"Diplomat," said O'Mara in a voice suggesting that he had just used a dirty word. For a moment he looked around the large, beautiful, and well-appointed room, and through the transparent wall that revealed his mixed-species secretarial staff busy at their consoles, then went on. "If you do eventually make it to this office, Lieutenant, you'll like it. Once the initial panic is over and you realize that you can be polite when you choose and not because you have to please others, you'll be able to apply the diplomatic oil that will keep the hospital running smoothly. I can't do that, and always feel happier when I'm somewhere else."

He stood up suddenly and circumnavigated his enormous desk to stand beside Braithwaite before he added, "This is still your show. Lead the way, Lieutenant."

Valleschni was the off-duty charge nurse on Tunneckis's recovery ward, which meant that, when they asked and received permission to talk to it in its private quarters, they had to wear their protective suits while the chlorine-breather wore nothing. The personal nature of the conversation made it impossible for one of them not to look at the obnoxious thing. After a brief nod of greeting, O'Mara kept his attention fixed on a lank bunch of something oily and decaying hanging from one wall (it was probably decorative vegetation and, for a chlorine-breather, sweet-smelling) while he allowed Braithwaite to do the talking.

"I had thought," said the Illensan when the lieutenant had finished, "that a visit from two psychiatrists presaged important and perhaps fearful revelations concerning my own mental state. Instead you want to know precisely how much nursing time has been spent on Patient Tunneckis, which in my own case is only a few minutes per day, and whether there have been any self-observed changes in my own personality or behavior or in members of my subordinate nursing staff who, you say, may or may not require therapy; and you tell me that these changes that are so subtle that I could be forgiven for missing them.

"Are you quite sure," it added, squelching closer on legs that looked like stubby columns of yellow-green, oozing seaweed, "that it isn't the psychiatrists who are in need of therapy?"

O'Mara started to laugh softly, then thought better of it. Unlike Kelgians, the Illensans were capable of polite conversation when they felt like it. Perhaps this one wasn't in the mood. Or maybe it was feeling hostile and uncooperative because it had developed a low order of xenophobia after being exposed to Tunneckis's psychological contagion, whose existence Braithwaite had still to prove. But more likely it was simply irritated at them for wasting its off-duty time.

"I am aware of mood swings and behavioral changes in myself and my staff every day," Valleschni went on, "and some of them aren't subtle. They can be caused by many things—worry about a tutor's remarks in lectures, a sex-based relationship with a colleague that is not progressing well so that the ward work is suffering, or many things that have a purely subjective importance to the people concerned. These minor losses of temper or flashes of insubordination are directed toward myself as a person. My culture is fortunate in its scientific accomplishments, particularly in other-species medicine, and unfortunate in that the stupid, small-minded majority of oxygen-breathers like yourselves considers us less than physically beautiful. Even your own superior prefers to look at a stupid flower rather than at me. This being the case, it is understandable that we dislike each other, but I do not believe that xenophobia is the problem."

"And I believe," said Braithwaite, momentarily losing his temper, "that xenophobia *is* the problem and that ..."

O'Mara cut him off by gently clearing his throat. The lieutenant caught what was plainly a nonverbal signal to disengage.

"Now that we have made you officially aware of the problem," said Braithwaite, regaining his calm, "our department would appreciate having any further information you can provide. We will, of course, be interviewing the other members of the ward staff who have had close contact with patient Tunneckis. Thank you for your cooperation, Charge Nurse."

When they were in the corridor, the lieutenant shook his head, nodded toward Valleschni's door, and said, "Illensans are not usually so impolite, sir. That could be an early indication of a xenophobic reaction."

"It's still your case, Lieutenant," said O'Mara. "Where to next?"

Normally O'Mara did not use the dining hall, because he had always been uncomfortable making polite small talk with people discussing a subject—medicine—in which he had no training, or whose conversation might reveal the early symptoms of an emotional disturbance, or who were merely swapping hospital gossip, of which he might also have to take professional cognizance. His well-known irascibility and impatience with people, although they never suspected it, was principally due to the fact that he still carried the memories and personality of his mind partner, Marrasarah, and over the years that honest and intensely forthright Kelgian tape donor and himself had become very close in their thinking. He had chosen therefore to eat privately in his office or living quarters, and so now all the diners were going to stare at him and wonder why the hell he was breaking with precedent. But in the event he and Braithwaite might just as well have been invisible, because the center of attention was elsewhere.

Practically all the staffers in the vast room were on their feet and raising a multispecies din while gesticulating with arms, tentacles, or whatever, towards a table close to one wall, where he saw a sight that he had hoped he would never see in Sector General: an all-out, no-holds-barred, mixed-species fight.

"Call for a security detail," O'Mara snapped as he hurried towards it. "Armed and with heavy restraints." But the lieutenant was already talking urgently into the nearby communicator and doing just that.

They were mixing it up so thoroughly that O'Mara had difficulty at first in seeing who and how many were involved among the debris of the partially demolished table and furniture, and the volume of untranslatable noise they were making gave no clue as to the reason for the fighting. But it was immediately obvious that they were fighting indiscriminately among themselves and not ganging up on one individual. That, O'Mara hoped, might reduce the severity if not the number of casualties. A Tralthan was trying to batter in the bony carapace of a Melfan, who was snapping with its pincers at the other's leathery hide while jabbing with a stiffened leg at the lower torso of a large, bear-like Orligian, who was hanging onto one of the Tralthan's free tentacles and trying to kick its elephantine legs out from under it. A well-muscled Earth-human charge nurse with blood that was probably his own running down his face and white tunic was in there somewhere using fists and feet. The Orligian's fur was also showing patches of blood and one of the Melfan's limbs was hanging limp. As O'Mara moved closer, a Nidian he hadn't noticed until then was expelled from the affray and came to a skidding halt at his feet.

He went down on one knee and grabbed the tiny, red-furred figure by the shoulders.

"Why the hell are you *fighting?*" he yelled above the din. "Stop it, stop it at once or you'll wreck your careers here."

"I know that, dammit," said the other crossly. "I was trying to stop it, but they have the advantage of weight. *You* try to talk some sense into them."

O'Mara growled an apology, lifted the Nidian to its feet, and began circling the group of combatants, who were completely ignoring the advice he was shouting at them. Suddenly he saw his chance and moved in on the Earth-human and gave him a hard double kidney punch. As the other gasped and buckled at the knees, he grabbed him around the waist and dragged him backward onto the floor a few yards away.

"Don't move from there, Charge Nurse," he said furiously, "or I'll damn well stamp on your stupid face."

As he returned to the fracas he felt so furious at the stupidity of these people who had started the first inter-species fight in Sector General's history that he almost meant what he had said.

He took out the Melfan by encircling its underside with his arms and, keeping the side of his face close to the carapace so that it couldn't reach around to poke him in the eyes, immobilized it by sliding it onto its back at a safe distance from the Earth-human charge nurse. Moving the Orligian was going to be much more difficult. Even in the old, wild days when his body weight was made up of muscle rather than fat, he had rarely bested one of them. Feeling ashamed of himself because he might almost be enjoying what he was doing after all the years of civilized behavior, he grabbed the other by its long, furry ears, planted a knee between its shoulder blades, and pulled back hard.

The Orligian gave a growling bellow, released its hold on the Tralthan's tentacle, dropped onto its hands and knees, and tried to throw O'Mara over its head like a maddened horse trying to unseat its rider. It might have succeeded if a pair of slim, iron-hard Hudlar tentacles hadn't encircled his waist and legs suddenly and dragged him away from it and high into the air. Another pair of tentacles were doing the same to the Orligian.

"What the hell are you *doing?*" said O'Mara, startled. "Put me down, dammit."

Below and between the suspended bodies of the Orligian and himself the Hudlar's speaking membrane vibrated as it replied politely, "Only if you promise to forgo your attempt to settle your dispute by physical means. You are guilty of behavior unbecoming to civilized beings."

"It's all right, Nurse," said Braithwaite to the Hudlar, trying hard to keep from smiling. "The Earth-human was trying to separate the combatants. He's one of the good guys."

When O'Mara's feet were on the floor again, he glowered at the other and said, "Are you enjoying this, Lieutenant?"

"Only a small part of it, sir; the rest is much too serious," Braithwaite replied, unabashed, then went on quickly, "While I was calling Security a Hudlar nurse was passing along the corridor and I asked for its help to . . ."

He broke off and waved at six massive Orligians with a selection of pacifiers suspended from their equipment harnesses as they came through the dining-hall entrance at a dead run.

"Here's the security detail now," he went on. "I suggest we take care of the wounded—at least there's no shortage of medical assistance in here—then confine them under guard to their quarters until we can interview them individually and get to the bottom of this business."

"Then do that," said O'Mara. "Is there something else on your mind?"

"Yes, sir," Braithwaite replied worriedly. "The Earth-human charge nurse and the Orligian I recognized, and the other two I'm fairly sure about even though Melfans and Tralthans still look the same to me. They are all currently attached to Tunneckis's recovery ward."

# CHAPTER 30

Padre Lioren was a Wearer of the Blue Cloak of Tarla which, in Earth academic circles, would have been placed on the same level of professional achievement as the old-time Nobel Prize for Medicine—although, since the Cromsaggar Incident, it had forsworn the practice of the art. Everyone on the Sector General staff knew the reason that he was the Psychology Department's other-species religious counselor rather than a senior physician, but no-body until now, not even a Kelgian like this one, had ever been so crassly insensitive and stupid as to remind him of it to his face.

Lioren took a firm grip on his anger with all eight hands and said gently, "What is troubling you, friend?"

"You are troubling me," said the Kelgian, its fur heaving into angry tufts, "you sanctimonious bloody murdering hypocrite. Go away, and stop trying to poison my mind with one of your stupid religions. I won't tell you anything or listen to a thing that looks like a diseased shumpid tree. Leave me alone."

In general configuration his tall, cone-shaped body with the four stubby, rootlike legs, four medial and four upper arms could be described as resembling a Kelgian shumpid tree if the describer wished to be offensive, which for some reason this one did. But it was the reason for the other's totally uncharacteristic behavior that interested him.

"I'll leave you alone," said Lioren quietly, "if that is what you really want. But what I want to do is to listen to your troubles, and personal insults if they are part of the problem, not try to teach you anything you don't want to learn. And there are many trees on Tarla that look a little like me, and some of them are infested by small, furry creatures that resemble you. Both species live and grow in the manner originally ordained for them with no choice in the matter. Unlike them, we are self-willed, civilized, and sapient."

"Supposedly," he couldn't help adding.

The Kelgian's fur continued to ripple and tuft in what was plainly intense agitation, but it remained silent.

"Please remember," Lioren went on, "even though I am attached to the Psychology Department, I am not bound by its rules nor am I required to report anything you may tell me to my superior or include it in your psych file unless you give your permission to do so. There is complete confidentiality. Plainly something is troubling you that is serious enough to affect your behavior toward your superiors, the other ward staff, and, I've been told, your off-duty other-species friends. Whether the problem is personal, ethical, or even criminal in nature, it will go no further than we two unless or until you allow otherwise. Now would you like to tell me about it?"

"No," said the other. "I wouldn't like to, because I don't like you. I don't want you near me and I don't believe what you say. You'll just go back and talk about me to the Earth-humans and that horrible Sommaradvan in your department. Everybody in this place says things they don't mean and they don't have the fur to show what they truly feel. I don't trust any of you because the only people I can trust are other Kelgians. For your information there is absolutely nothing wrong with me. I don't have a personal or ethical or any other kind of problem. Just go away."

After that tirade, Lioren thought sadly, there was nothing else to do.

And in another part of the hospital Cha Thrat, recently described as the department's horrible Sommaradvan, was beginning tactfully to probe the suspected emotional difficulties of an Earth-human trainee nurse. Her great size and disposition of limbs made it necessary for her to interview the subject through the other's open door.

"I'm sorry for calling during an off-duty period, Nurse Patel," said Cha Thrat, "but Senior Tutor Cresk-Sar is becoming increasingly concerned about your recent inattention and general behavior during lectures. Since you joined the hospital it tells me that your multi-species anatomical studies and general practical work on the wards has been exemplary, but recently there has been a marked deterioration both in the quality of your work and in your professional contacts with other-species colleagues and patients. So far none of this is serious enough for the Psychology Department to take official notice of it, which means that it hasn't gone into your psych file, but I was asked to have an unofficial word with you about it and, perhaps, give you a word of advice. Cresk-Sar wonders if the cause lies outside the training program. Is there anything that you would like to tell me, Nurse?"

The other's already dark facial skin coloration darkened some more. In Earth-humans, Cha Thrat had learned, this was an indication of the presence of a strongly felt emotion such as anger or embarrassment.

"Yes," said the nurse loudly, "I would like to tell you that Cresk-Sar is a nosy, small-minded, flea-bitten runt . . ." She twitched her shoulders. ". . . who gives me the creeps every time it comes near me. And you're as bad as it is, only bigger."

As a Nidian, the senior tutor possessed just over half the body mass of the Earth-human female, but Cha Thrat doubted that its tight, curly body fur harbored insect parasites. Plainly it was the other's emotions rather than its reason that was talking. Like the warrior-surgeon she had been and the trainee ruler-wizard she had become, she tried to bury her own emotional response under a deep layer of reason and, above all, control her usually short temper.

"I have need of information about you, Nurse Patel," said Cha Thrat, "not Senior Tutor Cresk-Sar."

"Then you still need it," the other replied, speaking too loudly considering the short distance separating them. "Why should I tell you anything about me, you outsized pervert? We know all about you, how your own people got you sent here by pulling political strings, and how you cut off one of your own arms during an op and, and . . . A warrior-surgeon, indeed. You're a bloody sword-swinging, Sommaradvan savage. Go away."

Cha Thrat forced herself to speak in a quiet, reasonable voice as she said, "I am not a warrior, a wielder of weapons, or, as it is in these civilized times, a user of dangerous technology. The term signifies my medical rank only. At the bottom are the menial-physicians, who deal out potions and poultices to the workers; then there are the warrior-surgeons like myself who used to treat the wounds of those hurt in battle before warfare was outlawed; and then, the most important, are the wizards, the healers of the mind, that is, whose duty it is to keep the mentalities of the rulers and sub-rulers in stable good health. Naturally, if a menial were to sustain a serious injury or a mental dysfunction, the nearest warrior-surgeon or ruler-wizard would attend . . ."

Cha Thrat stopped speaking when Nurse Patel's door hissed shut in her face. After a moment's pause for thought, she moved quickly to the nearest communicator and keyed for staff information.

"I require the present location of Administrator O'Mara," she said briskly, "and, if it is in a meeting or on rest period, use the Code Orange One priority break-in."

Just over three standard minutes passed before the screen lit with the image of O'Mara. It was out of uniform, wearing a soft, loose garment over the visible portion of its body and rubbing at the fleshy flaps that covered its Earth-human eyes.

"Dammit, Cha Thrat," it said angrily when she had finished talking, "why is a psychiatrist reporting the suspected presence of a contagious disease to me, another bloody psychiatrist? Since you joined the department you no longer practice medicine, but if you're moonlighting and have found something then tell your suspicions to one of the medics and hope that you've something to back them up. It's the middle of my night and I shall have harsh things to say to you in the morning. Off."

"Wait, sir," said Cha Thrat quickly. "I believe that we are faced with the presence of an unsuspected contagion, how limited or widespread it is I don't know, because up until a few minutes ago it would have been based only on hearsay and staff gossip. But now I think there is a solid basis to the rumors."

"Then tell me why you think that," said O'Mara in a quieter voice. "And, Cha Thrat, this had better be good."

"I'm not sure what is going on, sir," she said, "because what I'm thinking isn't possible. Normally a mental or emotional dysfunction, however serious, cannot be transmitted to the mind of another person unless there has been protracted association with the troubled personality and the other mind is extremely weak-willed and open to suggestion. I've already studied the psych files of the people mentioned in the rumors as well as that of my last interviewee and none of them, or for that matter any other member of the staff, would be allowed to work here if they had minds like that. I believe it to be a purely psychological xenophobic contagion, sir, and a nonmedical Code Orange One was the closest I could come to describing it. Did I do wrong?"

"You didn't," said O'Mara. Its eyes were no longer partially covered by their lids and Cha Thrat could hear the sound of its fingers tapping as if it was impatient to use the call keys. "Return to the department at once. Discuss your suspicions with Padre Lioren and Lieutenant Braithwaite and pool your information until I arrive. Off."

When the Sommaradvan's image flicked off his screen, O'Mara asked for the location and duty roster of Senior Physician Prilicla and found that the Cinrusskin was awake and about to begin its day. When faced with the possibility of a nonmedical illness, an empathic doctor should know best.

It was three hours later. For various nonmedical reasons, like the pressures of his new administrative job spilling over into his free time, O'Mara had already missed two nights' sleep. His mind ached from chasing itself in circles and he would have given a good chunk of his month's salary if he could have allowed himself the luxury of a large, jaw-dislocating yawn. Instead he held up one hand for silence and looked slowly from Braithwaite to Cha Thrat to Lioren and finally at Prilicla, the only person there who knew exactly how tired he felt, and tried to speak like an administrator rather than the chief psychologist three of them thought they knew and loathed.

"My compliments on the psychological detective work all of you have performed," he said, "and on the evidence you have gathered, which seems to point to an impossible conclusion. But now we have to stop reminding each other endlessly of how impossible it is and do something about the situation.

"Item," he went on. "We have three members of the medical staff and another who is currently being assessed for my job and who may or may not become a staff member. Without prior behavioral indications, it and several other members of the staff have suddenly exhibited xenophobia of a degree which cannot be tolerated in this hospital and must, if left untreated, lead to their dismissal. About twenty other members of the staff, whom I am ignoring for the moment, are displaying similar symptoms at a lower intensity. So we are faced with evidence that some form of mental contagion is present in the hospital which, by its very nature, is impossible.

"But if two inexplicable events occur at the same time," he said, "there is a strong possibility that they have a common cause. And when four or more of them occur within a few days of each other, that possibility becomes a probability amounting to virtual certainty. So let us consider how this impossible, nonmedical, mental disorder entered the hospital and how it is being propagated. Well?"

Braithwaite looked toward Prilicla, giving the senior physician the chance to speak first, but plainly the empath was feeling his impatience. It waved a delicate insectile hand for him to go on.

"Sir," said Braithwaite, "if it is a contagious disease, whether medical or mental, then we must assume the presence of a carrier who was originally infected and is transmitting the disease to everyone it contacts. But this disease isn't behaving like that, because so far the evidence points to a single source with the victims exhibiting diminishing degrees of infection depending on the time they spent, or are presently spending, in contact with the source, whom—I believe—we can now identify."

Cha Thrat dipped its head in agreement, Lioren made a gesture with its medial hands that meant the same thing, and Prilicla, who usually tried to agree with everyone so as to keep the ambient emotional radiation pleasant, did nothing.

"Go on," said O'Mara impatiently.

"The source," Braithwaite continued, "has to be the recently arrived VBGM classification, patient Tunneckis from Kerm, who is recuperating from brain surgery and postoperative emotional complications, which Dr. Cerdal asked for and was given my permission to treat. The Kermi are a telepathic species and this, in my opinion, is the crucial datum.

"Dr. Cerdal," he went on, "has spent several hours every day, the longest time that anyone has spent in its company, interviewing the patient, so far without any success in solving its problems. But Cerdal, without any previous history of mental disorder, is displaying symptoms of xenophobia so severe that it has been confined to its quarters. Less seriously affected are the Illensan PVSJ charge nurse Valleschni, who has ward responsibility for Tunneckis's aftercare and who checks on its condition at frequent intervals, and the Earth-human DBDG trainee nurse, Patel, who was also in regular attendance checking the wound dressings, serving meals, and such. These three have been withdrawn from duty and confined to their quarters, as have the people who were fighting in the dining hall. Their symptoms were not as marked as the others, but they had no close contact with the patient and were simply on duty nearby. Would you all agree that this suggests that the mental infection or whatever it is has a single radiant source and that its effects are time-cumulative? Not only that, the sudden worsening of the observed symptoms in everyone concerned suggests that the source is strengthening and increasing its effective range. But how do we isolate a nonmaterial infection?

"Doctor," Braithwaite said, turning suddenly to face Prilicla, "is there anything in the emotional radiation of the peripheral victims you observed which suggests otherwise?"

"No, friend Braithwaite," said Prilicla, "it is as you say. There is a coarsening, a lack in the more subtle shading and structuring of their emotions, as if the finer and, for want of a better word to describe it to a non-empath, more civilized feelings are being stripped away. However, removal from the source seems to have halted the process, which may be reversible. The mind as well as the body has ways of rebuilding itself, but perhaps I am erring on the side of optimism."

It looked at O'Mara for a moment, then went on, "This is a nice piece of observation and deduction on the Lieutenant's part, friend O'Mara, and I hope it will be rewarded accordingly. Now I know why you would not allow me to approach Tunneckis for an emotional reading even though the results might have been helpful. You were afraid I might catch it, whatever it is."

"That was the Lieutenant's idea, too," said O'Mara, scowling and refusing to join in complimenting his subordinate, "and I'm still thinking about how best to give him his just deserts while making sure he doesn't enjoy them."

O'Mara knew that Prilicla was fully aware of his feeling of admiration for the quality of Braithwaite's work but he had, after all, a reputation for nastiness to maintain. The empath returned its attention to the Lieutenant. A faint tremor began to move along its limbs and wings.

"I feel your suspicions, friend Braithwaite," it said. "What is troubling you?

"What troubles me," Braithwaite said, "is that, apart from viewing its operation and being asked to provide psychiatric postoperative support, we know nothing about Patient Tunneckis. Why was the patient isolated in the first place? Was someone already suspicious about what might happen and taking precautions? Doctor Prilicla, it is impossible to hide emotional radiation from you. As an empath, have you been able to pick up any feelings from anyone regarding this case, feelings that may have a bearing on the problem and that you are at liberty to disclose? Or better still, do you yourself know anything at all about the patient's emotional background?"

The tremor in Prilicla's wings and legs spread to its fragile, egg-shell body.

"Your feeling of suspicion is unjustified, friend Braithwaite," it said. "The isolation of the patient was intended to minimize the level of telepathic noise generated by its medical staff, noise that it may no longer be able to hear. But I can tell you a little more about the case."

# CHAPTER 31

By the time Prilicla had finished telling them everything it knew and they had devised a plan, not for solving the problem but for finding a method of containing it in the hope that an answer might somehow be found, O'Mara was feeling more than usually irascible through lack of sleep. As it was, the partial solution was going to turn a large number of the hospital's medical, maintenance, and security staff on their collective ear and even the new, self-assured Braithwaite could not be expected to order so many senior staff around without someone telling him exactly where to put his instructions. That was why O'Mara kept the Lieutenant at his side while he made noises like a hospital administrator to the person primarily responsible for the mess.

It was strange, he thought as the long-familiar Earth-human face appeared on his viewscreen, how many of the hospital's past emergencies had begun by this man either trying to do or often doing the medically impossible.

"Conway," O'Mara said sourly, "you and your telepathic patient have really landed us in it this time. Arrangements are being made as we speak to isolate Tunneckis from all contact with the medical and maintenance staff. Except for the few minutes spent with it by the bare minimum personnel needed to make its isolation as comfortable as possible, it is not to be approached by any living person. Remote-controlled monitoring and medical-treatment servos and a mobile food dispenser will be provided. Fortunately it has recovered sufficiently to use its own toilet facilities. If you have any other patients on Levels One-Ninety-Nine through Two-Zero-Three, they aren't there anymore and you'll probably find them on Two-Eighty-Five. But first I have orders for you which must be obeyed without argument or delay if—"

"Wait," Conway broke in. "You can't do that. I have three patients in that area and one of them is tricky. . . . Dammit, this isn't a convenient time for holding a stupid evacuation drill. You should have consulted me first. So forget your bloody orders, O'Mara, and tell me what the hell is going on!"

Listening to such an angry exchange between two of the hospital's top people was a brand-new experience for Braithwaite, and he was looking very uncomfortable. Before O'Mara could reply, the Lieutenant leaned forward so as to bring his face into visual range of O'Mara's communicator and tried to pour a little diplomatic oil over a manner that his chief's fatigue was making more abrasive than usual.

"Sir," he said quietly, with an apologetic glance at O'Mara beside him, "a dangerous situation has arisen which, among other things, has caused us to lose a lot of sleep and caused tempers to fray while we tracked it to its source. Rather than waste time trying to tell you about it in detail, I suggest you speak with Dr. Prilicla, who is now fully informed and who will be able to describe the emergency much better than we can. There is nothing to stop you attending your other patients once their new locations are known, and Administrator O'Mara doesn't wish to give offense . . ."

"Hah!" said Conway.

". . . but," Braithwaite continued firmly, "he must still forbid Di-

agnostician Thornnastor, Senior Physician Prilicla, and yourself
physical contact with patient Tunneckis. Security has orders to forbid access to this patient by any sapient life-forms or any approach
to within one hundred meters in any direction of its present location, although we expect this distance limit to be reviewed and extended in the light of further reports on the progress of the
infection. With respect, sir, you, too, must be bound by these orders."

"With respect, Lieutenant," said Conway, "what bloody infection? Tunneckis isn't infected with anything. I suppose you could
best describe the case as a road traffic accident, or maybe as an act
of its planetary God. It was just driving home when its ground vehicle was struck by lightning. Tunneckis wasn't even sick."

"It is now," said Braithwaite very seriously. "We have incon-
trovertible evidence that a form of mental contagion is radiating
from Tunneckis's present location and that, according to Dr. Prilicla, who is charting the rate of expansion for us, it is spreading at
an accelerating rate into the adjacent levels of the hospital and beyond. In effect, it seems to strip away the more sensitive layers of
consciousness, those which we use to make friends, or to trust
rather than fear strangers, and, in short, enable us to behave like civilized individuals. I mentioned earlier to you that Tunneckis might
not be telepathically dumb. Now we know that it is producing a
loud, incoherent, telepathic shout that is slowly destroying the
minds within its increasing range. We don't know what the final
stage will be, almost certainly a condition of rampant xenophobia
with possibly a descent into pre-sapience. That is why we cannot
allow the hospital's best medical minds to be affected, because we
will need them to find a solution.

"If they can," he added.

"Ignore the Lieutenant's clumsy attempt at flattery, Conway,"
O'Mara joined in suddenly. "According to Prilicla, it was you agreeing to accept and treat the hospital's first Kerma patient that got us
into this mess, so you can use your fine mind to help us get out of
it. Right?"

Conway frowned, then nodded. "But it isn't a medical condition," he said. "It's a, a state of mind in an emotionally disturbed patient who happens to be a telepath. What is Psychology Department doing about it?"

"All we can," O'Mara replied.

"Of course you are," said Conway. "I'll talk to Prilicla at once. And Thornnastor, who's also involved. But if this mental infection is radiating and strengthening as you say, how long before we start transferring patients to another hospital?"

"Or move Tunneckis out of this one?" said O'Mara. "But if its present condition continues to worsen, I doubt whether the Kermi or anyone else will want it. You have to find the answer to this one, Doctor, or you'll be faced with an interesting and very urgent ethical dilemma."

Braithwaite cleared his throat and looked back to O'Mara. "It might not be all that urgent, sir," he said. "I didn't have the opportunity to get your approval, but I used your name freely with the engineering and medical-technology people to put them to work on a temporary solution. They are currently modifying a four-person survival pod I—I mean we—commandeered from one of the Orligian supply ships and are installing Kerma life-support, medical monitoring, and the equipment that will enable the pod to be supplied and serviced by remote-control devices sensitive enough for patient care. That will take them at least three days. They might trim a few hours off that estimate, sir, if you were to speak sternly to them in person."

O'Mara's immediate reaction should have been to lift the skin off the Lieutenant's back with a tongue-lashing for using his superior's name and rank without permission. But it was a good idea that he might have thought of himself given time, and his feelings were too desensitized with fatigue to be hurt.

Instead he just nodded and said, "I'll do that."

"With Tunneckis in the pod outside the hospital," Braithwaite went on, turning back to Conway on the screen, "You can maintain the medical treatment necessary at long range while the department tries to provide psychotherapy over the communicator. Dr. Prilicla will tell us if and when the patient has to be moved farther out."

Conway shook his head, in puzzlement rather than negation, and said, "Well done, Lieutenant; at least that will give us time to think. But how can a case that began as a simple vehicular casualty with suspected brain injuries turn suddenly into something that, without the patient being aware of what it's doing, is sucking out the higher levels of intelligence and sensitivity from the people around it like some kind of mental black hole? This doesn't make sense."

"With respect, sir," said Braithwaite, "what was the exact nature of its injuries?"

"Apart from minor scorching of the body surface, which was healing well before it was admitted," said Conway, apparently taking no offense at a mere lieutenant daring to question a senior diagnostician, "I couldn't find anything serious enough to treat. The problem was an impairment of its telepathic faculty, which we couldn't cure, accompanied by a major psychological component to the case which we passed to Psychology to see if you people could help."

"Then the condition may have been present before Tunneckis arrived here," said Braithwaite, still saying all the things O'Mara was too tired to say, "and you just inherited the problem without knowing it was there."

"A comforting thought," said Conway, dividing his attention between them, "but as the physician-in-charge I'm looking for answers, not excuses for my negative behavior. First I'm going to contact the Monitor base on Kerm for more details on Tunneckis's accident, and to find out if anything like this has ever happened there in the past and what, if anything, the Kermi were able to do about it. Even with a triple-A medical-emergency coding, that will take several hours. In the meantime I'll talk to Prilicla and the medical and engineering teams to get a detailed assessment of the extent of this nonmedical contagion and its rate of progression, then call a meeting with the senior staff concerned for this time tomorrow in the administrator's conference room. That will impress them with the importance we're placing on this job. Sorry for making free with your offices, sir, but as you know, in an emergency of this kind it is the medic in charge who has the rank."

He smiled faintly and went on, "I wouldn't presume to give you an order, Administrator O'Mara, but my present medical advice is to stop working and even thinking and catch up on your sleep while you can. For the next few days we're going to need your fresh, rested, devious, and nasty mind. Yours, too, Lieutenant. Off."

In the event, O'Mara thought, his stale, partially rested, devious, and nasty mind had very little to contribute during the first two hectic hours of that meeting, and Braithwaite, who always looked fresh and rested, did nothing but listen attentively to the sometimes heated exchanges between the senior engineering and medical staff.

Major Okambi of Engineering reported good progress with the installation of the Kerma VBGM's life-support and medical monitoring because it was a simple, warm-blooded oxygen-breather, but its small body mass meant that the long-stay furnishings, communicator, and facilities had to be modified to fit its tiny digits, and the fact that it could be approached only by a variety of remotely controlled devices meant that the pod's entry lock had to be completely rebuilt. Okambi said that his people were doing their best, but the original three-day estimate had been a trifle optimistic and the pod would not be operational for at least five days.

Prilicla, its limbs trembling with the effort of saying something that would cause unpleasant emotional radiation, said, "At its present rate of propagation, friend Okambi, in five days we will have to evacuate eight levels above and below friend Tunneckis's present location. The inconvenience to patients and staff during the transfer of treatment and catering facilities will be immense, because the levels to be vacated will also include the main dining hall. If the hospital personnel are not to risk their minds as well as their digestive processes, the food-service operation will have to be made from the ward kitchens or to the staff living quarters. Should your estimate overrun by a single day, the hospital's entire kitchen and food-storage level would have to be evacuated as well. That would add considerably to the already serious disruption."

The empath's trembling increased as its words caused an upsurge of unpleasant emotional radiation in the room. Most of it, O'Mara thought as he looked at the faces whose expressions he could read, must be the dark negation of barely controlled fear for the personal safety of themselves and the thousands of beings who were their direct responsibility. It was Okambi who spoke first.

"I know we're supposed to care for our patients, Doctor," he said angrily, "but this one is causing trouble out of all proportion to its individual importance. Why don't you just chalk it up as one of the few failures and send it home?"

"Sir," said Braithwaite before the other could reply, "you're forgetting the nature of the patient's disease. By the time the ship got back to Kerm, the crew might not have enough of their minds left to land it. And if they did, we would be returning a being that is capable of destroying Kerma minds over a presently unknown but large radius, perhaps even their entire civilization." Turning to Prilicla, he said, "Doctor, is there any possible way to contain this nonmaterial contagion other than by sheer distance? By enclosing it in a modified hush field, perhaps, that deadens mental rather than sound radiation?"

"That was the first thing we tried, Lieutenant," said Okambi impatiently. "Telepathy uses a delicate, organic transmitter and receiver whose radiation cannot so far be reproduced, much less shielded." He looked at O'Mara. "You've had several sessions by communicator with Dr. Cerdal, the first and so far worst-affected victim, as well as Tunneckis itself. Is there any possibility of a psychiatric solution?"

O'Mara shook his head. "Unfortunately, Dr. Cerdal is a clear case of mind being ruled by emotion rather than reason, and the emotions are those of a frightened child being plagued by the most horrible nightmares, the other-species nightmares all around it who are trying to help. Its xenophobia is extreme. My staff talked to the others who had shorter exposure to Tunneckis. They exhibit the same symptoms in lesser degree depending on their distance and total time of exposure, which appears to be cumulative. Tunneckis itself is emotionally disturbed, completely and utterly despairing as a result of the accident that left it telepathically deaf and dumb. For several minutes at a time it is coherent and communicative, but is so far unresponsive to my attempts at providing therapy. It is totally unaware of the mental havoc it is causing. Unless I can think of a strong therapeutic reason for telling it, I intend not to do so because, well, it feels bad enough already."

For a moment the personality, feelings, and memories of Marrasarah surged into the forefront of his mind. The loss of fur mobility was the worst thing short of death that could happen to a once-beautiful Kelgian, but Tunneckis's situation was much worse. He found himself blinking a couple of times to clear a sudden fogginess in his vision, but he tried to conceal the pain and anger in his voice with a thick layer of sarcasm when he spoke.

"It would be a nice change if my psychologists instead of you wonder-working doctors could produce a medical miracle," he said, dividing his attention between Conway, Thornnastor, and Prilicla, "but the very best we can do is salvage what we can from a mind damaged as a result of the original accident, or by your subsequent surgical intervention, or both. Even if it is successful, the psychotherapy would be palliative, an attempt to help the patient make the best of its sensory impairment, and not curative. Its present condition was the result of physical trauma, the shock of a lightning strike, and the effect that had on its brain or nervous system. So the problem is basically a medical one and the primary responsibility for solving it is yours."

Thornnastor began stamping angrily with its medial feet, while Prilicla's trembling increased. Conway jumped to his feet, then sat down again and said quietly, "Sir, we're not trying to shift responsibility here. It is ours and we accept it, but that doesn't help solve the problem. As the chief psychologist as well as the administrator, what do *you* suggest we do?"

*Of course you're not trying to shift the responsibility,* O'Mara thought wryly, *except to make me responsible for finding the answer.* Aloud, he said, "The serious postoperative developments in this case may be blinding you to some of the factors of the original causation. Patient Tunneckis's condition is rare, perhaps unique, and certainly nothing like it has occurred in recent Kerma history. Why is this? What is there different about the physical circumstances or the surroundings or some other undiscovered factor of Tunneckis's accident that did not happen, or perhaps could not have happened, in the past?

"Are you sure you have all the facts, Doctors?"

Thornnastor stopped vibrating the floor with its feet. Prilicla's trembling diminished. Conway was frowning and looking as though he was thinking hard. But O'Mara wasn't finished with them yet.

"As chief psychologist I've probably known what you have been thinking before you knew it yourselves," he said, looking at each of them in turn, "but as your hospital administrator I'm obliged to make the position and the decisions required of you as clear and unequivocal as possible. Sector General may be faced with the greatest threat in its history, not to its structure but to its personnel and continued existence as the greatest multi-species hospital in the Federation. The duration of this threat is presently unknown and totally dependent on the life expectancy of patient Tunneckis, which is likely to be short and mentally unpleasant if it is condemned to solitary confinement inside a vast, deserted hospital with only robot devices to feed and care for it until they malfunction beyond their ability to self-repair. So we may well be absent from the hospital for only a few months or years.

"We must therefore ask ourselves," he went on, "whether the indeterminate lifetime of one patient is worth the financial and emotional cost and the physical disruption it is causing to the establishment, the staff, and the other patients, some of whom, particularly the water-breathing Chalders and ultra-low-temperature crystalline life-forms, may not survive the necessarily hasty evacuation. There is a very simple, completely sensible option if the answer to this problem isn't found. It is the easiest answer to our problem, although ethically it is a little tricky, but all of you must have considered it or are considering it now."

O'Mara paused for a moment, then ended grimly, "Should we assist patient Tunnekis to terminate painlessly without further waste of time?"

Prilicla's body was shaking in the emotional gale that was sweeping the room. O'Mara looked at it apologetically, knowing that it would know exactly how he was feeling, too. But strangely, the emotional radiation was causing the empath's quivering body gradually to grow still.

"Friend O'Mara," it said finally, "there is nobody here or, I believe, anywhere else in the hospital, who will accept that option."

# CHAPTER 32

Patient Tunneckis was transferred from the otherwise empty recovery ward and through the silent and deserted adjoining levels to the original OR on a remotely controlled litter and immobilized on the operating table. Sensor pads were attached to its oval, sluglike body and it was prepped for the operation, all without being touched by human or any other hands. It was totally relaxed by the local anesthetic but it was and would remain fully conscious.

Watching it intently on a large lecture screen ten levels away were Diagnosticians Conway and Thornnastor, Senior Physician Prilicla, Lieutenant Braithwaite, and O'Mara himself. It was O'Mara who spoke first, and solely to the patient.

"Tunneckis," he said with gentle reassurance, "we are trying to cure you. Even though you may think that you are telepathically deaf and dumb you are not, at least not completely. Since shortly after you arrived here you have been unknowingly transmitting a continuous, sense-free telepathic shout, a sound so loud, so intensely unpleasant and far-reaching that our medical staff and patients have had to be moved beyond its range. That is why re-motely controlled devices instead of people have been taking care of you."

Beside him he heard Conway give a quiet, incredulous grunt at his massive understatement of the situation. O'Mara ignored him and went on, "But if you can still use your telepathic faculty to shout then it is not completely lost. That is promising because it may be only a short step from being able to shout to being able to speak, and listen, normally. That is why the hospital's two best doc-tors are going into your brain to try to rectify the fault. You will be fully conscious during the operation, but as the brain interior has no pain receptors you should feel no physical discomfort. You may, however, feel sensory changes while the doctors are working there. It would be helpful if you told us what they are or how they are af-fecting your mind. Tenneckis, do you agree to us performing this operation and will you help us during it?"

He knew that they were going to do the operation anyway, with or without the patient's cooperation, but it would be kinder to let it think that it still had a say in the matter.

"I'm, I'm afraid," the distant Tenneckis replied. It made a low, hissing sound that did not translate, then went on, "I'm afraid of this place, and your cold, shiny, clicking machines that do things to me, and of all the horrible people in the hospital including you. Mostly I'm afraid of going on living this way. Please, I just want this black, awful, continual fear of everybody and everything to stop."

O'Mara thought of Dr. Cerdal as he had seen it last, heavily se-dated but still babbling and crying and completely out of control, and of the others, who had had less protracted contact with Tun-neckis and who were in proportionately better shape. He could have said that he understood because others were feeling the same intense and unreasoning fear of all those around them that mani-fested itself as manic xenophobia, but that would have been adding guilt to the patient's already crushing mental load.

Instead he said gently, "We want to cure you, Tunneckis, and remove the cause of that fear. Will you help us?"

The silence seemed to last much longer than the few seconds shown on the room's chronometer, but finally the answer came.

"Yes."

O'Mara gave an almost explosive sigh of relief and looked away from the screen. Braithwaite was looking quietly pleased, Thornnastor was stamping a forefoot against the floor in agitation, the emotional radiation from some person or persons in the room was giving Prilicla the shakes again, and Conway was frowning and chewing at his lower lip. O'Mara sighed again more quietly.

"Conway," he said dryly, "I know the signs. You are thinking about doing something stupid. Well?"

"I've been too busy to thank you properly or bring you up to date on the later developments," said Conway quickly. "That was a really good steer you gave us about reinvestigating Tunneckis's accident. The Orligian medical officer on Kerm base was once a forensic scientist, and it took the scene of the crime—I mean the accident—and related circumstances apart and used a microscopic sieve on the evidence. It sent us detailed analyses of the metal structure—the padding, and even the body paintwork of Tunneckis's groundcar following the lightning strike, and of an undamaged vehicle of the same type. There were also the results of a complete physical examination on a normally healthy Kerm volunteer to serve as an organic benchmark. But it was you who pointed us in the right direction in the first place and . . ."

"Flattery doesn't work on me," O'Mara broke in sharply, "so get to the point."

"The point," said Conway, beginning to sound excited, "is that nothing like the Tunneckis accident had ever happened before because their technology isn't advanced and ground vehicles are a recent development. The brief, ultra-high temperature and exposure to the electrical discharge of the lightning strike vaporized sections of the internal padding so that toxic material was inhaled and eventually circulated to the brain. Mistakenly I thought that the minor scorching of Tunneckis's body surface was the only symptom. But now I know differently, and Thornnastor has come up with a specific that will detoxify the brain area involved. I'm confident—well, let's say I'm guardedly optimistic—of effecting a cure."

O'Mara looked at him steadily for a moment, then said, "You are about to say 'but.' "

"But it will be very delicate work," said Conway, "work I would rather not do at a distance with remotely controlled instruments. It will have to be a hands-on job. I fully realize the risks of a lengthy exposure to Tunneckis's mental contagion, but I don't foresee it being a long operation. Sir, I'll have to be there."

"And I," said Thornnastor and Prilicla, practically making it a duet.

O'Mara was silent for a moment. He was wondering how it would feel at first hand, rather than listening to Cerdal or the others trying to describe it, when the higher levels of one's mind began to dissolve away and one became more and more suspicious and afraid of all the other-species staff in the hospital, people he had known and respected and liked for a great many years. He took a firm grip on the mind he still had and spoke.

"And I," he said gruffly. "Somebody will be needed there with enough sense to pull the plug if we look like we're running out of time." He turned to Prilicla. "But not you, little friend. You will stay well clear and only fly in for a few seconds at fifteen-minute intervals to monitor and report on our emotional radiation. You will be aware of trouble developing long before we are. And if you detect the slightest sign of a coarsening of the intellect, or insensitive or ill-mannered or antisocial behavior, no matter what we say to you or how we excuse it, you tell the security team to pull us out at once. Is that understood?"

"Yes, friend O'Mara," said the empath.

Thornnastor stamped three of its feet in rapid succession and turned one of its eyes toward Conway. Aged Tralthans were notoriously hard of hearing and assumed other species to be the same, with the result that its whisper was loud and penetrating.

"Insensitive and ill-mannered behavior," it said. "With O'Mara, how will we know the difference?"

OR One-Twelve was in all respects ready and waiting for them as Conway, Thornnastor, and O'Mara entered and moved quickly to their positions. The microsurgery instruments, high-magnification scanner, the recorder, and Pathology's modified crystalline suspension had been checked and double-checked at a distance so that all they had to do was go to work.

Without wasting time.

"Try to relax, Tunneckis," said O'Mara reassuringly. "This time we know where we're going because we've been there before. The entry-wound area will be anesthetized and there will be no physical sensation from inside your brain. Talk to me whenever you feel like it, and don't worry. Ready?"

"Yes," said Tunneckis, "I think."

Once again the big operating screen showed the tremendously magnified view from the internal vision pickup as Conway's instruments negotiated the cavernous inner ear, pierced the membrane, and opened a path into the area of the telepathic faculty. Sweating with the effort of making his hands move even more slowly inside the reduction gauntlets, Conway went into the series of liquid-filled, interconnected tunnels with the slender-stemmed clusters of crystalline flowers growing from their mottled pink-and-yellow walls and stirring in the microscopic turbulence caused by the invading instruments.

Even to O'Mara's untutored eye they didn't look healthy.

"This is a mess," said Conway in unknowing confirmation. "The mistake we made during the first op was in analyzing, reproducing, and replacing the ambient fluid and crystal structures without realizing that they were contaminated by a higher than normal concentration of toxic material, the complex of vaporized metal and plastic inhaled by the patient following the lightning strike to its vehicle, that was carried by the blood supply from the lungs to the brain. Thornnastor has injected a specific which has neutralized the toxicity and no more will be arriving. But we can't simply suck out the contaminated fluid and replace it with the new material in case emptying the area collapses or otherwise damages the brain structure. So we'll have to do both at the same time and gradually dilute and replace the old, contaminated fluid with the proper mix of minerals and trace elements which will enable the crystals to regrow in their correct but inevitably still slightly toxic medium.

"As you can see, there are two distinct types of crystals present . . ."

One type was a small, stunted, almost colorless crystalline flower that barely filled the cuplike receptor on the top of its stalk, O'Mara saw. The other was large and dark red and overhung its cup-shaped attachment point like a misshapen black cabbage. He was pretty sure of which one was responsible for the mental contagion spreading throughout the hospital, and again Conway was agreeing with him.

". . . My guess is that the smaller, less developed type are the telepathic receptors," Conway went on, "and the larger, which have been growing out of control in the contaminated fluid since we were last in here, are the transmitters that are radiating the continuous telepathic shouting that is causing our other problems. We'll have to remove them from their stalks, very carefully, and withdraw them with the contaminated fluid. Dammit, there are a lot of them. How are we for time? And how is the patient?"

"You have been working for half an hour," said Prilicla, who had flown silently into the room. "During my last visit you were all too busy to notice me so I left without speaking when I found that the emotional-radiation levels were optimum."

"Half an *hour?*" said Conway, incredulously. "It shows how fast time passes when you're enjoying yourself."

"Conway!" said O'Mara sharply. "That was a particularly insensitive remark to make in the presence of a conscious patient, especially one who might not understand Earth-human sarcasm."

"Insensitive?" said Conway, looking suddenly worried. "Am I being ... affected?"

"I don't think so, friend Conway," Prilicla broke in. "Your emotional radiation, like that of everyone else here, is being distorted by fear, but it is diffuse and may be based on your general fear for the patient's well-being. Friend Tunneckis is also feeling intense fear, but that is normal for the circumstance and it is trying hard to keep it under control."

"And I do understand sarcasm," Tunneckis added, "wherever it originates, so an apology is unnecessary."

Conway gave a short, relieved laugh and was back at work before it ended.

The procedure was slow, painstaking, and seemingly endless. As Conway used his microinstruments carefully to crush and detach the large crystals from their stalks, large only because of the ultra-high magnification, and withdraw them through a tiny suction tube, O'Mara thought that it was like watching a particularly inefficient underwater vacuum cleaner at work. But with the crystalline debris was going a measured quantity of the toxin-filled liquid that Thornnastor was replacing with the uncontaminated fluid in which, they were hoping, the new, healthy crystals would grow. Slowly and steadily the proportion of toxic material was diminishing, and it seemed that a few of the crystalline flowers of both kinds were attaching themselves to empty stalks. Conway was sweating in concentration and all four of Thornnastor's eyes were directed at its instruments. Prilicla paid four more visits but came and went without comment. It was not until the seventh visit that it spoke.

"The security detail is standing by at a safe distance," it said, maintaining a stable hover just inside the entrance, "but they can be here within three minutes. I must remind you that you have been in close proximity to your patient for nearly two hours and—"

"No, dammit!" Conway broke in. "We could be nearly there. I'm not stopping now."

"Nor I," rumbled Thornnastor.

"The ambient emotional radiation here is—" Prilicla began, when Conway broke in again.

"Thornnastor," he said urgently, "if our empathic friend calls in the security heavies, will you block the door with your body? They won't dare do anything too violent to the hospital's senior diagnostician even if our administrator tells them otherwise. Right?"

"Right," said Thornnastor.

"Your administrator," said O'Mara firmly, "will order them to keep their distance."

Conway's expression was puzzled but very pleased as he looked up briefly at O'Mara and then at Prilicla before going on, "Please listen to me. I'm not afraid of anybody here, or anywhere else for that matter. There's no xenophobia that I'm aware of . . ." For a moment his voice was tinged with doubt. ". . . unless losing my temper like this with a good friend is an early symptom. But I don't feel that there's anything wrong with my mind. How is the patient feeling?"

"I know exactly what and how you feel, friend Conway," said Prilicla, "and friend Tunneckis is feeling frightened, disoriented, and badly confused."

"Tunneckis," said Conway urgently, "what's happening?"

"I don't know what's happening," the other replied angrily. "My mind is flashing pictures and sounds. They are disconnected, unrelated, and, and *nonverbal*. What, what did you just do to me?"

"It would take too long to explain right now," Conway replied, "but I intend doing it again for as long as I can." Keeping his hands inside the stepdown gauntlets and his eyes fixed on the operating screen, he said excitedly, "The patient's reaction proves it. We're beginning to get results."

"Friend Conway, I don't know what's happening, either," said Prilicla. "Based on the staff distance and exposure tables we worked out for friend Tunneckis's telepathic, ah, shouting, all of you should be showing marked changes in emotional radiation and behavior by now. Instead your symptoms, with one exception, are minimal. I can only attribute this to the presence of several tape-donor entities within your minds. These tapes, which are the recordings of the past donors' knowledge and memories, are not subject to modification by a mental influence of the present, so they may be serving as a mental anchor for the minds concerned. As diagnosticians in possession of many mind partners, you are being kept stable by the thoughts and feelings of your taped entities. But this is buying you only a little time, how much exactly I can't say, because I can already feel your minds being affected. You will need to leave soon."

"And one of us," said Conway, with his eyes still fixed on the operating screen, "is not a diagnostician. Administrator, for your own mental safety you must leave at once. You can talk to the patient by communicator, and keep Security off our backs, when you're at a safe distance."

"No," said O'Mara.

Prilicla was the only person in the hospital who knew that O'Mara had a mind partner, one single mental anchor called Marrasarah that might or might not save his sanity, but the empath was sworn to silence on that subject. One strong-willed, Kelgian anchor, he told himself, should be enough. He knew that Prilicla was feeling his doubts, but it left without mentioning them.

It was insidious.

He was watching Conway and Thornnastor at work and trying with little success to find reassuring words to say to Tunneckis, whose confusion and fear and despair hung around it like an unseen, smothering, and terrifying cloud that was almost palpable. He felt a growing urge to leave the room, if only to get the chance to breathe some clean air. More and more he found himself wondering if they were wasting their time, and he was gradually coming to the decision that they were. This Tunneckis creature was suffering because it had been the victim of a fluke accident that none of its own people could do anything about, and it was wrecking the sanity of the hospital staff who were trying to cure it. One had to keep a sense of proportion in these things. And an overgrown, sluglike, loathsome thing was all that Tunneckis was, a telepath who was eating away at his mind, a foul thing that could never go home and must not be allowed to stay here. The solution was obvious, the decision simple, and he had the rank to see that it was carried out. He would tell this self-opinionated young upstart Conway and the stupid elephant assisting him that the Kerma slug was expendable and to abort the procedure forthwith.

But suddenly O'Mara felt afraid, more afraid than he had ever been in his entire life. The fear was formless, unfocused but intense, and reinforced with a feeling of utter despair. He didn't want to make a decision or give orders because he was sure Conway, who had always managed to do things his own way, would refuse to obey them; and Thornnastor would grip him in its long, warty tentacles and stamp him to a pulp under its elephant's feet. He just wanted to run away and hide, from everything and every horrible, frightening, and alien person in this terrible place. Even Prilicla, so soft and fragile and so outwardly friendly, was forever crawling into his mind with its empathic faculty and uncovering the deepest, most shameful feelings that nobody should ever know while it waited its chance to tell everybody the truth about him. He was no good, O'Mara told himself bitterly, despairingly and fearfully, and useless to himself and everybody else. He was nothing.

O'Mara gripped the edge of the operating table so tightly that his fingers and hands turned white. He wasn't aware that when he spoke it was closer to being a shout of anguish.

"Marrasarah, please *help* me!"

Conway looked up, his expression furious. "You bloody fool, O'Mara! Don't make sudden loud noises like that, this is a delicate operation. Who the hell is Marrasarah? Never mind, just stand there and keep quiet."

A tiny, cool, and aloof group of brain cells that were unaffected by the storm of fear and despair sweeping his tortured mind noted the disrespectful words and manner and decided that this was totally uncharacteristic of Conway, and that the Tunneckis contagion was getting to him, too. Suddenly the other shouted even louder than had O'Mara.

"Dammit, my *head!*"

Conway's teeth were clenched and his face contorted with pain, but he had not taken his hands out of the operating gauntlets. Then slowly he relaxed.

For some reason the intensity of O'Mara's fear and despair was beginning to ease. Concerned, he said, "What's wrong with your head?"

"A deep, unlocalized itching between the ears that felt as if somebody was working in my brain with a wire brush," Conway replied. Suddenly recovering his respectful manners, he went on excitedly, "Sir, I've felt that itching sensation before. It was Tunneckis trying to communicate telepathically with nontelepaths. It lasted only for an instant. Didn't you feel it, too? And hear the message?"

"No," said O'Mara.

"I felt the cranial itching," said Thornnastor, being ponderously clinical, "but not from between my ears, which are, as you must know, differently situated in my species. It was accompanied by a confusion of mental noise but no message. What did it say?"

Conway had returned all of his attention to the operating screen and was speaking quickly as he worked.

"It said an awful lot in such a short time," he said, "and I'll tell you all about it later. Right now we need about twenty minutes to complete this procedure and withdraw, but we could stay here all day if need be without suffering any mental ill effects. For a while there I was off the mental rails, feeling useless and afraid and suspicious of everybody. I apologize for anything I said. You two must have been having similar feelings. But now we're all back to normal and our troubles, *all* of our troubles, are over. We can begin repopulating the evacuated levels. Tunneckis is no longer telepathically deaf and dumb and is feeling fine."

"Much as I dislike having to disagree with a colleague, friend Conway," said Prilicla as it flew into the room to hover above the operating table, "I must say that you are guilty of a gross understatement. Friend Tunneckis is radiating feelings of relief, gratitude, and intense happiness."

# CHAPTER 33

They met early on the following day in his old office because that was where he felt most comfortable and that was where he wanted to begin saying his good-byes. Conway, Thornnastor, Prilicla, and all the members of the Psychology Department staff were distributed over the available furniture and making the place look crowded and more untidy than usual. Conway was standing beside the big diagnostic screen and summing up his report on the Tunneckis operation.

". . . During the first procedure," he was saying, "we assumed that analyzing the mineral and crystal content of the brain fluid in the area and reintroducing it in concentrated form would encourage the natural healing process but, unknowingly at the time, we were simply replacing it with more contaminated material in a much higher concentration. The result was that the growth of the clusters of pale crystals, which we now know were the telepathic receivers, became increasingly stunted while the darker ones, the transmitters, became grossly enlarged, structurally deformed, and grew out of control. In that state they were increasingly amplifying their telepathic output, but they could not transmit thoughts, only feelings. At the time Tunneckis was in bad mental shape, fearful of its surroundings, of its unthinkable future as a telepathic mute, and was suffering from a deep, clinical depression that seemingly would continue for the rest of its life. It would be difficult for normal people like us to imagine such depths of despair, but we don't have to imagine it because for a while we, and a number of others beginning with the patient's medical attendants, shared it.

"Tunneckis felt really bad, and so did we.

"But now the patient is recuperating and feeling well," he went on. "During the few seconds when my atrophied Earth-human telepathic faculty was kicked into life, we learned a lot about each other, and especially that it is impossible for a telepath to lie with the mind. The mental contagion of senseless fear and utter despair that it was broadcasting with increasing intensity over the past days ceased with its cure and, without the continual reinforcement of that signal, the effects will gradually disappear. Knowing and agreeing with my idea for keeping it here for a period of clinical observation and recuperation, it also said that bringing the most severe cases into close proximity with it for a few hours at a time would actively advance the curative process. I was thinking, sir, that as Cerdal is the worst-affected being in the hospital as well as a contender for your job, you should give it the first chance with the Tunneckis treatment."

"That will be done," said O'Mara, and added silently, *But not by me.*

Conway moved away from the screen to sit on the edge of a Melfan relaxer before he went on, "The base commander on Kerm has asked me to spend a few months there. It says that my glimpse into Tunneckis's mind will reduce their cultural contact problems as well as giving me the chance to gather information on native Kerma medicine in case another one turns up in Sector General, hopefully with something less disrupting. Maybe by the time I get back you'll have made your choice and I might be calling Dr. Cerdal 'sir.' "

"You won't," said O'Mara, "for two reasons. Dr. Cerdal wishes to remain in Sector General but has withdrawn its application for the administrator's position, and I've already made my choice. Having done so I shall, of course, be leaving the hospital as soon as suitable transport can be arranged."

Conway was so surprised that he nearly fell through the Melfan chair. Thornnastor made a sound like an interrogatory foghorn; Prilicla began trembling faintly as the Psychology Department staff showed surprise in their various fashions. O'Mara cleared his throat.

"It wasn't an easy decision," he said, looking at Padre Lioren and Cha Thrat, "but I should have realized that it was inevitable from the beginning. This is the first and probably the only time that I will say nice things to you people, because politeness doesn't come easily to me. But I must say that I have, I mean had, an exceptionally fine staff. You are hardworking, dedicated, caring, adaptable, and imaginative . . ." His eyes rested for a moment on Braithwaite. ". . . and one of you has recently displayed these qualities more strongly than the others. All three of you have the medical qualifications that are now required and, without exception, you are all capable of doing the job. But as is sometimes the case with truly committed people who have found their purpose in life and are content, those who could do the job don't want it. This applies especially to my successor, who will consider my choice an honor but not an act of kindness. Tough. But in his case I must insist.

"My congratulations, Administrator Braithwaite."

Cha Thrat and the padre made their species' equivalent gestures of approval, Prilicla trilled, Conway applauded, and Thornnastor stamped all its feet in turn, softly for a Tralthan. Conway stood up suddenly and leaned toward Braithwaite with his hand outstretched.

"Nice going, Administrator," he said. "After the way you uncovered the Tunneckis problem, you really deserve this." He laughed. "But a well-mannered chief psychologist that nobody dislikes will take a bit of getting used to."

Speaking for the first time, Padre Lioren turned all its eyes on O'Mara and said, "Sir, you said that you wanted to leave without delay. The hospital has been your life for longer than most of us can remember. I, we that is, wonder what you intend to do with the rest of that life?"

"I have plans," he replied seriously. "They include continuing my professional work and living happily ever after."

"But, sir," Conway said, "surely you're not obliged to leave right away? Braithwaite will need a settling-in period of a few weeks or more likely months, and you should allow your mind to get used to the idea of doing nothing. Or maybe you won't be allowed to sever all connections with Sector General. We run into nonmedical problems from time to time and may need you to come back for a while on a consultancy basis. And stop shaking your head, sir. At the very least we need time to juggle with the staffing schedules so we can throw a proper farewell party."

"No," said O'Mara firmly. "No settling-in period, because the best way of doing the job is to be dropped in at the deep end. No temporary detachments, no consultancies, and most of all, no long and embarrassing farewells for someone nobody likes. Prilicla knows my feelings about this. I insist. Thank you, but no."

Braithwaite cleared his throat. It was a polite but authoritative sound. He said, "I'm not an empath like Dr. Prilicla, sir, but I know the feelings of every person in the hospital toward you. This time it is I who must insist. Your departure will be delayed by a few days because none of the outgoing ships can take you without first clearing it with me, so there will be time to organize a farewell party that all of us will remember.

"As the newly appointed hospital administrator," Braithwaite added, "I am making that my first executive order."

# CHAPTER 34

Eventually he was allowed to board the Monitor Corps supply ship *Cranthor*, a regular and frequest visitor to the hospital. It had an all-Tralthan crew and one passenger cabin that was environmentally suited to Earth-human DBDGs. Those members of the crew who had not met him knew who he was and what he had been, and they were so eager to please him that they offered to start another farewell party on board. He told them that he just wanted to rest without company or conversation or entertainment tapes while he tried to recover from the first one. But the truth was that he wanted to watch the vast, dazzling spectacle of the hospital complex as it shrank to become a tiny, multicolored jewel in the aft viewscreen, while reminding himself that he was seeing it for the last time and remembering back to the time when he had been in a construction gang working on the empty structure, and the strange, weird, and exciting events and people he had met on his way up to his recent and brief appointment and sendoff as its retiring administrator.

The party had taken three days and two nights, because all

the people who wanted to say good-bye to him had not been off-duty at the same time. He could not understand the reason for all the fuss, because he knew that he was an intensely unlikable person even if he had been good at his job, but some of the things the senior and very junior staff of many species had said to him had almost wrecked his emotional self-control. He had been respected much more than he had ever imagined and, while nobody would admit to liking much less loving him, the intensity of that dislike had manifested itself in some strange and often touching ways.

Love, he thought, was supposed to be akin to hate. In their own particular fashion they must have hated him very much.

He stayed with *Cranthor* while it refilled its holds on Traltha, Orligia, and Nidia, but left it there because its next destination would be a return trip to Sector General. Over the years he had become an expert at hopping from ship to ship and, although he was still able to travel as a retired space officer and Sector General administrator, he had accrued enough back salary over the years to be able to pay his way if he wanted to keep a low profile. This time it wasn't necessary, because *Korallan,* a tour ship larger and better appointed and, presumably, less likely to have operational mishaps than the old *Kreskhallar,* was berthed at Nidia's Retlin spaceport while its passengers saw the sights, and was due to depart for O'Mara's final destination in three days' time. He was already familiar with Retlin from earlier stopovers, but used the time to reaccustom himself since his last leave to shopping and staying in low-ceilinged buildings where he had to bend almost double, and to public-transport vehicles in which he had to either kneel or squat.

On the first night out he discovered that the multi-species dining room contained seven other Earth-human passengers, three females and four males, all of them young. He was given a seat at the end of their table but deliberately avoided joining in their conversation. Unlike the situation in *Kreskhallar*'s dining room, this time he wasn't the only male show in town and he had no intention of engaging in a shipboard romance. His life was complicated enough as it was.

He left the ship when it was disembarking at Kelgia's main spaceport and took a private groundcar into its capital city. The driver was used to Earth-human and many other strange shapes squeezing themselves into its vehicle and politely, for a Kelgian, described items of scenic or architectural interest, not realizing that O'Mara had traveled this way many times and was already familiar with them. Even so, he could not help watching as the sprawling expanse of Kelgia's largest multi-species hospital complex, looking like an open, beautifully landscaped, and aseptically clean white township, moved slowly past.

Even though he had never actually visited the place, every stretch of parkland, garden, and tree-shaded walkway, as well as the layout of the wards, operating theaters, and staff accommodation in every building, was known to him through the memories of his mind partner, who had trained and served there.

Kledenth, its fur rippling in a combination of impatience and pleasure, was already waiting for him at the entrance to its house when he paid off his driver and began stretching to ease his stiffened leg and back muscles. The Kelgian indicated its own larger and more comfortable vehicle parked a few meters away.

It said, "I had to pull, as you Earth-humans say, a few strings, but I got it. All the equipment you wanted is loaded on board. Now, I suppose you're in a hurry to use it?"

"Eager to use it, Kledenth," O'Mara replied, "but not in a tearing hurry. This time I'm not on leave and don't have to return to Sector General, so hopefully I'm on this world to stay. There is time now, and there will be more later, to talk to you and your family and to thank you yet again for everything you've done for us over the years. The debt for saving your fur after that accident on *Kreskhallar* is more than repaid."

"Look at the way my fur moves," said Kledenth. "In spite of my age is it not beautiful? It could so easily have been otherwise. My life and successful career subsequent to that accident, my loving life-mate and children, I owe to your specialist knowledge and gross insubordination toward that ship's captain, and to the skill of the Earth-human female. That debt will never be repaid. But I think you are making one of your stupid and unnecessary Earth-human pretenses, so get into my groundcar and stop wasting time being polite to someone who doesn't understand the concept."

Their vehicle was picking up speed and Kledenth's home was shrinking behind them when it said, "How fares the Joan entity?"

"She congratulates you on the birth of your latest grandchild," O'Mara replied, "and she says she is well. Reading between the lines I could detect no evidence of serious emotional upsets between her life-mate and herself or their two matured offspring. Her last few letters, as you would put it, were showing happy fur."

They had traveled more than a mile before Kledenth spoke again.

"Myself I thought it visually quite repulsive," it said, "but when I showed the shipboard photographs I had taken to an Earth-human business acquaintance, it said that she was a dish and that you had been a very fortunate man. O'Mara, why didn't you continue and develop the relationship instead of . . ."

"You know why," said O'Mara.

"I know," said the other, "but I think you're mad."

O'Mara smiled. "I'm a psychologist."

"And a very good one," said Kledenth. "I know that, too. But we've arrived. I won't go in with you because the place makes me feel very uncomfortable. It reminds me of how I might have been."

The Retreat was a large establishment surrounded by lawns and gardens whose occupants were hidden by a thick screen of aromatic foliage from the view of chance passersby who would otherwise have been seriously distressed by seeing them. O'Mara used his key to open the high, opaque gate and, carrying his luggage in one hand and the equipment container in the other, walked slowly toward the house. He recognized some of the people who were lying curled up on the grass like furry question marks or undulating between the flower beds, because he had long since learned how to tell Kelgians apart. He spoke to them in passing and some of them were feeling well enough to speak back.

Inside the building he climbed the tiny steps of the Kelgian staircase. His room was exactly as he had left it a year earlier except that it was tidy and she had attached sprigs of festive aromatic vegetation to his favorite pictures. The tidiness, they both knew, would be a temporary condition. He dumped his bag on the tiny, low-ceilinged room's single, narrow bed, but held on to the equipment container while he went back downstairs to her office.

There was only one person in the establishment whose feet made a sound like his, so he wasn't surprised that she was already watching him as he came through the doorway. He placed the container on a side table and, with one hand still resting on it, turned to look back at her. The silence lengthened. Another person might have said hello, or asked if he'd had a good trip or verbally eased the situation in some other fashion, but Kelgians didn't go in for small talk.

"It will take a few minutes to unpack and assemble," he said, "after which it will be ready for use. Will you allow me to use it?"

"I don't know," said Marrasarah. The small areas of her fur that still retained mobility were spiking in indecision.

"You've had a year since my last visit to think about it," said O'Mara quietly, "and now that I've severed all professional contact with Sector General and I plan to stay on Kelgia for the rest of our lives, you can take a little more time to think about it. What's the problem? Remember, I know your mind as well as you do yourself."

"You *knew* my mind," said Marrasarah, "at the time I donated the Educator tape. In the intervening time that mind has changed, for the better. This was due entirely to your curative therapy and never-ending patience with me. But I, apart from the thoughts and feelings that I have been able to deduce from your words and actions, know nothing of your mind. But that may be enough for me."

"But it isn't enough for me," said O'Mara, gesturing toward the container. "At the hospital I used my influence with Prilicla, who is the only other being who knows about us, to have a tape made of my mind. I have it with me. I can talk to you and try to describe them in words, but I don't have the fur to show you the true depth of my feelings for you and why I've held them over these many years. In a few minutes you could know everything."

"I am afraid," she replied, "to know everything."

As he waited for her to go on, even the dead areas of fur seemed to be twitching in her agitation. With one of his own kind he would have moved closer and placed a reassuring hand on her shoulder, but that would not happen here.

During the thirty-odd years that she had been his patient and more than friend there had been no physical contact between them.

"You know everything about me because you carry my donor tape within your mind," she said finally, "but you are forgetting that it is no longer the same mind and you, O'Mara, have changed it. For reasons which you described to me in words and which still don't make sense to me, you took on my case. It was not through pity for my deformity, you insisted, but because I represent a problem which, because of your growing affection for the personality I had been, you wanted to spend all of your leaves of absence from the hospital, except for the first one when you and the Earth-human female Joan saved Kledenth's fur, trying to solve . . ."

"It was, is, much more than affection," said O'Mara.

"Don't interrupt me," she continued. "I cannot tell a lie, but the truth is complicated and difficult for me to speak. You solved my problem, not by performing a medically impossible miracle on a grossly deformed body but by repairing the wreckage of the mind within. And by working patiently you gave it, and many other minds here, a reason to go on living instead of existing in pain and self-loathing and cut off from friends and families until a usually self-inflicted death ended it.

"With me," she went on, the undamaged parts of her fur writhing at the memories, "you began by morally blackmailing Kledenth into tracing the whereabouts of this Retreat through my old hospital. Then you talked. And talked. It was cruel at first, but you reminded me of the great medical future that had streched in front of me before the accident ended it, except that you insisted that the mind inside my deformed body had a future, too, one that did not depend on visual contact and social interaction with my undamaged colleagues. Then over the years, without allowing anyone outside to know of your presence here or what you were doing for us, you reorganized this place of the living dead and, instead of it being a trash can filled with social outcasts that our people preferred not to think about, you gradually changed it into a consultancy that uses the newly healed and multidisciplined minds of its occupants to perform services that are increasingly in demand. The outgoing vision channels are switched off, naturally, so that nobody has to look at the experts they are consulting, but our clients are used to that now. I don't know what type of mind-changing therapy you used on the others, because their former specialties aren't medicine and they won't talk about it, but with me you talked about nothing but Sector General.

"You told me about the wonderful and often dangerous events that took place there," Marrasarah went on, "and the strange beings who work there, and the even stranger entities and conditions that they are called on to treat, and the challenging problems and ingenious solutions that were and are a daily routine. The staff and patients you described with the feeling of a great and dedicated psychiatrist while the events were related with the medical insight and purely Kelgian viewpoint possible only to one who shares my mind. In the beginning I, too, wanted an excuse to die and leave this deformed body. Instead I began counting the days until your next leave so as to hear more of your life. And now you want me to share that life by copying all of your memories into my mind, including this strange attraction you feel for me. I am greatly honored that you should offer this, but I don't think I want to share all the knowledge and innermost secrets and the true, unspoken thoughts of the psychologist O'Mara's mind.

"I am afraid."

O'Mara tried not to look at the pitifully few mobile patches of fur that were reflecting her fear. Even though it would not alter their future together or his feelings for her, he was becoming afraid, too, of her rejecting a gift that would lead to her full understanding of the rough, untutored, and complex person that was himself.

"Of what?" he said gently.

"I know you through your words and actions," she replied. "They were healing words and kindly actions spread out over many years. But now you are giving me the chance to know the true thinking and reasons behind those words and actions, and of that I am afraid. I am afraid of discovering a small selfishness or imperfection in a being I have long regarded with respect, admiration, and deep affection, or of discovering in you a strange, psychological abnormality that your Earth-human words have unwittingly concealed from me. I—I am afraid of being disappointed."

O'Mara smiled, knowing that over the years she had learned to understand the meaning behind that Earth-human grimace, and ordered his thoughts for a moment before speaking. He had been looking forward to this moment ever since he had illegally impressed himself with the Marrasarah mind tape to aid the therapy on the then-young trainee, Thornnastor, and he was afraid, too, but of the disappointment of rejection.

He said, "My words and actions toward you have been those of a therapist with one physically impaired, emotionally disturbed, and professionally challenging patient who, for many years, has ceased to require therapy or be a patient. So I admit that I am selfish and imperfect and not admirable or worthy of respect, and there isn't a psychologist in the Federation who would not consider me as anything but abnormal because I do need your affection, and more than that.

"Within the first few hours of taking your mind tape," he went on, "I formed a strong, emotional attachment to you. It was love at first meeting, but it was a nonphysical love that had nothing to do with sexual attraction because, if it had, that really would have been abnormal. I loved, and love, the Marrasarah personality who had worked and studied hard to rise to the top of a profession which, even on enlightened Kelgia, is predominantly male. I loved the unselfish way you helped your fellow students, your most difficult patients, and eventually your colleagues who had professional or personal problems, and the larger the problems the more you strove to solve them. In spite of your youth when you donated the mind tape, you were widely respected and loved because you couldn't help being a counselor and friend and at times a mother to everyone who needed help. If I had met an Earth-human who was like you, my early life would have been different and certainly happier. But instead you became my mind partner. Everything about you became part of me and I was more contented and happy than I could have believed possible.

"Since that time," he continued when she seemed about to interrupt, "your experience has helped me in my work, given me a greater understanding in my professional dealings with other-species patients, and generally kept me emotionally stable under stress, especially during my last job with Tunneckis, which as yet you don't know about.

"But long before I realized how much you were helping me," he continued, "I was angry at the way that cruel accident to your fur had ended an extremely promising career. So I decided to attempt something that the psychiatric source material in our library computer insisted was impossible. I tried to rebuild the otherwise brilliant mind of a fur-damaged Kelgian from the inside, and over half our lifetimes that is what we did. I say 'we' because you helped me by controlling the anger and fighting the bitter despair that was pulling you toward the inevitable ending of your own life.

"I owe you for that, too, because I could not have borne losing you as person even though your mind will be in mine as long as I live.

"Many times when I was telling you about Sector General," he went on, "I tried to tell you everything about me in poor, limping, inadequate words. But now, if you will agree to take my mind tape, you can discover the complete truth about me. I have had faults, bad habits, no social skills, secret fears, and phobias since a very early age, and now you can learn about them all. The result may be uncomfortable, frightening, even mentally repugnant to you. If you find it so, the mind tape can be erased again in a few minutes. But be warned. The result will be much deeper and more intimate than the lying together of two people during the act of physical mating, because it will be a true marriage of minds. I have known and will always know you in that way, Marrasarah, and I want you to know me. Please say yes. Or do you need more time to consider?"

"No," she said.

Without hesitation she moved to the relaxer beside the table holding his equipment container. He didn't trust himself to speak while he assembled and double-checked and calibrated the equipment for an Earth-human to Kelgian mind transfer. Still without speaking, he fitted the helmet comfortably onto her delicate, cone-shaped head and switched on. A few minutes later he removed the helmet again, thinking that this had been the first and hopefully the only physical contact he would have with her. If there was a second contact it would be because she wanted the contents of his mind to be erased from hers. But all she did was look up at him while the small patches of still-mobile fur rippled in slow, even waves. He let the silence run for as long as he could.

"Is there a problem?" he blurted out finally. "Are you all right? Do you want an erasure?"

"No, yes, and no," she replied. "I *know* you now, O'Mara, and everything you have ever experienced and thought about yourself, the others in your life, and especially about me. Your mind lies close and comfortably with mine, and I want it to do so until the day I die. But there is something about you that I will never understand."

"What?" he said, feeling the wave of happiness that her earlier words had sent sweeping through him check itself suddenly as if it might be about to collapse and ebb away. "You know and should understand everything. What don't you understand about me?"

"I don't understand, mind partner O'Mara," she replied, "how you are able to balance yourself on just two feet."

# TOR
# BOOKS The Best in Science Fiction

### LIEGE-KILLER • Christopher Hinz
"*Liege-Killer* is a genuine page-turner, beautifully written and exciting from start to finish....Don't miss it."—*Locus*

### HARVEST OF STARS • Poul Anderson
"A true masterpiece. An important work—not just of science fiction but of contemporary literature. Visionary and beautifully written, elegaic and transcendent, *Harvest of Stars* is the brightest star in Poul Anderson's constellation."
—Keith Ferrell, editor, *Omni*

### FIREDANCE • Steven Barnes
SF adventure in 21st century California—by the co-author of *Beowulf's Children*.

### ASH OCK • Christopher Hinz
"A well-handled science fiction thriller."—*Kirkus Reviews*

### CALDÉ OF THE LONG SUN • Gene Wolfe
The third volume in the critically-acclaimed Book of the Long Sun.
"Dazzling."—*The New York Times*

### OF TANGIBLE GHOSTS • L.E. Modesitt, Jr.
Ingenious alternate universe SF from the author of the *Recluce* fantasy series.

### THE SHATTERED SPHERE • Roger MacBride Allen
The second book of the Hunted Earth continues the thrilling story that began in *The Ring of Charon*, a daringly original hard science fiction novel.

### THE PRICE OF THE STARS • Debra Doyle and
### James D. Macdonald
Book One of the Mageworlds—the breakneck SF epic of the most brawling family in the human galaxy!